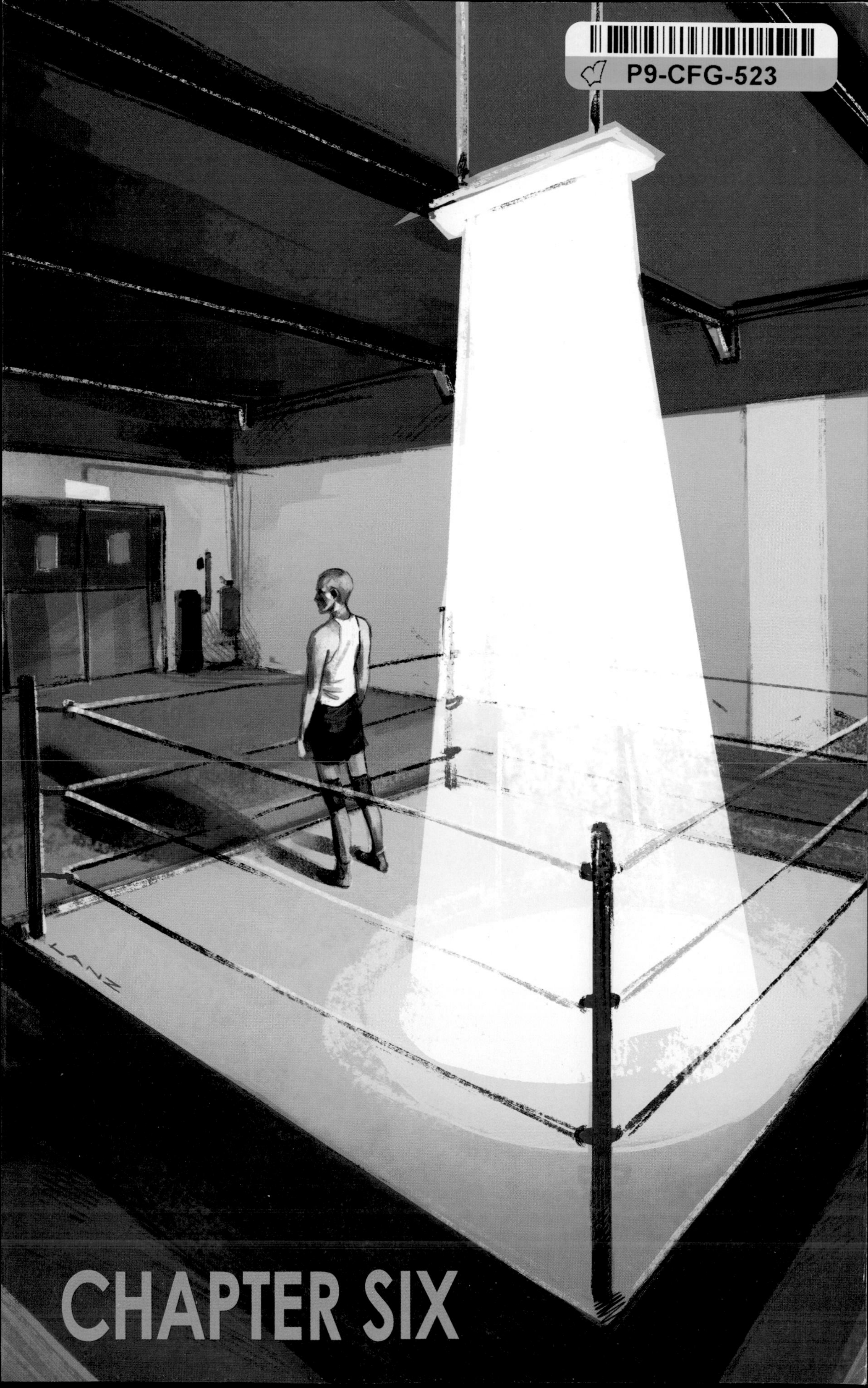
LANZ

CHAPTER SIX

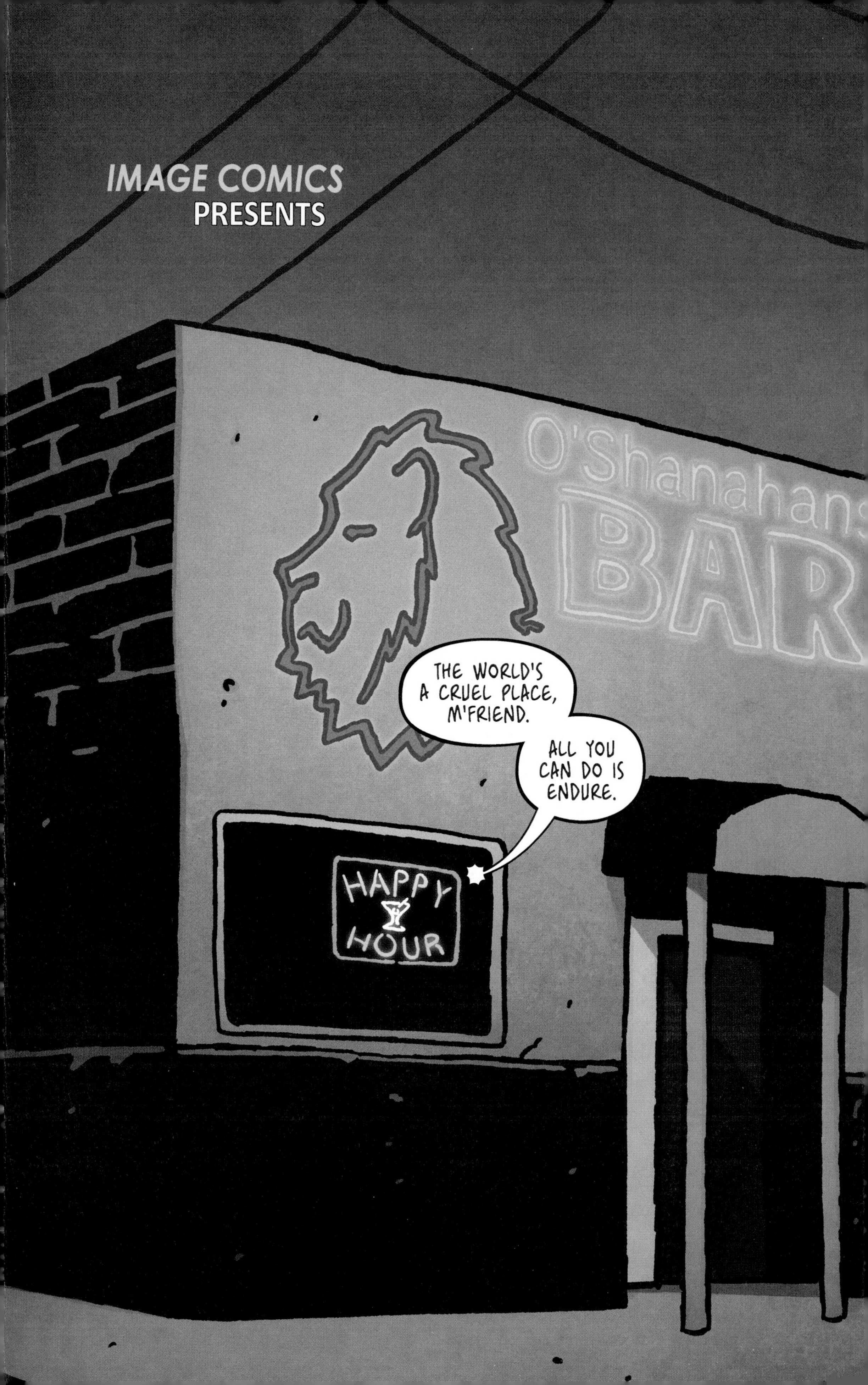
IMAGE COMICS
PRESENTS
O'Shanahans
BAR
THE WORLD'S A CRUEL PLACE, M'FRIEND.
ALL YOU CAN DO IS ENDURE.
HAPPY HOUR

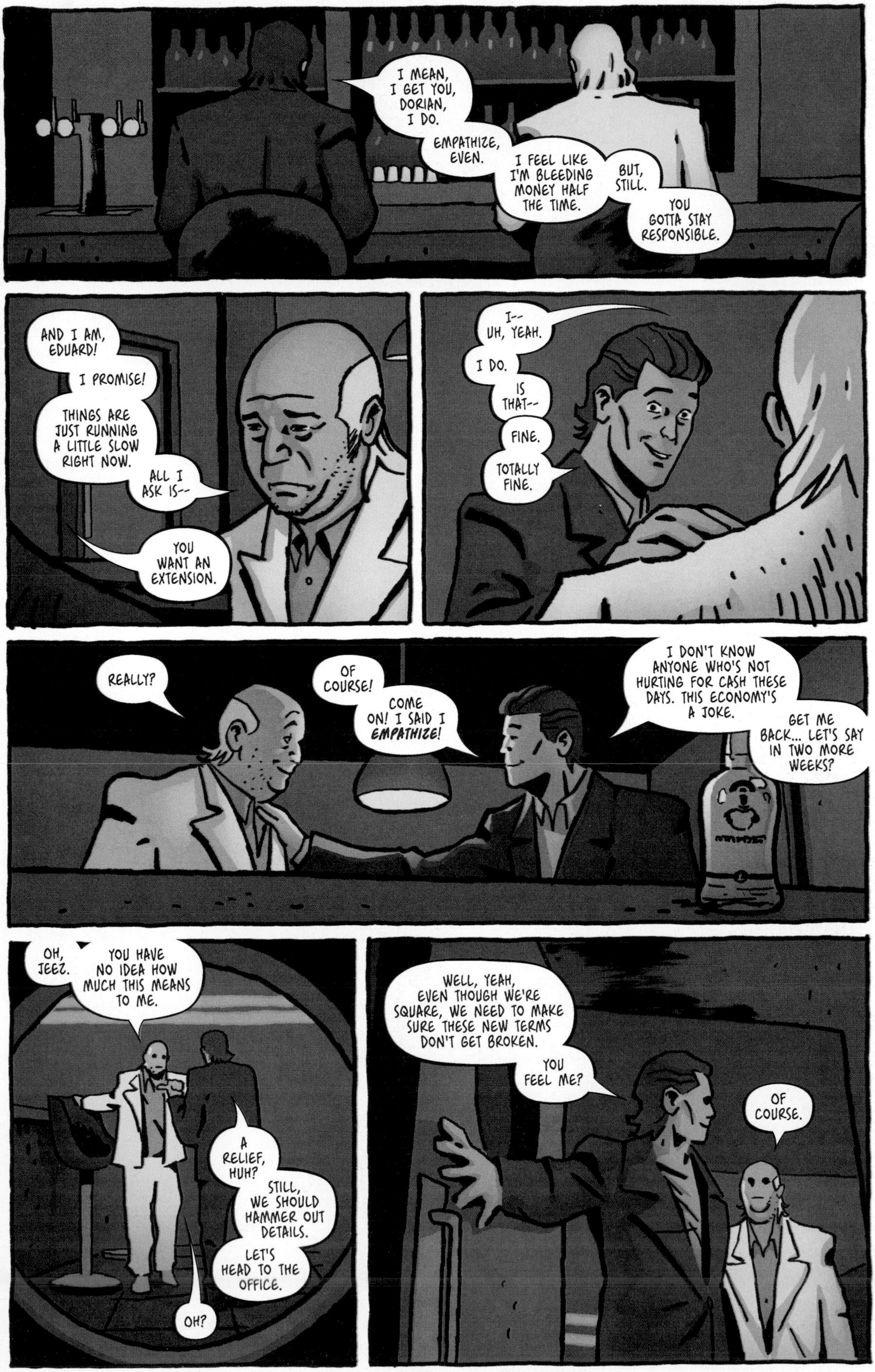
I MEAN, I GET YOU, DORIAN, I DO.
EMPATHIZE, EVEN.
I FEEL LIKE I'M BLEEDING MONEY HALF THE TIME.
BUT, STILL.
YOU GOTTA STAY RESPONSIBLE.
AND I AM, EDUARD!
I PROMISE!
THINGS ARE JUST RUNNING A LITTLE SLOW RIGHT NOW.
ALL I ASK IS--
YOU WANT AN EXTENSION.
I-- UH, YEAH.
I DO.
IS THAT--
FINE.
TOTALLY FINE.
REALLY?
OF COURSE!
COME ON! I SAID I *EMPATHIZE!*
I DON'T KNOW ANYONE WHO'S NOT HURTING FOR CASH THESE DAYS. THIS ECONOMY'S A JOKE.
GET ME BACK... LET'S SAY IN TWO MORE WEEKS?
OH, JEEZ.
YOU HAVE NO IDEA HOW MUCH THIS MEANS TO ME.
A RELIEF, HUH?
STILL, WE SHOULD HAMMER OUT DETAILS.
LET'S HEAD TO THE OFFICE.
OH?
WELL, YEAH, EVEN THOUGH WE'RE SQUARE, WE NEED TO MAKE SURE THESE NEW TERMS DON'T GET BROKEN.
YOU FEEL ME?
OF COURSE.

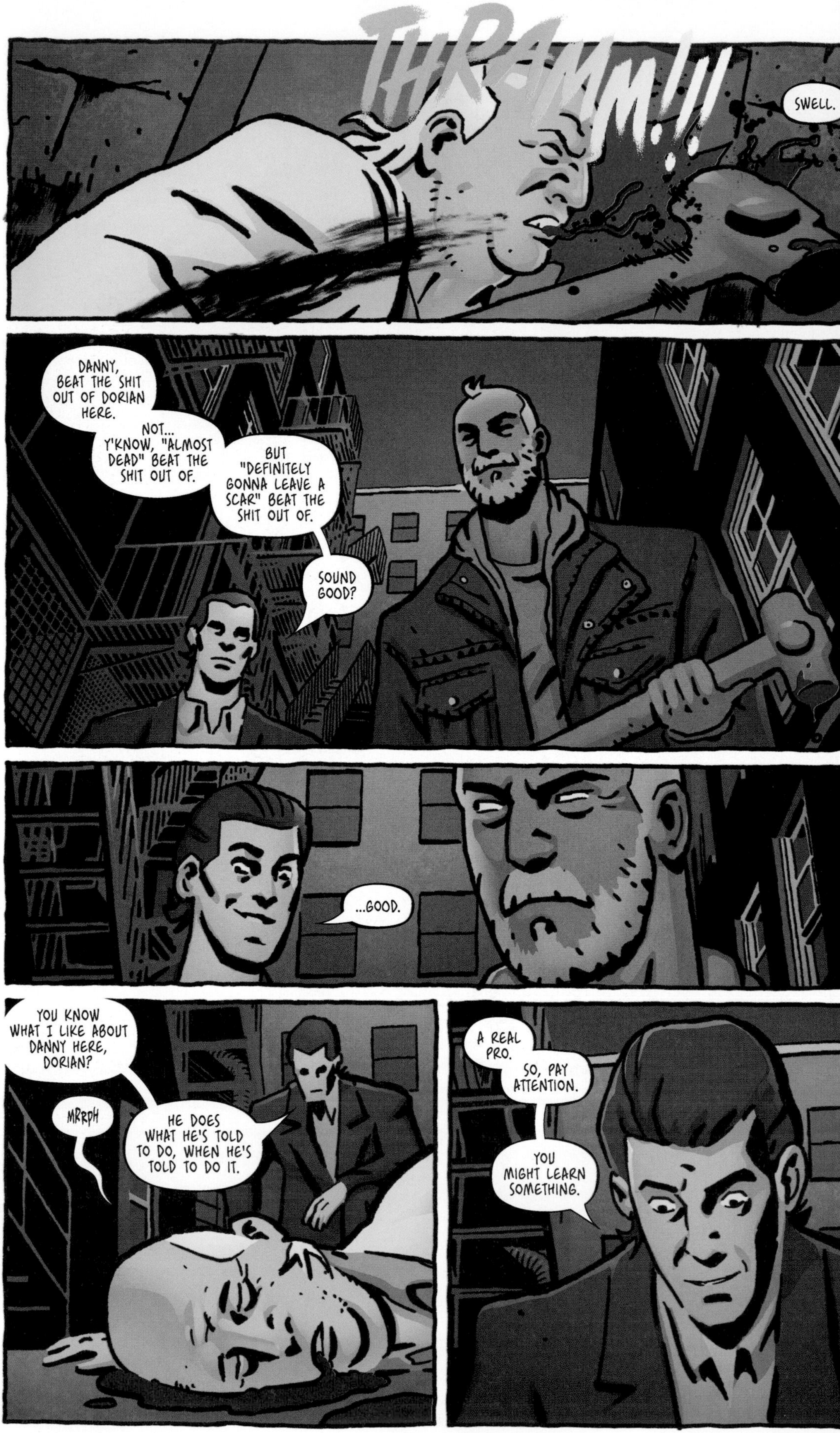
THRAMM!!!
SWELL.
DANNY, BEAT THE SHIT OUT OF DORIAN HERE.
NOT... Y'KNOW, "ALMOST DEAD" BEAT THE SHIT OUT OF.
BUT "DEFINITELY GONNA LEAVE A SCAR" BEAT THE SHIT OUT OF.
SOUND GOOD?
...GOOD.
YOU KNOW WHAT I LIKE ABOUT DANNY HERE, DORIAN?
MRRPH
HE DOES WHAT HE'S TOLD TO DO, WHEN HE'S TOLD TO DO IT.
A REAL PRO.
SO, PAY ATTENTION.
YOU MIGHT LEARN SOMETHING.

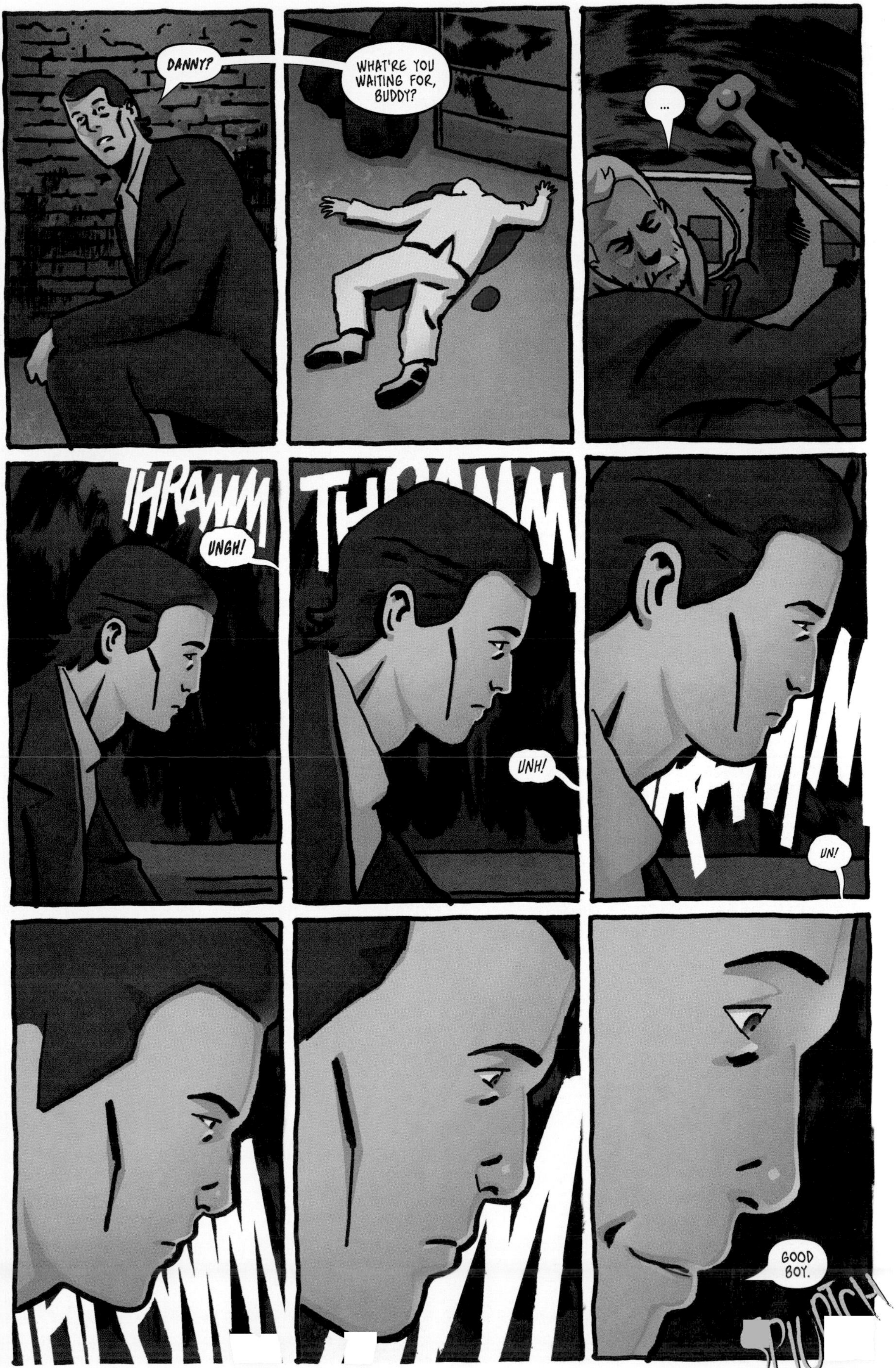
DANNY?
WHAT'RE YOU WAITING FOR, BUDDY?
...
THRAWM
UNGH!
UNH!
UN!
GOOD BOY.
SPLUTCH

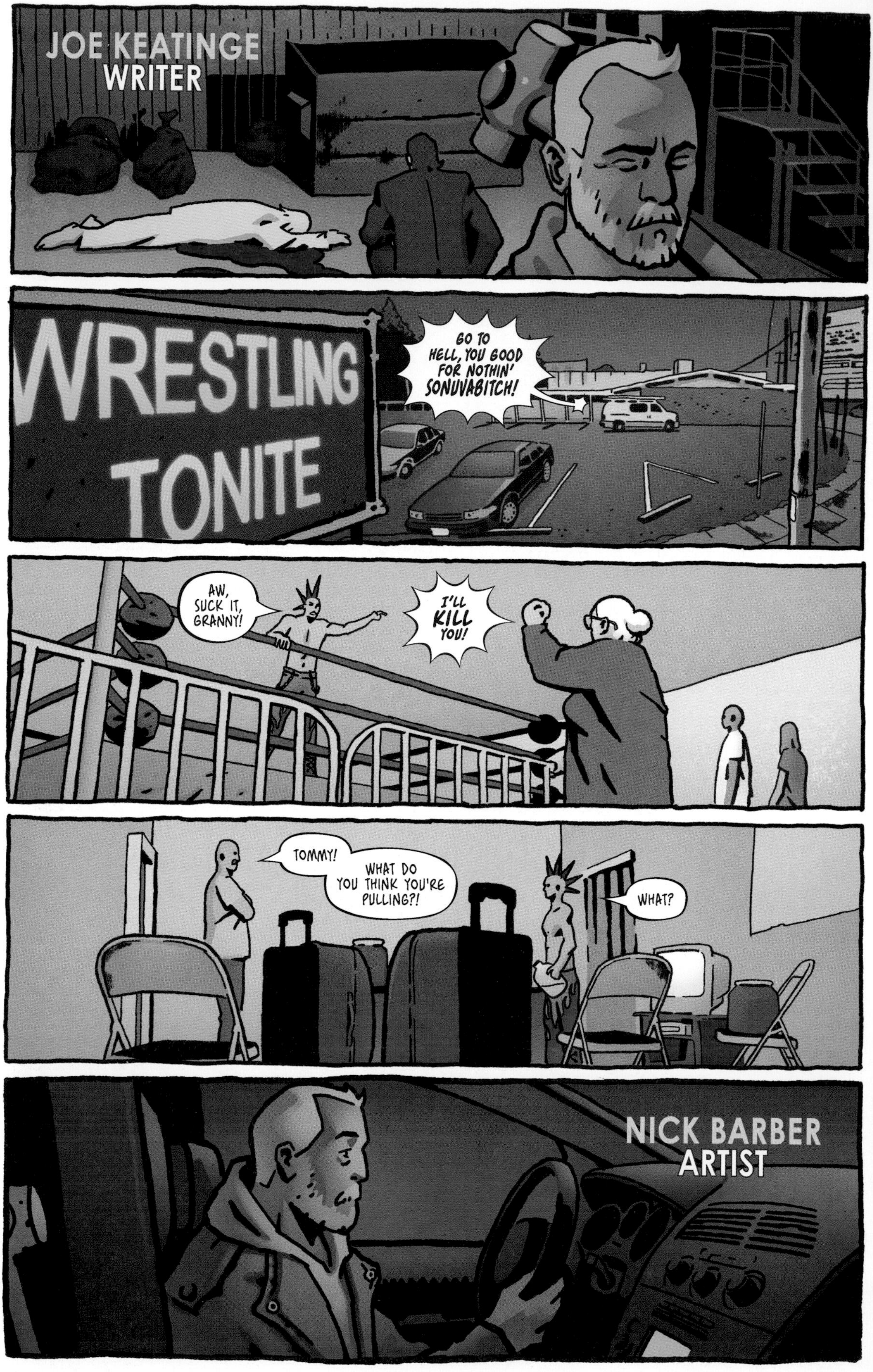
JOE KEATINGE
WRITER
WRESTLING TONITE
GO TO HELL, YOU GOOD FOR NOTHIN' SONUVABITCH!
AW, SUCK IT, GRANNY!
I'LL KILL YOU!
TOMMY!
WHAT DO YOU THINK YOU'RE PULLING?!
WHAT?
NICK BARBER
ARTIST

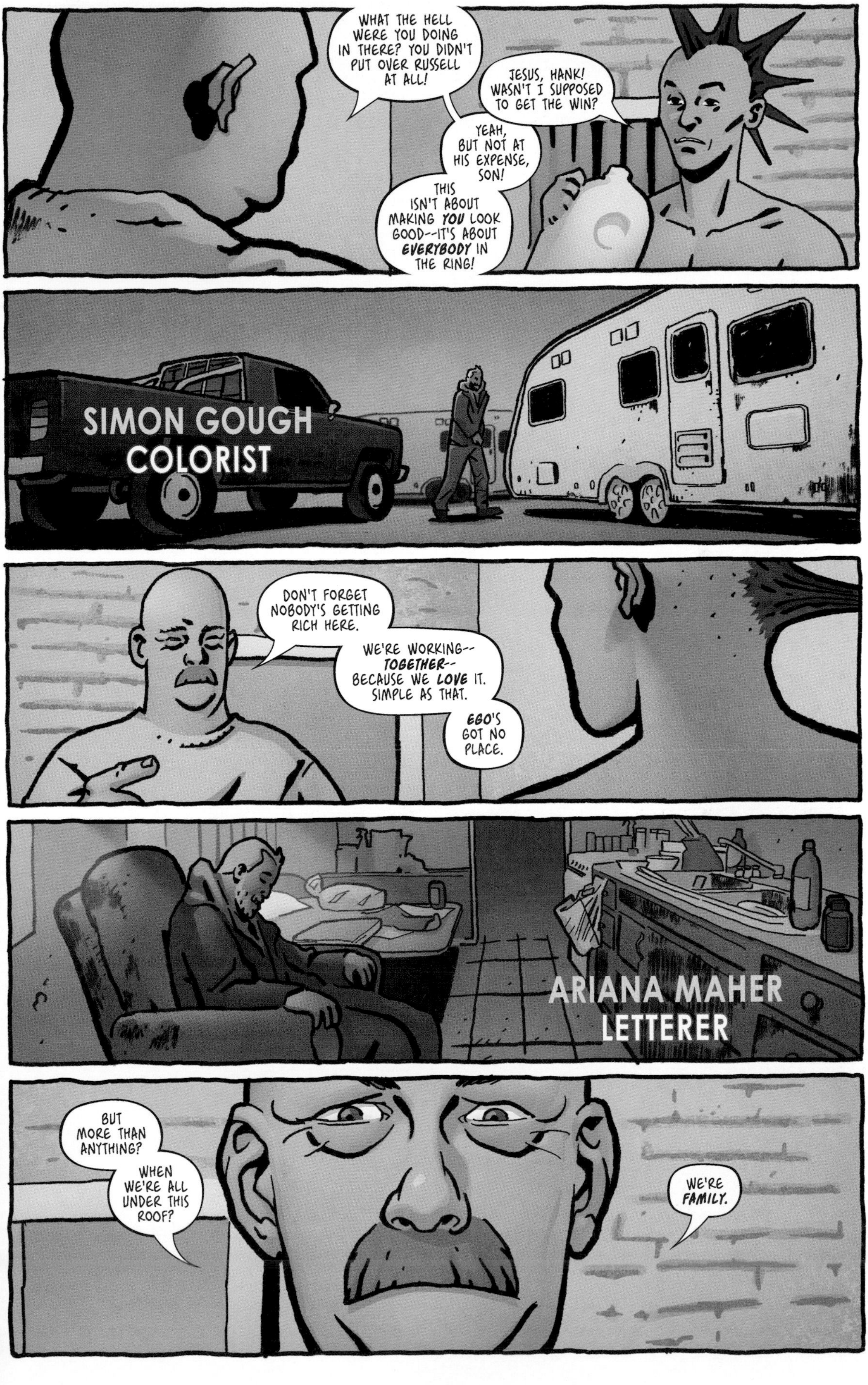
WHAT THE HELL WERE YOU DOING IN THERE? YOU DIDN'T PUT OVER RUSSELL AT ALL!
JESUS, HANK! WASN'T I SUPPOSED TO GET THE WIN?
YEAH, BUT NOT AT HIS EXPENSE, SON!
THIS ISN'T ABOUT MAKING YOU LOOK GOOD--IT'S ABOUT EVERYBODY IN THE RING!
SIMON GOUGH
COLORIST
DON'T FORGET NOBODY'S GETTING RICH HERE.
WE'RE WORKING--TOGETHER--BECAUSE WE LOVE IT. SIMPLE AS THAT.
EGO'S GOT NO PLACE.
ARIANA MAHER
LETTERER
BUT MORE THAN ANYTHING?
WHEN WE'RE ALL UNDER THIS ROOF?
WE'RE FAMILY.

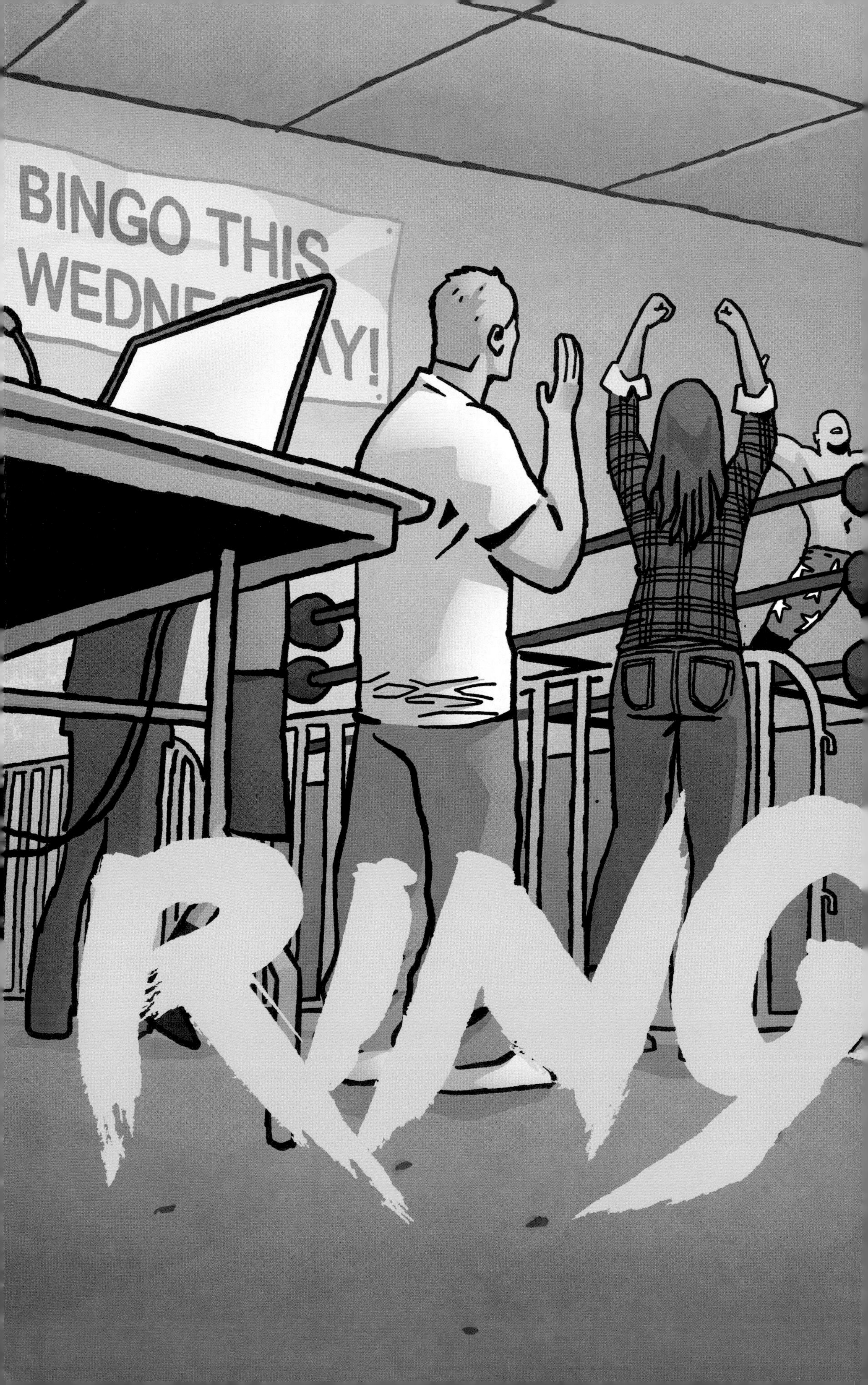
BINGO THIS
WEDNE AY!
RING

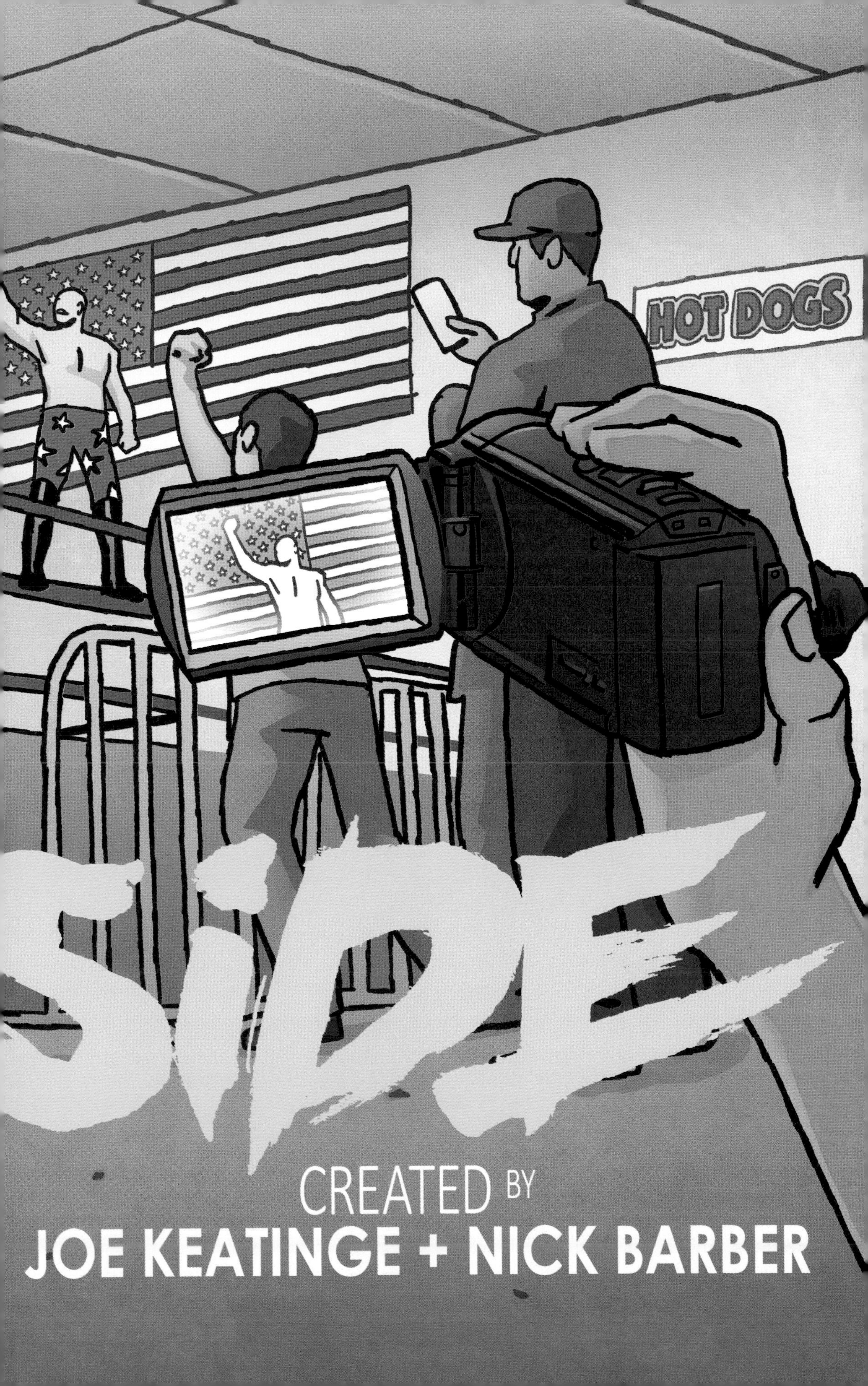
HOT DOGS
SIDE
CREATED BY
JOE KEATINGE + NICK BARBER

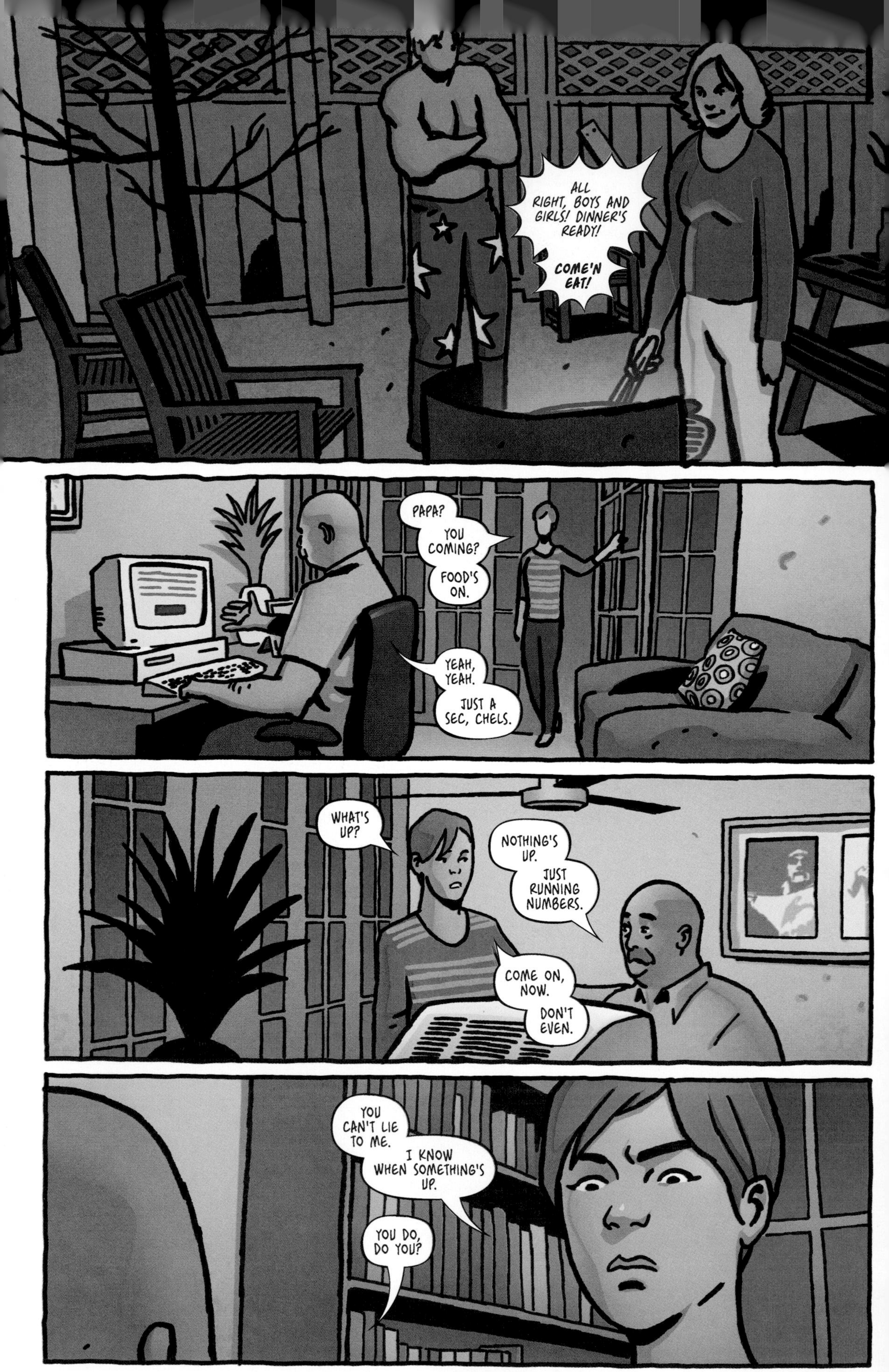
ALL RIGHT, BOYS AND GIRLS! DINNER'S READY!
COME'N EAT!
PAPA?
YOU COMING?
FOOD'S ON.
YEAH, YEAH.
JUST A SEC, CHELS.
WHAT'S UP?
NOTHING'S UP.
JUST RUNNING NUMBERS.
COME ON, NOW.
DON'T EVEN.
YOU CAN'T LIE TO ME.
I KNOW WHEN SOMETHING'S UP.
YOU DO, DO YOU?

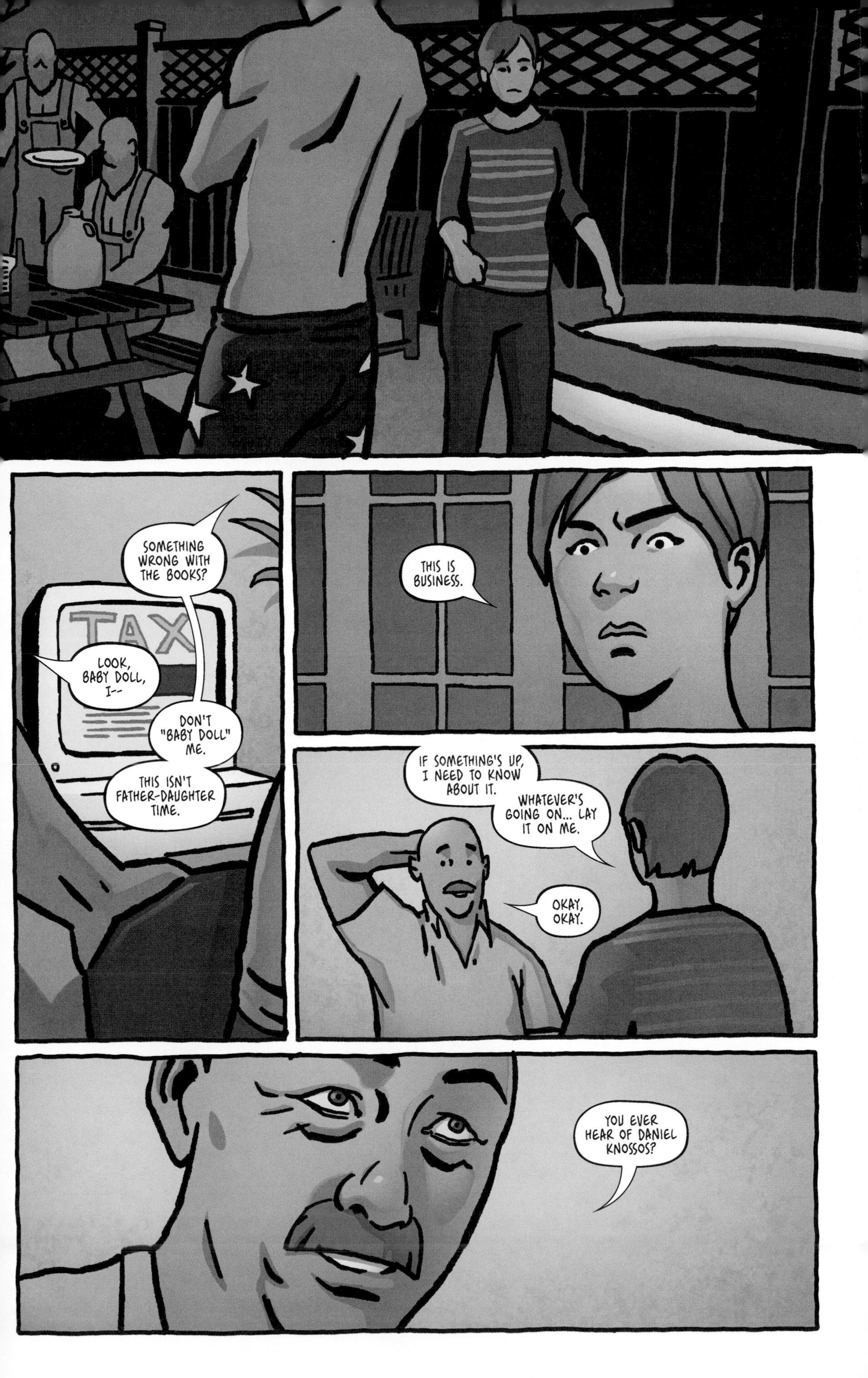
SOMETHING WRONG WITH THE BOOKS?
LOOK, BABY DOLL, I--
DON'T "BABY DOLL" ME.
THIS ISN'T FATHER-DAUGHTER TIME.
THIS IS BUSINESS.
IF SOMETHING'S UP, I NEED TO KNOW ABOUT IT.
WHATEVER'S GOING ON... LAY IT ON ME.
OKAY, OKAY.
YOU EVER HEAR OF DANIEL KNOSSOS?

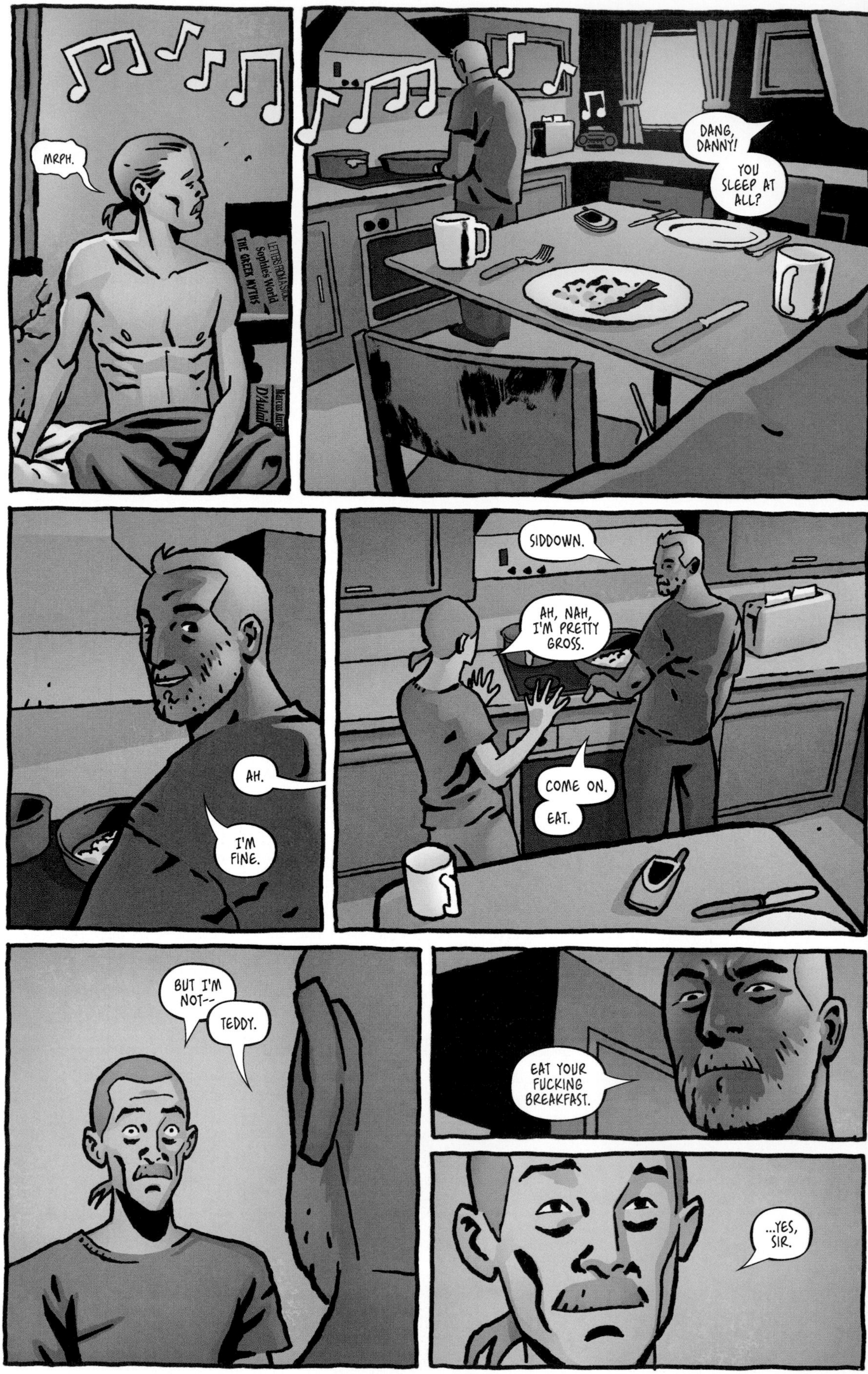
MRPH.
Sophie's World
THE GREEK MYTHS
DANG, DANNY!
YOU SLEEP AT ALL?
AH.
I'M FINE.
SIDDOWN.
AH, NAH, I'M PRETTY GROSS.
COME ON.
EAT.
BUT I'M NOT--
TEDDY.
EAT YOUR FUCKING BREAKFAST.
...YES, SIR.

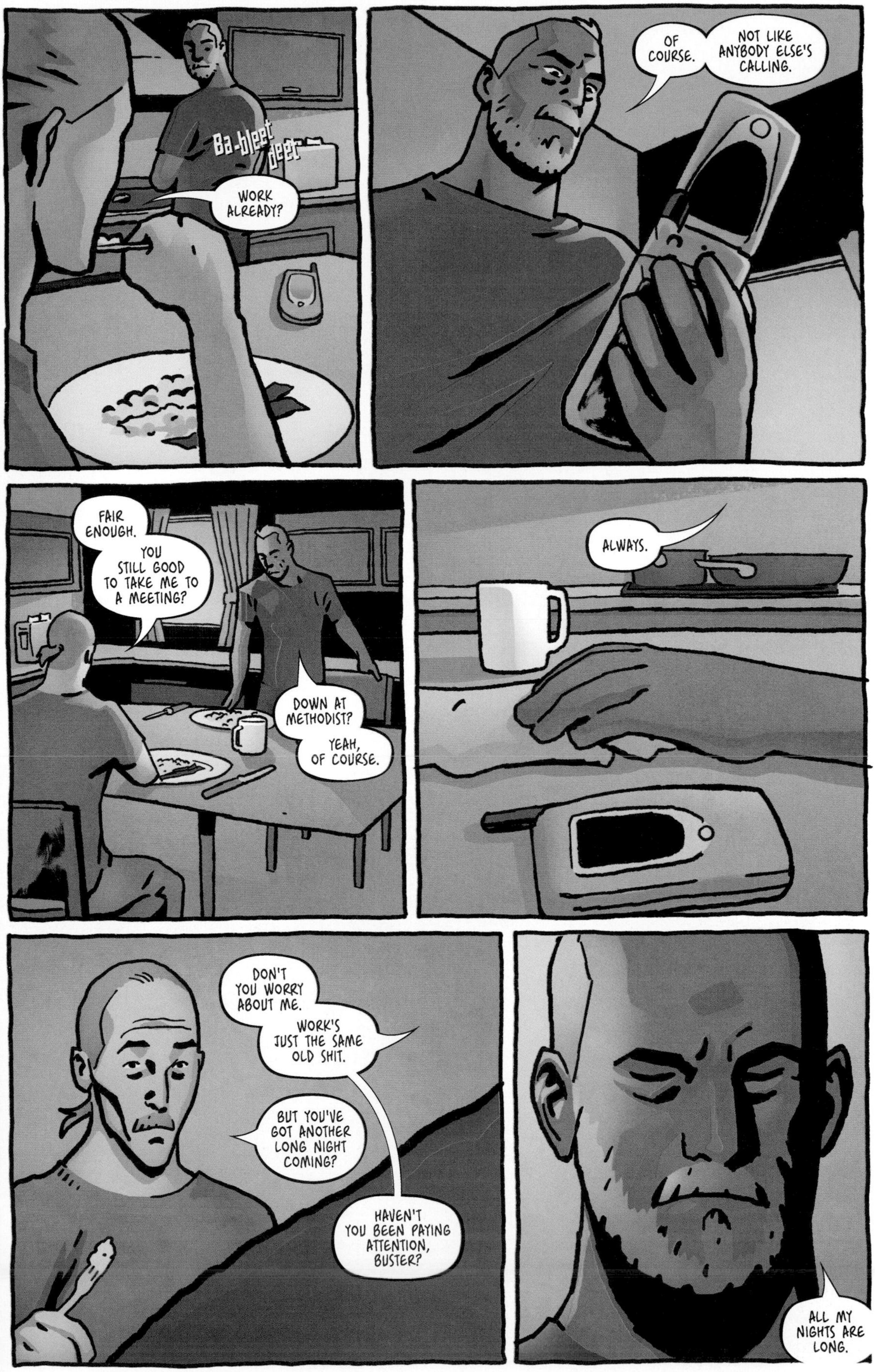
Ba-bleet deet
WORK ALREADY?
OF COURSE.
NOT LIKE ANYBODY ELSE'S CALLING.
FAIR ENOUGH.
YOU STILL GOOD TO TAKE ME TO A MEETING?
DOWN AT METHODIST?
YEAH, OF COURSE.
ALWAYS.
DON'T YOU WORRY ABOUT ME.
WORK'S JUST THE SAME OLD SHIT.
BUT YOU'VE GOT ANOTHER LONG NIGHT COMING?
HAVEN'T YOU BEEN PAYING ATTENTION, BUSTER?
ALL MY NIGHTS ARE LONG.

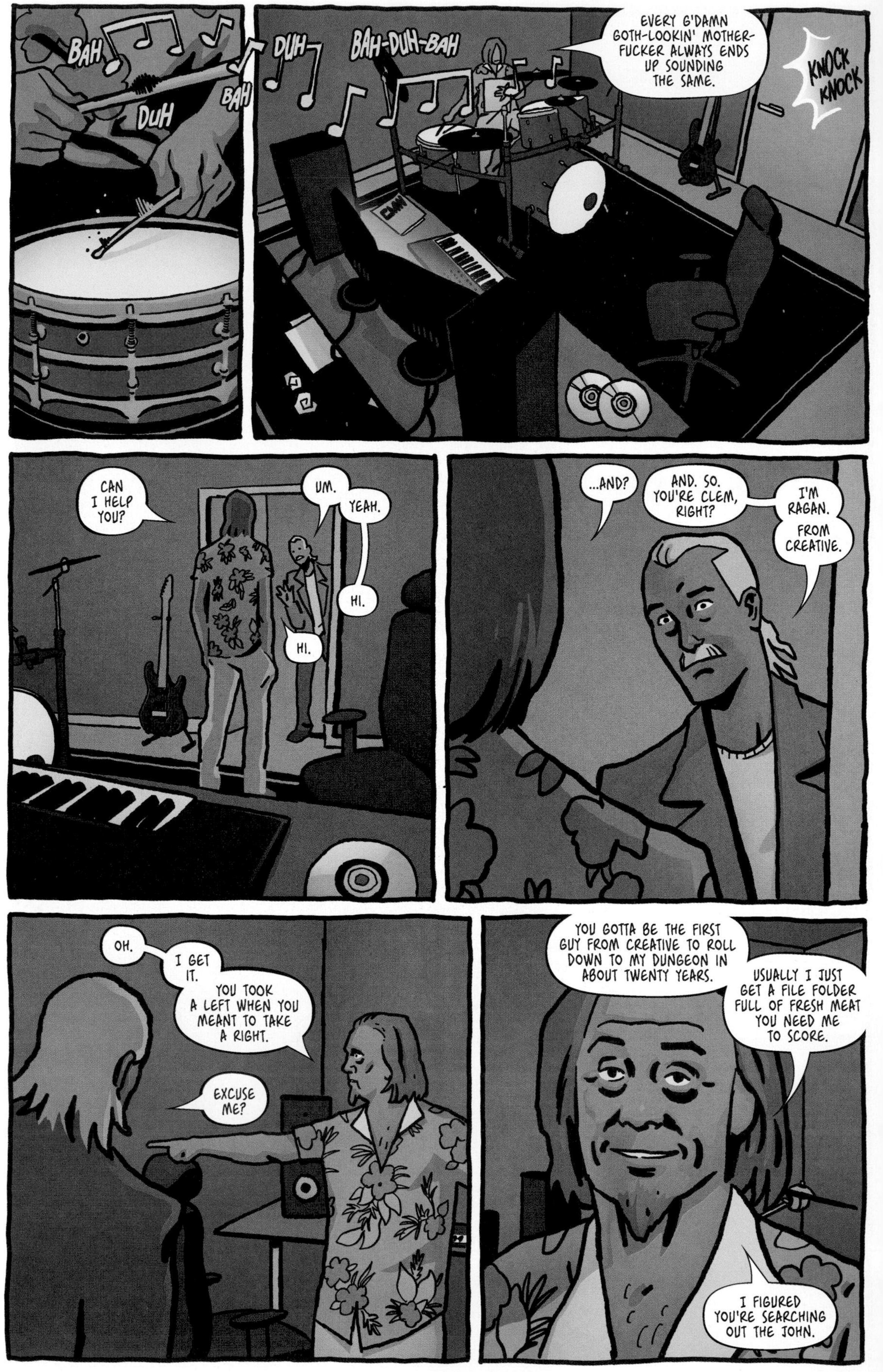
BAH
DUH
BAH
DUH
BAH-DUH-BAH
EVERY G'DAMN GOTH-LOOKIN' MOTHER-FUCKER ALWAYS ENDS UP SOUNDING THE SAME.
KNOCK KNOCK
CAN I HELP YOU?
UM.
YEAH.
HI.
HI.
...AND?
AND. SO. YOU'RE CLEM, RIGHT?
I'M RAGAN.
FROM CREATIVE.
OH.
I GET IT.
YOU TOOK A LEFT WHEN YOU MEANT TO TAKE A RIGHT.
EXCUSE ME?
YOU GOTTA BE THE FIRST GUY FROM CREATIVE TO ROLL DOWN TO MY DUNGEON IN ABOUT TWENTY YEARS.
USUALLY I JUST GET A FILE FOLDER FULL OF FRESH MEAT YOU NEED ME TO SCORE.
I FIGURED YOU'RE SEARCHING OUT THE JOHN.

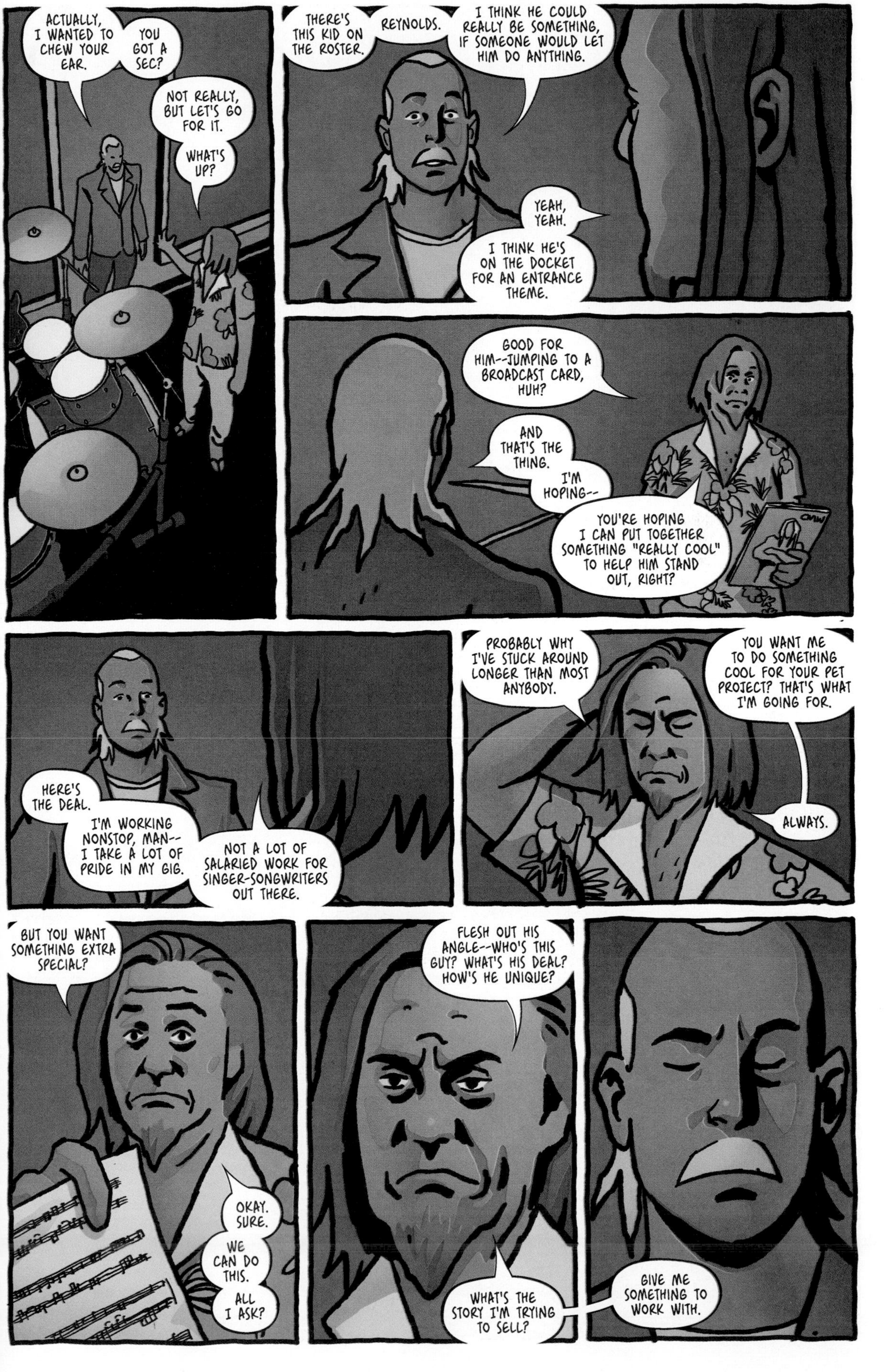

ACTUALLY, I WANTED TO CHEW YOUR EAR.
YOU GOT A SEC?
NOT REALLY, BUT LET'S GO FOR IT.
WHAT'S UP?
THERE'S THIS KID ON THE ROSTER.
REYNOLDS.
I THINK HE COULD REALLY BE SOMETHING, IF SOMEONE WOULD LET HIM DO ANYTHING.
YEAH, YEAH.
I THINK HE'S ON THE DOCKET FOR AN ENTRANCE THEME.
GOOD FOR HIM--JUMPING TO A BROADCAST CARD, HUH?
AND THAT'S THE THING.
I'M HOPING--
YOU'RE HOPING I CAN PUT TOGETHER SOMETHING "REALLY COOL" TO HELP HIM STAND OUT, RIGHT?
HERE'S THE DEAL.
I'M WORKING NONSTOP, MAN--I TAKE A LOT OF PRIDE IN MY GIG.
NOT A LOT OF SALARIED WORK FOR SINGER-SONGWRITERS OUT THERE.
PROBABLY WHY I'VE STUCK AROUND LONGER THAN MOST ANYBODY.
YOU WANT ME TO DO SOMETHING COOL FOR YOUR PET PROJECT? THAT'S WHAT I'M GOING FOR.
ALWAYS.
BUT YOU WANT SOMETHING EXTRA SPECIAL?
OKAY. SURE.
WE CAN DO THIS.
ALL I ASK?
FLESH OUT HIS ANGLE--WHO'S THIS GUY? WHAT'S HIS DEAL? HOW'S HE UNIQUE?
WHAT'S THE STORY I'M TRYING TO SELL?
GIVE ME SOMETHING TO WORK WITH.

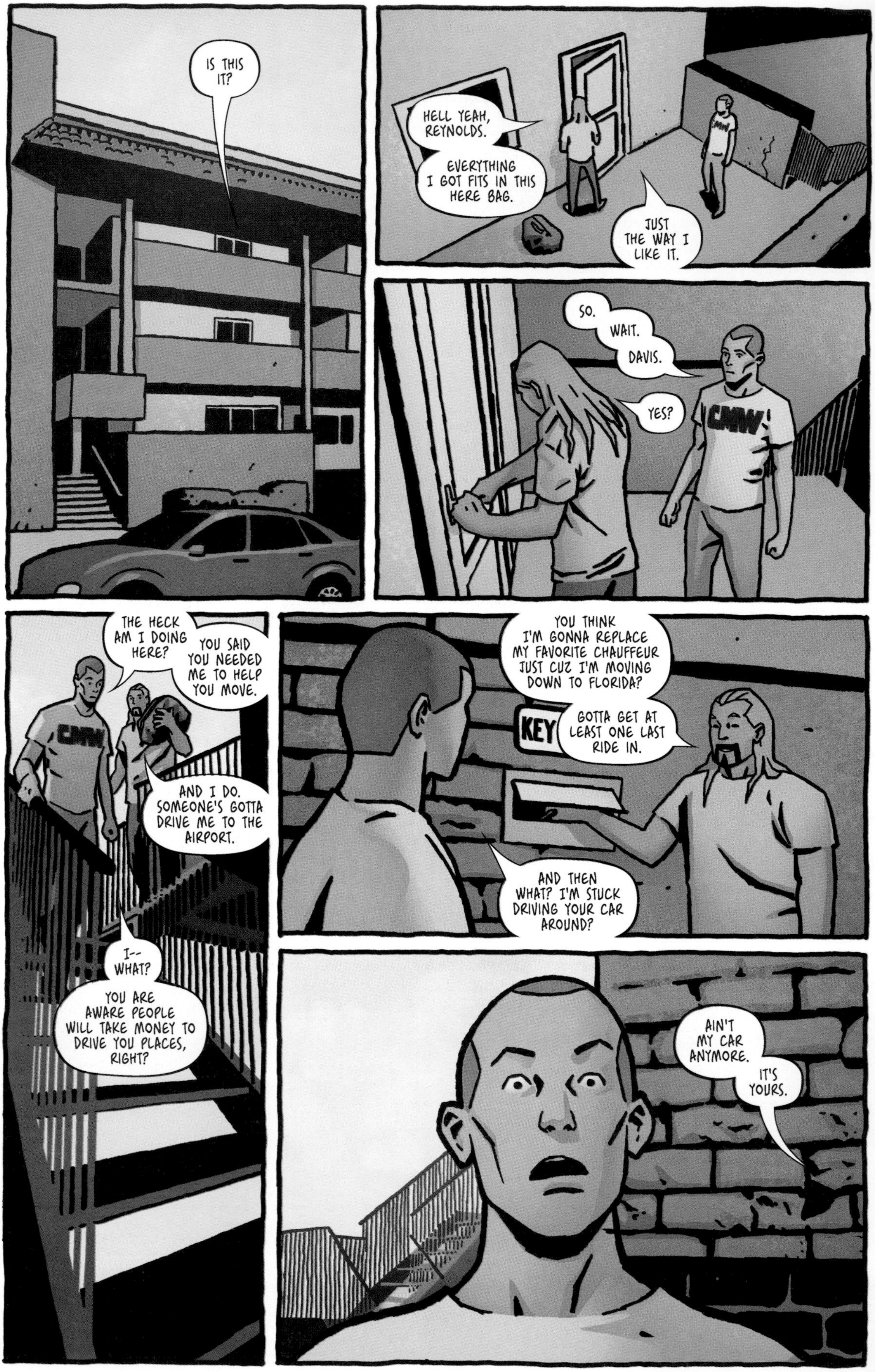
IS THIS IT?
HELL YEAH, REYNOLDS.
EVERYTHING I GOT FITS IN THIS HERE BAG.
JUST THE WAY I LIKE IT.
SO.
WAIT.
DAVIS.
YES?
THE HECK AM I DOING HERE?
YOU SAID YOU NEEDED ME TO HELP YOU MOVE.
AND I DO. SOMEONE'S GOTTA DRIVE ME TO THE AIRPORT.
I-- WHAT?
YOU ARE AWARE PEOPLE WILL TAKE MONEY TO DRIVE YOU PLACES, RIGHT?
YOU THINK I'M GONNA REPLACE MY FAVORITE CHAUFFEUR JUST CUZ I'M MOVING DOWN TO FLORIDA?
KEY
GOTTA GET AT LEAST ONE LAST RIDE IN.
AND THEN WHAT? I'M STUCK DRIVING YOUR CAR AROUND?
AIN'T MY CAR ANYMORE.
IT'S YOURS.

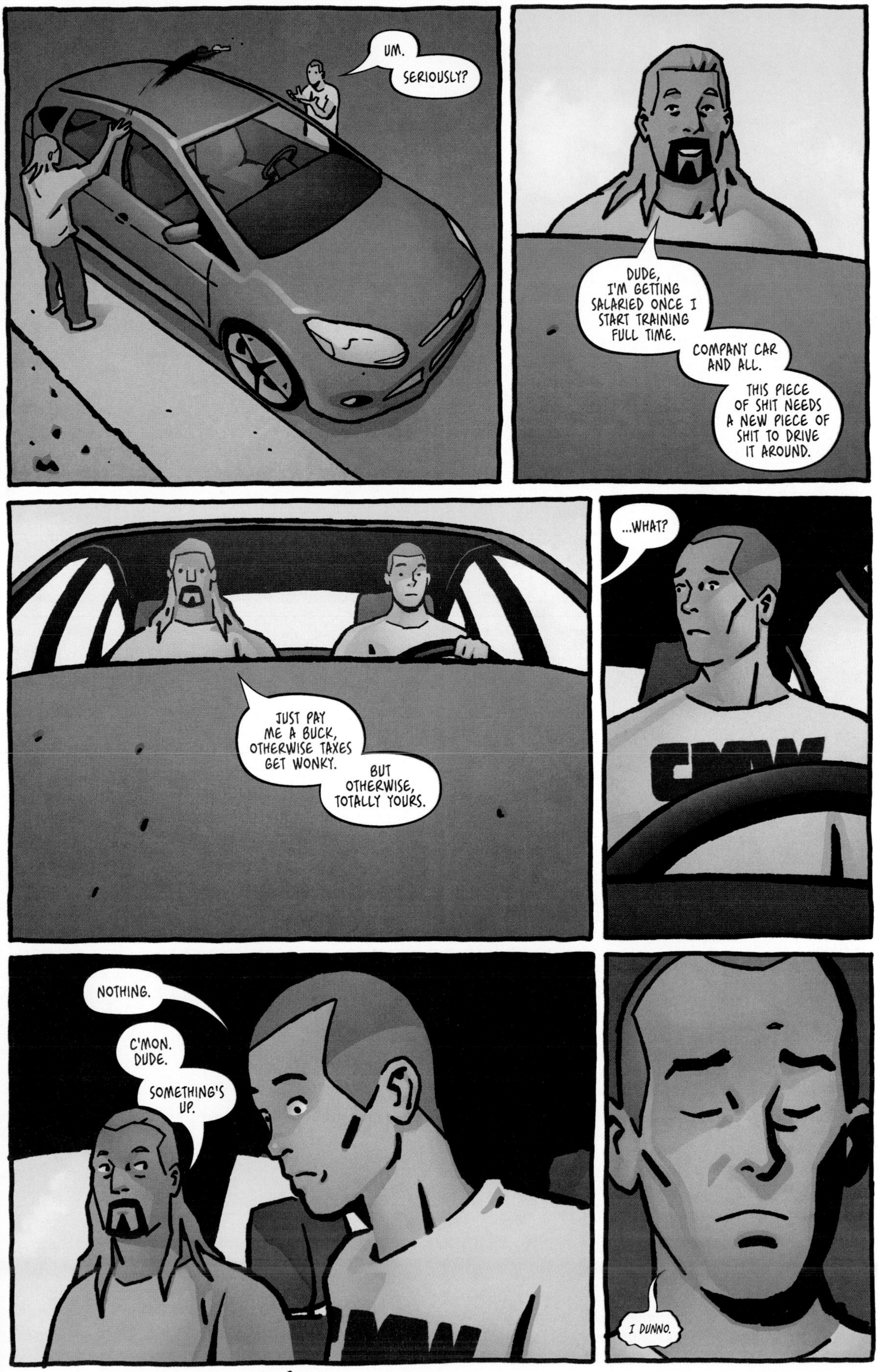
UM.
SERIOUSLY?
DUDE, I'M GETTING SALARIED ONCE I START TRAINING FULL TIME.
COMPANY CAR AND ALL.
THIS PIECE OF SHIT NEEDS A NEW PIECE OF SHIT TO DRIVE IT AROUND.
JUST PAY ME A BUCK, OTHERWISE TAXES GET WONKY.
BUT OTHERWISE, TOTALLY YOURS.
...WHAT?
NOTHING.
C'MON. DUDE.
SOMETHING'S UP.
I DUNNO.

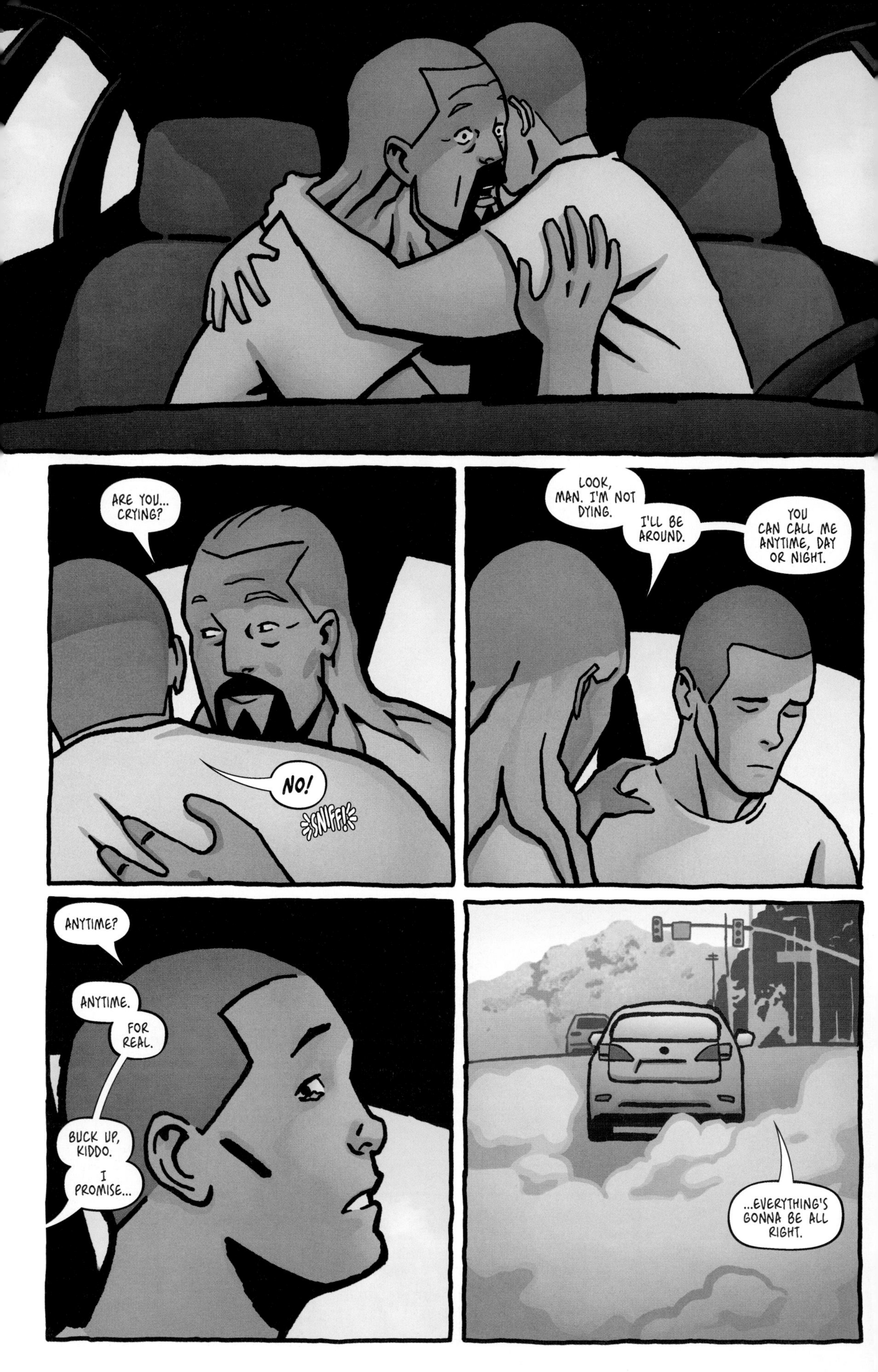
ARE YOU... CRYING?
NO!
SNIFF!
LOOK, MAN. I'M NOT DYING.
I'LL BE AROUND.
YOU CAN CALL ME ANYTIME, DAY OR NIGHT.
ANYTIME?
ANYTIME.
FOR REAL.
BUCK UP, KIDDO.
I PROMISE...
...EVERYTHING'S GONNA BE ALL RIGHT.

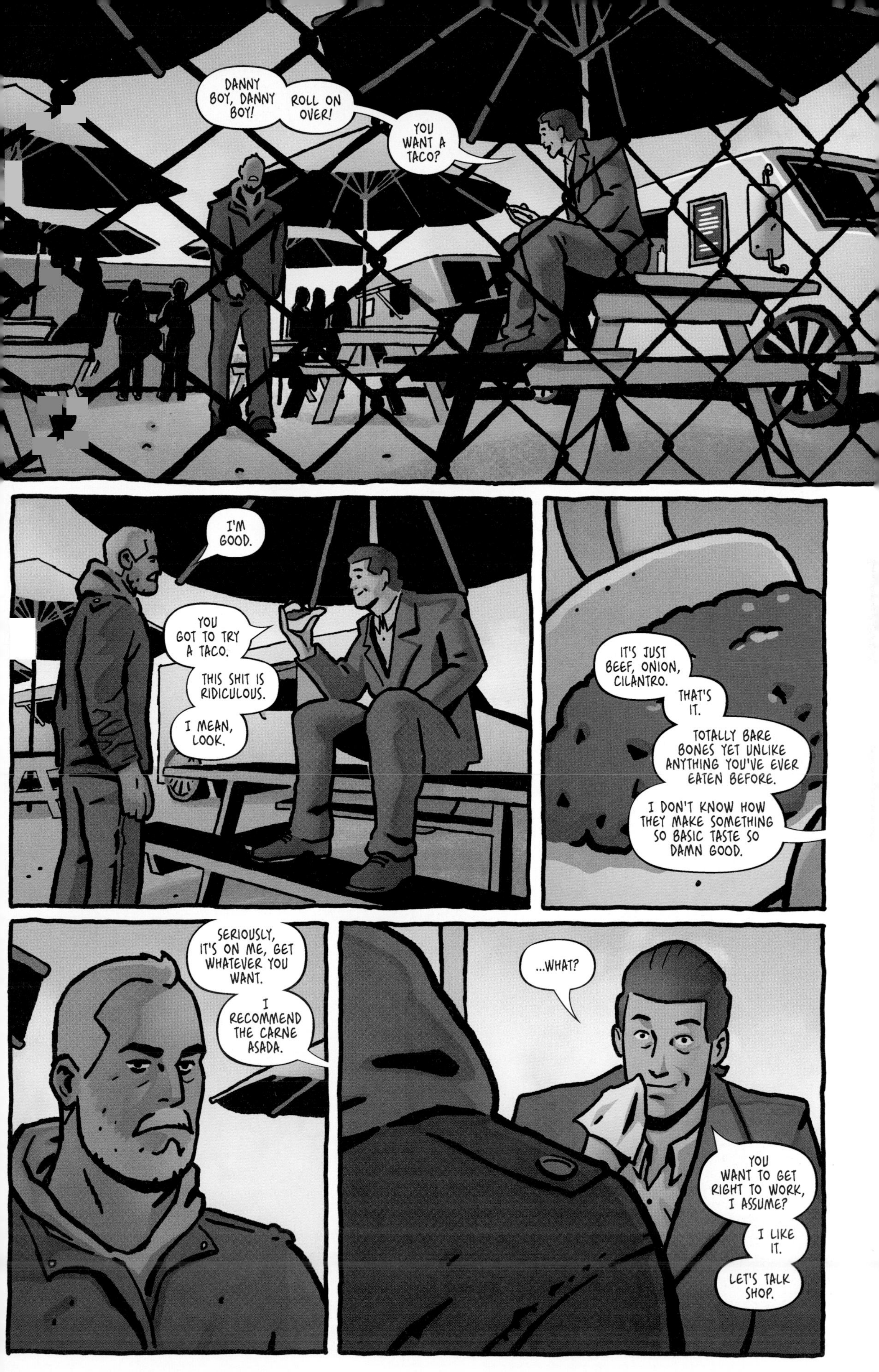
DANNY BOY, DANNY BOY!
ROLL ON OVER!
YOU WANT A TACO?
I'M GOOD.
YOU GOT TO TRY A TACO.
THIS SHIT IS RIDICULOUS.
I MEAN, LOOK.
IT'S JUST BEEF, ONION, CILANTRO.
THAT'S IT.
TOTALLY BARE BONES YET UNLIKE ANYTHING YOU'VE EVER EATEN BEFORE.
I DON'T KNOW HOW THEY MAKE SOMETHING SO BASIC TASTE SO DAMN GOOD.
SERIOUSLY, IT'S ON ME, GET WHATEVER YOU WANT.
I RECOMMEND THE CARNE ASADA.
...WHAT?
YOU WANT TO GET RIGHT TO WORK, I ASSUME?
I LIKE IT.
LET'S TALK SHOP.

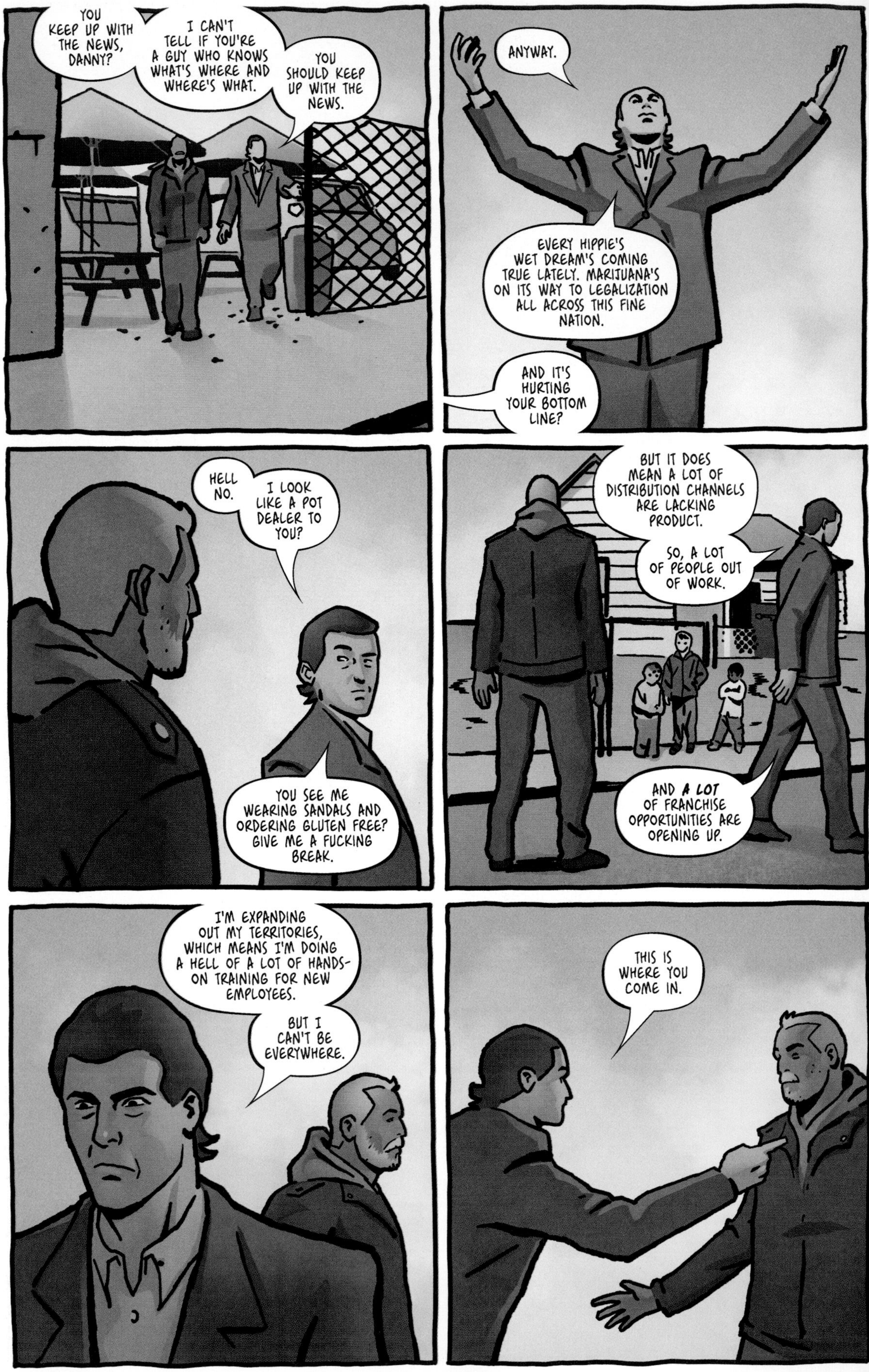
YOU KEEP UP WITH THE NEWS, DANNY?
I CAN'T TELL IF YOU'RE A GUY WHO KNOWS WHAT'S WHERE AND WHERE'S WHAT.
YOU SHOULD KEEP UP WITH THE NEWS.
ANYWAY.
EVERY HIPPIE'S WET DREAM'S COMING TRUE LATELY. MARIJUANA'S ON ITS WAY TO LEGALIZATION ALL ACROSS THIS FINE NATION.
AND IT'S HURTING YOUR BOTTOM LINE?
HELL NO.
I LOOK LIKE A POT DEALER TO YOU?
YOU SEE ME WEARING SANDALS AND ORDERING GLUTEN FREE? GIVE ME A FUCKING BREAK.
BUT IT DOES MEAN A LOT OF DISTRIBUTION CHANNELS ARE LACKING PRODUCT.
SO, A LOT OF PEOPLE OUT OF WORK.
AND ***A LOT*** OF FRANCHISE OPPORTUNITIES ARE OPENING UP.
I'M EXPANDING OUT MY TERRITORIES, WHICH MEANS I'M DOING A HELL OF A LOT OF HANDS-ON TRAINING FOR NEW EMPLOYEES.
BUT I CAN'T BE EVERYWHERE.
THIS IS WHERE YOU COME IN.

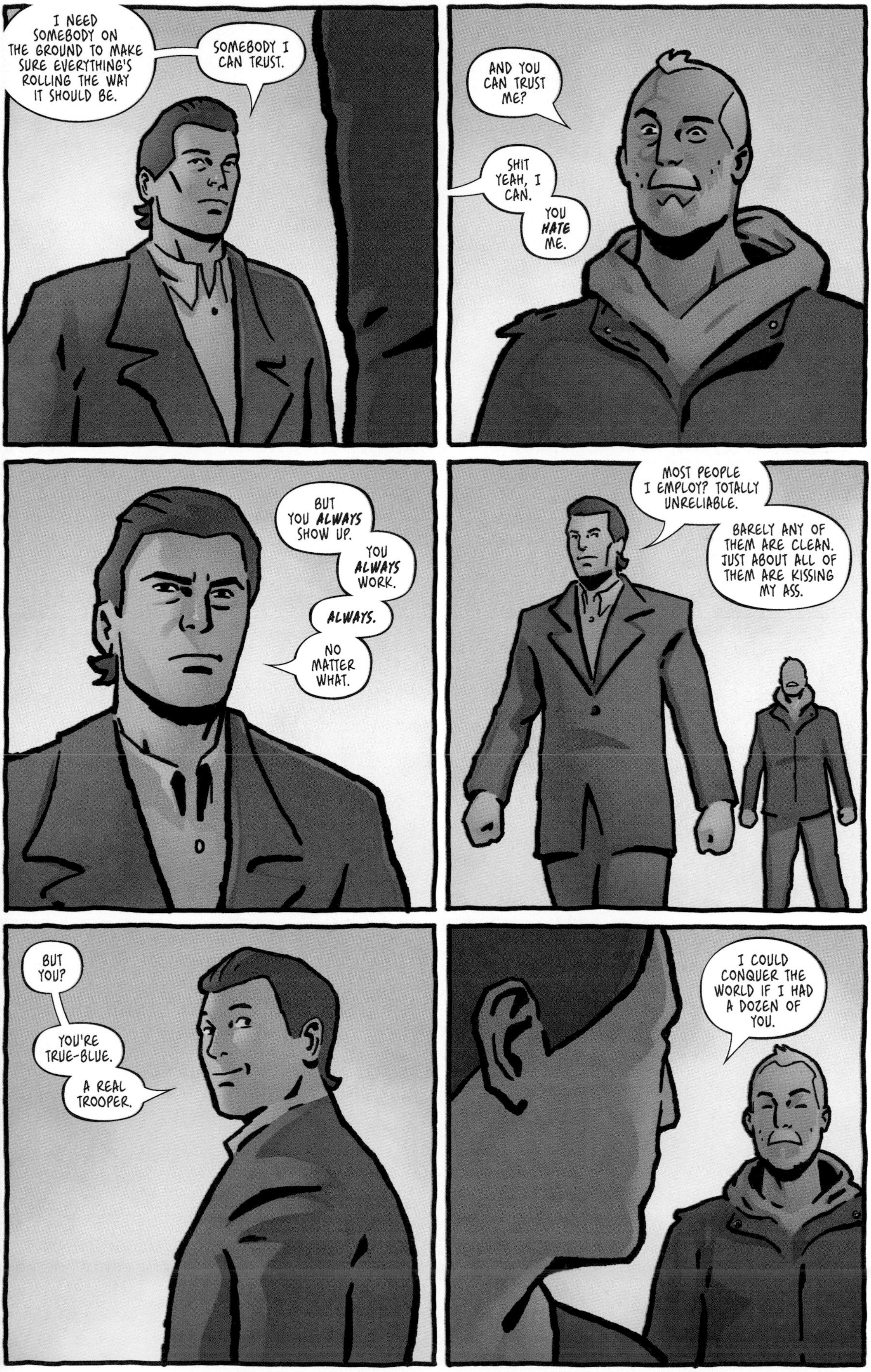

I NEED SOMEBODY ON THE GROUND TO MAKE SURE EVERYTHING'S ROLLING THE WAY IT SHOULD BE.
SOMEBODY I CAN TRUST.
AND YOU CAN TRUST ME?
SHIT YEAH, I CAN.
YOU **HATE** ME.
BUT YOU **ALWAYS** SHOW UP.
YOU **ALWAYS** WORK.
ALWAYS.
NO MATTER WHAT.
MOST PEOPLE I EMPLOY? TOTALLY UNRELIABLE.
BARELY ANY OF THEM ARE CLEAN. JUST ABOUT ALL OF THEM ARE KISSING MY ASS.
BUT YOU?
YOU'RE TRUE-BLUE.
A REAL TROOPER.
I COULD CONQUER THE WORLD IF I HAD A DOZEN OF YOU.

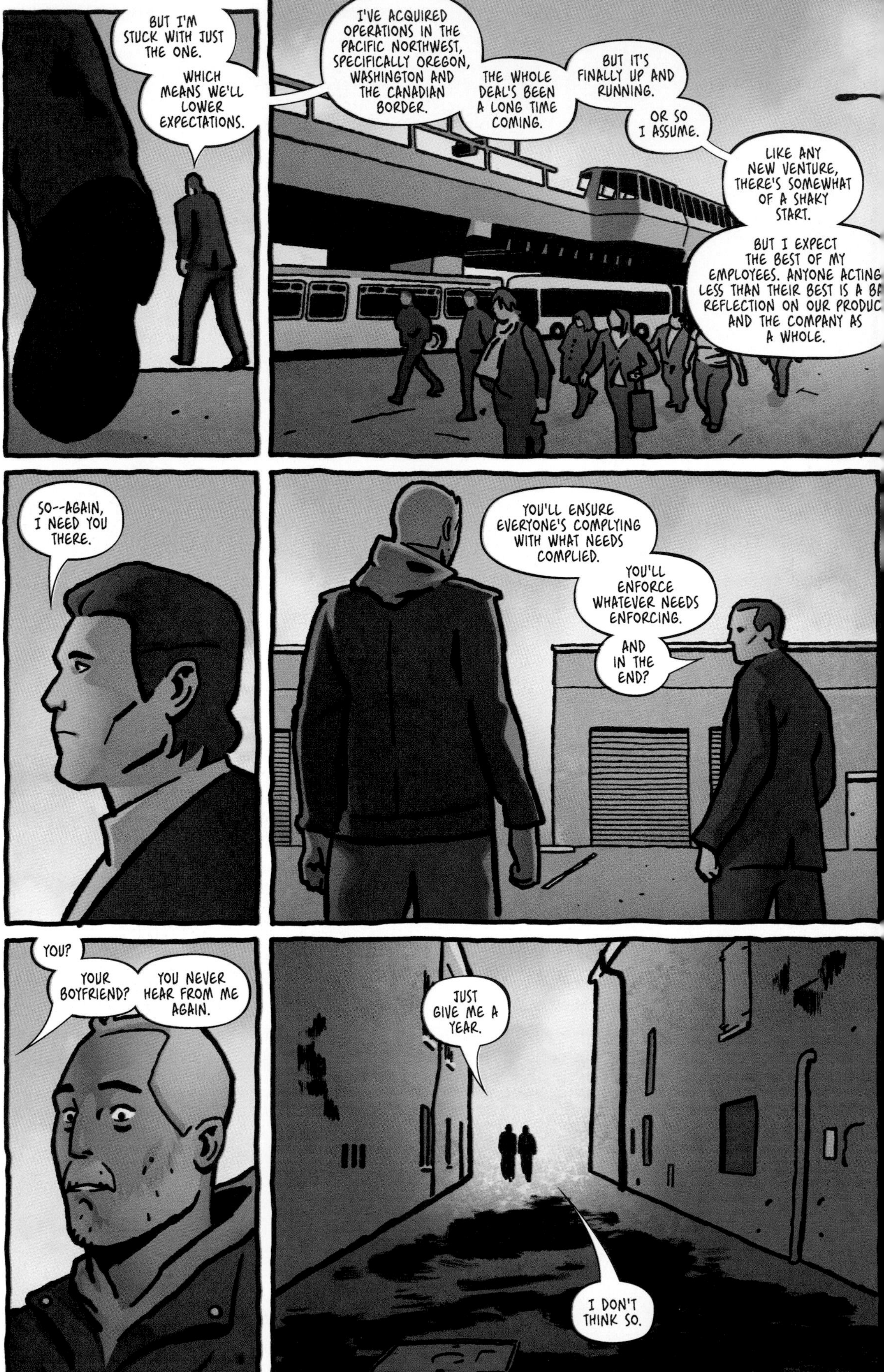
BUT I'M STUCK WITH JUST THE ONE.
WHICH MEANS WE'LL LOWER EXPECTATIONS.
I'VE ACQUIRED OPERATIONS IN THE PACIFIC NORTHWEST, SPECIFICALLY OREGON, WASHINGTON AND THE CANADIAN BORDER.
THE WHOLE DEAL'S BEEN A LONG TIME COMING.
BUT IT'S FINALLY UP AND RUNNING.
OR SO I ASSUME.
LIKE ANY NEW VENTURE, THERE'S SOMEWHAT OF A SHAKY START.
BUT I EXPECT THE BEST OF MY EMPLOYEES. ANYONE ACTING LESS THAN THEIR BEST IS A BA REFLECTION ON OUR PRODUC AND THE COMPANY AS A WHOLE.
SO--AGAIN, I NEED YOU THERE.
YOU'LL ENSURE EVERYONE'S COMPLYING WITH WHAT NEEDS COMPLIED.
YOU'LL ENFORCE WHATEVER NEEDS ENFORCING.
AND IN THE END?
YOU?
YOUR BOYFRIEND?
YOU NEVER HEAR FROM ME AGAIN.
JUST GIVE ME A YEAR.
I DON'T THINK SO.

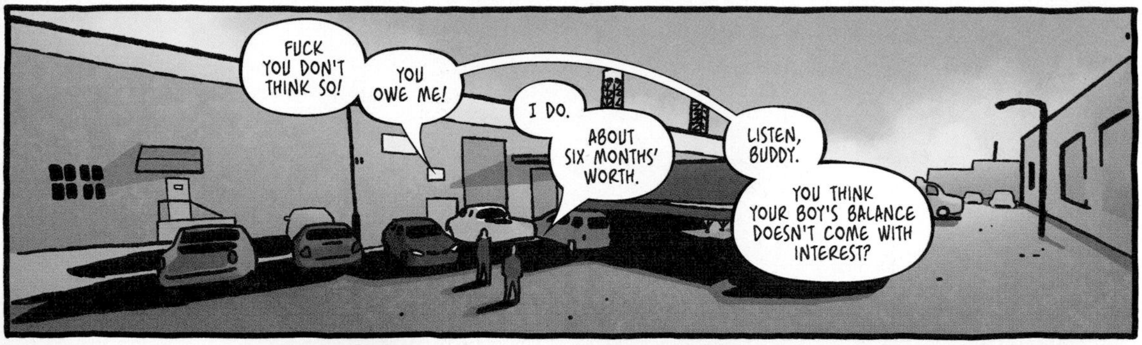
FUCK YOU DON'T THINK SO!
YOU OWE ME!
I DO.
ABOUT SIX MONTHS' WORTH.
LISTEN, BUDDY.
YOU THINK YOUR BOY'S BALANCE DOESN'T COME WITH INTEREST?
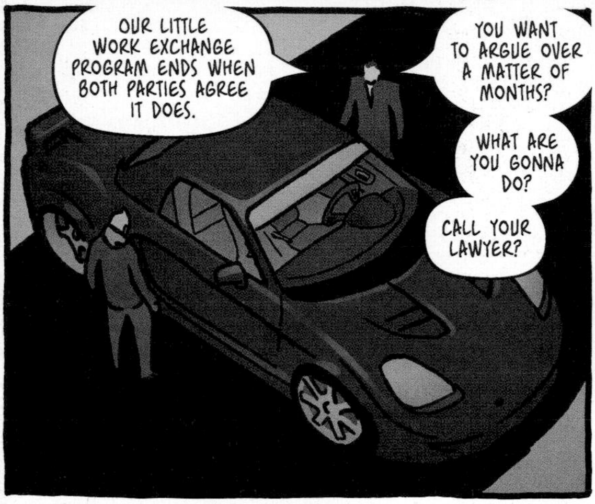
OUR LITTLE WORK EXCHANGE PROGRAM ENDS WHEN BOTH PARTIES AGREE IT DOES.
YOU WANT TO ARGUE OVER A MATTER OF MONTHS?
WHAT ARE YOU GONNA DO?
CALL YOUR LAWYER?
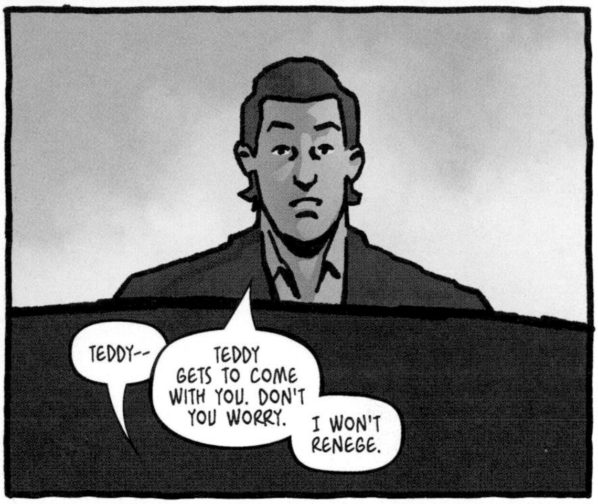
TEDDY--
TEDDY GETS TO COME WITH YOU. DON'T YOU WORRY.
I WON'T RENEGE.
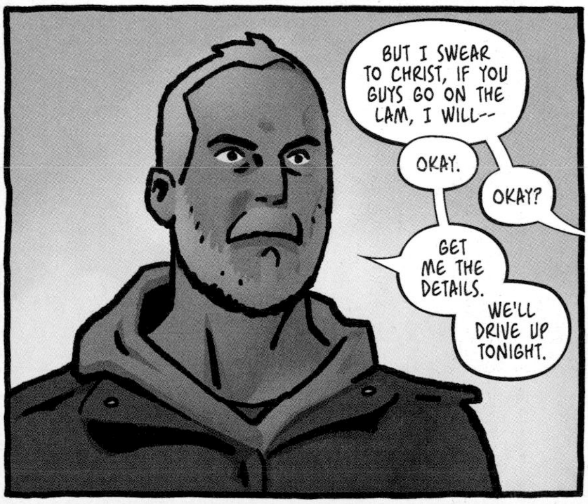
BUT I SWEAR TO CHRIST, IF YOU GUYS GO ON THE LAM, I WILL--
OKAY.
OKAY?
GET ME THE DETAILS.
WE'LL DRIVE UP TONIGHT.
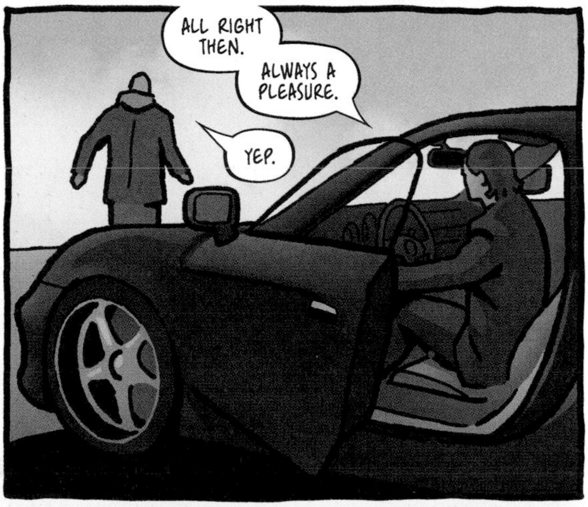
ALL RIGHT THEN.
ALWAYS A PLEASURE.
YEP.
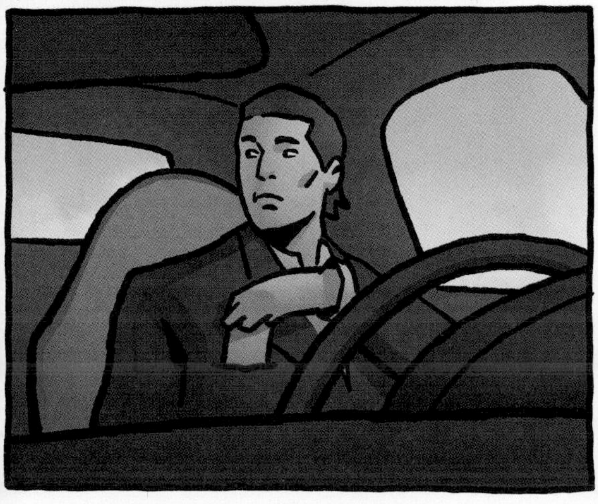
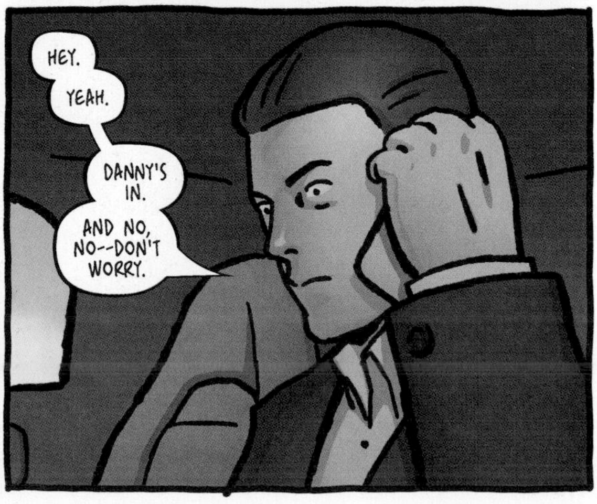
HEY.
YEAH.
DANNY'S IN.
AND NO, NO--DON'T WORRY.

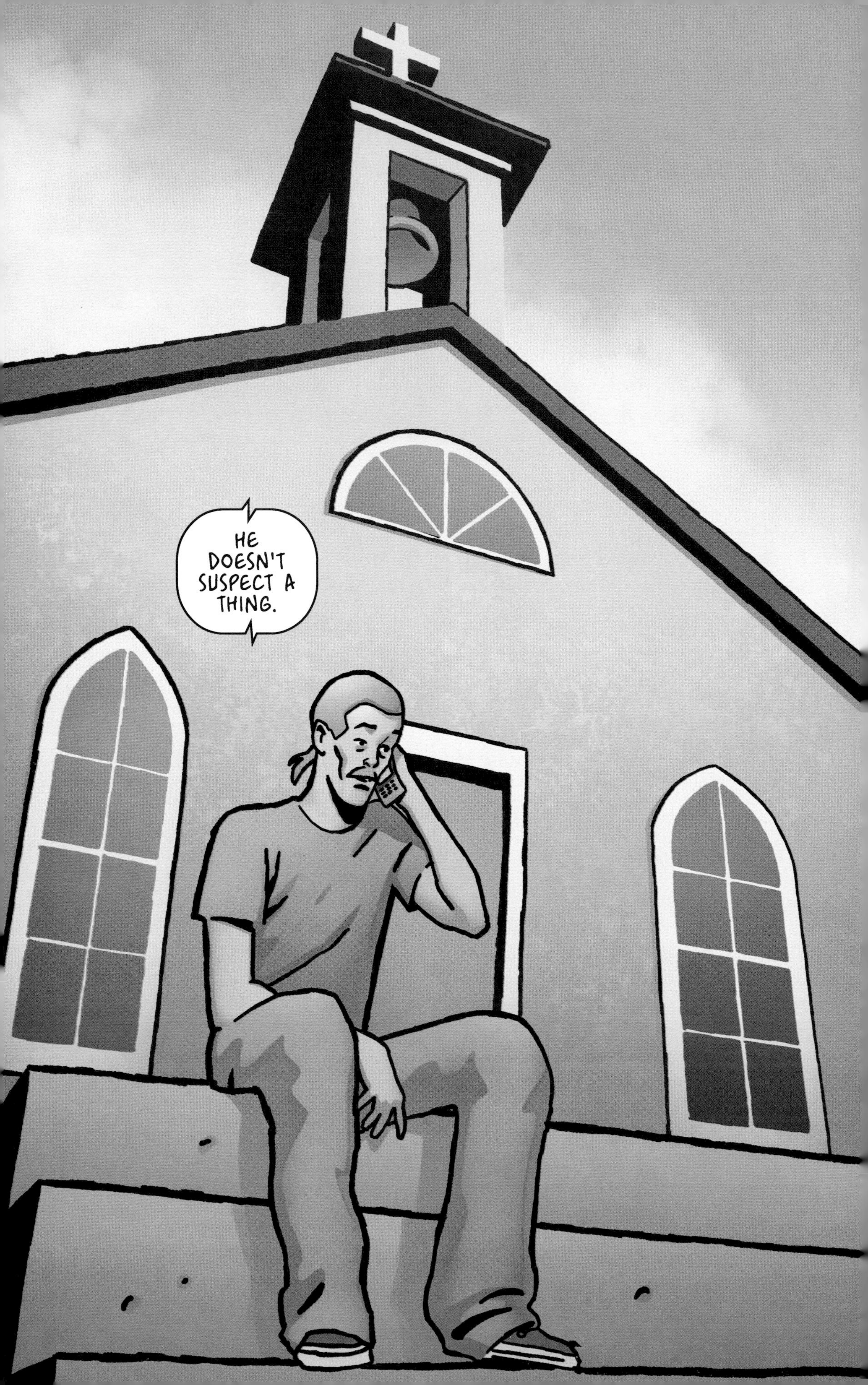
HE DOESN'T SUSPECT A THING.

CHAPTER SEVEN

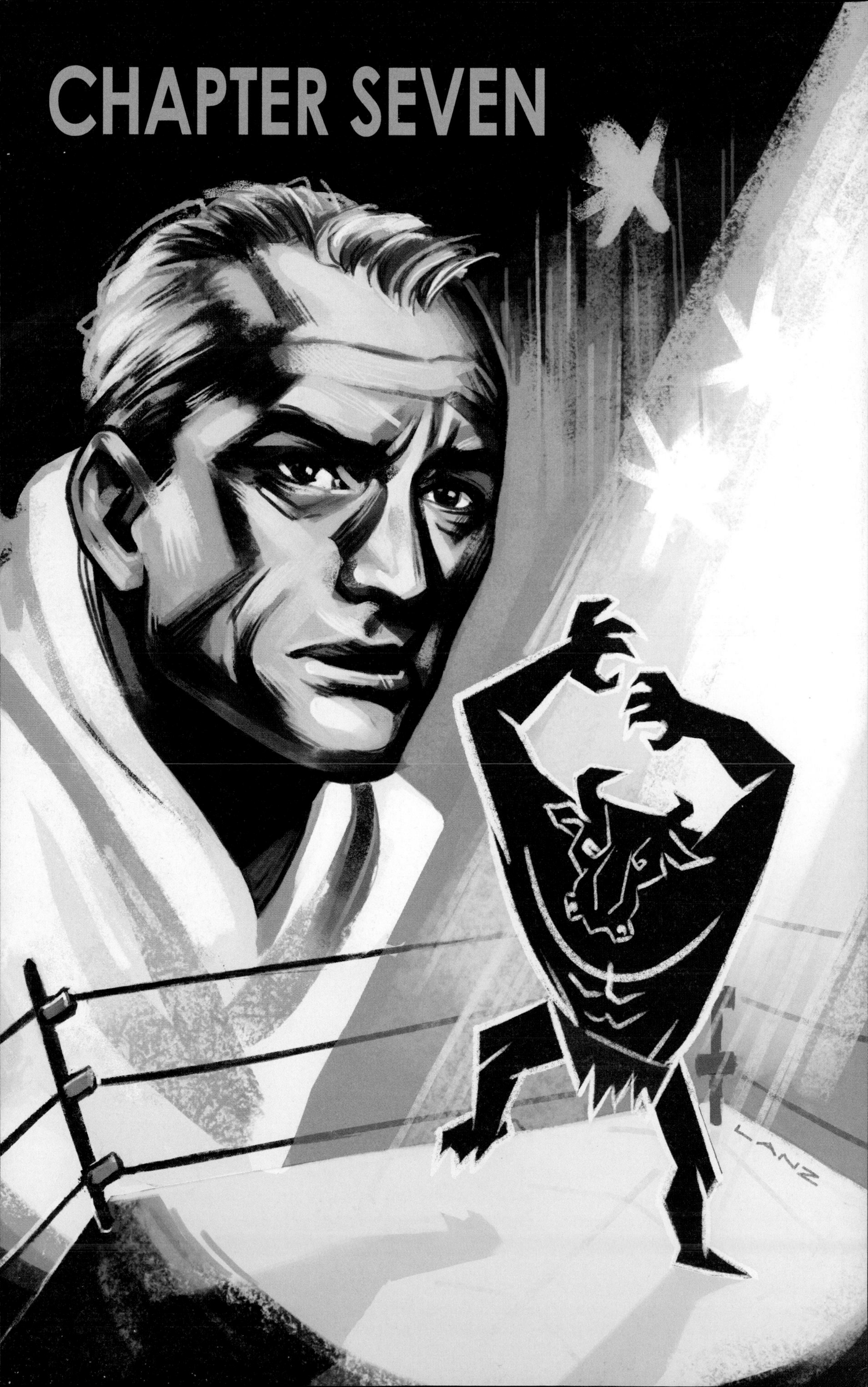
LANZ

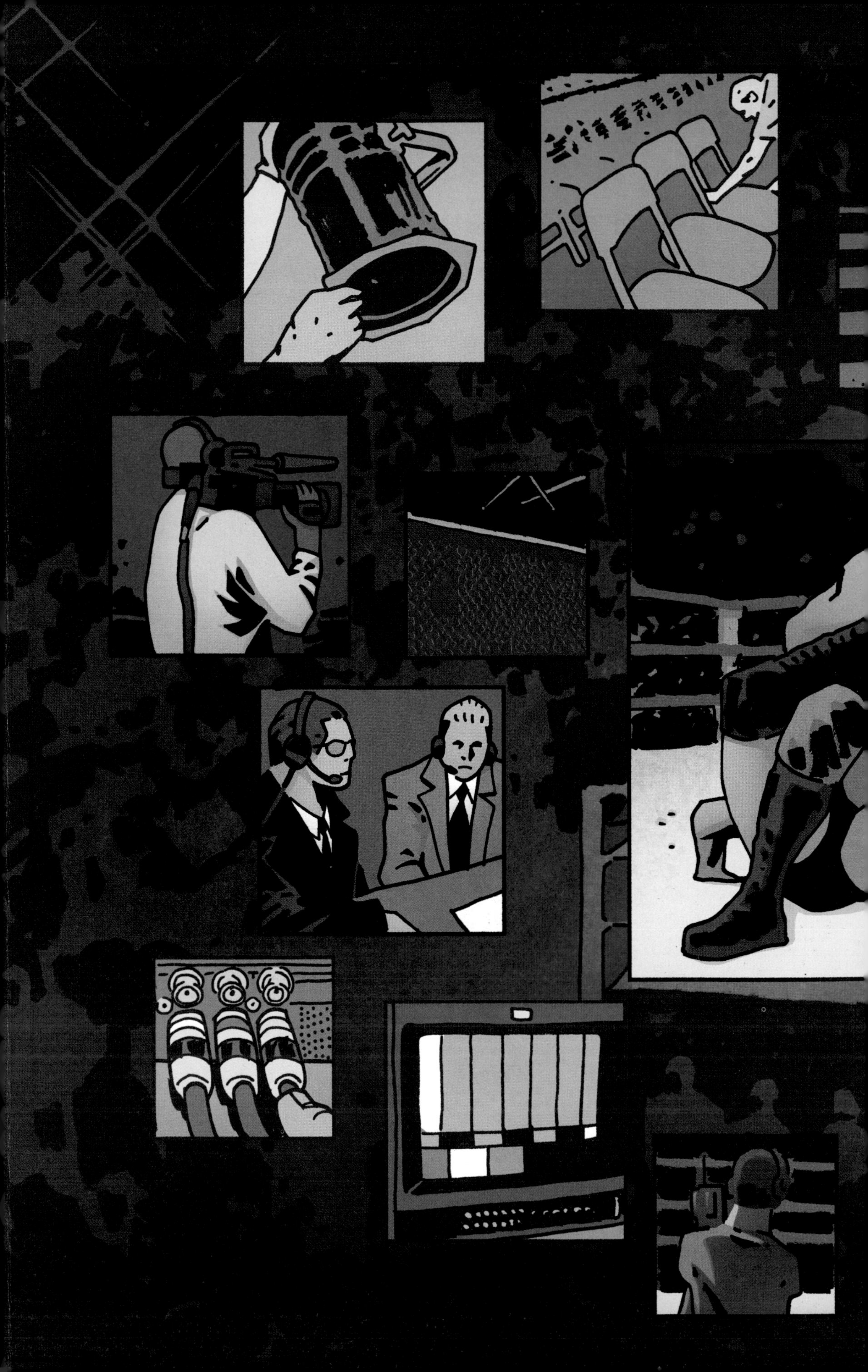

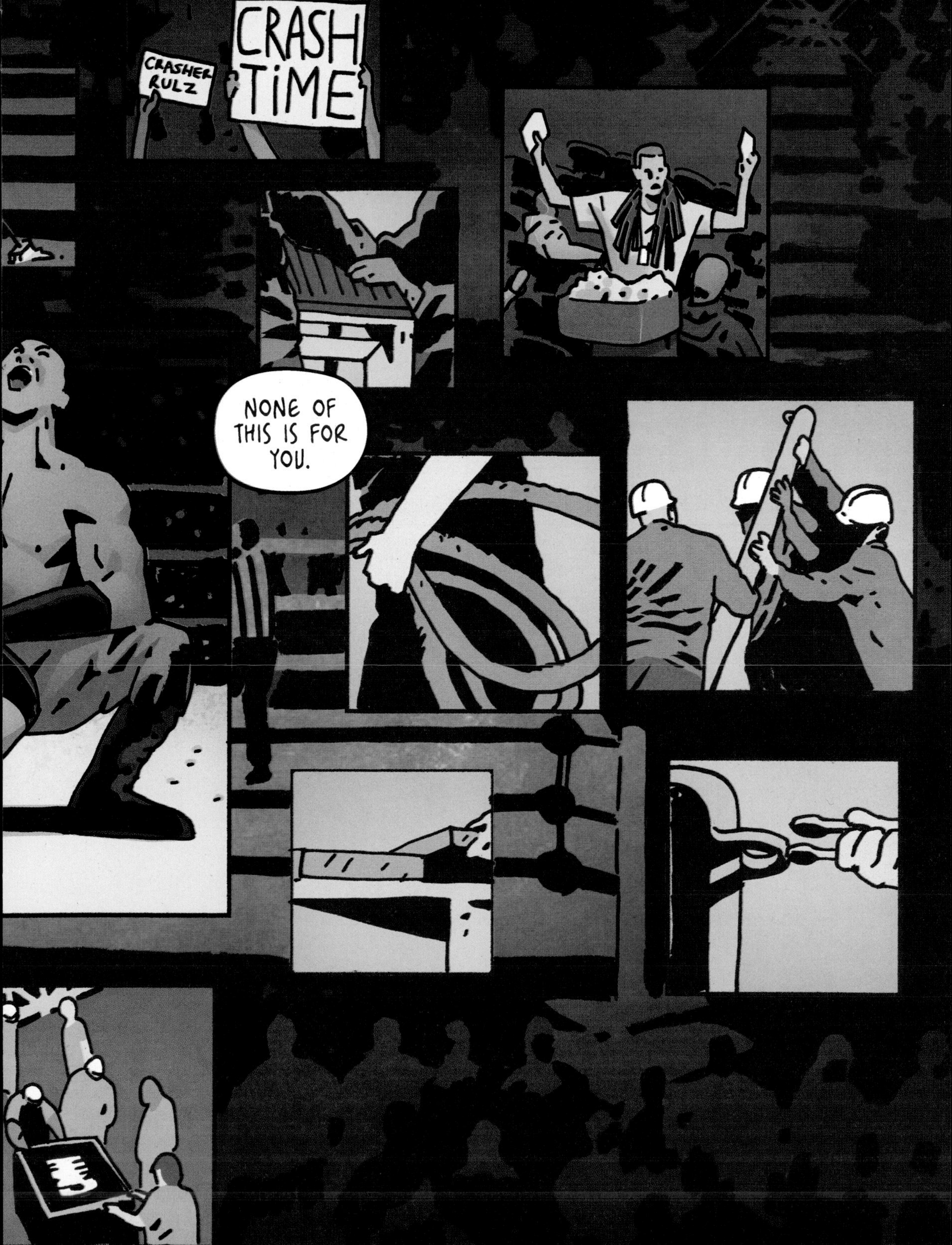
CRASHER RULZ
CRASH TIME
NONE OF THIS IS FOR YOU.

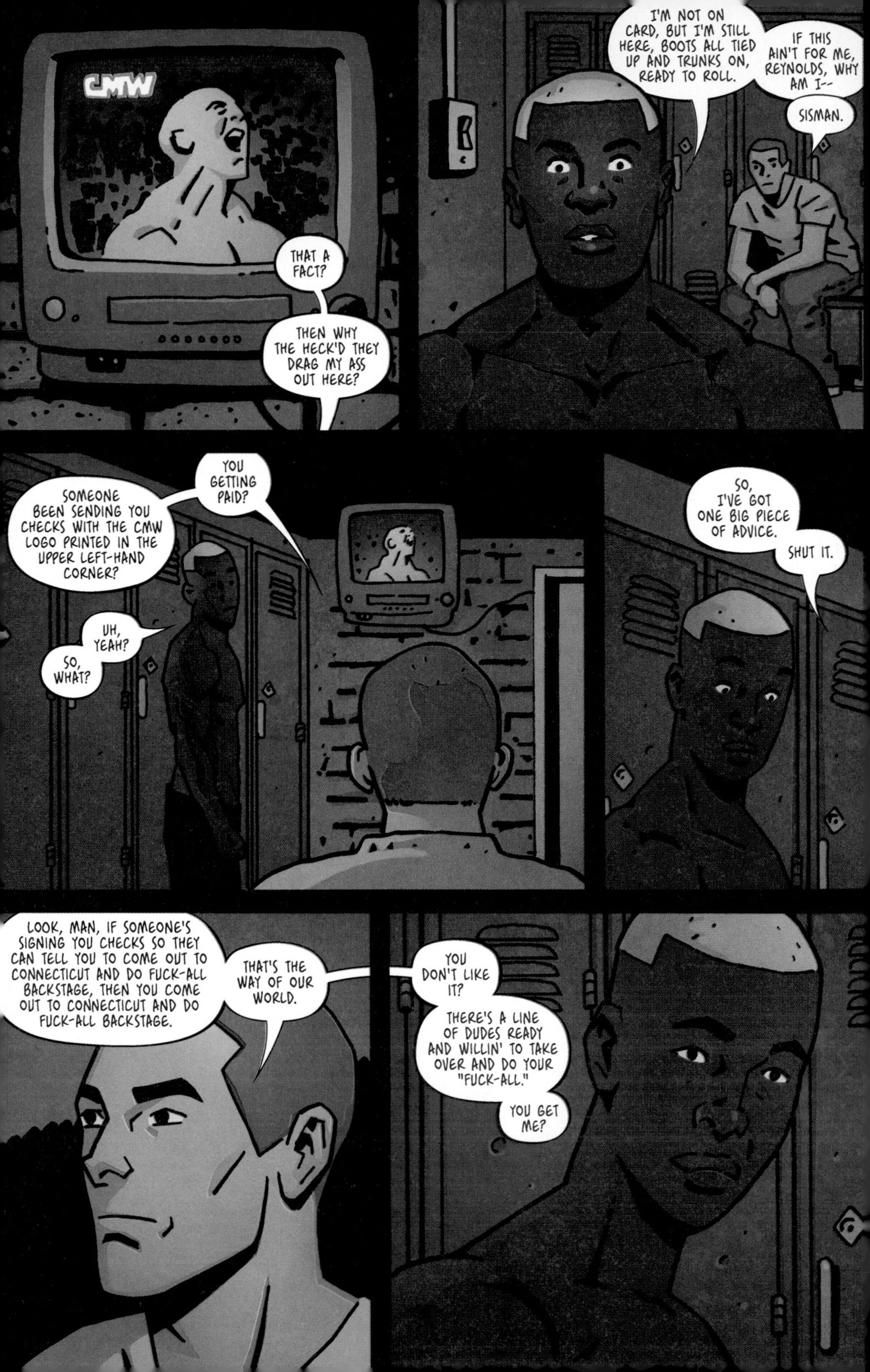
THAT A FACT?
THEN WHY THE HECK'D THEY DRAG MY ASS OUT HERE?
I'M NOT ON CARD, BUT I'M STILL HERE, BOOTS ALL TIED UP AND TRUNKS ON, READY TO ROLL.
IF THIS AIN'T FOR ME, REYNOLDS, WHY AM I--
SISMAN.
SOMEONE BEEN SENDING YOU CHECKS WITH THE CMW LOGO PRINTED IN THE UPPER LEFT-HAND CORNER?
YOU GETTING PAID?
UH, YEAH?
SO, WHAT?
SO, I'VE GOT ONE BIG PIECE OF ADVICE.
SHUT IT.
LOOK, MAN, IF SOMEONE'S SIGNING YOU CHECKS SO THEY CAN TELL YOU TO COME OUT TO CONNECTICUT AND DO FUCK-ALL BACKSTAGE, THEN YOU COME OUT TO CONNECTICUT AND DO FUCK-ALL BACKSTAGE.
THAT'S THE WAY OF OUR WORLD.
YOU DON'T LIKE IT?
THERE'S A LINE OF DUDES READY AND WILLIN' TO TAKE OVER AND DO YOUR "FUCK-ALL."
YOU GET ME?

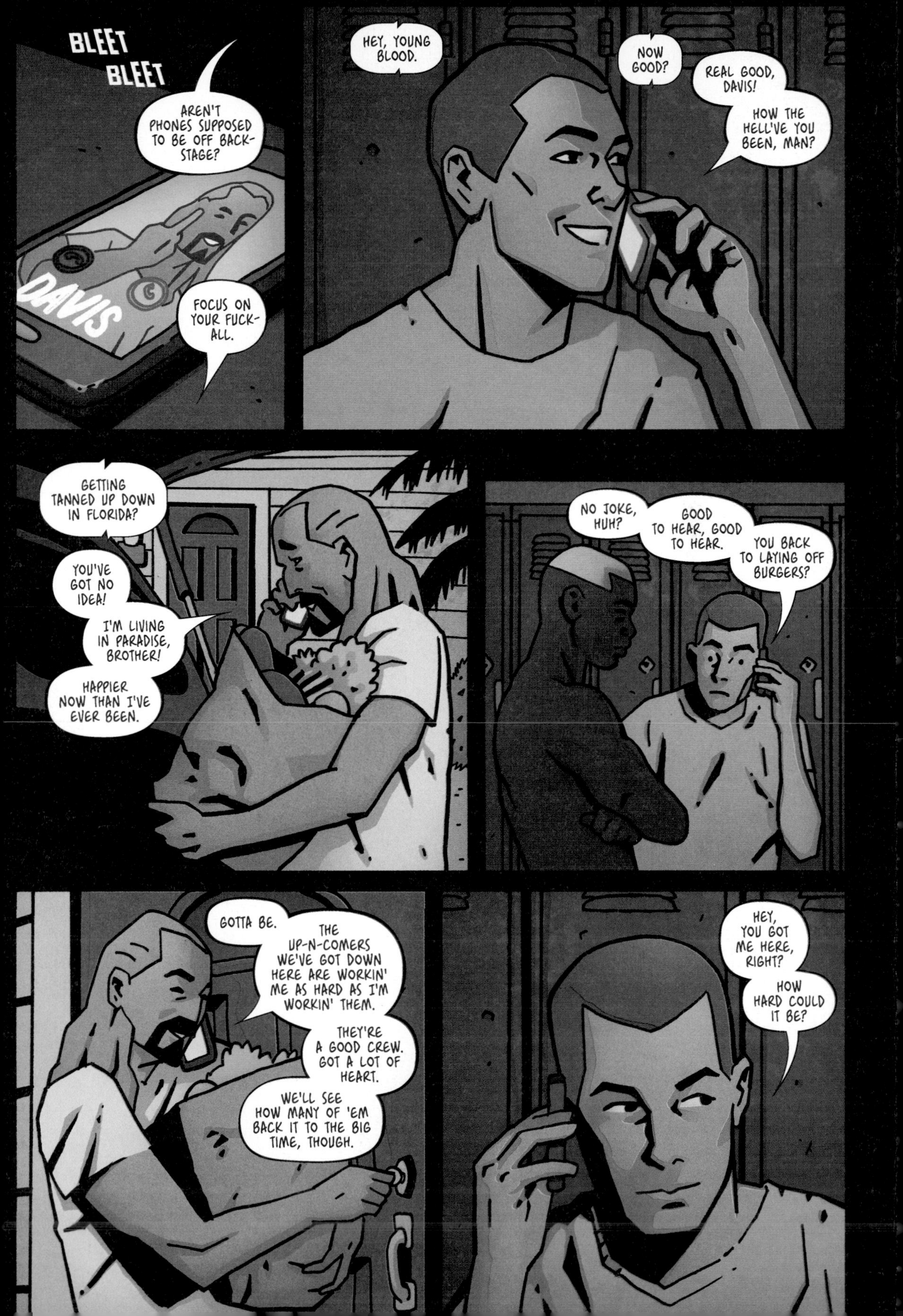
BLEET BLEET
AREN'T PHONES SUPPOSED TO BE OFF BACK-STAGE?
DAVIS
FOCUS ON YOUR FUCK-ALL.
HEY, YOUNG BLOOD.
NOW GOOD?
REAL GOOD, DAVIS!
HOW THE HELL'VE YOU BEEN, MAN?
GETTING TANNED UP DOWN IN FLORIDA?
YOU'VE GOT NO IDEA!
I'M LIVING IN PARADISE, BROTHER!
HAPPIER NOW THAN I'VE EVER BEEN.
NO JOKE, HUH?
GOOD TO HEAR, GOOD TO HEAR.
YOU BACK TO LAYING OFF BURGERS?
GOTTA BE.
THE UP-N-COMERS WE'VE GOT DOWN HERE ARE WORKIN' ME AS HARD AS I'M WORKIN' THEM.
THEY'RE A GOOD CREW. GOT A LOT OF HEART.
WE'LL SEE HOW MANY OF 'EM BACK IT TO THE BIG TIME, THOUGH.
HEY, YOU GOT ME HERE, RIGHT?
HOW HARD COULD IT BE?

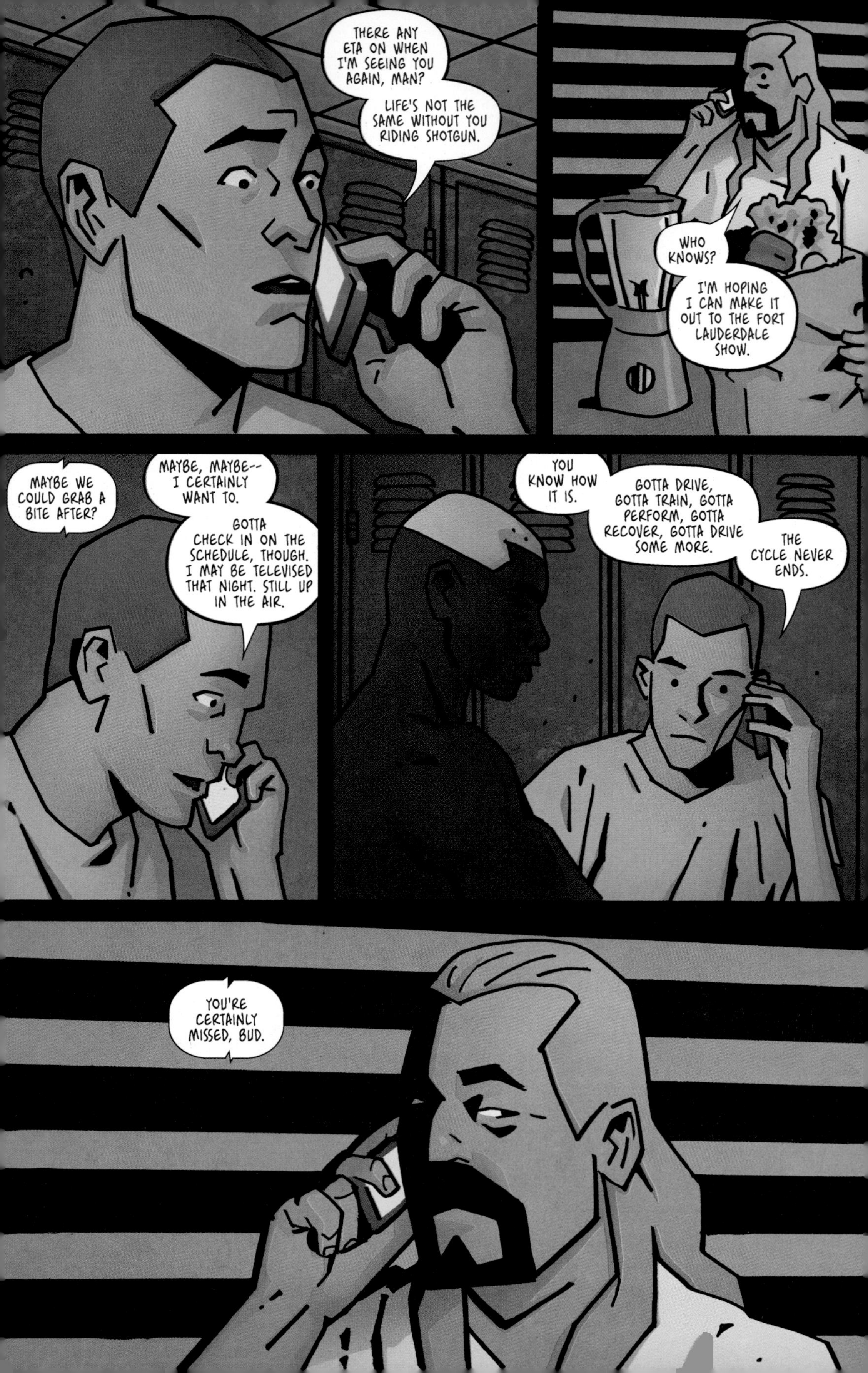
THERE ANY ETA ON WHEN I'M SEEING YOU AGAIN, MAN?
LIFE'S NOT THE SAME WITHOUT YOU RIDING SHOTGUN.
WHO KNOWS?
I'M HOPING I CAN MAKE IT OUT TO THE FORT LAUDERDALE SHOW.
MAYBE WE COULD GRAB A BITE AFTER?
MAYBE, MAYBE-- I CERTAINLY WANT TO.
GOTTA CHECK IN ON THE SCHEDULE, THOUGH. I MAY BE TELEVISED THAT NIGHT. STILL UP IN THE AIR.
YOU KNOW HOW IT IS.
GOTTA DRIVE, GOTTA TRAIN, GOTTA PERFORM, GOTTA RECOVER, GOTTA DRIVE SOME MORE.
THE CYCLE NEVER ENDS.
YOU'RE CERTAINLY MISSED, BUD.

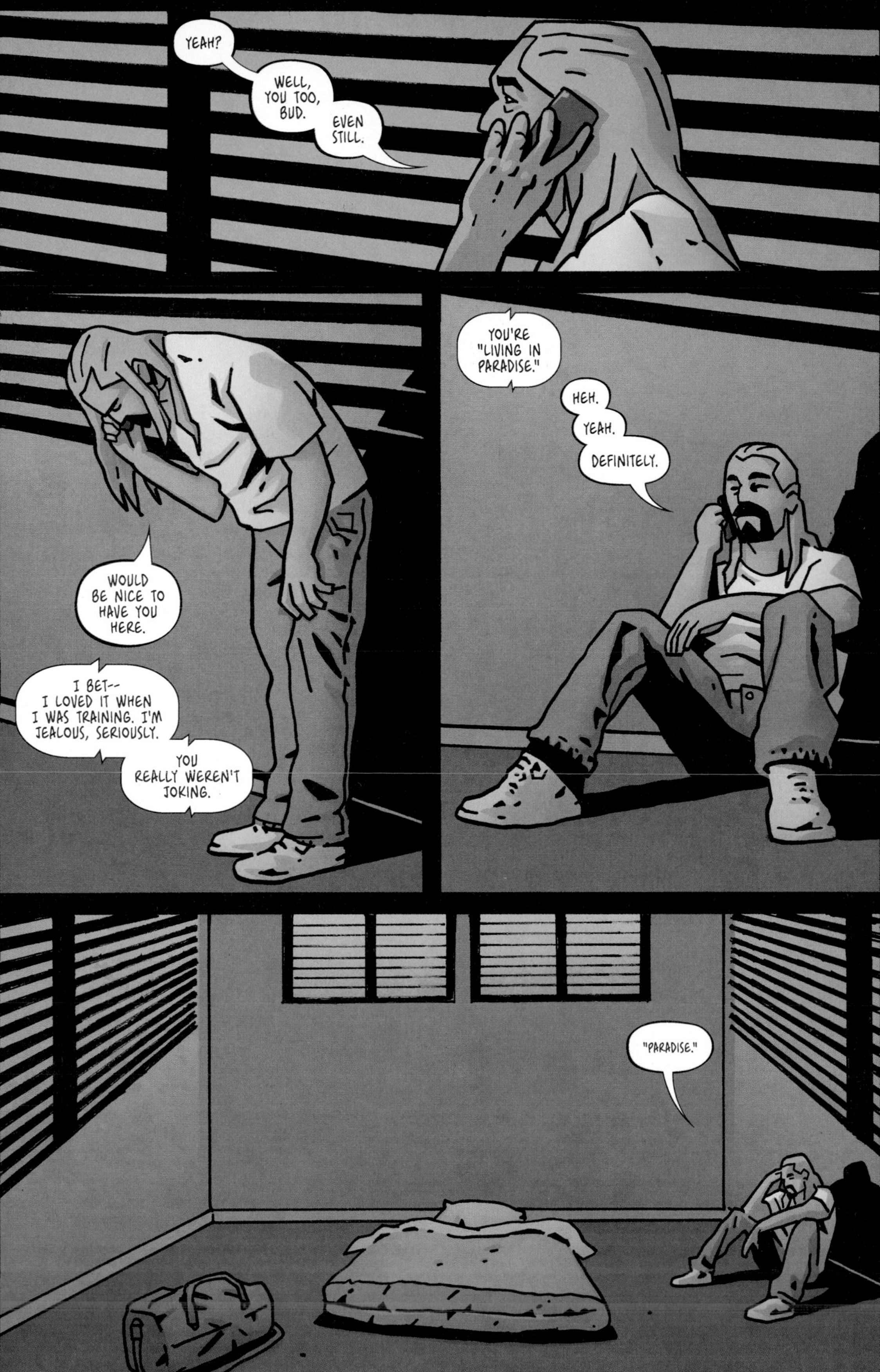
YEAH?
WELL, YOU TOO, BUD.
EVEN STILL.
YOU'RE "LIVING IN PARADISE."
WOULD BE NICE TO HAVE YOU HERE.
HEH.
YEAH.
DEFINITELY.
I BET-- I LOVED IT WHEN I WAS TRAINING. I'M JEALOUS, SERIOUSLY.
YOU REALLY WEREN'T JOKING.
"PARADISE."

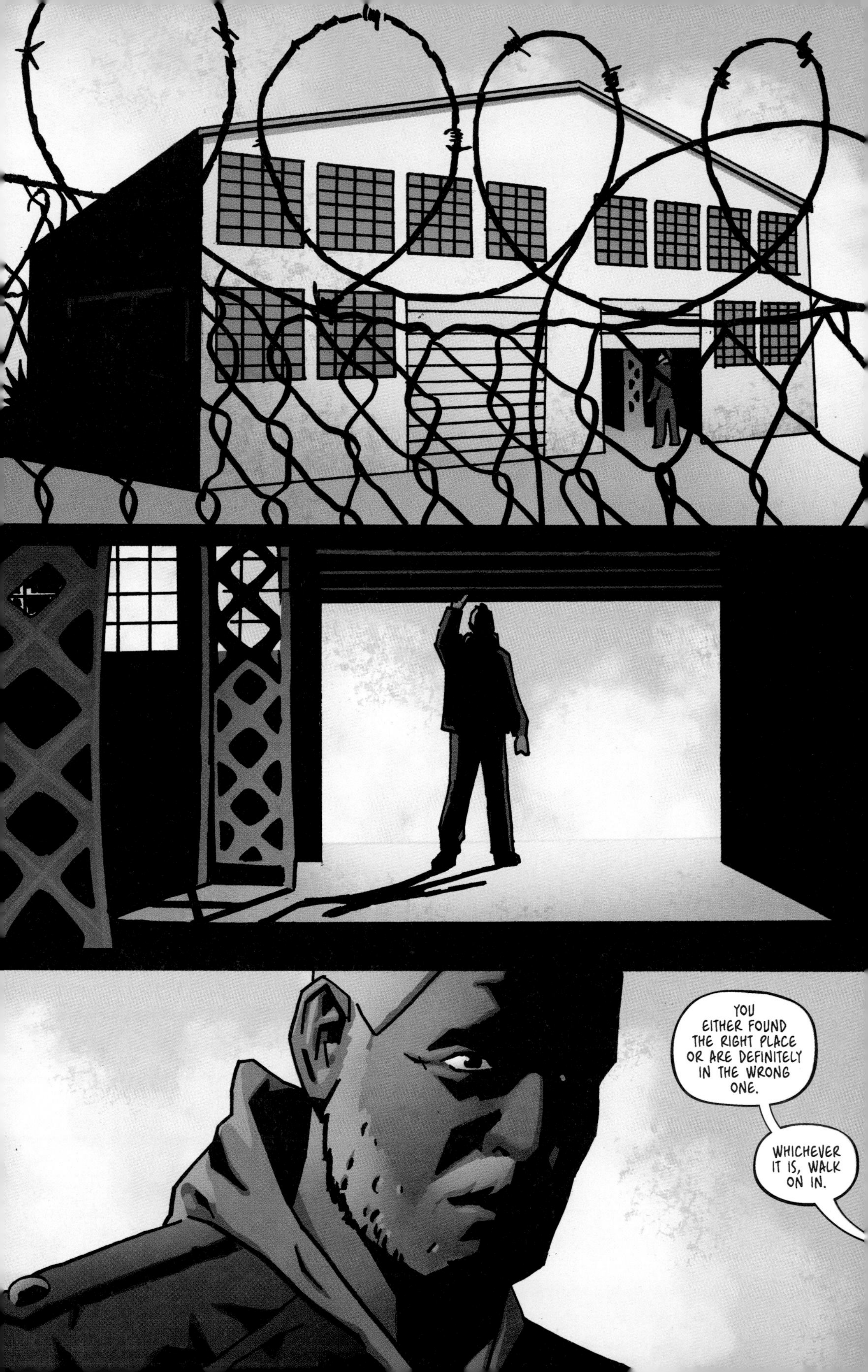
YOU EITHER FOUND THE RIGHT PLACE OR ARE DEFINITELY IN THE WRONG ONE.
WHICHEVER IT IS, WALK ON IN.

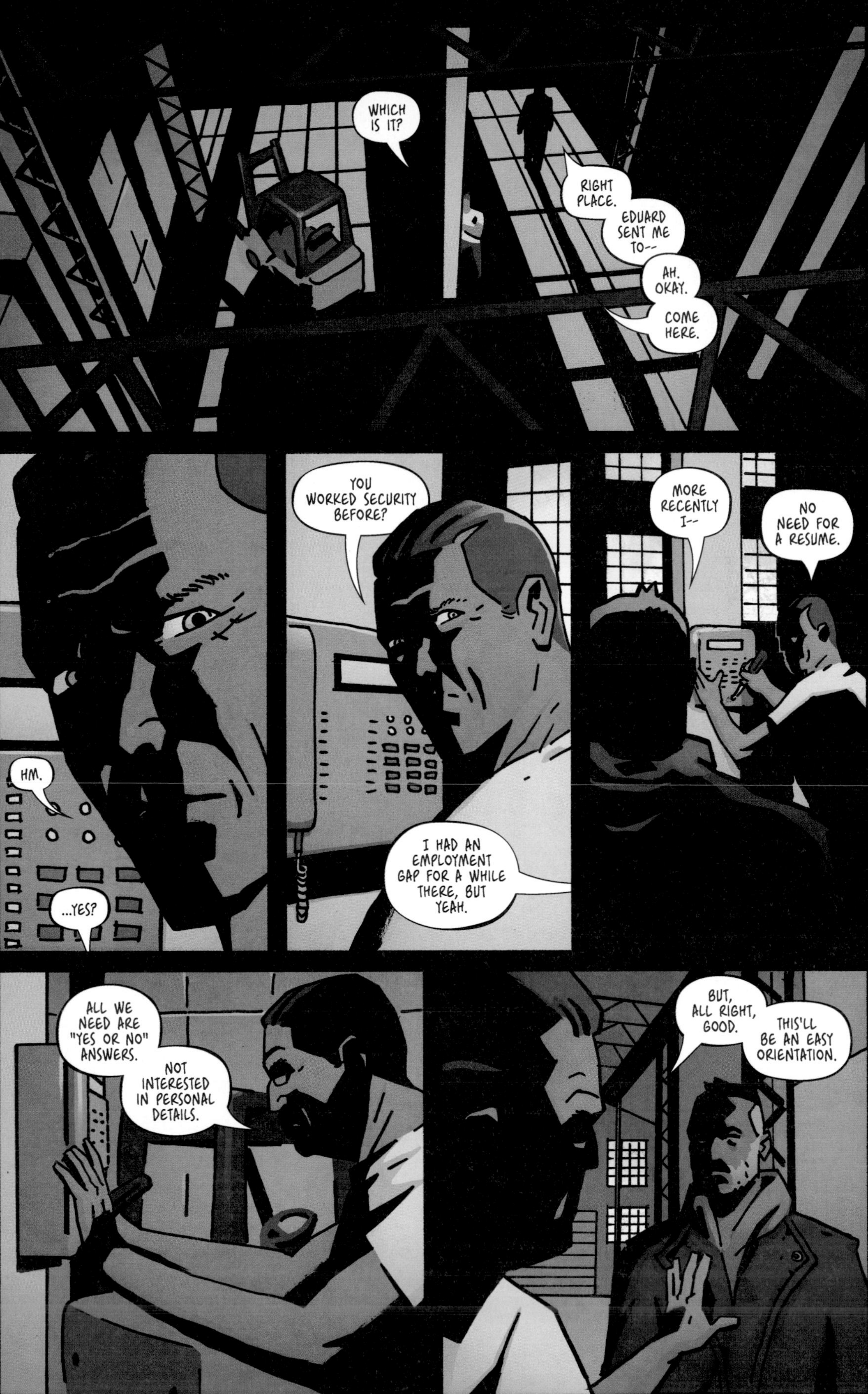
WHICH IS IT?
RIGHT PLACE.
EDUARD SENT ME TO--
AH. OKAY.
COME HERE.
HM.
...YES?
YOU WORKED SECURITY BEFORE?
I HAD AN EMPLOYMENT GAP FOR A WHILE THERE, BUT YEAH.
MORE RECENTLY I--
NO NEED FOR A RESUME.
ALL WE NEED ARE "YES OR NO" ANSWERS.
NOT INTERESTED IN PERSONAL DETAILS.
BUT, ALL RIGHT, GOOD.
THIS'LL BE AN EASY ORIENTATION.

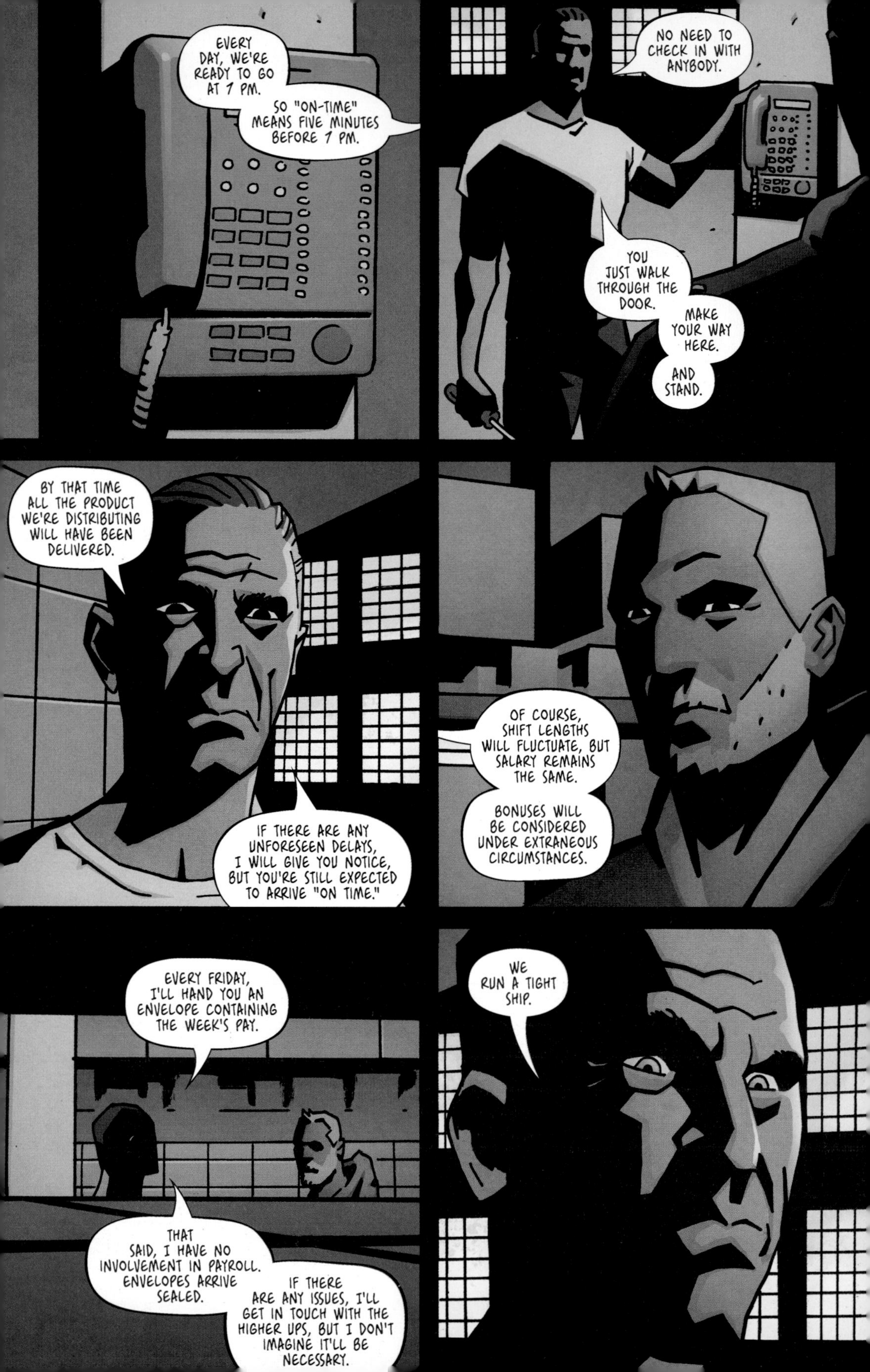
EVERY DAY, WE'RE READY TO GO AT 7 PM.
SO "ON-TIME" MEANS FIVE MINUTES BEFORE 7 PM.
NO NEED TO CHECK IN WITH ANYBODY.
YOU JUST WALK THROUGH THE DOOR.
MAKE YOUR WAY HERE.
AND STAND.
BY THAT TIME ALL THE PRODUCT WE'RE DISTRIBUTING WILL HAVE BEEN DELIVERED.
IF THERE ARE ANY UNFORESEEN DELAYS, I WILL GIVE YOU NOTICE, BUT YOU'RE STILL EXPECTED TO ARRIVE "ON TIME."
OF COURSE, SHIFT LENGTHS WILL FLUCTUATE, BUT SALARY REMAINS THE SAME.
BONUSES WILL BE CONSIDERED UNDER EXTRANEOUS CIRCUMSTANCES.
EVERY FRIDAY, I'LL HAND YOU AN ENVELOPE CONTAINING THE WEEK'S PAY.
THAT SAID, I HAVE NO INVOLVEMENT IN PAYROLL. ENVELOPES ARRIVE SEALED.
IF THERE ARE ANY ISSUES, I'LL GET IN TOUCH WITH THE HIGHER UPS, BUT I DON'T IMAGINE IT'LL BE NECESSARY.
WE RUN A TIGHT SHIP.

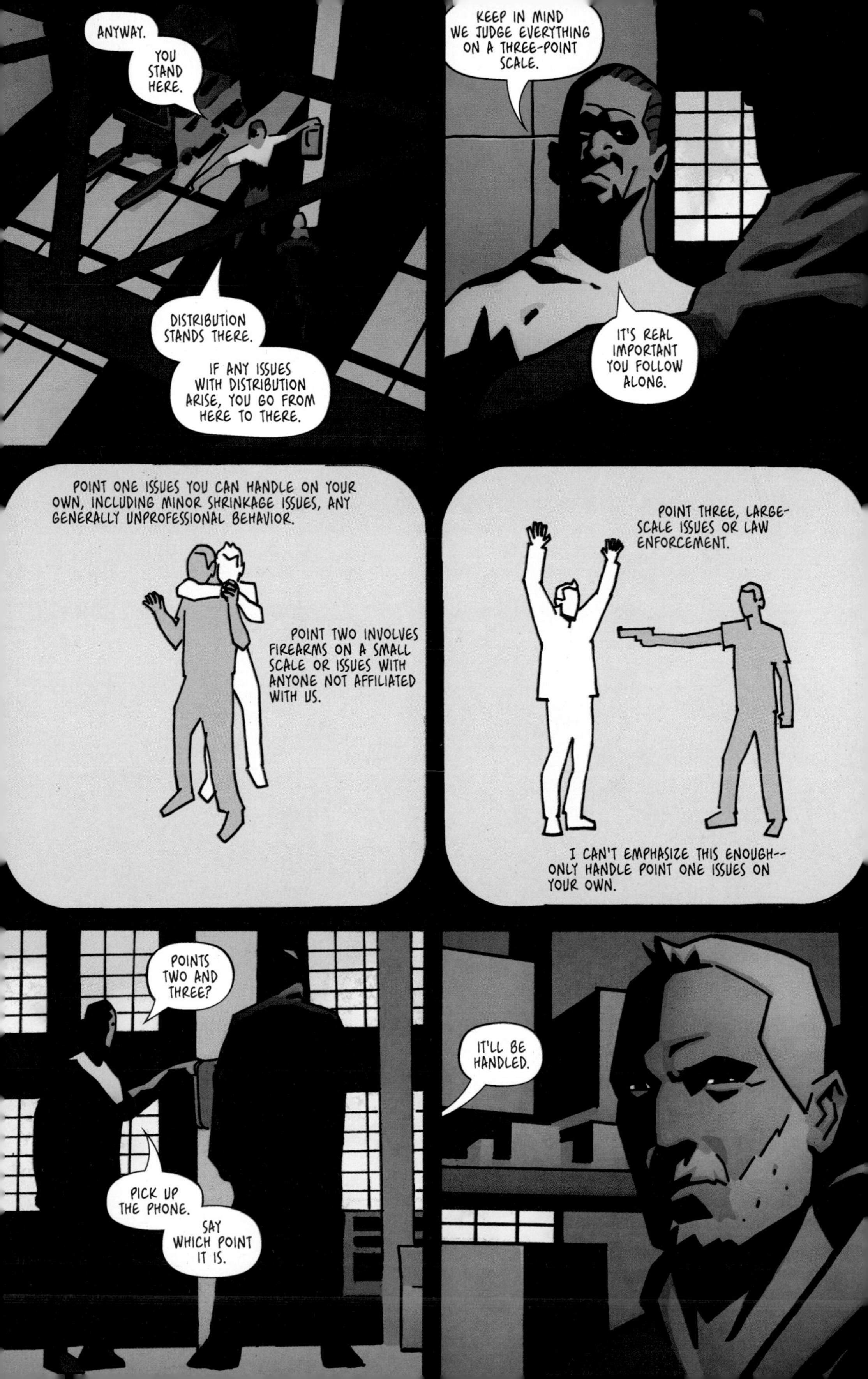
ANYWAY.
YOU STAND HERE.
DISTRIBUTION STANDS THERE.
IF ANY ISSUES WITH DISTRIBUTION ARISE, YOU GO FROM HERE TO THERE.
KEEP IN MIND WE JUDGE EVERYTHING ON A THREE-POINT SCALE.
IT'S REAL IMPORTANT YOU FOLLOW ALONG.
POINT ONE ISSUES YOU CAN HANDLE ON YOUR OWN, INCLUDING MINOR SHRINKAGE ISSUES, ANY GENERALLY UNPROFESSIONAL BEHAVIOR.
POINT TWO INVOLVES FIREARMS ON A SMALL SCALE OR ISSUES WITH ANYONE NOT AFFILIATED WITH US.
POINT THREE, LARGE-SCALE ISSUES OR LAW ENFORCEMENT.
I CAN'T EMPHASIZE THIS ENOUGH-- ONLY HANDLE POINT ONE ISSUES ON YOUR OWN.
POINTS TWO AND THREE?
PICK UP THE PHONE.
SAY WHICH POINT IT IS.
IT'LL BE HANDLED.

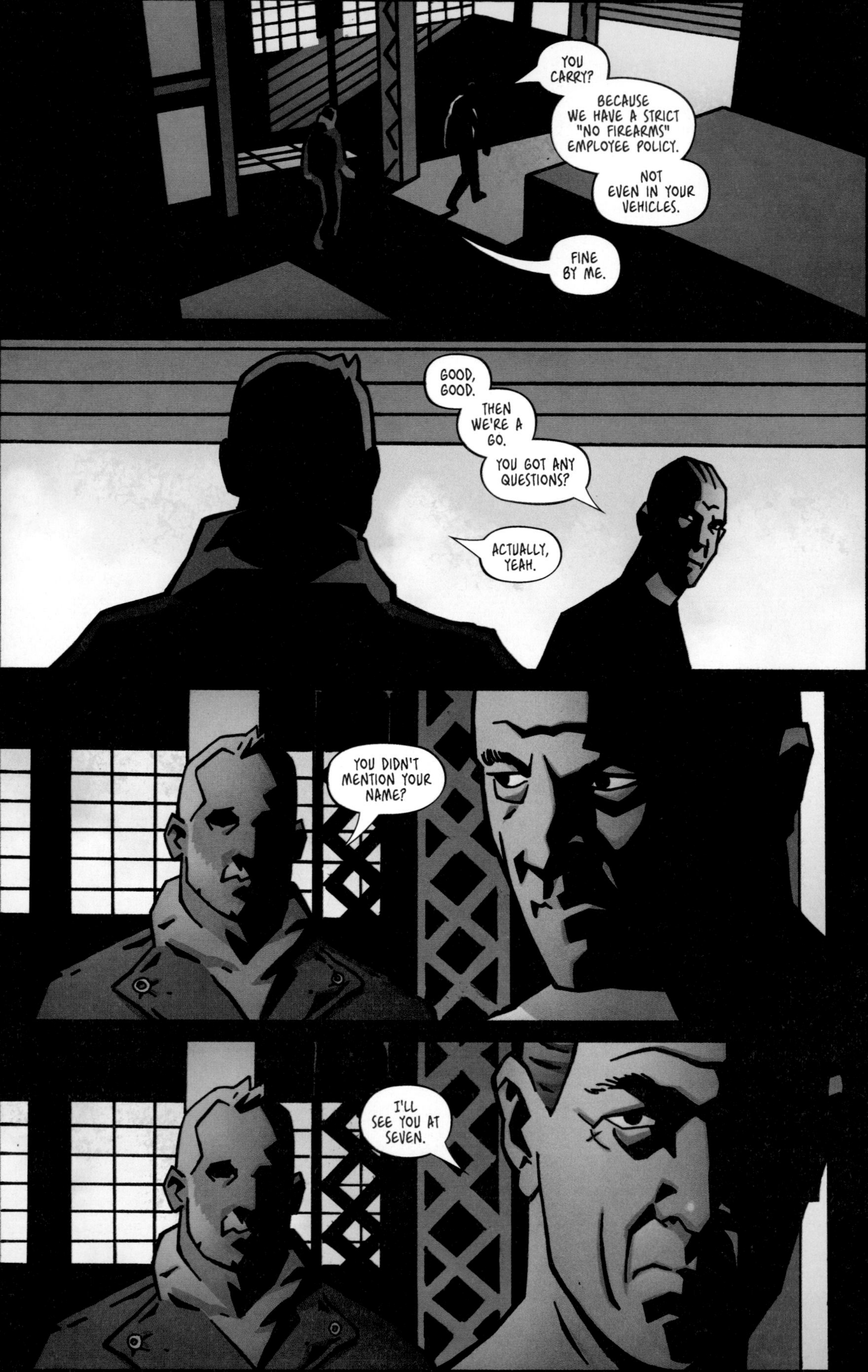
YOU CARRY?
BECAUSE WE HAVE A STRICT "NO FIREARMS" EMPLOYEE POLICY.
NOT EVEN IN YOUR VEHICLES.
FINE BY ME.
GOOD, GOOD.
THEN WE'RE A GO.
YOU GOT ANY QUESTIONS?
ACTUALLY, YEAH.
YOU DIDN'T MENTION YOUR NAME?
I'LL SEE YOU AT SEVEN.

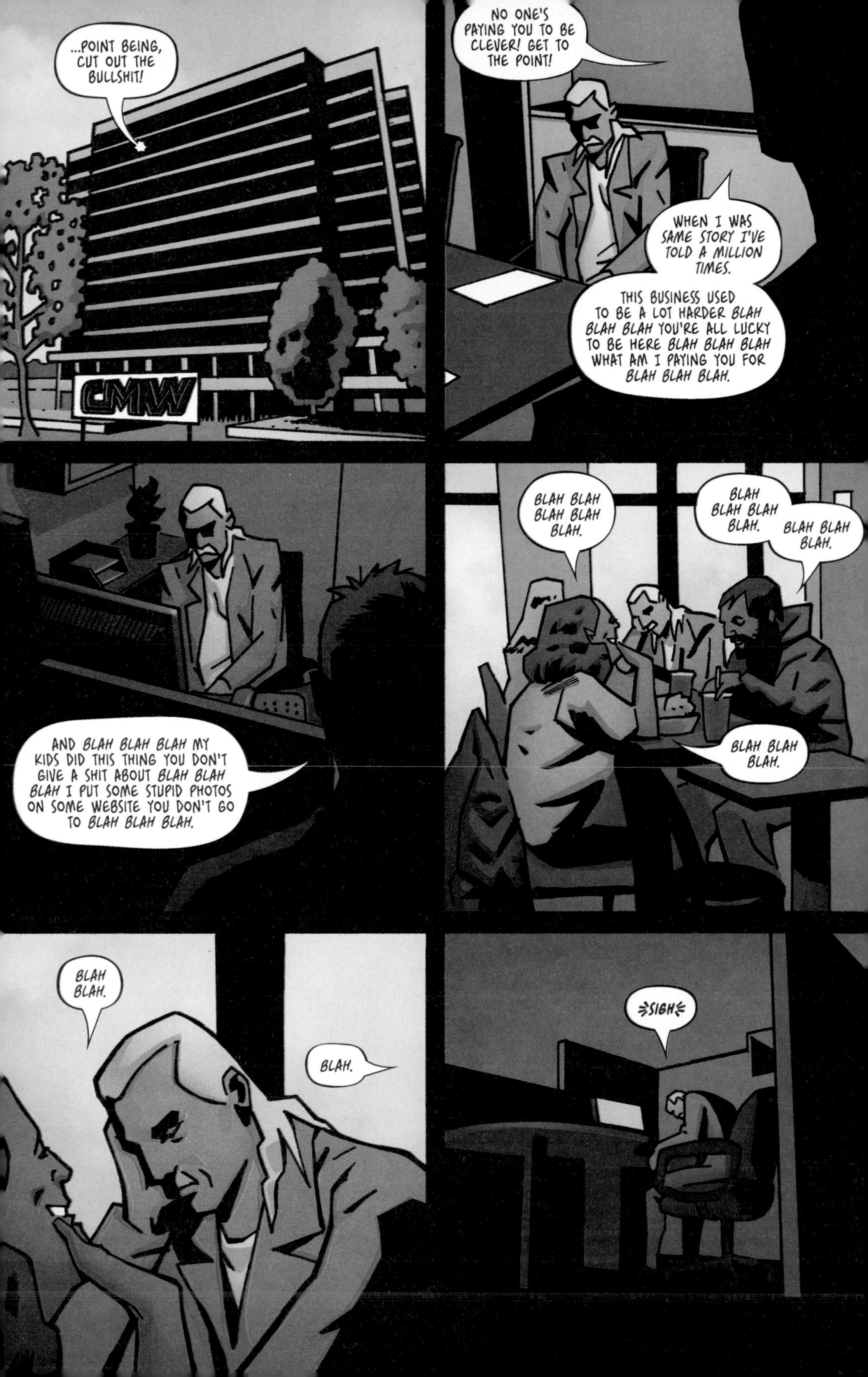

...POINT BEING, CUT OUT THE BULLSHIT!
CMW
NO ONE'S PAYING YOU TO BE CLEVER! GET TO THE POINT!
WHEN I WAS SAME STORY I'VE TOLD A MILLION TIMES.
THIS BUSINESS USED TO BE A LOT HARDER *BLAH BLAH BLAH* YOU'RE ALL LUCKY TO BE HERE *BLAH BLAH BLAH* WHAT AM I PAYING YOU FOR *BLAH BLAH BLAH.*
AND *BLAH BLAH BLAH* MY KIDS DID THIS THING YOU DON'T GIVE A SHIT ABOUT *BLAH BLAH BLAH* I PUT SOME STUPID PHOTOS ON SOME WEBSITE YOU DON'T GO TO *BLAH BLAH BLAH.*
BLAH BLAH BLAH BLAH BLAH.
BLAH BLAH BLAH BLAH.
BLAH BLAH BLAH.
BLAH BLAH BLAH.
BLAH BLAH.
BLAH.
SIGH

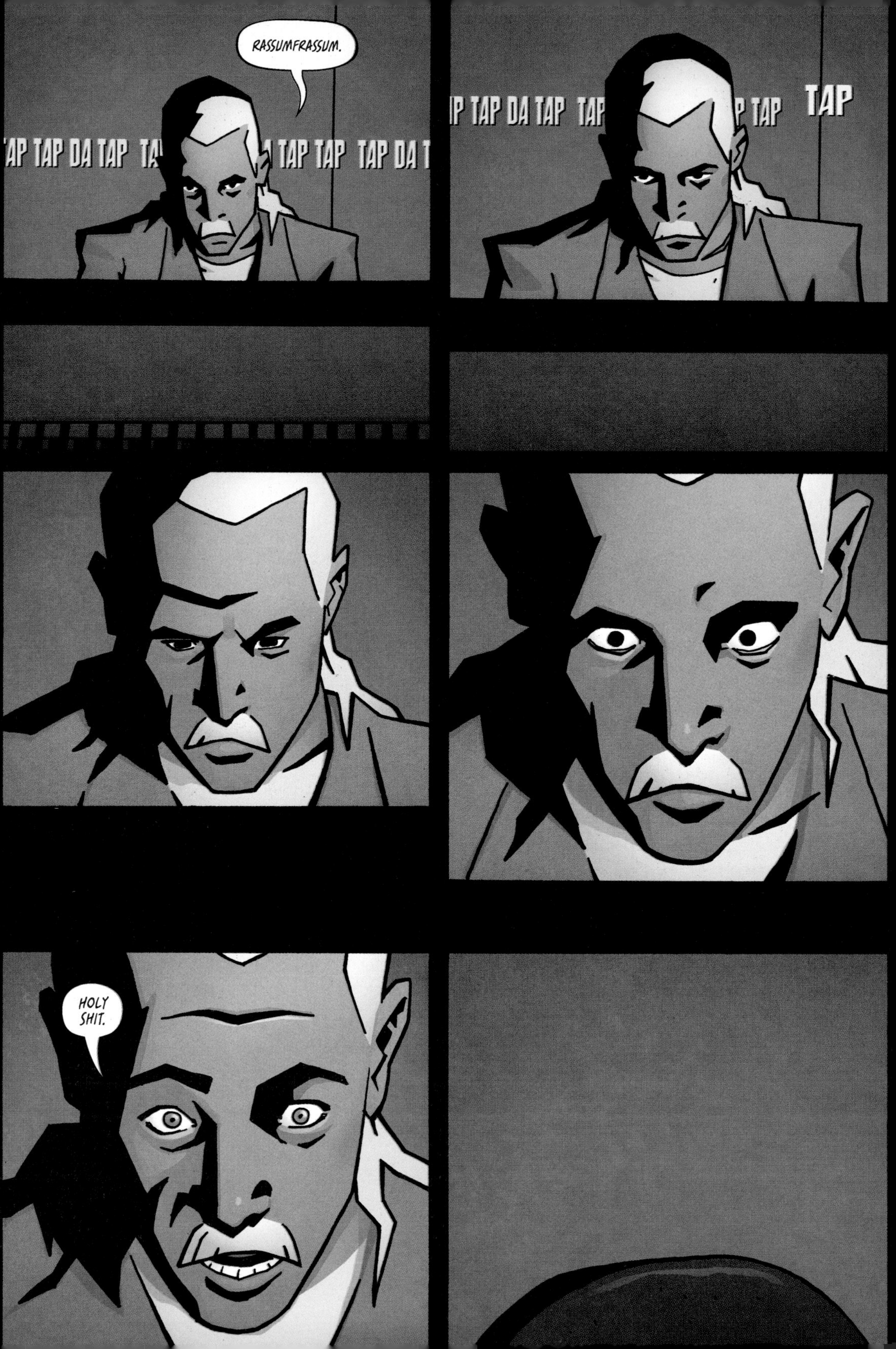
RASSUMFRASSUM.
TAP TAP DA TAP TAP TAP TAP TAP DA TAP
TAP TAP DA TAP TAP TAP TAP TAP
HOLY SHIT.

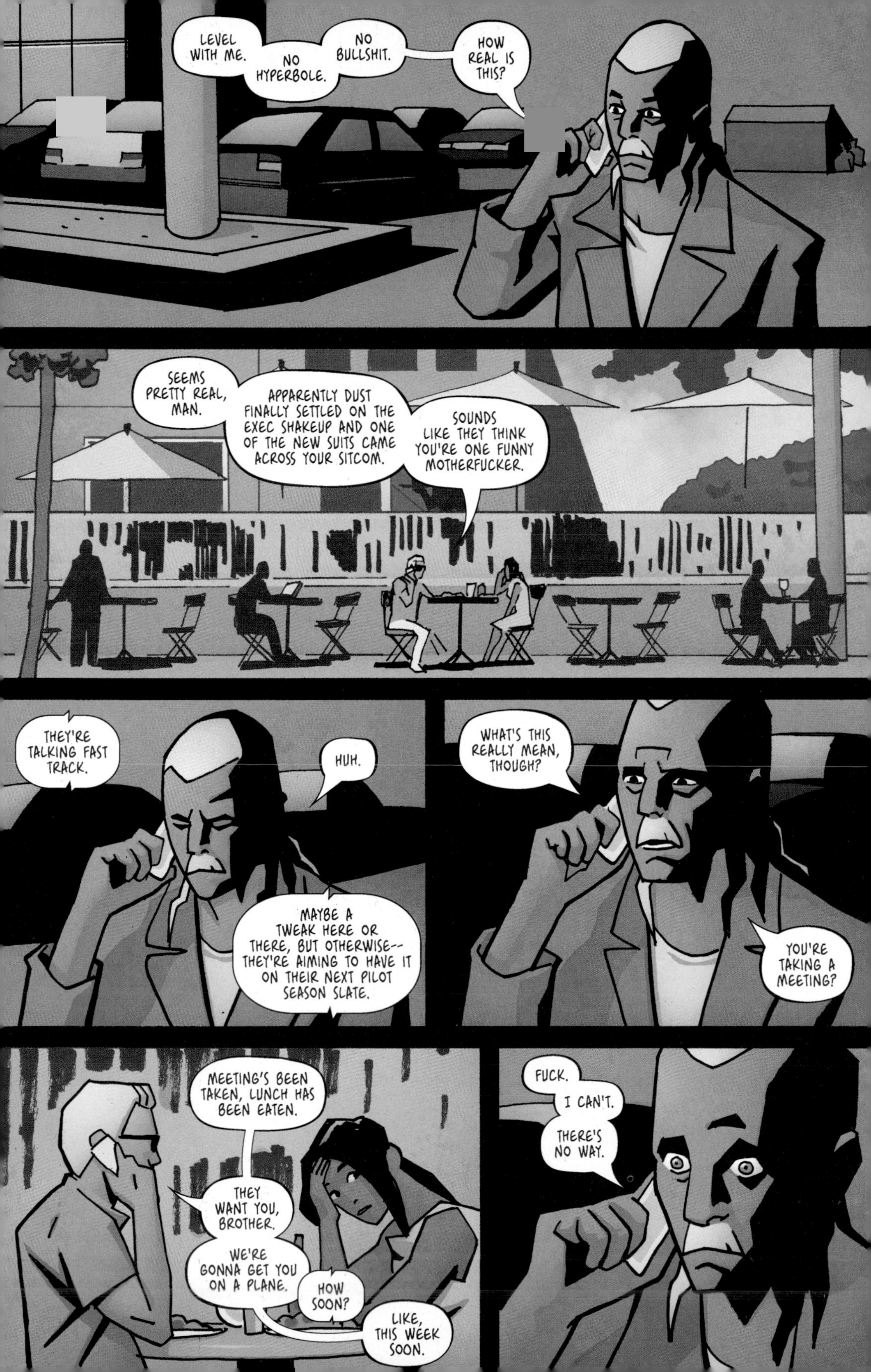
LEVEL WITH ME.
NO HYPERBOLE.
NO BULLSHIT.
HOW REAL IS THIS?
SEEMS PRETTY REAL, MAN.
APPARENTLY DUST FINALLY SETTLED ON THE EXEC SHAKEUP AND ONE OF THE NEW SUITS CAME ACROSS YOUR SITCOM.
SOUNDS LIKE THEY THINK YOU'RE ONE FUNNY MOTHERFUCKER.
THEY'RE TALKING FAST TRACK.
HUH.
MAYBE A TWEAK HERE OR THERE, BUT OTHERWISE-- THEY'RE AIMING TO HAVE IT ON THEIR NEXT PILOT SEASON SLATE.
WHAT'S THIS REALLY MEAN, THOUGH?
YOU'RE TAKING A MEETING?
MEETING'S BEEN TAKEN, LUNCH HAS BEEN EATEN.
THEY WANT YOU, BROTHER.
WE'RE GONNA GET YOU ON A PLANE.
HOW SOON?
LIKE, THIS WEEK SOON.
FUCK.
I CAN'T.
THERE'S NO WAY.

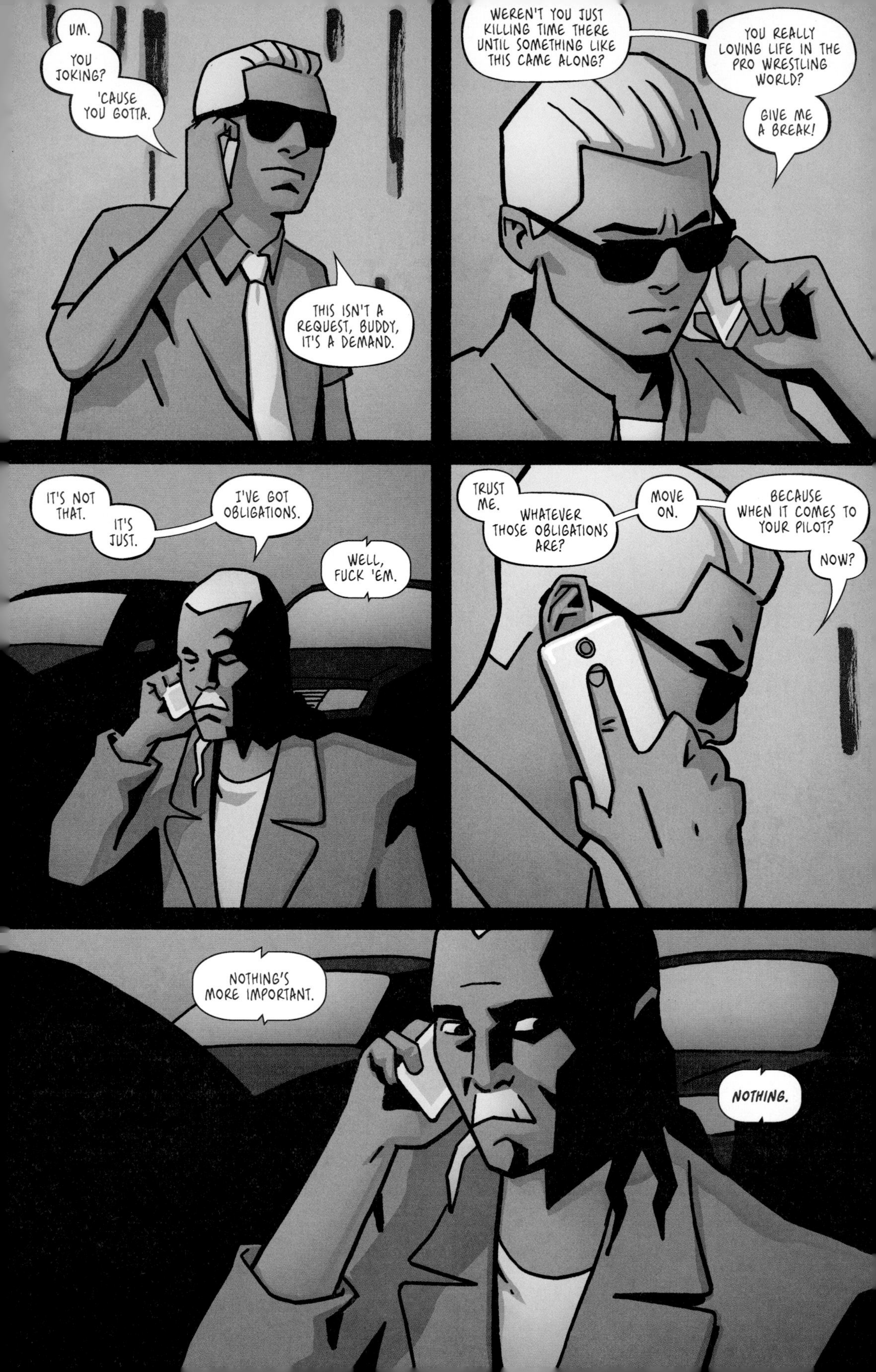
UM.
YOU JOKING?
'CAUSE YOU GOTTA.
THIS ISN'T A REQUEST, BUDDY, IT'S A DEMAND.
WEREN'T YOU JUST KILLING TIME THERE UNTIL SOMETHING LIKE THIS CAME ALONG?
YOU REALLY LOVING LIFE IN THE PRO WRESTLING WORLD?
GIVE ME A BREAK!
IT'S NOT THAT.
IT'S JUST.
I'VE GOT OBLIGATIONS.
WELL, FUCK 'EM.
TRUST ME.
WHATEVER THOSE OBLIGATIONS ARE?
MOVE ON.
BECAUSE WHEN IT COMES TO YOUR PILOT?
NOW?
NOTHING'S MORE IMPORTANT.
NOTHING.

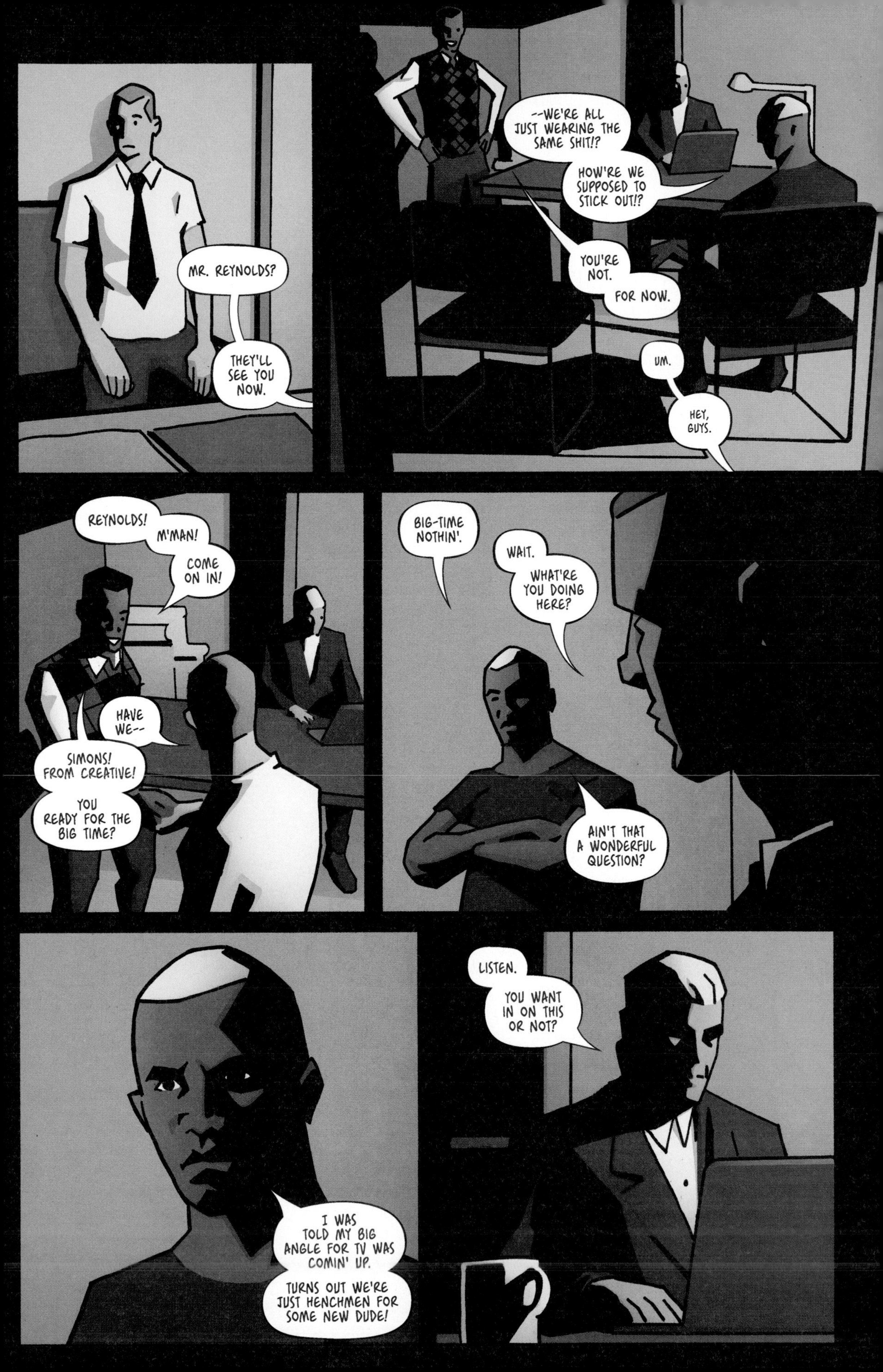
MR. REYNOLDS?
THEY'LL SEE YOU NOW.
--WE'RE ALL JUST WEARING THE SAME SHIT!?
HOW'RE WE SUPPOSED TO STICK OUT!?
YOU'RE NOT.
FOR NOW.
UM.
HEY, GUYS.
REYNOLDS!
M'MAN!
COME ON IN!
HAVE WE--
SIMONS! FROM CREATIVE!
YOU READY FOR THE BIG TIME?
BIG-TIME NOTHIN'.
WAIT.
WHAT'RE YOU DOING HERE?
AIN'T THAT A WONDERFUL QUESTION?
I WAS TOLD MY BIG ANGLE FOR TV WAS COMIN' UP.
TURNS OUT WE'RE JUST HENCHMEN FOR SOME NEW DUDE!
LISTEN.
YOU WANT IN ON THIS OR NOT?

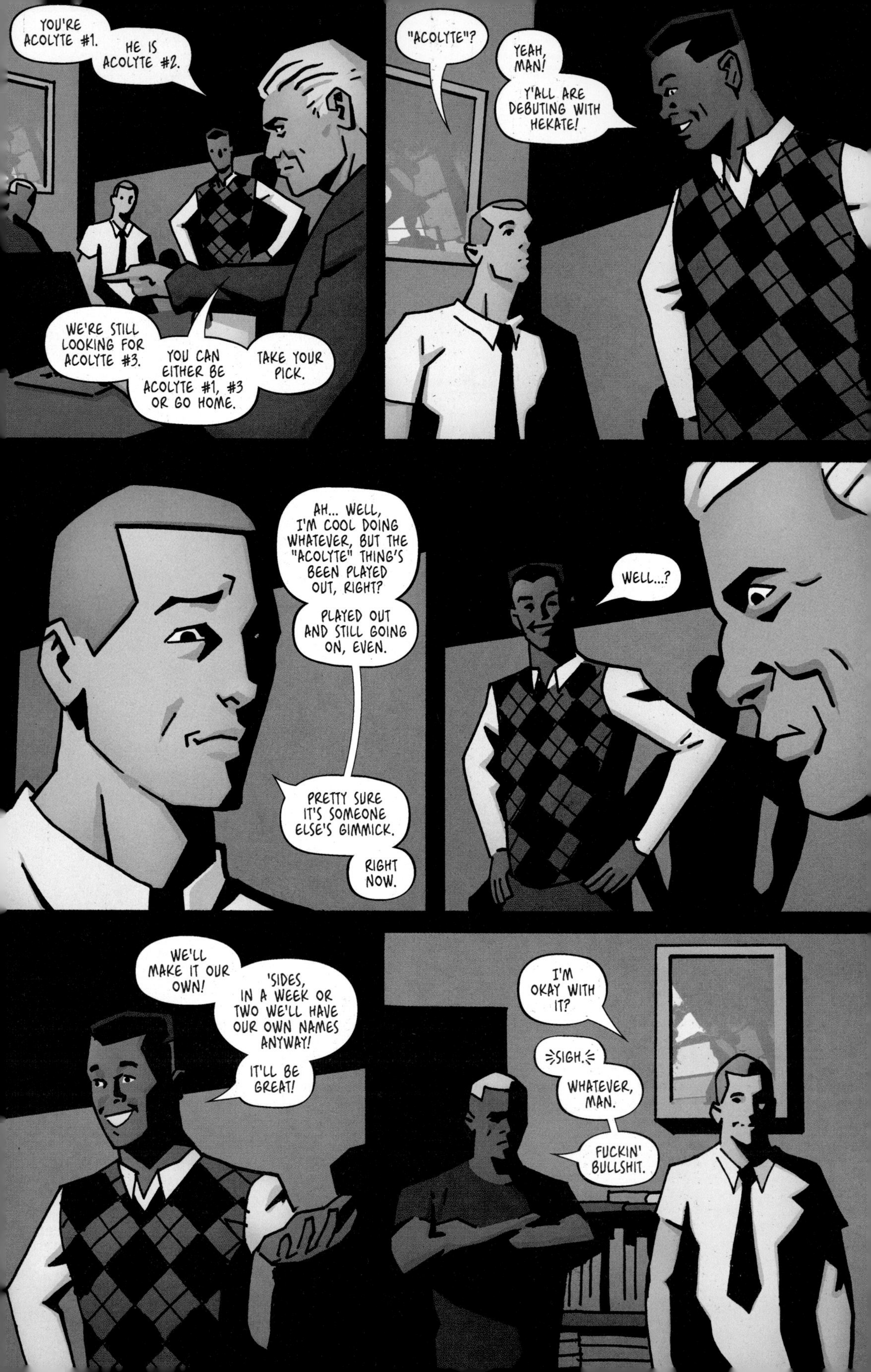
YOU'RE ACOLYTE #1.
HE IS ACOLYTE #2.
WE'RE STILL LOOKING FOR ACOLYTE #3.
YOU CAN EITHER BE ACOLYTE #1, #3 OR GO HOME.
TAKE YOUR PICK.
"ACOLYTE"?
YEAH, MAN!
Y'ALL ARE DEBUTING WITH HEKATE!
AH... WELL, I'M COOL DOING WHATEVER, BUT THE "ACOLYTE" THING'S BEEN PLAYED OUT, RIGHT?
PLAYED OUT AND STILL GOING ON, EVEN.
PRETTY SURE IT'S SOMEONE ELSE'S GIMMICK.
RIGHT NOW.
WELL...?
WE'LL MAKE IT OUR OWN!
'SIDES, IN A WEEK OR TWO WE'LL HAVE OUR OWN NAMES ANYWAY!
IT'LL BE GREAT!
I'M OKAY WITH IT?
SIGH.
WHATEVER, MAN.
FUCKIN' BULLSHIT.

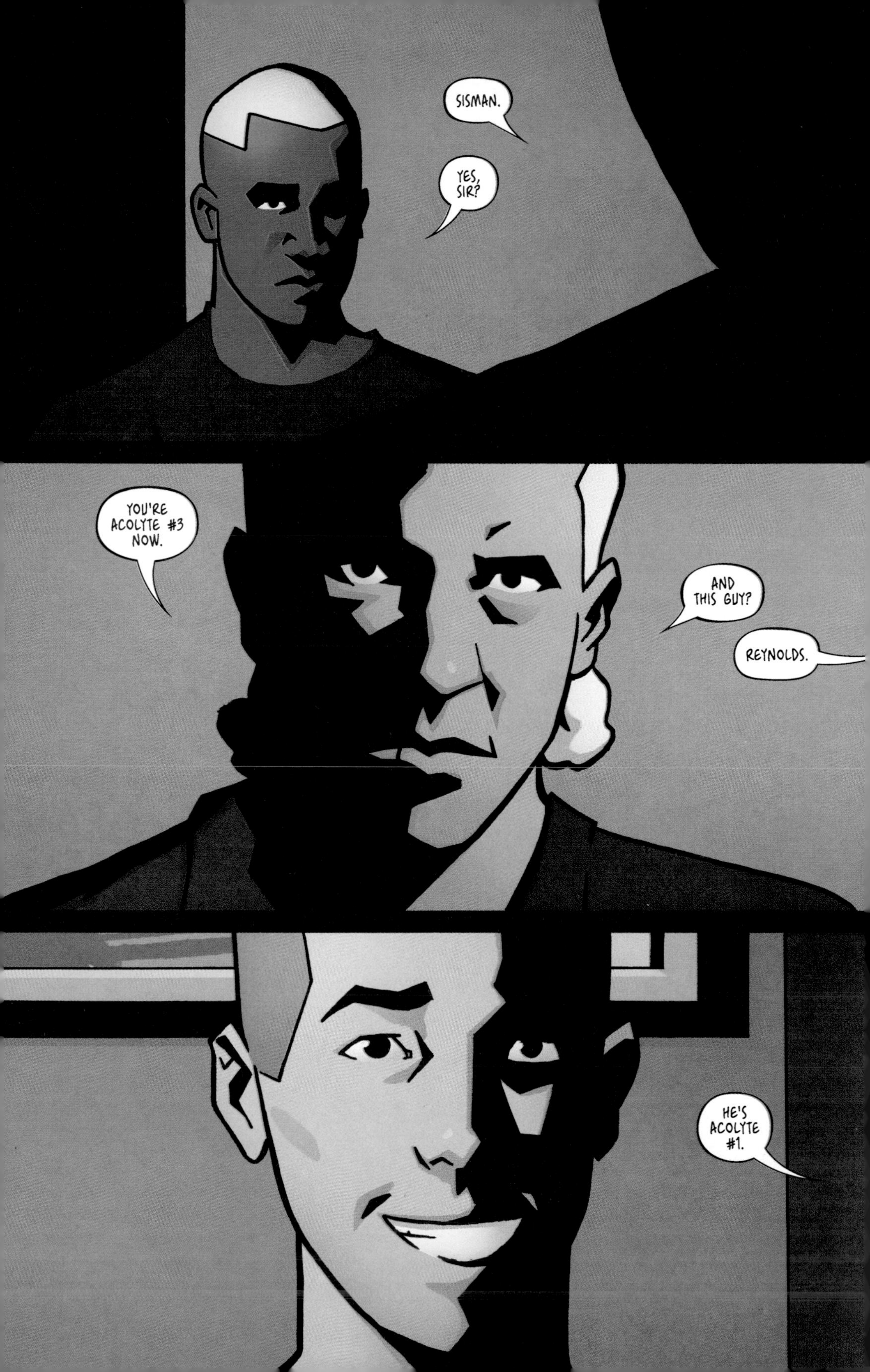
SISMAN.
YES, SIR?
YOU'RE ACOLYTE #3 NOW.
AND THIS GUY?
REYNOLDS.
HE'S ACOLYTE #1.

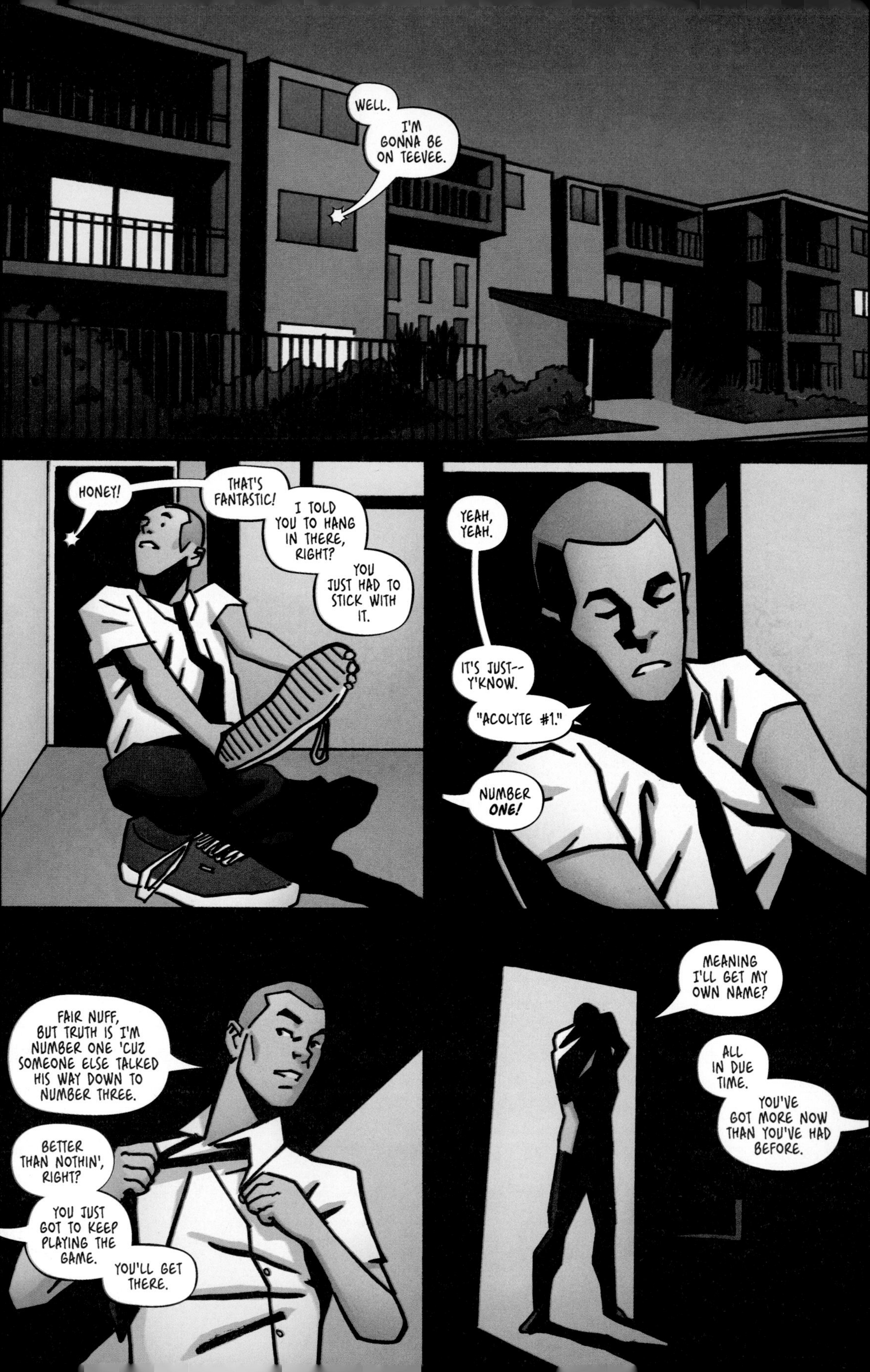
WELL.
I'M GONNA BE ON TEEVEE.
HONEY!
THAT'S FANTASTIC!
I TOLD YOU TO HANG IN THERE, RIGHT?
YOU JUST HAD TO STICK WITH IT.
YEAH, YEAH.
IT'S JUST-- Y'KNOW.
"ACOLYTE #1."
NUMBER ONE!
FAIR NUFF, BUT TRUTH IS I'M NUMBER ONE 'CUZ SOMEONE ELSE TALKED HIS WAY DOWN TO NUMBER THREE.
BETTER THAN NOTHIN', RIGHT?
YOU JUST GOT TO KEEP PLAYING THE GAME.
YOU'LL GET THERE.
MEANING I'LL GET MY OWN NAME?
ALL IN DUE TIME.
YOU'VE GOT MORE NOW THAN YOU'VE HAD BEFORE.

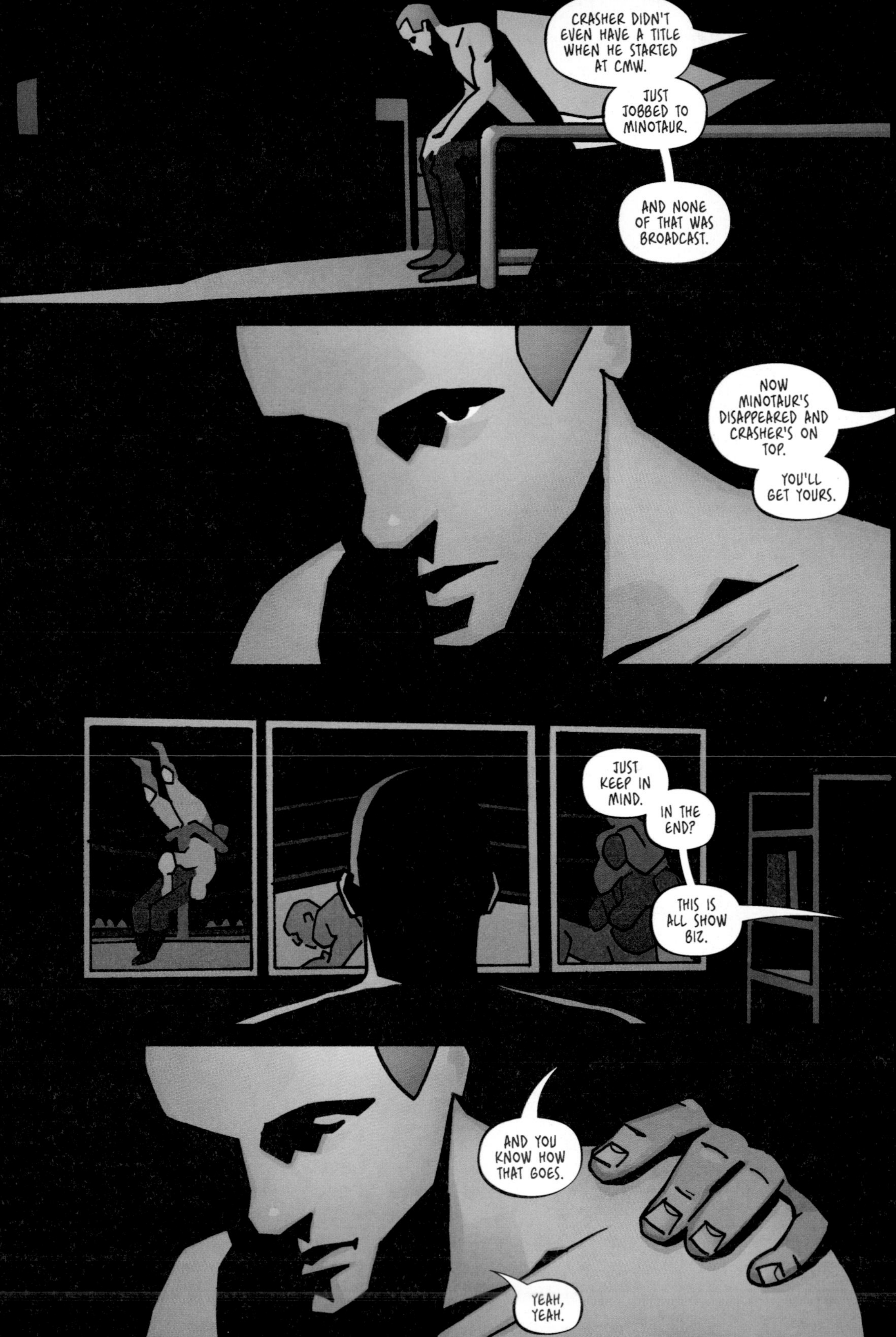
CRASHER DIDN'T EVEN HAVE A TITLE WHEN HE STARTED AT CMW.
JUST JOBBED TO MINOTAUR.
AND NONE OF THAT WAS BROADCAST.
NOW MINOTAUR'S DISAPPEARED AND CRASHER'S ON TOP.
YOU'LL GET YOURS.
JUST KEEP IN MIND.
IN THE END?
THIS IS ALL SHOW BIZ.
AND YOU KNOW HOW THAT GOES.
YEAH, YEAH.

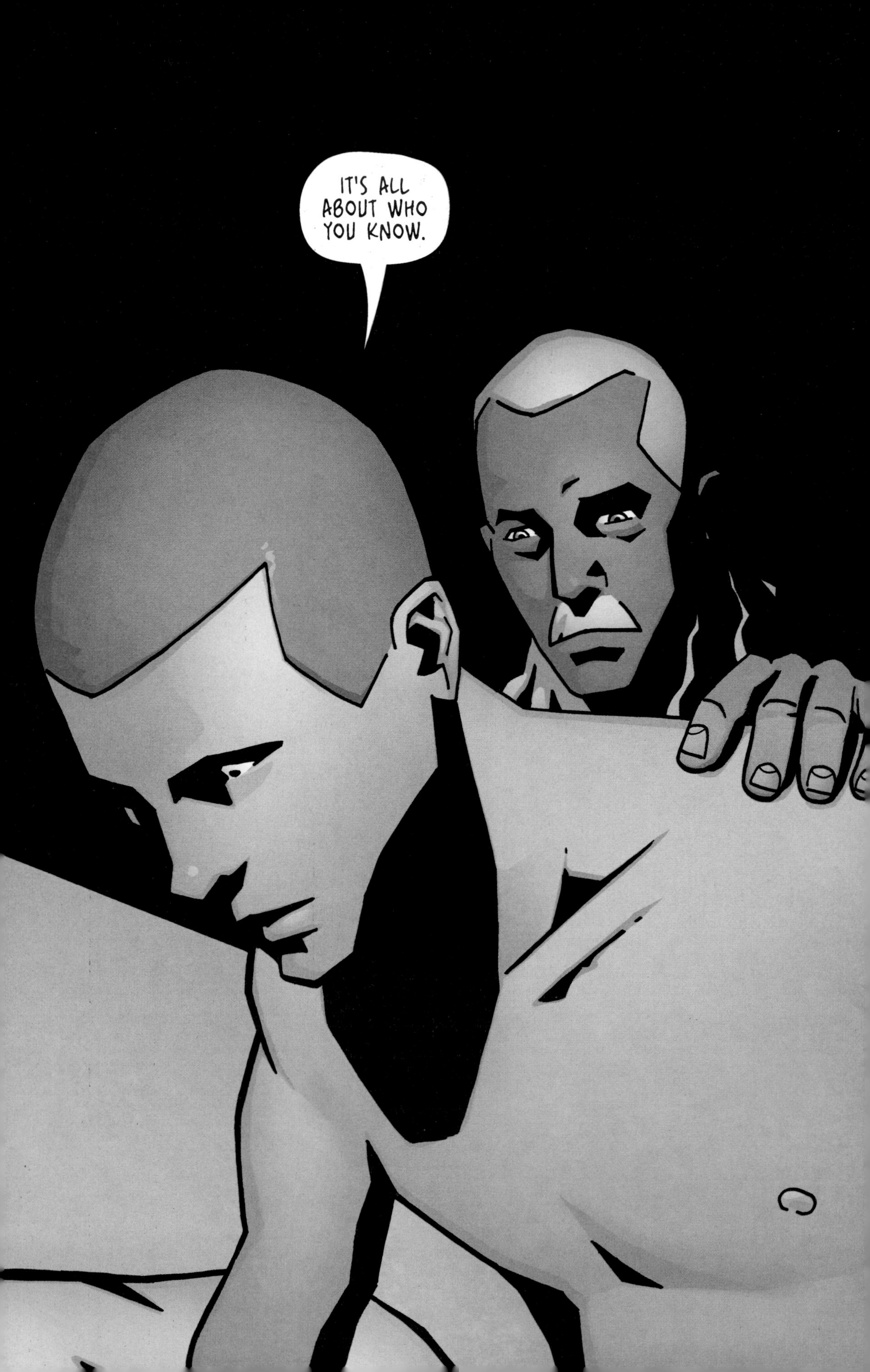
IT'S ALL ABOUT WHO YOU KNOW.

CHAPTER EIGHT

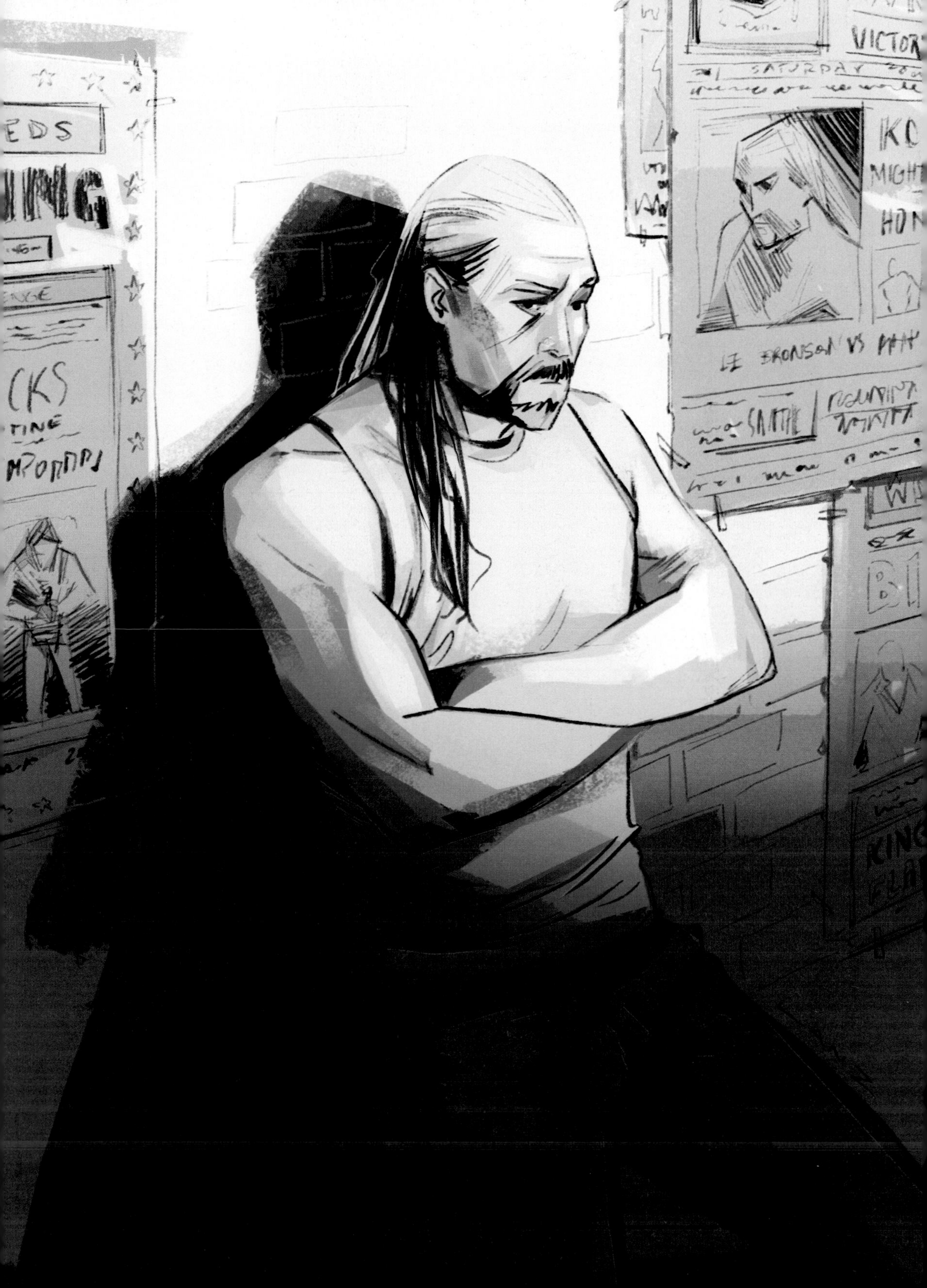
SATURDAY
BRONSON VS

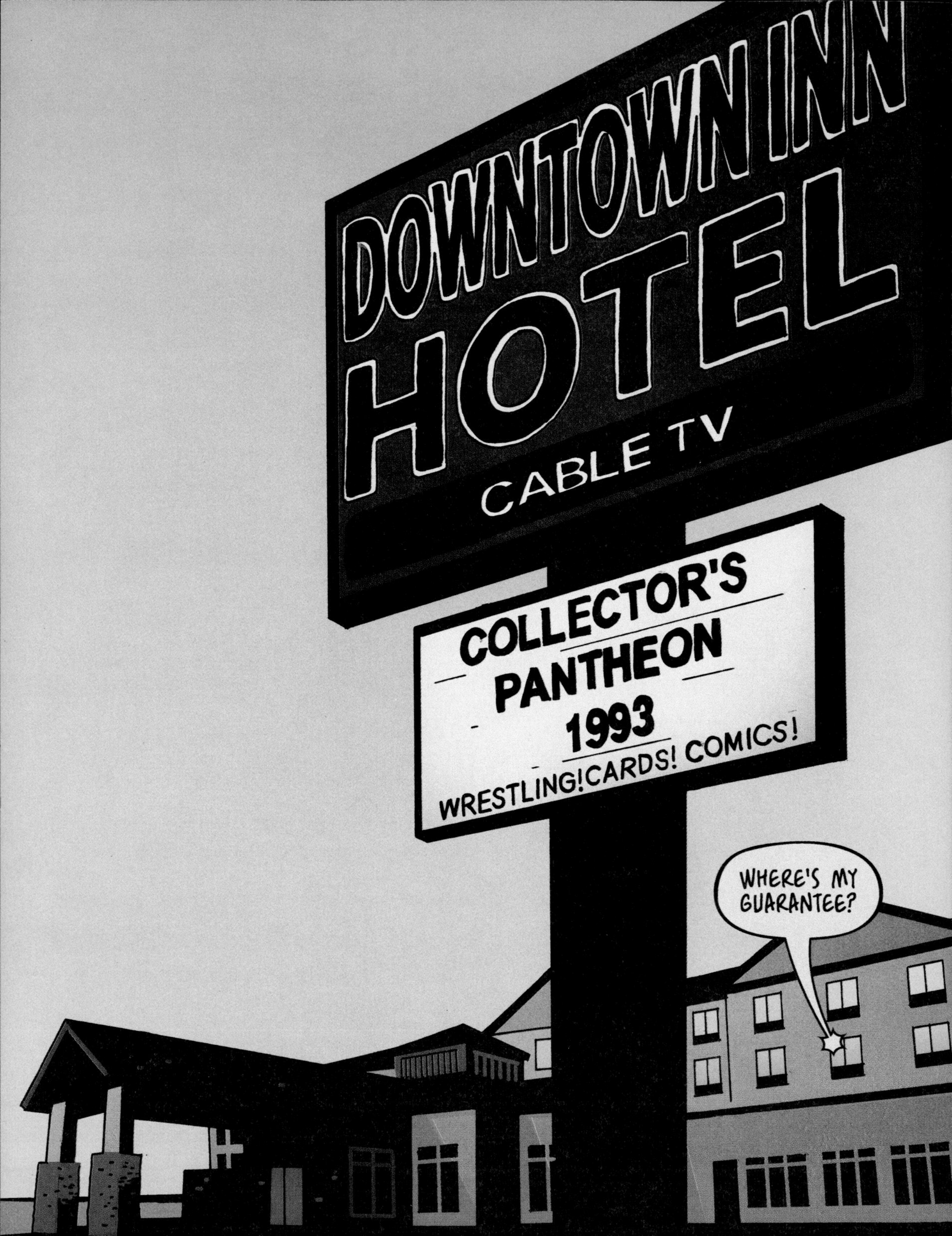
DOWNTOWN INN
HOTEL
CABLE TV
COLLECTOR'S
PANTHEON
1993
WRESTLING! CARDS! COMICS!
WHERE'S MY GUARANTEE?

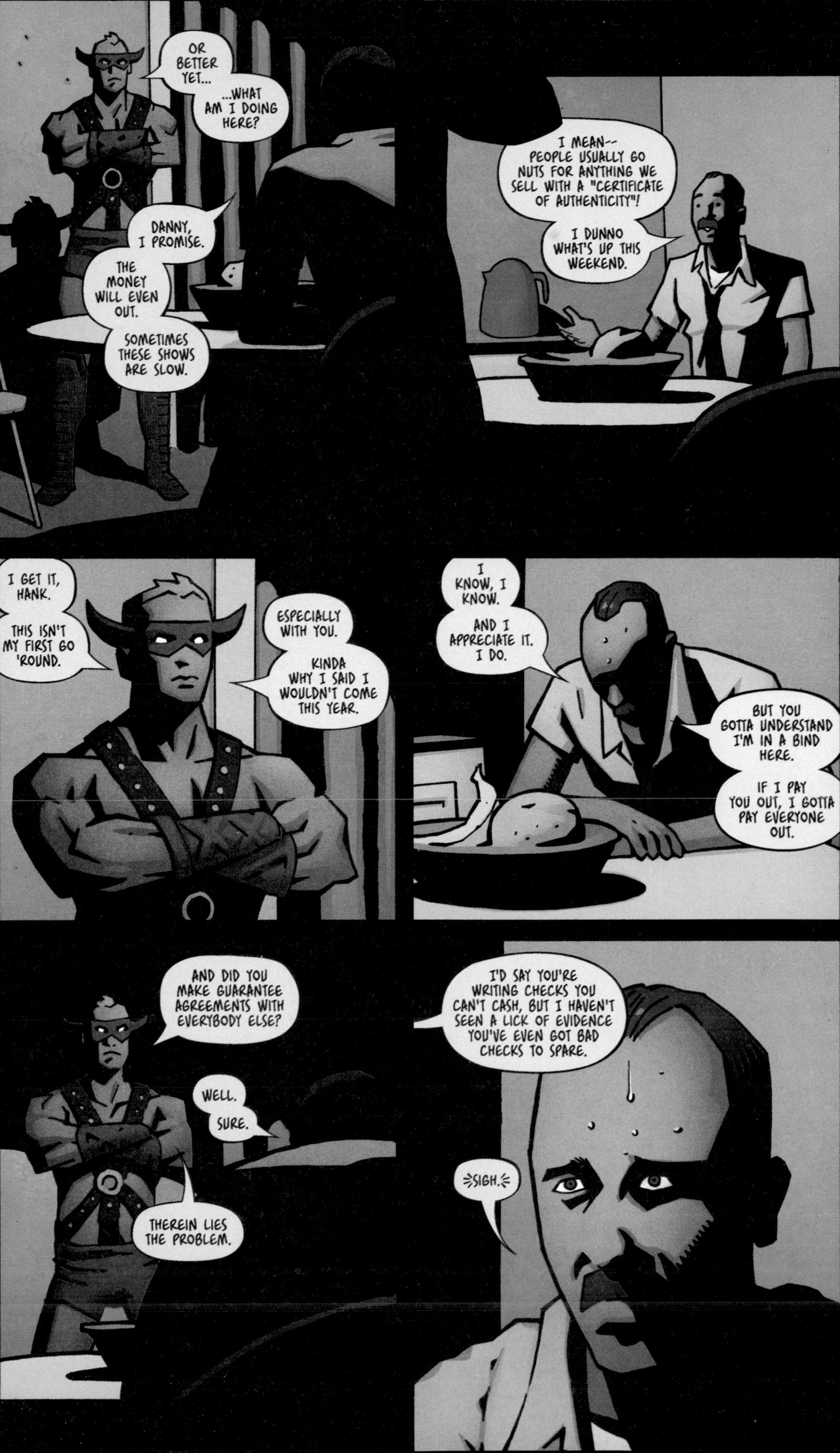
OR BETTER YET...
...WHAT AM I DOING HERE?
DANNY, I PROMISE.
THE MONEY WILL EVEN OUT.
SOMETIMES THESE SHOWS ARE SLOW.
I MEAN-- PEOPLE USUALLY GO NUTS FOR ANYTHING WE SELL WITH A "CERTIFICATE OF AUTHENTICITY"!
I DUNNO WHAT'S UP THIS WEEKEND.
I GET IT, HANK.
THIS ISN'T MY FIRST GO 'ROUND.
ESPECIALLY WITH YOU.
KINDA WHY I SAID I WOULDN'T COME THIS YEAR.
I KNOW, I KNOW.
AND I APPRECIATE IT. I DO.
BUT YOU GOTTA UNDERSTAND I'M IN A BIND HERE.
IF I PAY YOU OUT, I GOTTA PAY EVERYONE OUT.
AND DID YOU MAKE GUARANTEE AGREEMENTS WITH EVERYBODY ELSE?
WELL.
SURE.
THEREIN LIES THE PROBLEM.
I'D SAY YOU'RE WRITING CHECKS YOU CAN'T CASH, BUT I HAVEN'T SEEN A LICK OF EVIDENCE YOU'VE EVEN GOT BAD CHECKS TO SPARE.
SIGH.

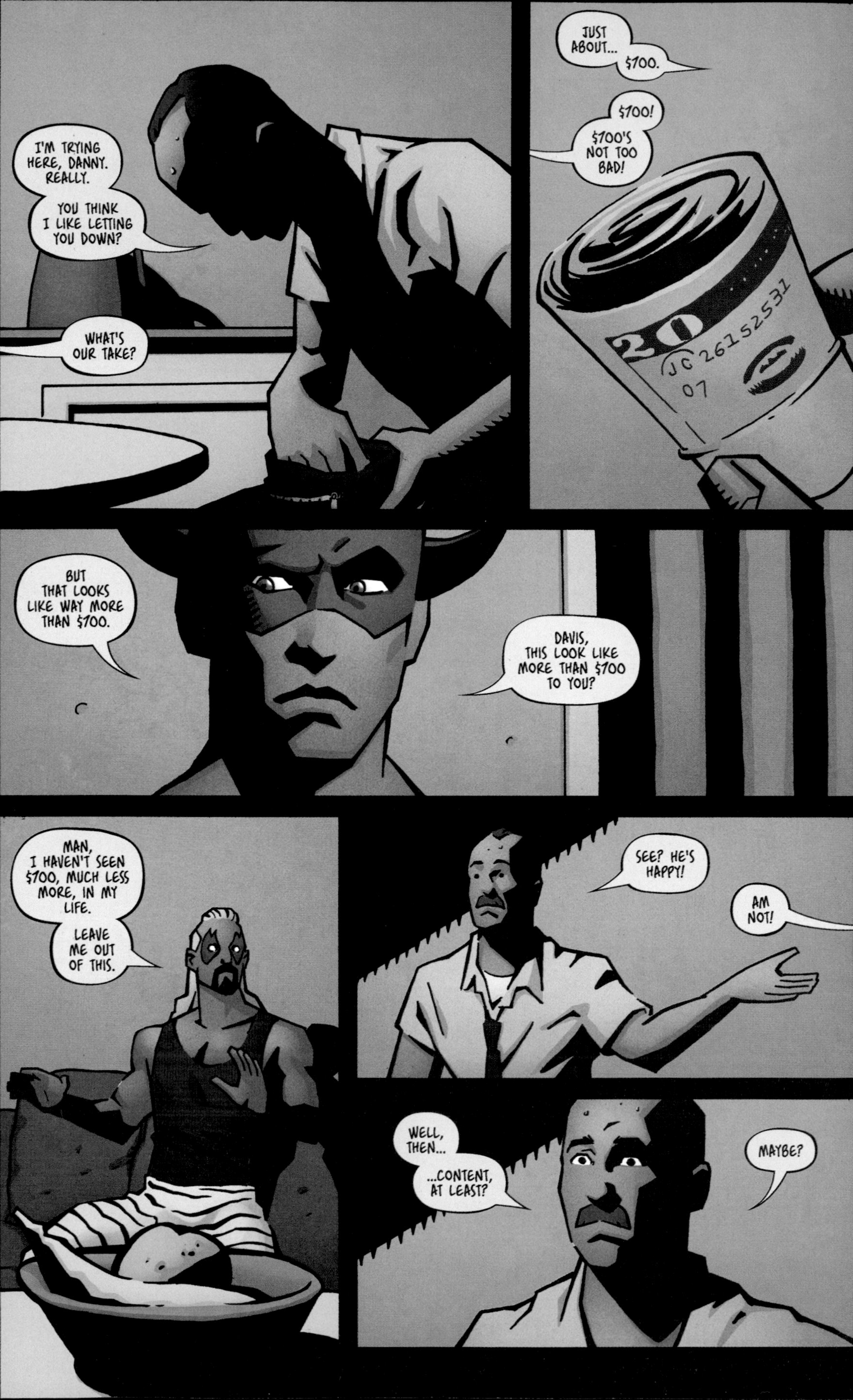
I'M TRYING HERE, DANNY. REALLY.
YOU THINK I LIKE LETTING YOU DOWN?
WHAT'S OUR TAKE?
JUST ABOUT... $700.
$700!
$700'S NOT TOO BAD!
20
JC 26152531
07
BUT THAT LOOKS LIKE WAY MORE THAN $700.
DAVIS, THIS LOOK LIKE MORE THAN $700 TO YOU?
MAN, I HAVEN'T SEEN $700, MUCH LESS MORE, IN MY LIFE.
LEAVE ME OUT OF THIS.
SEE? HE'S HAPPY!
AM NOT!
WELL, THEN...
...CONTENT, AT LEAST?
MAYBE?

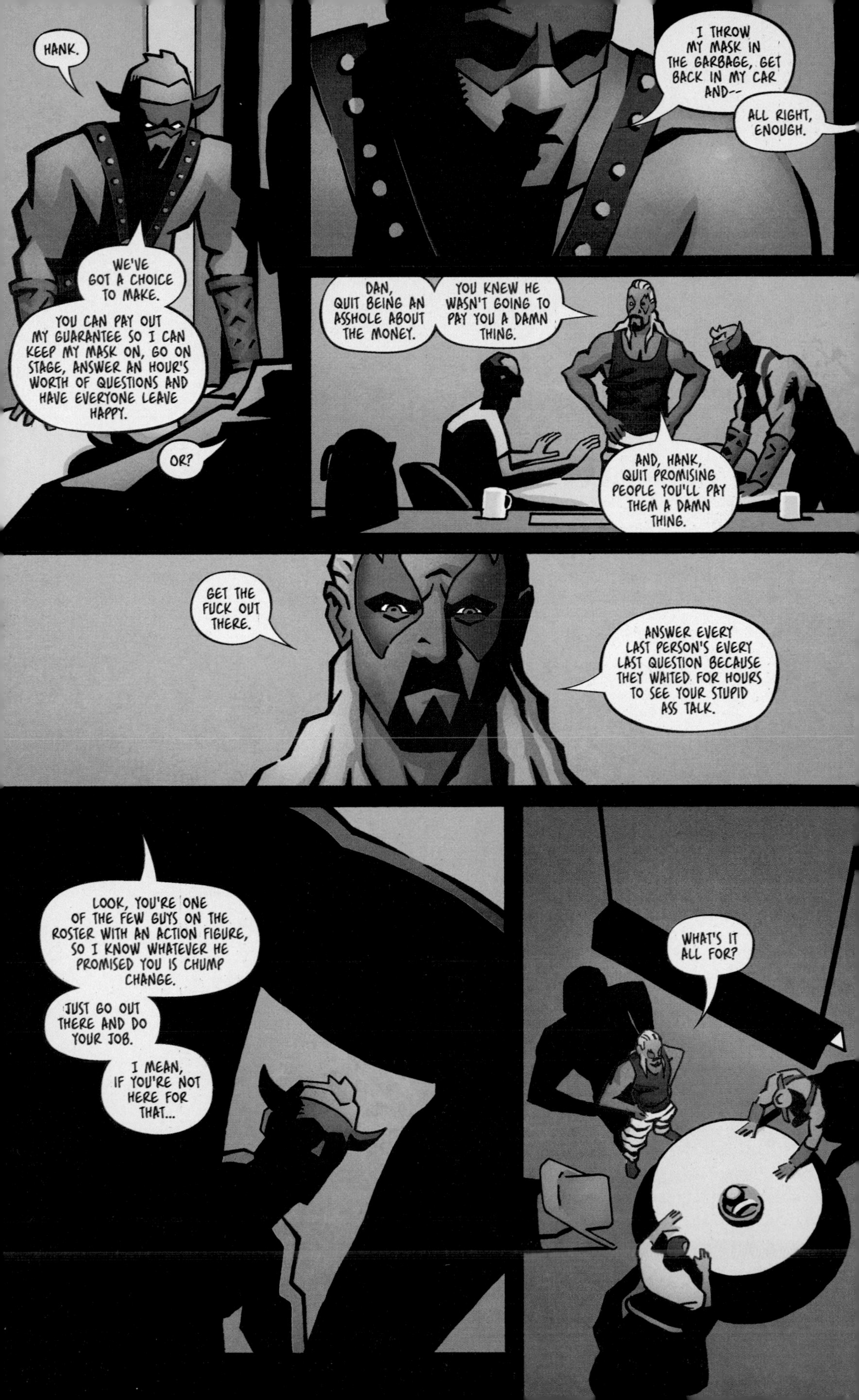
HANK.
I THROW MY MASK IN THE GARBAGE, GET BACK IN MY CAR AND--
ALL RIGHT, ENOUGH.
WE'VE GOT A CHOICE TO MAKE.
YOU CAN PAY OUT MY GUARANTEE SO I CAN KEEP MY MASK ON, GO ON STAGE, ANSWER AN HOUR'S WORTH OF QUESTIONS AND HAVE EVERYONE LEAVE HAPPY.
OR?
DAN, QUIT BEING AN ASSHOLE ABOUT THE MONEY.
YOU KNEW HE WASN'T GOING TO PAY YOU A DAMN THING.
AND, HANK, QUIT PROMISING PEOPLE YOU'LL PAY THEM A DAMN THING.
GET THE FUCK OUT THERE.
ANSWER EVERY LAST PERSON'S EVERY LAST QUESTION BECAUSE THEY WAITED FOR HOURS TO SEE YOUR STUPID ASS TALK.
LOOK, YOU'RE ONE OF THE FEW GUYS ON THE ROSTER WITH AN ACTION FIGURE, SO I KNOW WHATEVER HE PROMISED YOU IS CHUMP CHANGE.
JUST GO OUT THERE AND DO YOUR JOB.
I MEAN, IF YOU'RE NOT HERE FOR THAT...
WHAT'S IT ALL FOR?

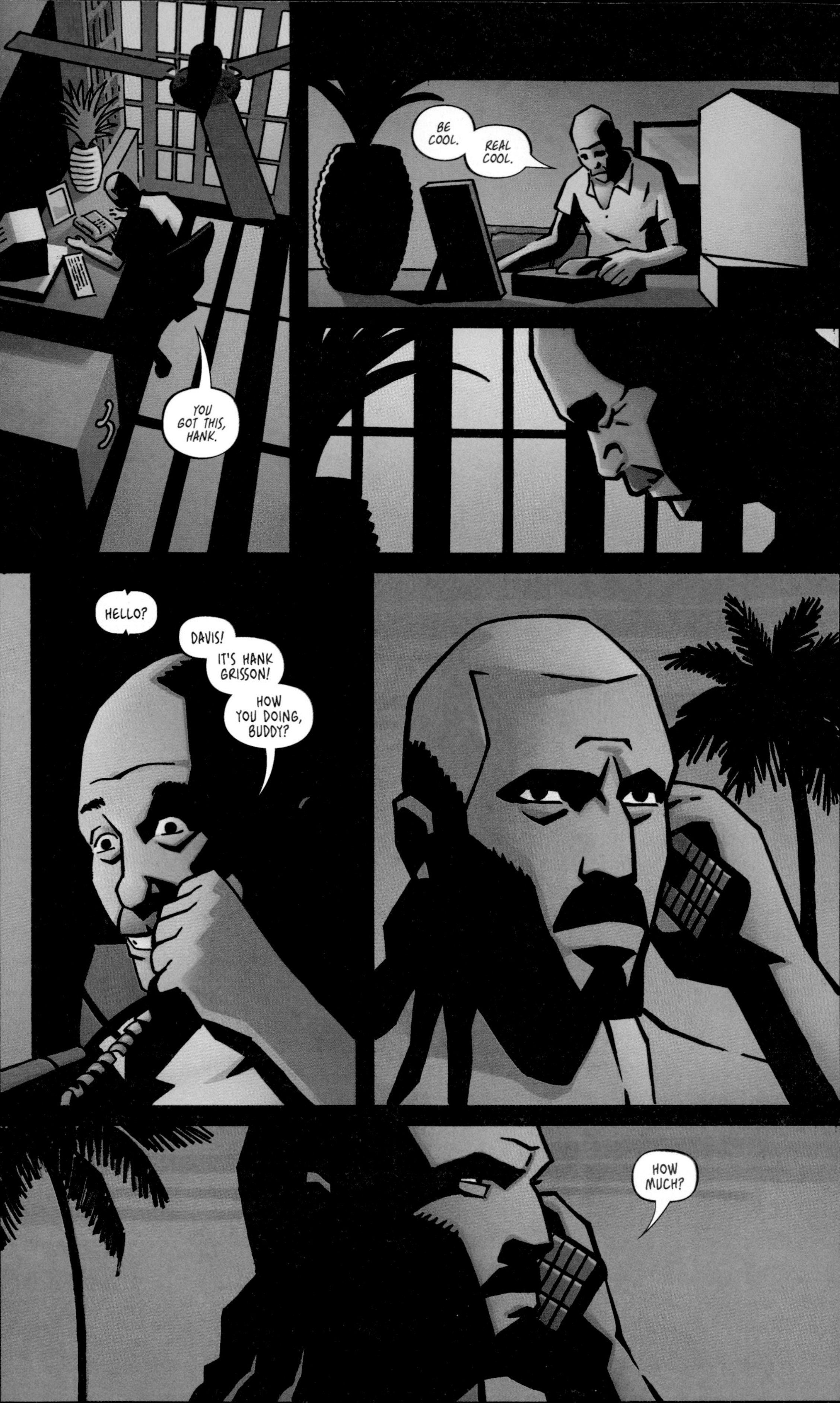
BE COOL.
REAL COOL.
YOU GOT THIS, HANK.
HELLO?
DAVIS!
IT'S HANK GRISSON!
HOW YOU DOING, BUDDY?
HOW MUCH?

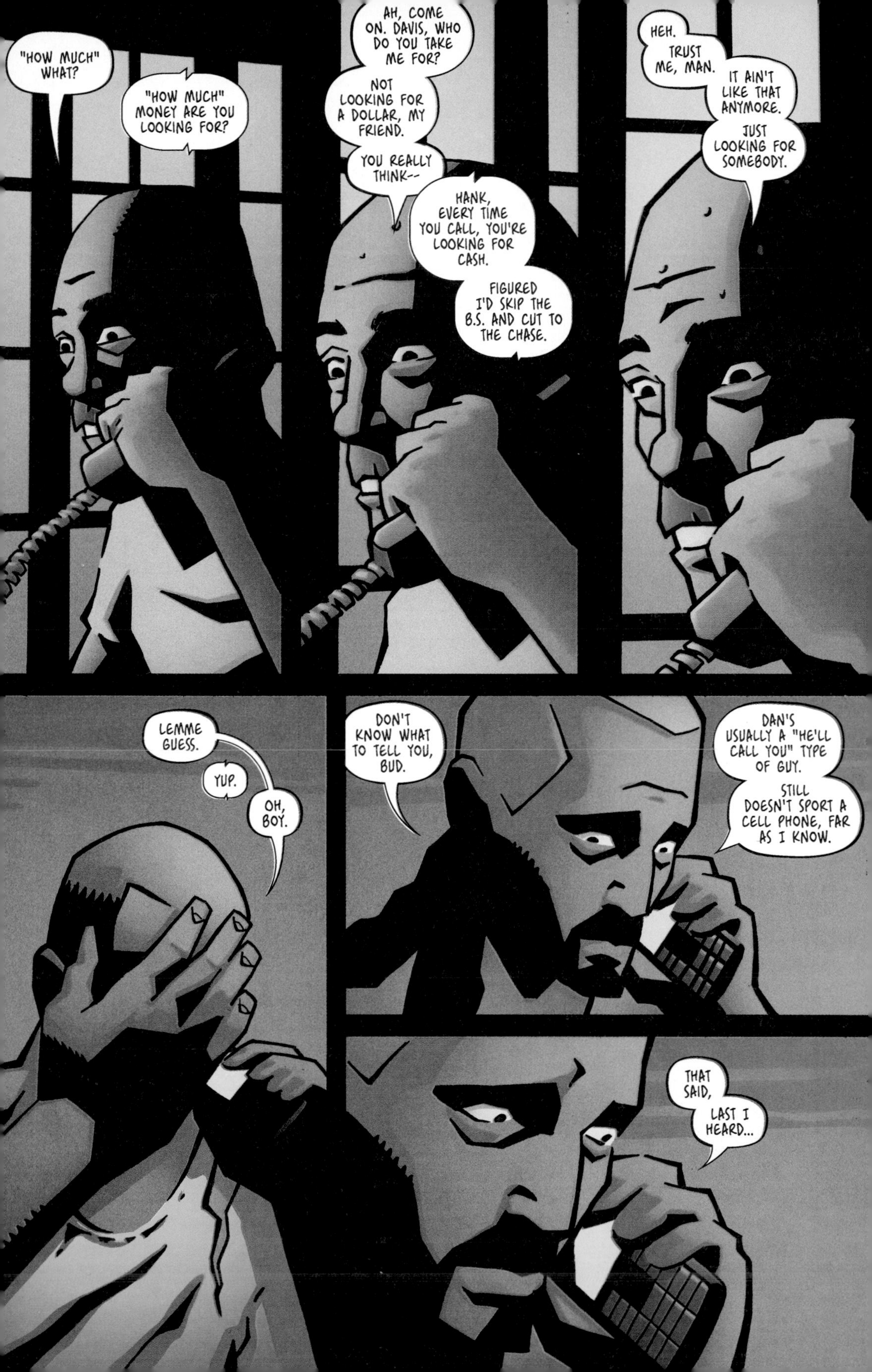
"HOW MUCH" WHAT?
"HOW MUCH" MONEY ARE YOU LOOKING FOR?
AH, COME ON. DAVIS, WHO DO YOU TAKE ME FOR?
NOT LOOKING FOR A DOLLAR, MY FRIEND.
YOU REALLY THINK--
HANK, EVERY TIME YOU CALL, YOU'RE LOOKING FOR CASH.
FIGURED I'D SKIP THE B.S. AND CUT TO THE CHASE.
HEH.
TRUST ME, MAN.
IT AIN'T LIKE THAT ANYMORE.
JUST LOOKING FOR SOMEBODY.
LEMME GUESS.
YUP.
OH, BOY.
DON'T KNOW WHAT TO TELL YOU, BUD.
DAN'S USUALLY A "HE'LL CALL YOU" TYPE OF GUY.
STILL DOESN'T SPORT A CELL PHONE, FAR AS I KNOW.
THAT SAID,
LAST I HEARD...

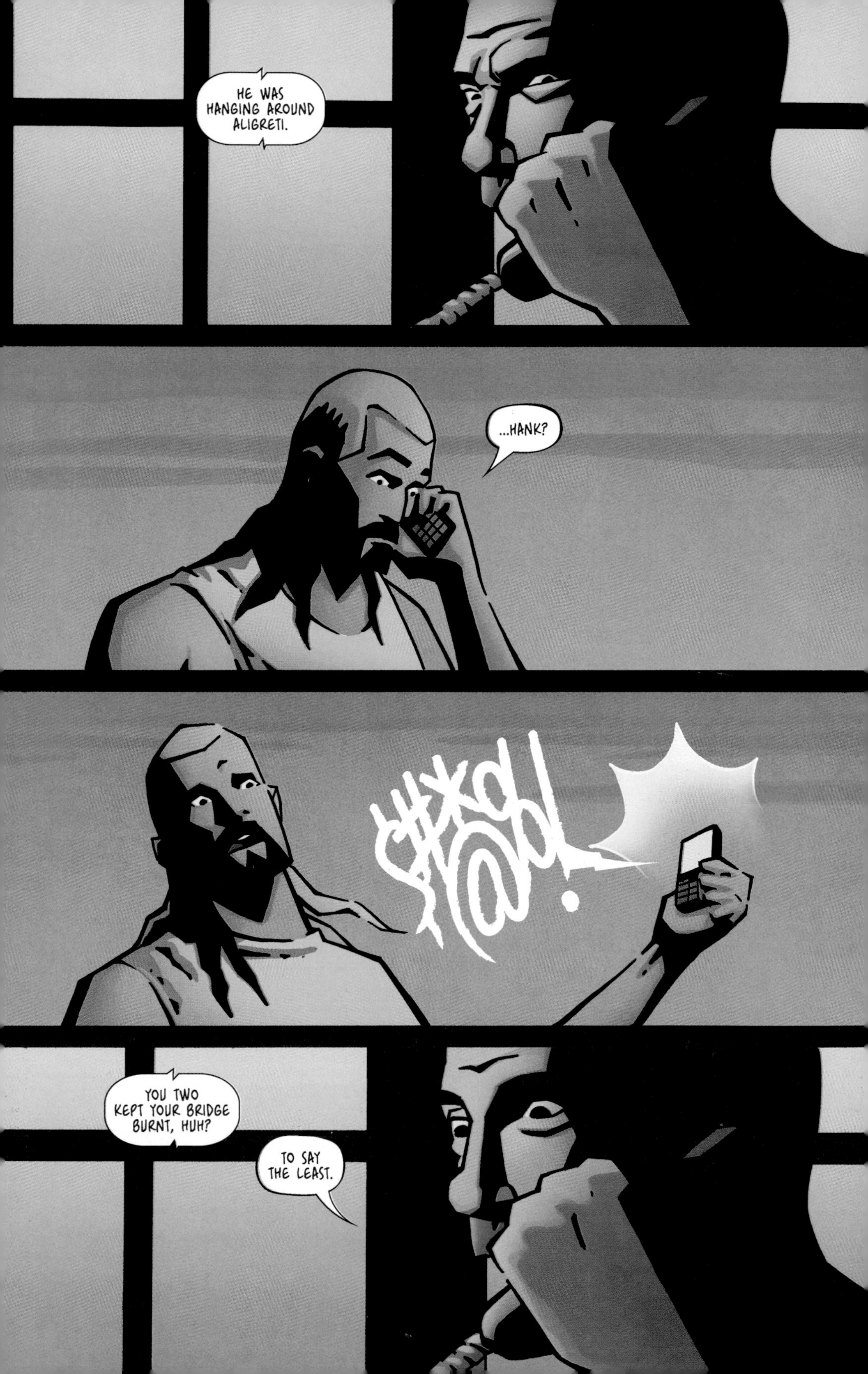
HE WAS HANGING AROUND ALIGRETI.
...HANK?
YOU TWO KEPT YOUR BRIDGE BURNT, HUH?
TO SAY THE LEAST.

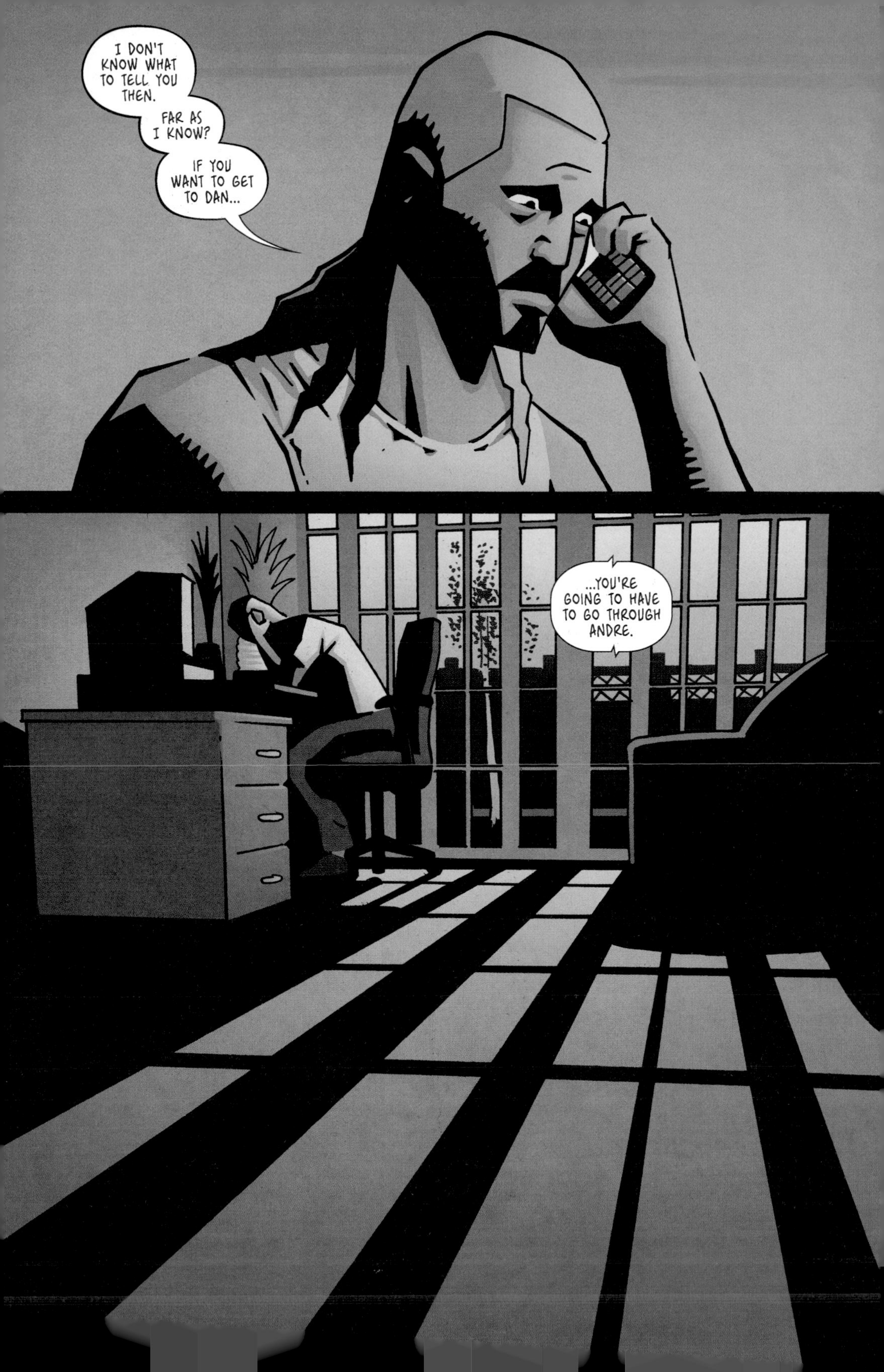
I DON'T KNOW WHAT TO TELL YOU THEN.
FAR AS I KNOW?
IF YOU WANT TO GET TO DAN...
...YOU'RE GOING TO HAVE TO GO THROUGH ANDRE.

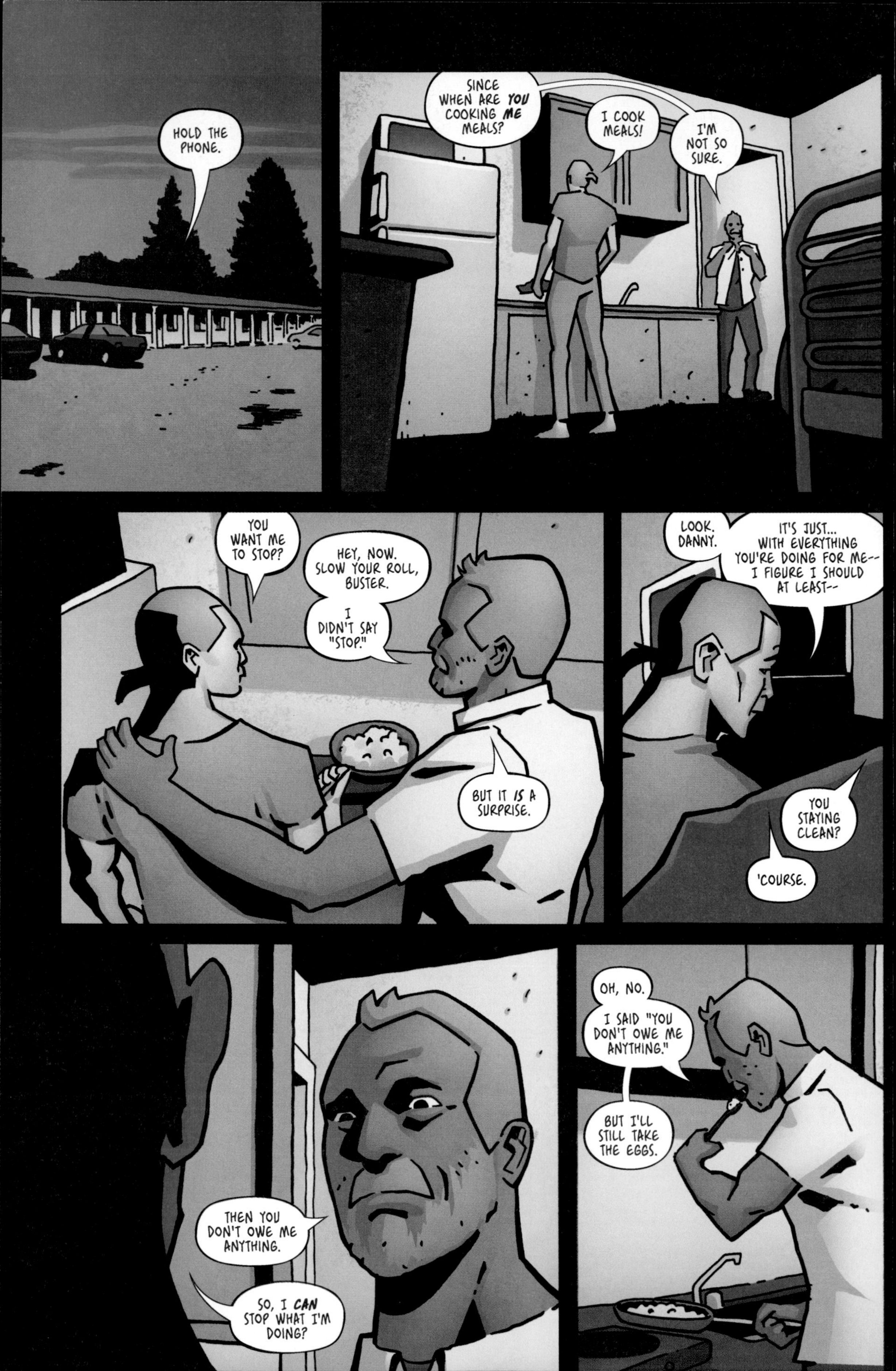
HOLD THE PHONE.
SINCE WHEN ARE YOU COOKING ME MEALS?
I COOK MEALS!
I'M NOT SO SURE.
YOU WANT ME TO STOP?
HEY, NOW. SLOW YOUR ROLL, BUSTER.
I DIDN'T SAY "STOP."
BUT IT IS A SURPRISE.
LOOK. DANNY.
IT'S JUST... WITH EVERYTHING YOU'RE DOING FOR ME-- I FIGURE I SHOULD AT LEAST--
YOU STAYING CLEAN?
'COURSE.
THEN YOU DON'T OWE ME ANYTHING.
SO, I CAN STOP WHAT I'M DOING?
OH, NO.
I SAID "YOU DON'T OWE ME ANYTHING."
BUT I'LL STILL TAKE THE EGGS.

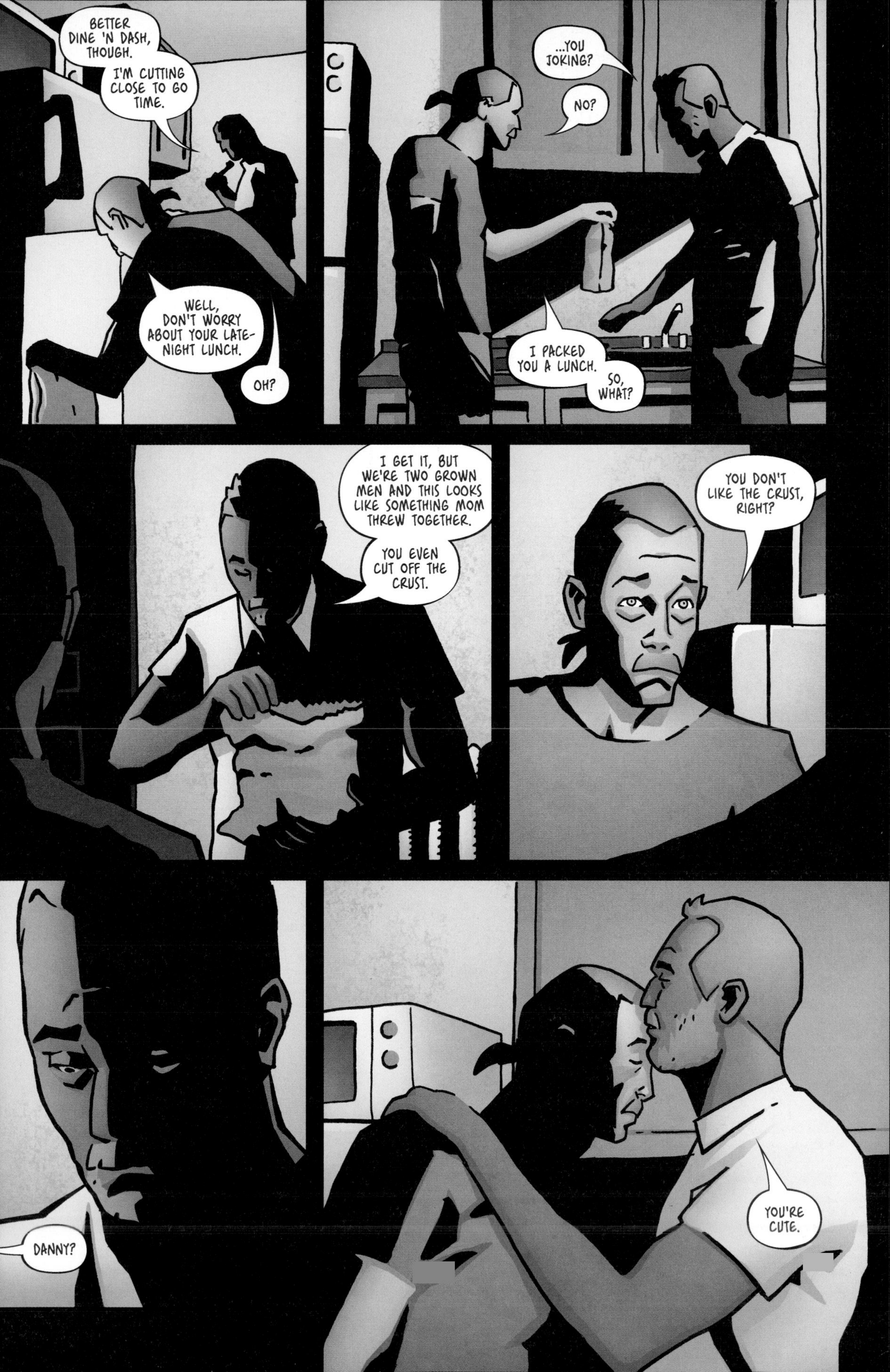
BETTER DINE 'N DASH, THOUGH.
I'M CUTTING CLOSE TO GO TIME.
WELL, DON'T WORRY ABOUT YOUR LATE-NIGHT LUNCH.
OH?
...YOU JOKING?
NO?
I PACKED YOU A LUNCH.
SO, WHAT?
I GET IT, BUT WE'RE TWO GROWN MEN AND THIS LOOKS LIKE SOMETHING MOM THREW TOGETHER.
YOU EVEN CUT OFF THE CRUST.
YOU DON'T LIKE THE CRUST, RIGHT?
DANNY?
YOU'RE CUTE.

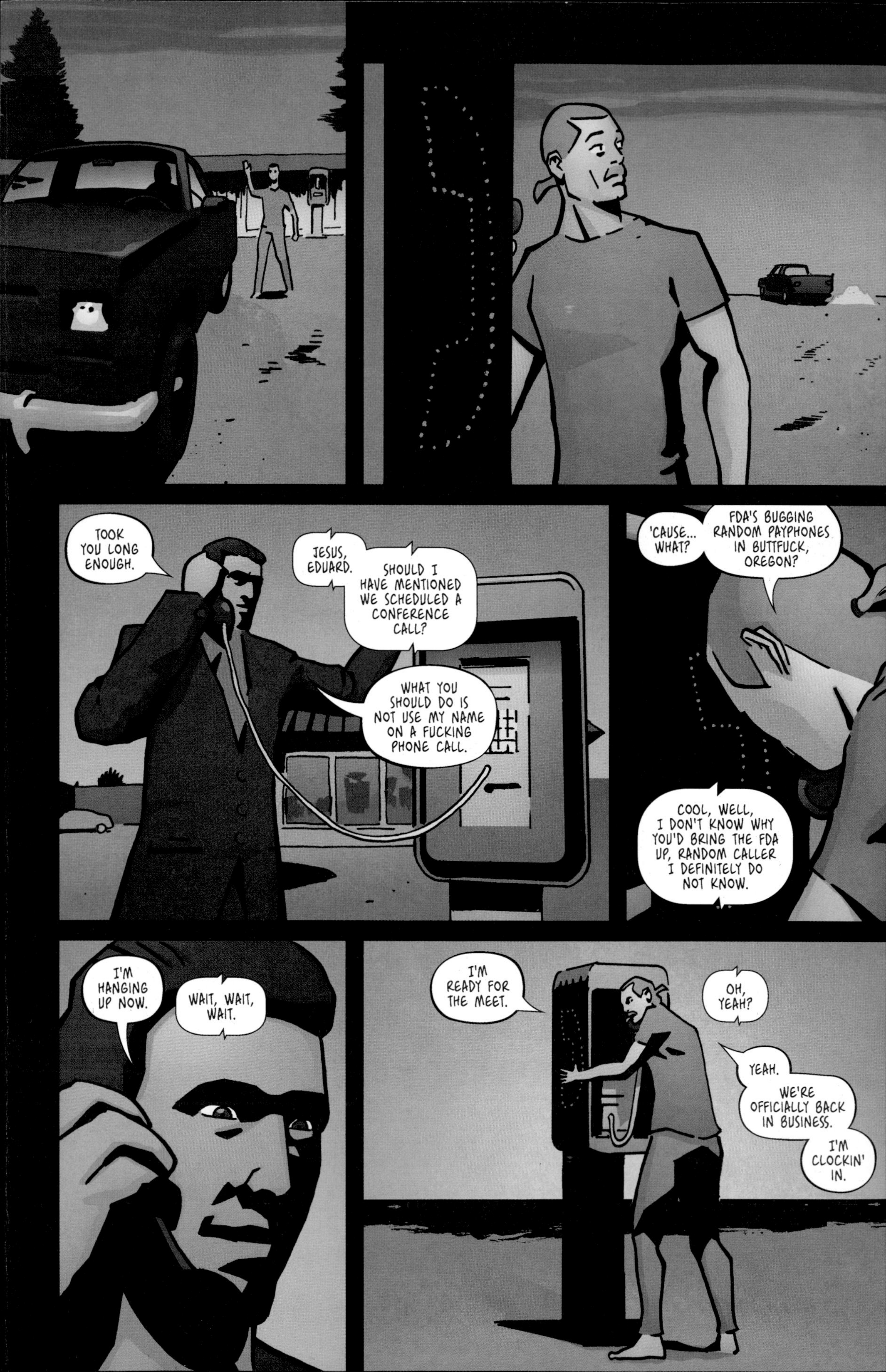
TOOK YOU LONG ENOUGH.
JESUS, EDUARD.
SHOULD I HAVE MENTIONED WE SCHEDULED A CONFERENCE CALL?
WHAT YOU SHOULD DO IS NOT USE MY NAME ON A FUCKING PHONE CALL.
'CAUSE... WHAT?
FDA'S BUGGING RANDOM PAYPHONES IN BUTTFUCK, OREGON?
COOL, WELL, I DON'T KNOW WHY YOU'D BRING THE FDA UP, RANDOM CALLER I DEFINITELY DO NOT KNOW.
I'M HANGING UP NOW.
WAIT, WAIT, WAIT.
I'M READY FOR THE MEET.
OH, YEAH?
YEAH.
WE'RE OFFICIALLY BACK IN BUSINESS.
I'M CLOCKIN' IN.

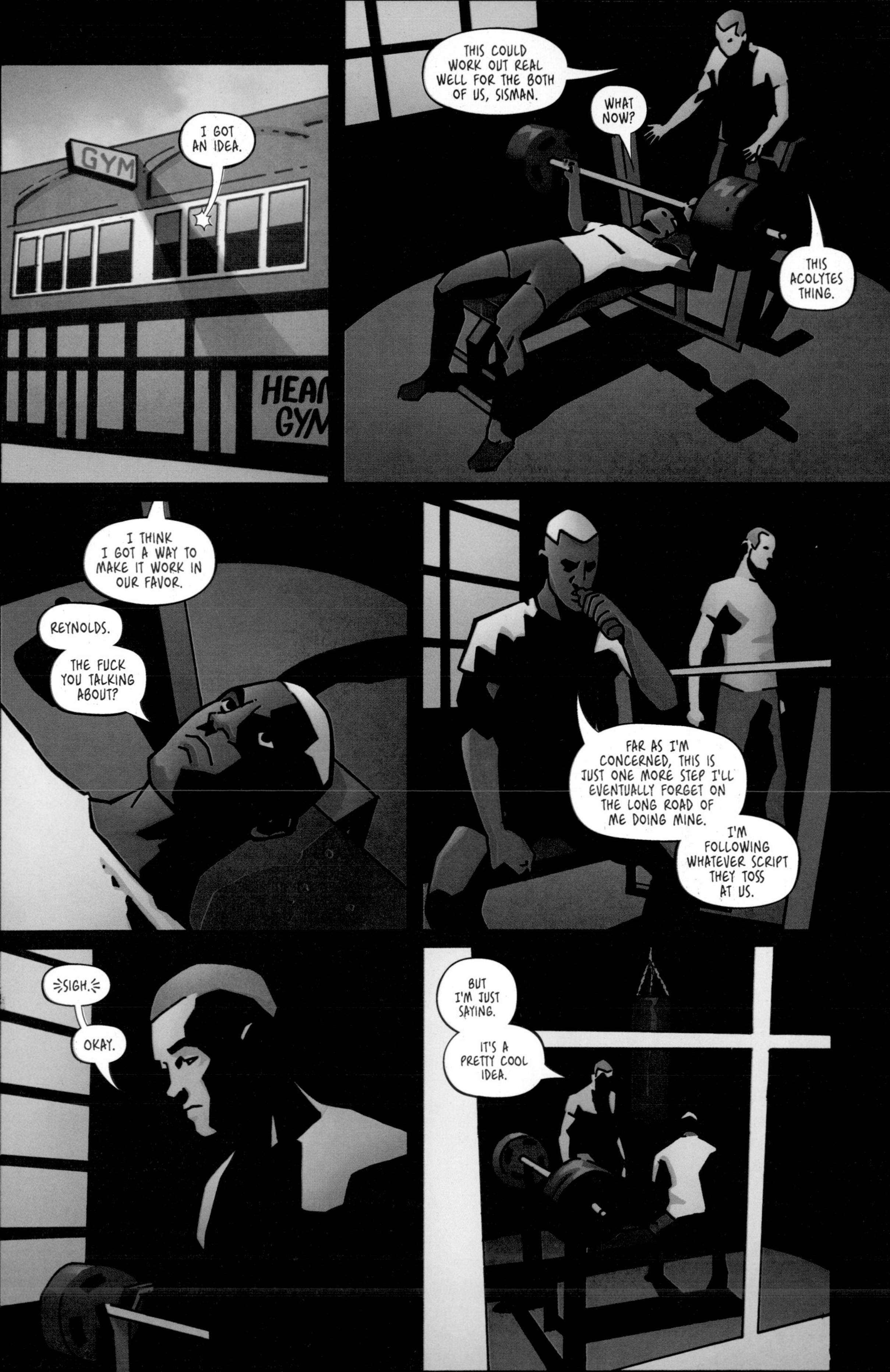

GYM
I GOT AN IDEA.
HEA
GYM
THIS COULD WORK OUT REAL WELL FOR THE BOTH OF US, SISMAN.
WHAT NOW?
THIS ACOLYTES THING.
I THINK I GOT A WAY TO MAKE IT WORK IN OUR FAVOR.
REYNOLDS.
THE FUCK YOU TALKING ABOUT?
FAR AS I'M CONCERNED, THIS IS JUST ONE MORE STEP I'LL EVENTUALLY FORGET ON THE LONG ROAD OF ME DOING MINE.
I'M FOLLOWING WHATEVER SCRIPT THEY TOSS AT US.
SIGH.
OKAY.
BUT I'M JUST SAYING.
IT'S A PRETTY COOL IDEA.

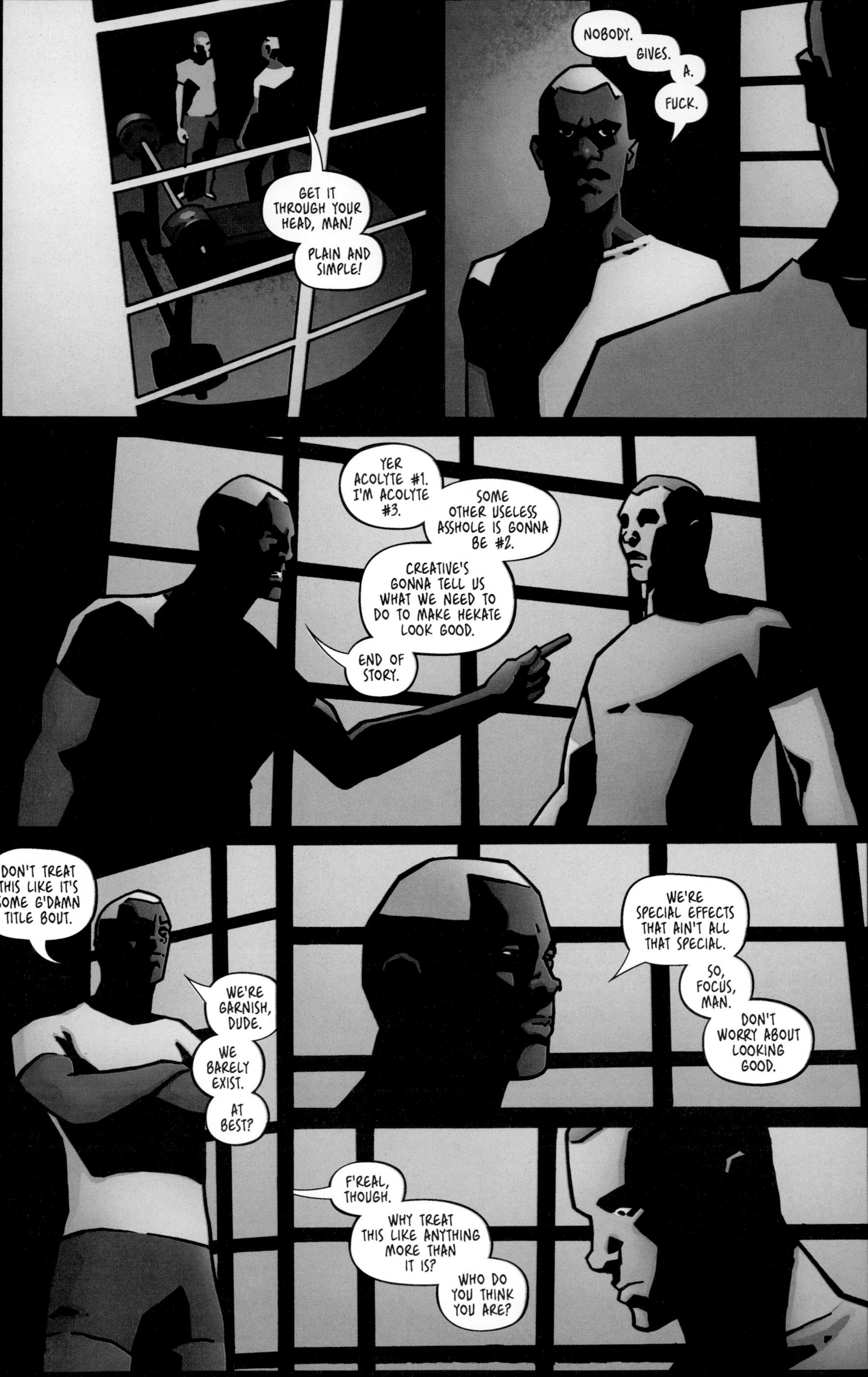
GET IT THROUGH YOUR HEAD, MAN!
PLAIN AND SIMPLE!
NOBODY.
GIVES.
A.
FUCK.
YER ACOLYTE #1. I'M ACOLYTE #3.
SOME OTHER USELESS ASSHOLE IS GONNA BE #2.
CREATIVE'S GONNA TELL US WHAT WE NEED TO DO TO MAKE HEKATE LOOK GOOD.
END OF STORY.
DON'T TREAT THIS LIKE IT'S SOME G'DAMN TITLE BOUT.
WE'RE GARNISH, DUDE.
WE BARELY EXIST.
AT BEST?
WE'RE SPECIAL EFFECTS THAT AIN'T ALL THAT SPECIAL.
SO, FOCUS, MAN.
DON'T WORRY ABOUT LOOKING GOOD.
F'REAL, THOUGH.
WHY TREAT THIS LIKE ANYTHING MORE THAN IT IS?
WHO DO YOU THINK YOU ARE?

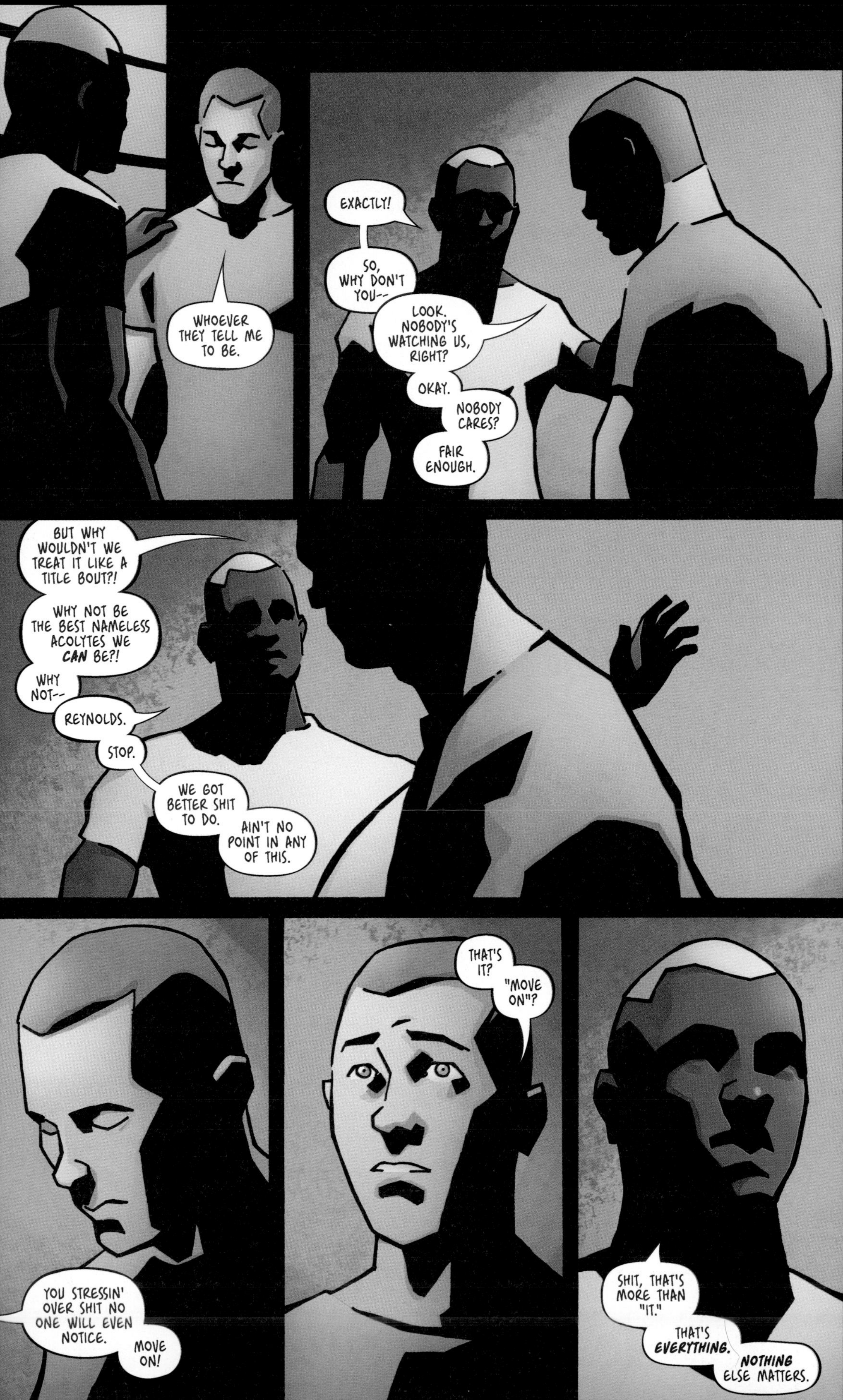
WHOEVER THEY TELL ME TO BE.
EXACTLY!
SO, WHY DON'T YOU--
LOOK. NOBODY'S WATCHING US, RIGHT?
OKAY.
NOBODY CARES?
FAIR ENOUGH.
BUT WHY WOULDN'T WE TREAT IT LIKE A TITLE BOUT?!
WHY NOT BE THE BEST NAMELESS ACOLYTES WE CAN BE?!
WHY NOT--
REYNOLDS.
STOP.
WE GOT BETTER SHIT TO DO.
AIN'T NO POINT IN ANY OF THIS.
YOU STRESSIN' OVER SHIT NO ONE WILL EVEN NOTICE.
MOVE ON!
THAT'S IT?
"MOVE ON"?
SHIT, THAT'S MORE THAN "IT."
THAT'S EVERYTHING.
NOTHING ELSE MATTERS.

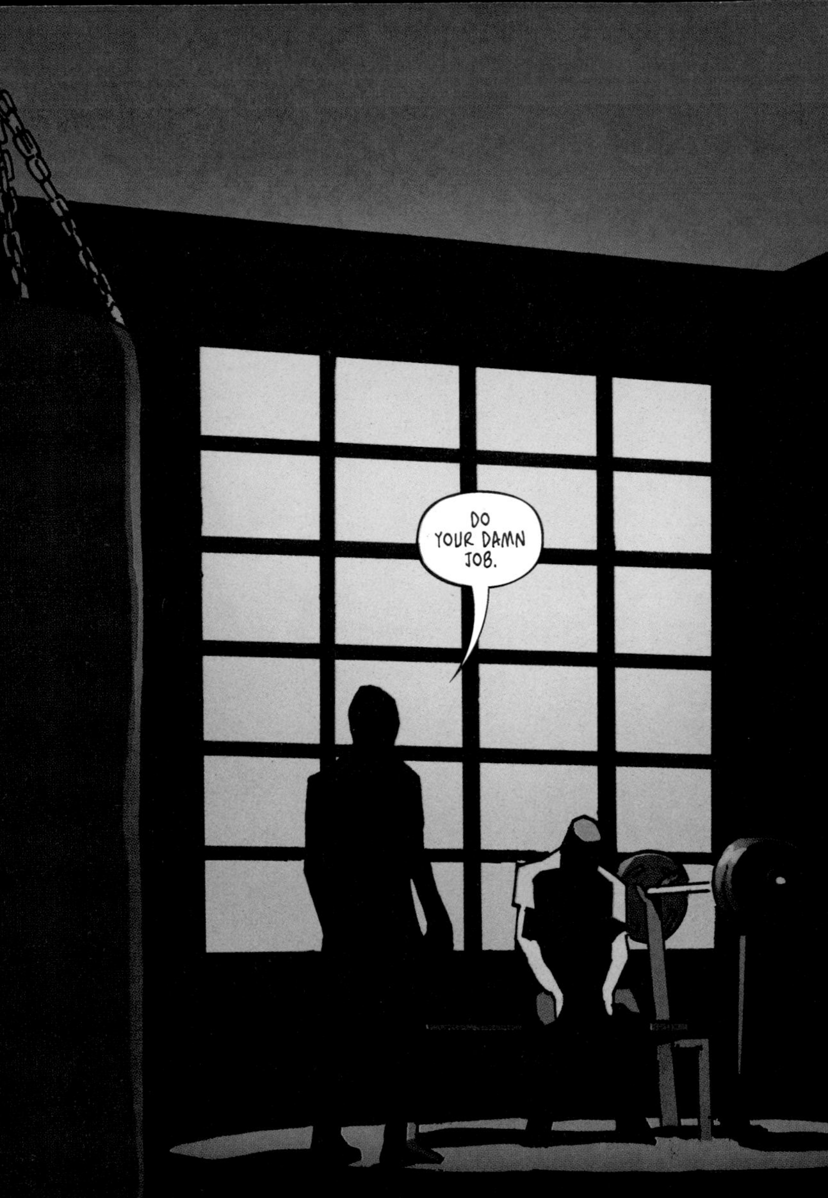
DO YOUR DAMN JOB.

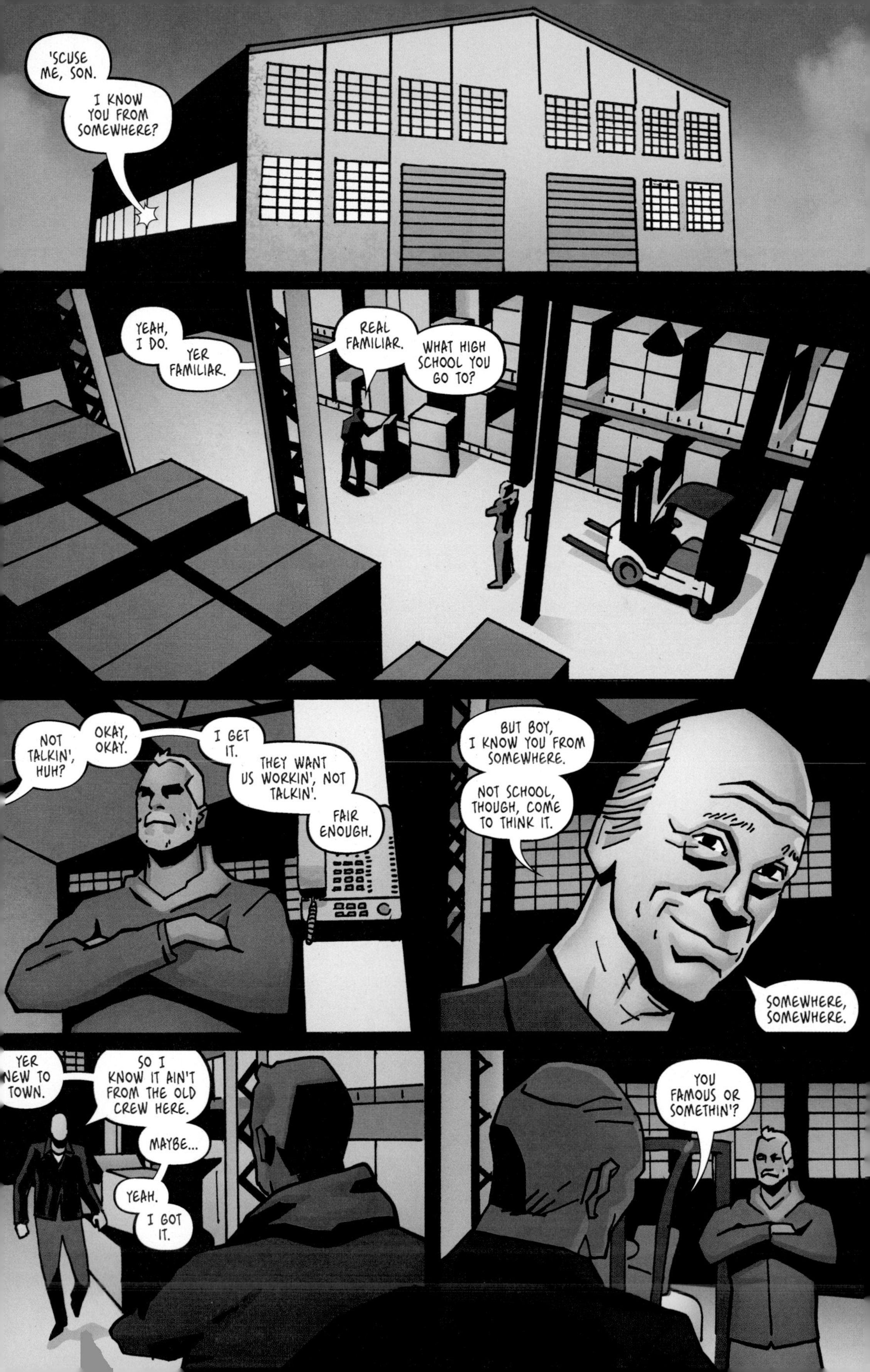
'SCUSE ME, SON.
I KNOW YOU FROM SOMEWHERE?
YEAH, I DO.
YER FAMILIAR.
REAL FAMILIAR.
WHAT HIGH SCHOOL YOU GO TO?
NOT TALKIN', HUH?
OKAY, OKAY.
I GET IT.
THEY WANT US WORKIN', NOT TALKIN'.
FAIR ENOUGH.
BUT BOY, I KNOW YOU FROM SOMEWHERE.
NOT SCHOOL, THOUGH, COME TO THINK IT.
SOMEWHERE, SOMEWHERE.
YER NEW TO TOWN.
SO I KNOW IT AIN'T FROM THE OLD CREW HERE.
MAYBE...
YEAH.
I GOT IT.
YOU FAMOUS OR SOMETHIN'?

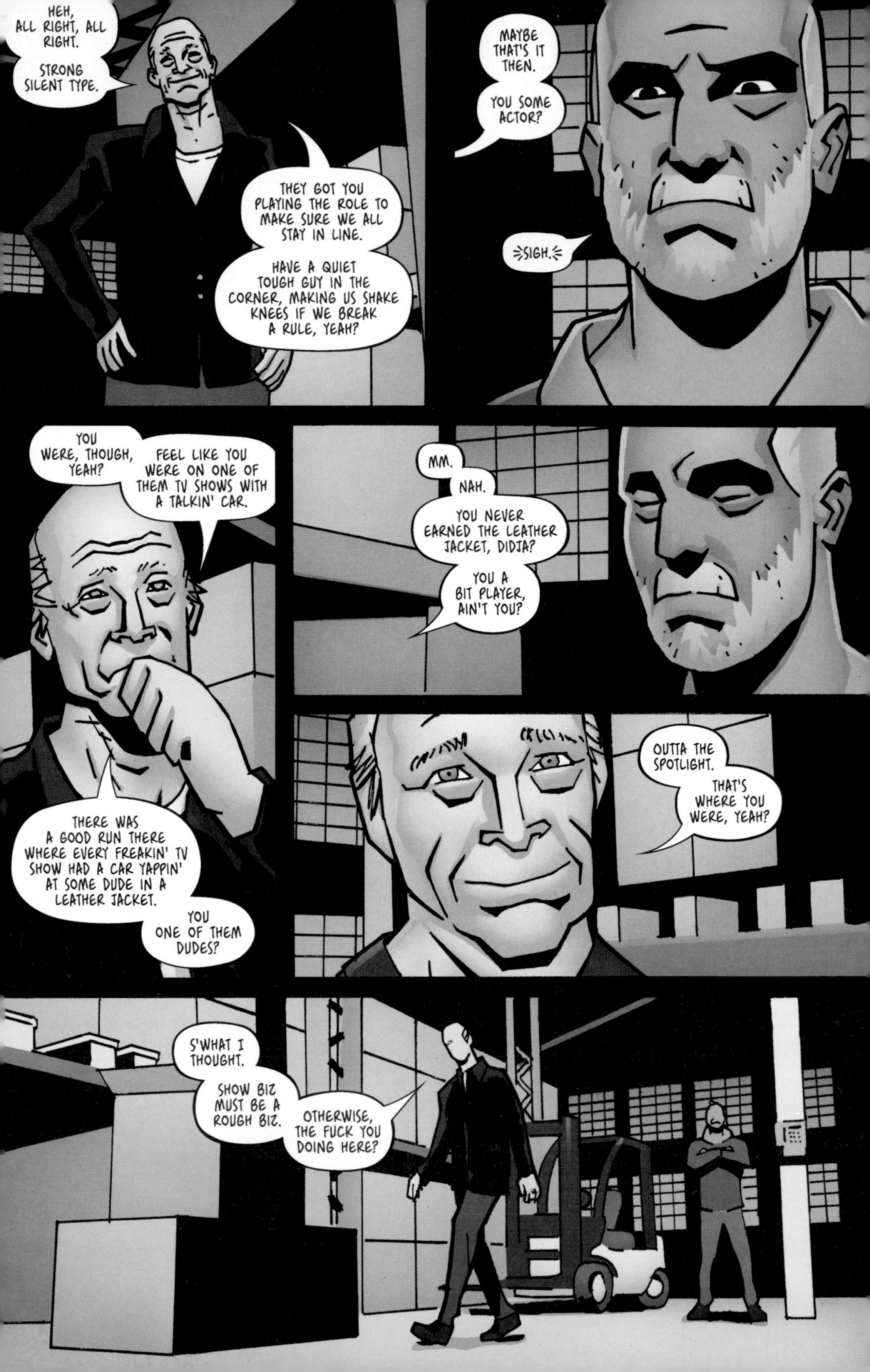
HEH, ALL RIGHT, ALL RIGHT.
STRONG SILENT TYPE.
THEY GOT YOU PLAYING THE ROLE TO MAKE SURE WE ALL STAY IN LINE.
HAVE A QUIET TOUGH GUY IN THE CORNER, MAKING US SHAKE KNEES IF WE BREAK A RULE, YEAH?
MAYBE THAT'S IT THEN.
YOU SOME ACTOR?
SIGH.
YOU WERE, THOUGH, YEAH?
FEEL LIKE YOU WERE ON ONE OF THEM TV SHOWS WITH A TALKIN' CAR.
THERE WAS A GOOD RUN THERE WHERE EVERY FREAKIN' TV SHOW HAD A CAR YAPPIN' AT SOME DUDE IN A LEATHER JACKET.
YOU ONE OF THEM DUDES?
MM.
NAH.
YOU NEVER EARNED THE LEATHER JACKET, DIDJA?
YOU A BIT PLAYER, AIN'T YOU?
OUTTA THE SPOTLIGHT.
THAT'S WHERE YOU WERE, YEAH?
S'WHAT I THOUGHT.
SHOW BIZ MUST BE A ROUGH BIZ.
OTHERWISE, THE FUCK YOU DOING HERE?

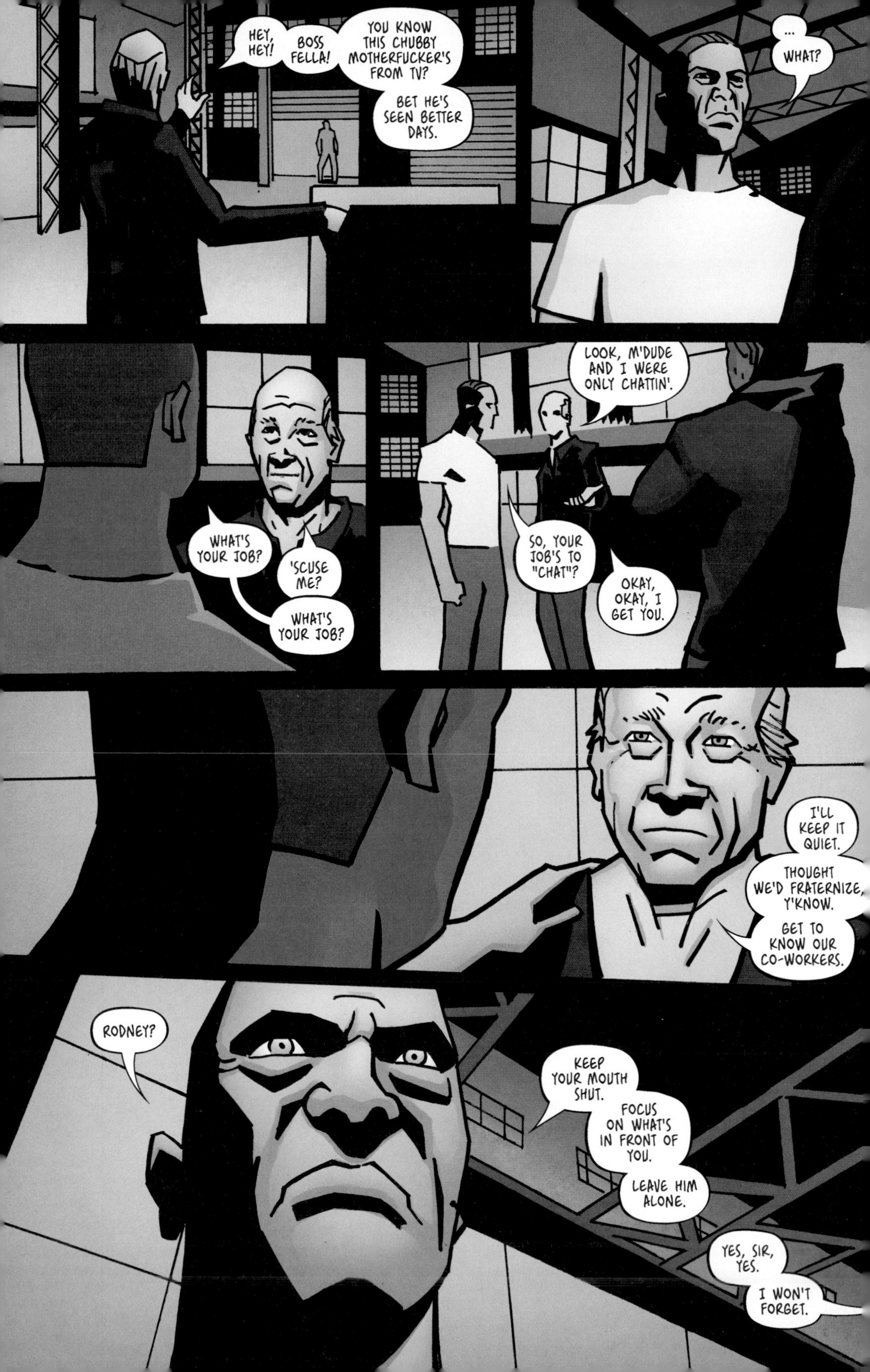
HEY, HEY!
BOSS FELLA!
YOU KNOW THIS CHUBBY MOTHERFUCKER'S FROM TV?
BET HE'S SEEN BETTER DAYS.
... WHAT?
WHAT'S YOUR JOB?
'SCUSE ME?
WHAT'S YOUR JOB?
LOOK, M'DUDE AND I WERE ONLY CHATTIN'.
SO, YOUR JOB'S TO "CHAT"?
OKAY, OKAY, I GET YOU.
I'LL KEEP IT QUIET.
THOUGHT WE'D FRATERNIZE, Y'KNOW.
GET TO KNOW OUR CO-WORKERS.
RODNEY?
KEEP YOUR MOUTH SHUT.
FOCUS ON WHAT'S IN FRONT OF YOU.
LEAVE HIM ALONE.
YES, SIR, YES.
I WON'T FORGET.

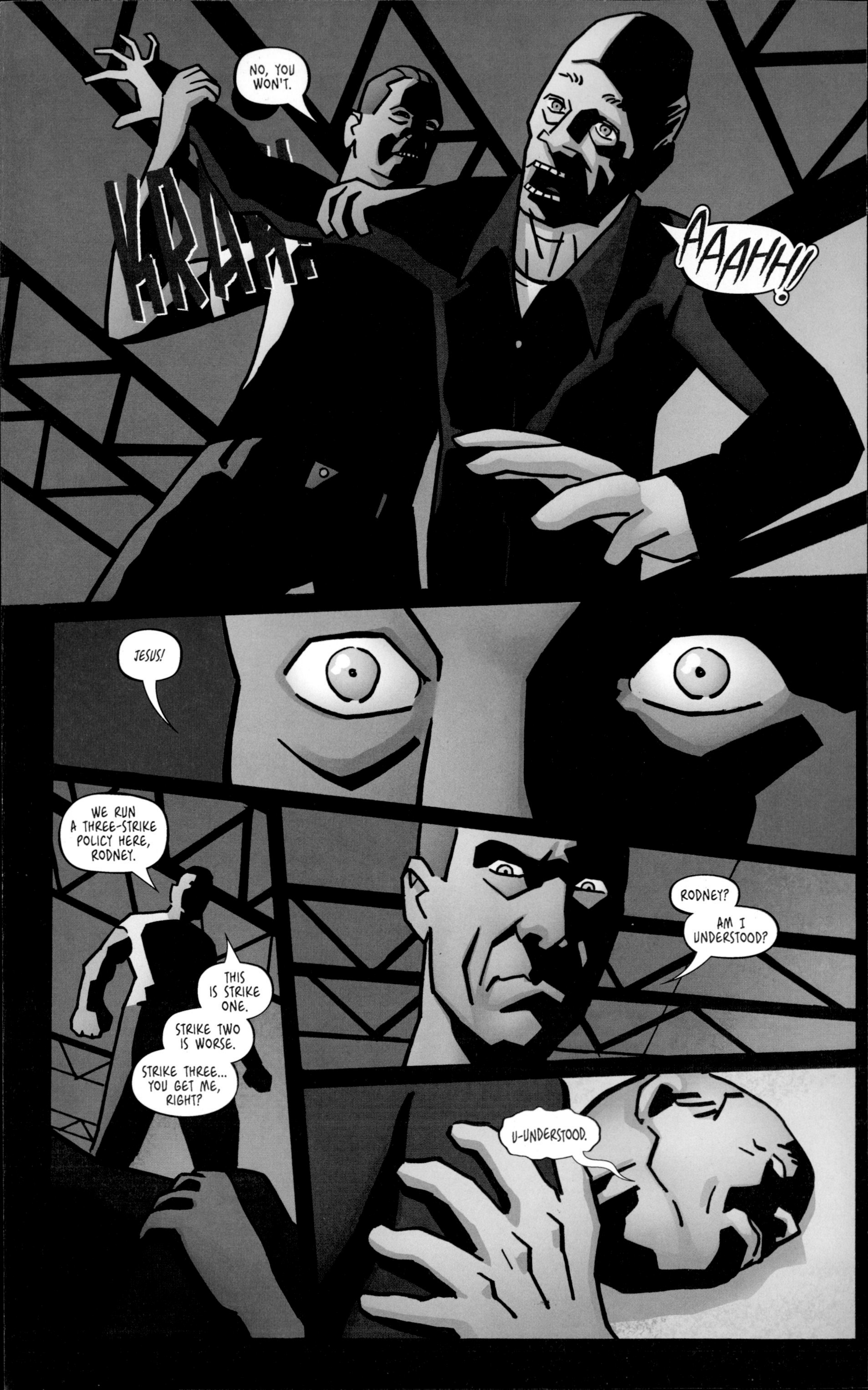
NO, YOU WON'T.
KRAK!
AAAHH!
JESUS!
WE RUN A THREE-STRIKE POLICY HERE, RODNEY.
THIS IS STRIKE ONE.
STRIKE TWO IS WORSE.
STRIKE THREE... YOU GET ME, RIGHT?
RODNEY?
AM I UNDERSTOOD?
U-UNDERSTOOD.

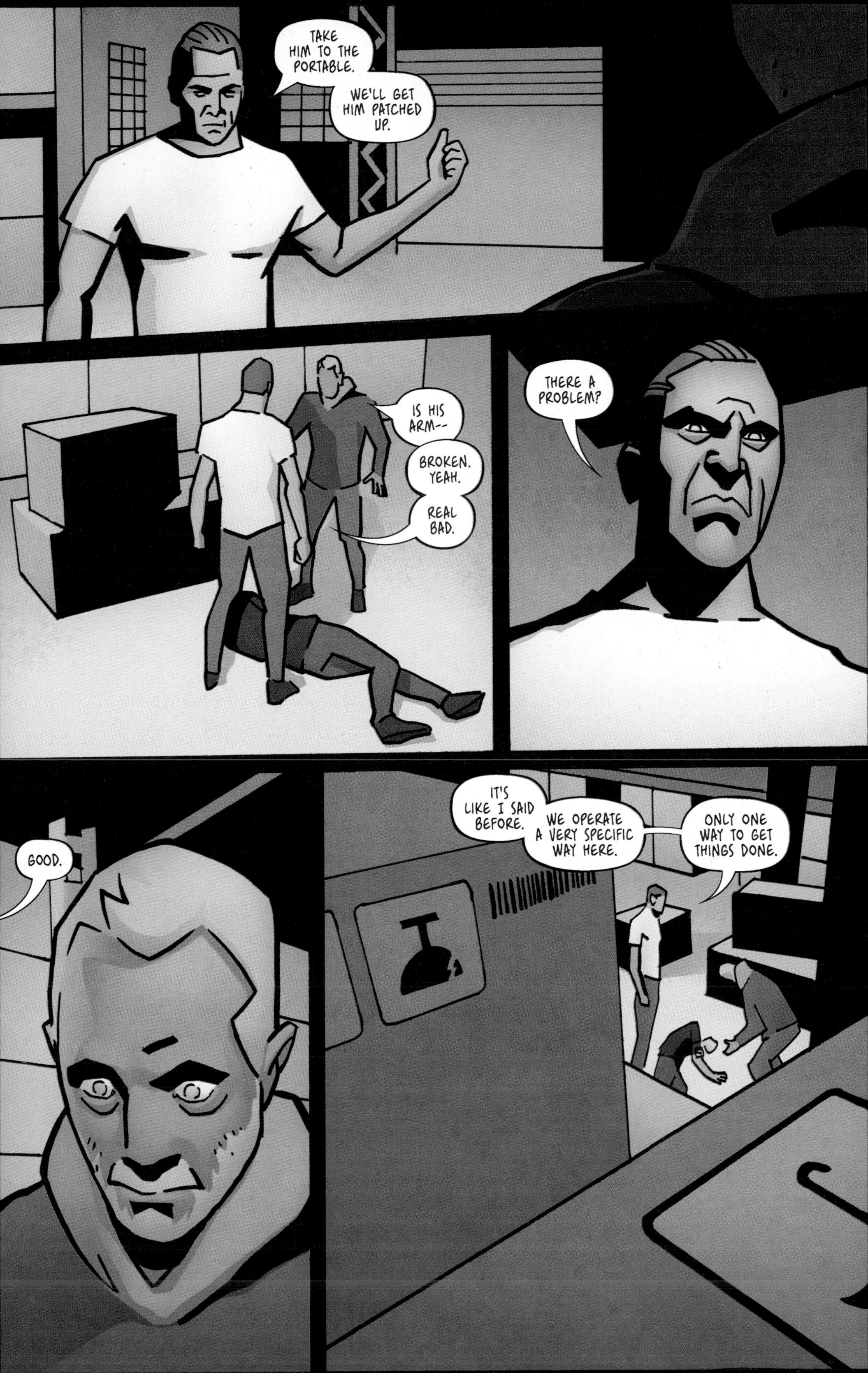
TAKE HIM TO THE PORTABLE.
WE'LL GET HIM PATCHED UP.
IS HIS ARM--
BROKEN. YEAH.
REAL BAD.
THERE A PROBLEM?
GOOD.
IT'S LIKE I SAID BEFORE.
WE OPERATE A VERY SPECIFIC WAY HERE.
ONLY ONE WAY TO GET THINGS DONE.

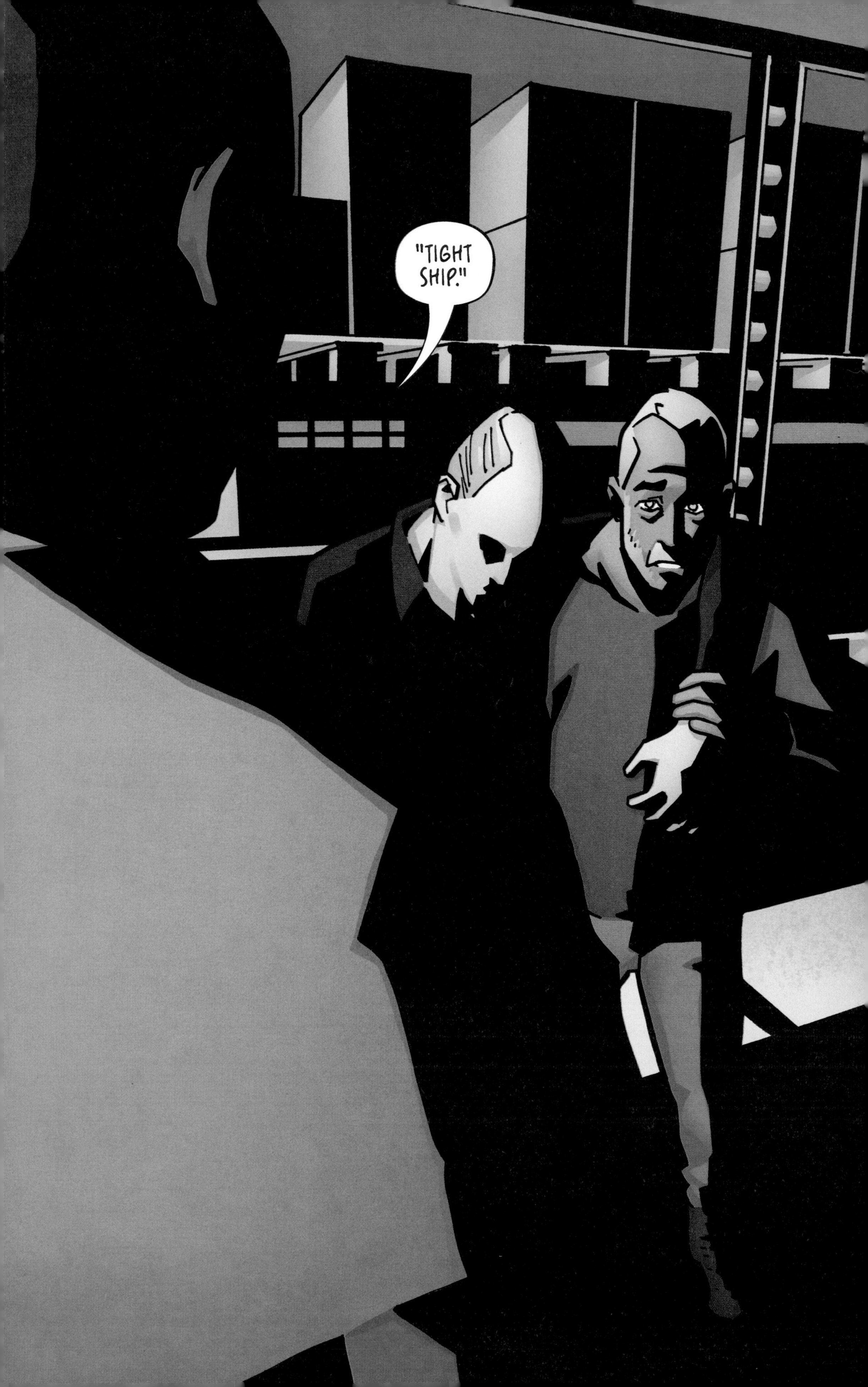
"TIGHT SHIP."

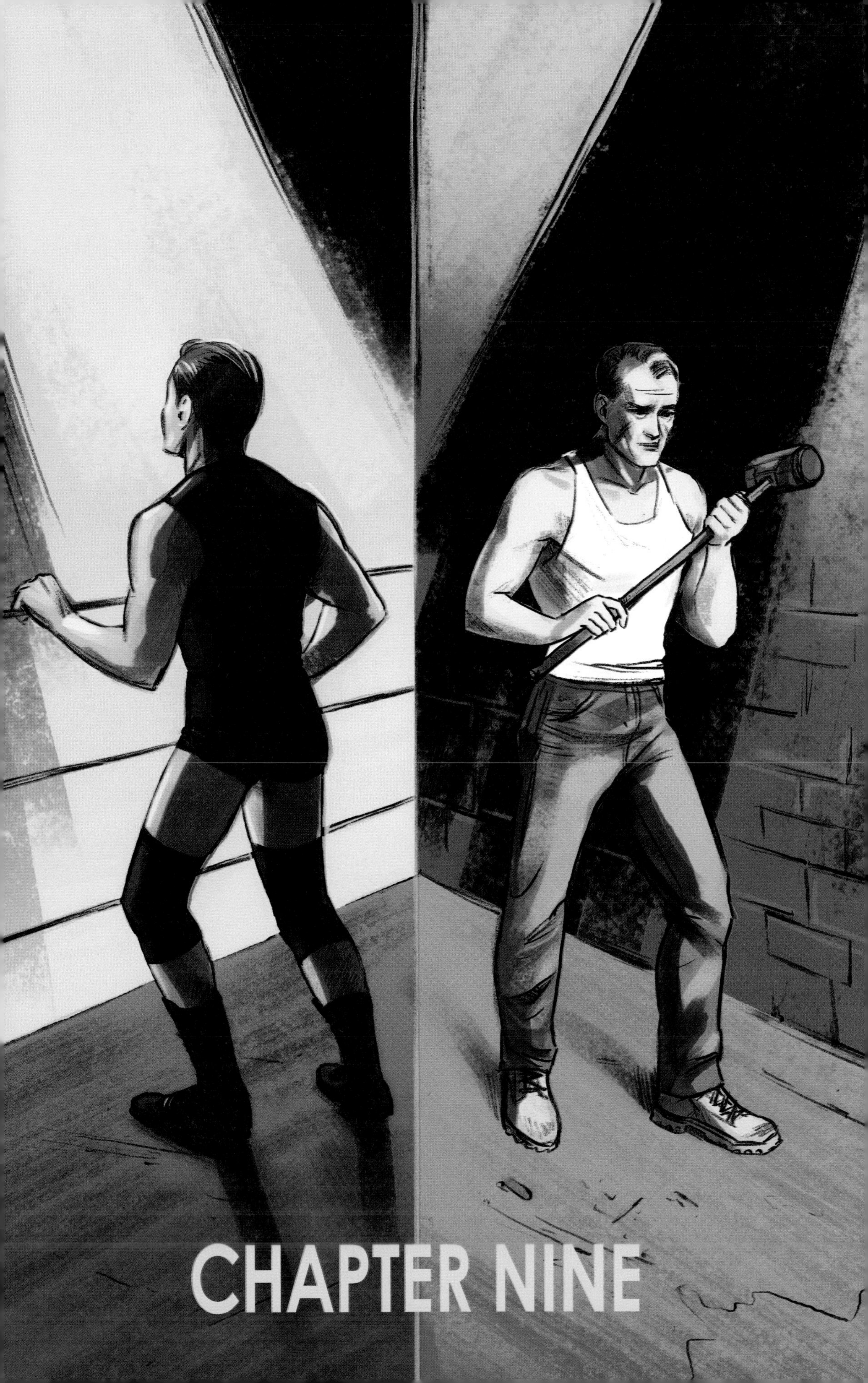

CHAPTER NINE

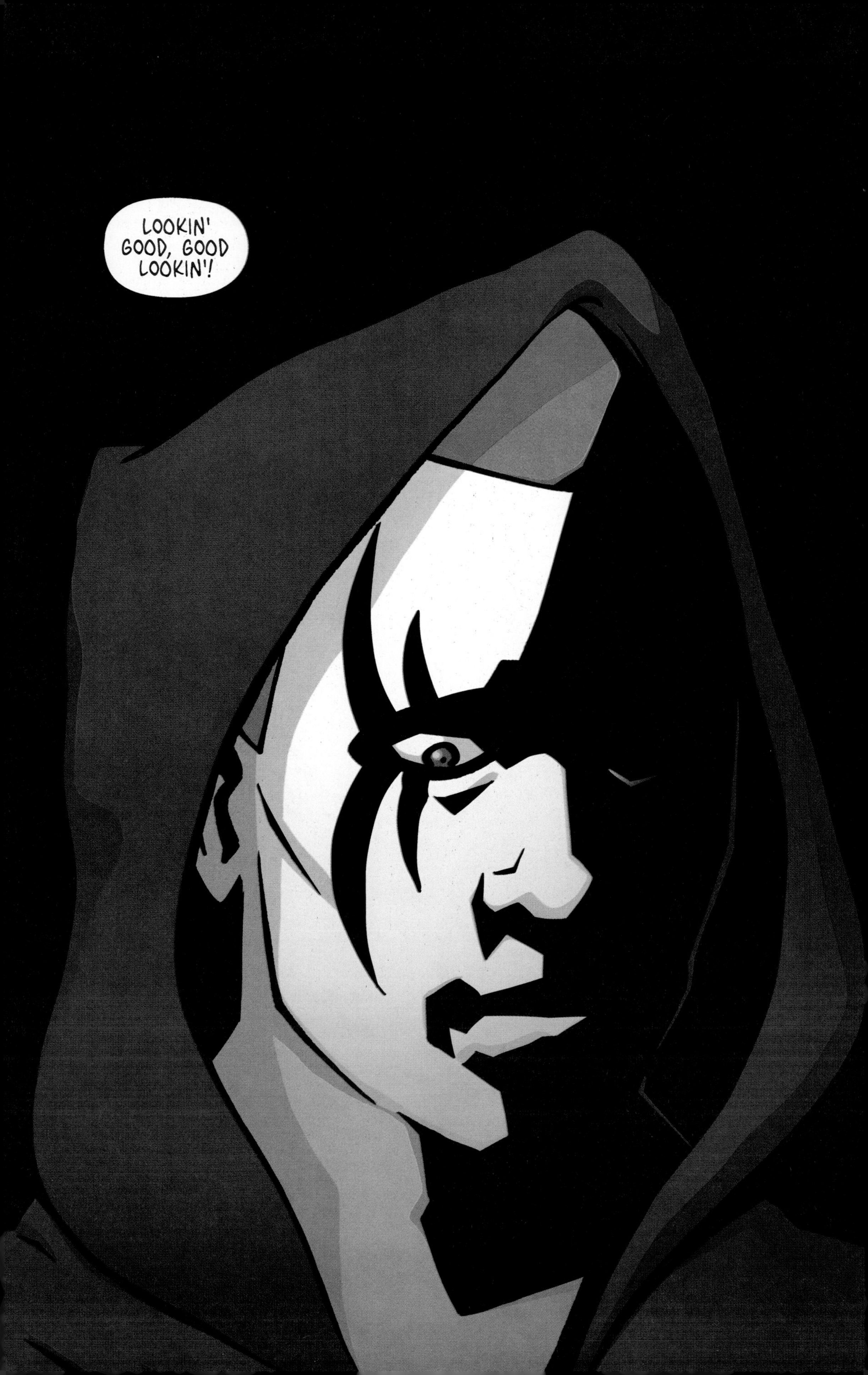
LOOKIN' GOOD, GOOD LOOKIN'!

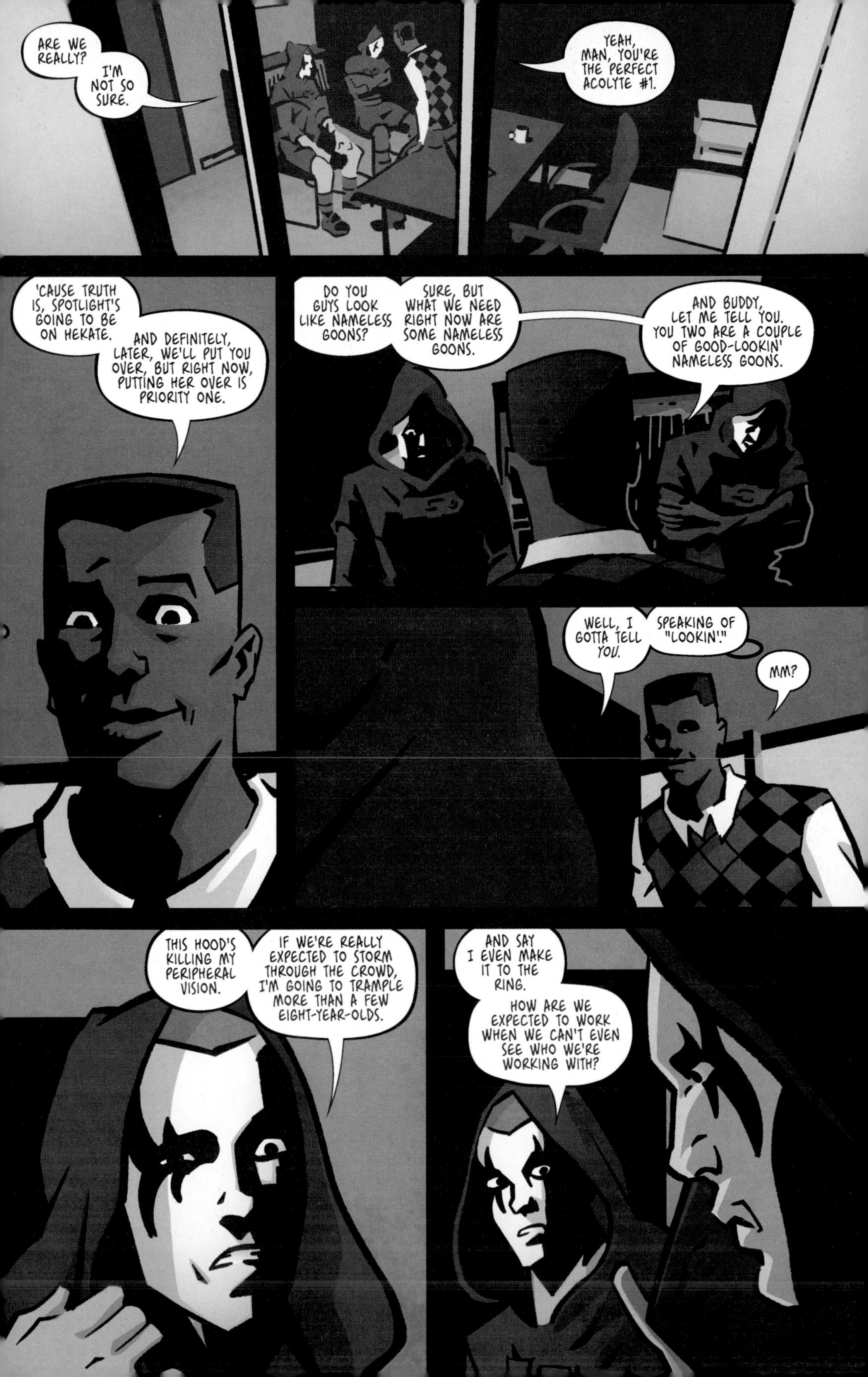

ARE WE REALLY?
I'M NOT SO SURE.
YEAH, MAN, YOU'RE THE PERFECT ACOLYTE #1.
'CAUSE TRUTH IS, SPOTLIGHT'S GOING TO BE ON HEKATE.
AND DEFINITELY, LATER, WE'LL PUT YOU OVER, BUT RIGHT NOW, PUTTING HER OVER IS PRIORITY ONE.
DO YOU GUYS LOOK LIKE NAMELESS GOONS?
SURE, BUT WHAT WE NEED RIGHT NOW ARE SOME NAMELESS GOONS.
AND BUDDY, LET ME TELL YOU. YOU TWO ARE A COUPLE OF GOOD-LOOKIN' NAMELESS GOONS.
WELL, I GOTTA TELL YOU.
SPEAKING OF "LOOKIN'."
MM?
THIS HOOD'S KILLING MY PERIPHERAL VISION.
IF WE'RE REALLY EXPECTED TO STORM THROUGH THE CROWD, I'M GOING TO TRAMPLE MORE THAN A FEW EIGHT-YEAR-OLDS.
AND SAY I EVEN MAKE IT TO THE RING.
HOW ARE WE EXPECTED TO WORK WHEN WE CAN'T EVEN SEE WHO WE'RE WORKING WITH?

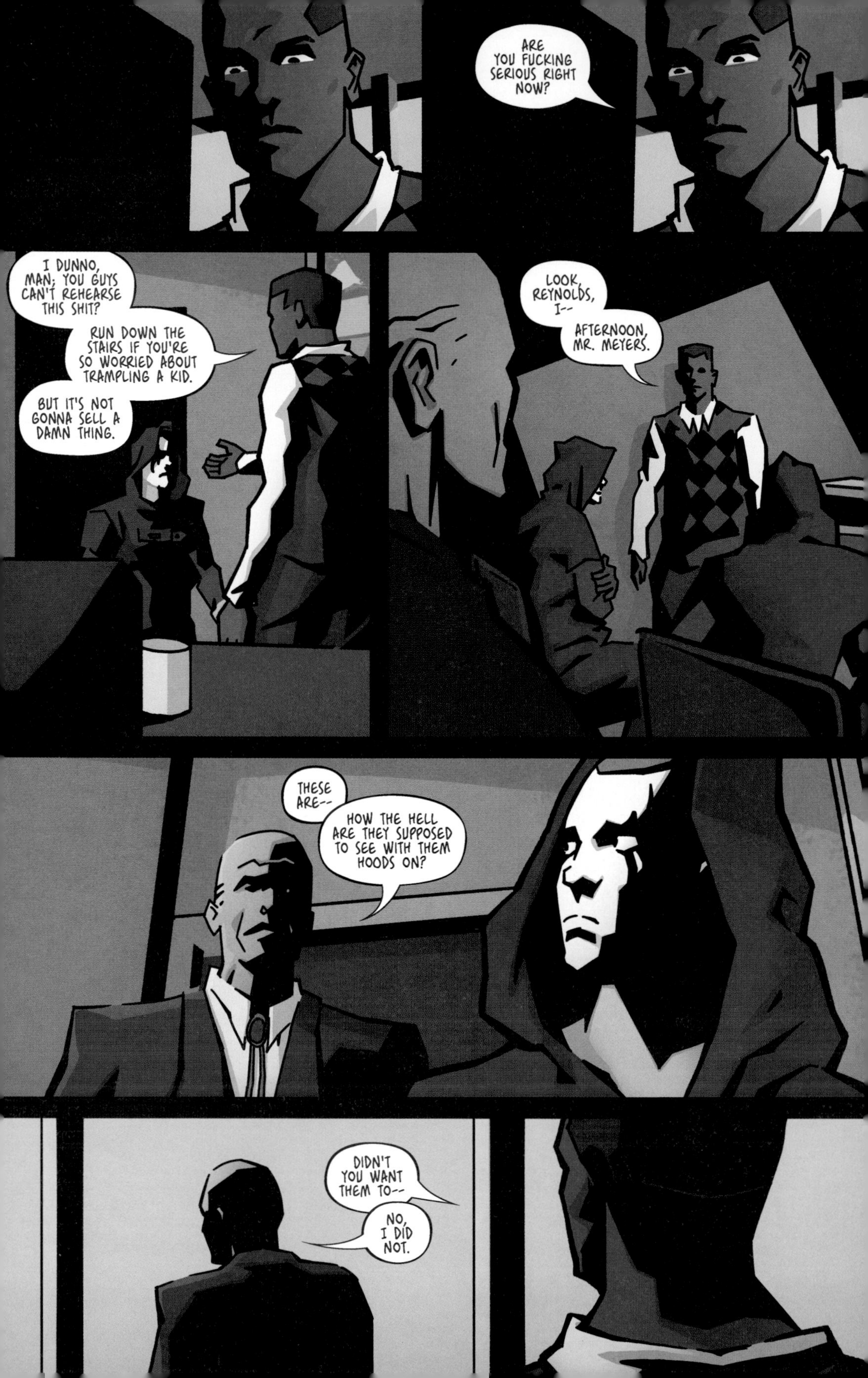
ARE YOU FUCKING SERIOUS RIGHT NOW?
I DUNNO, MAN; YOU GUYS CAN'T REHEARSE THIS SHIT?
RUN DOWN THE STAIRS IF YOU'RE SO WORRIED ABOUT TRAMPLING A KID.
BUT IT'S NOT GONNA SELL A DAMN THING.
LOOK, REYNOLDS, I--
AFTERNOON, MR. MEYERS.
THESE ARE--
HOW THE HELL ARE THEY SUPPOSED TO SEE WITH THEM HOODS ON?
DIDN'T YOU WANT THEM TO--
NO, I DID NOT.

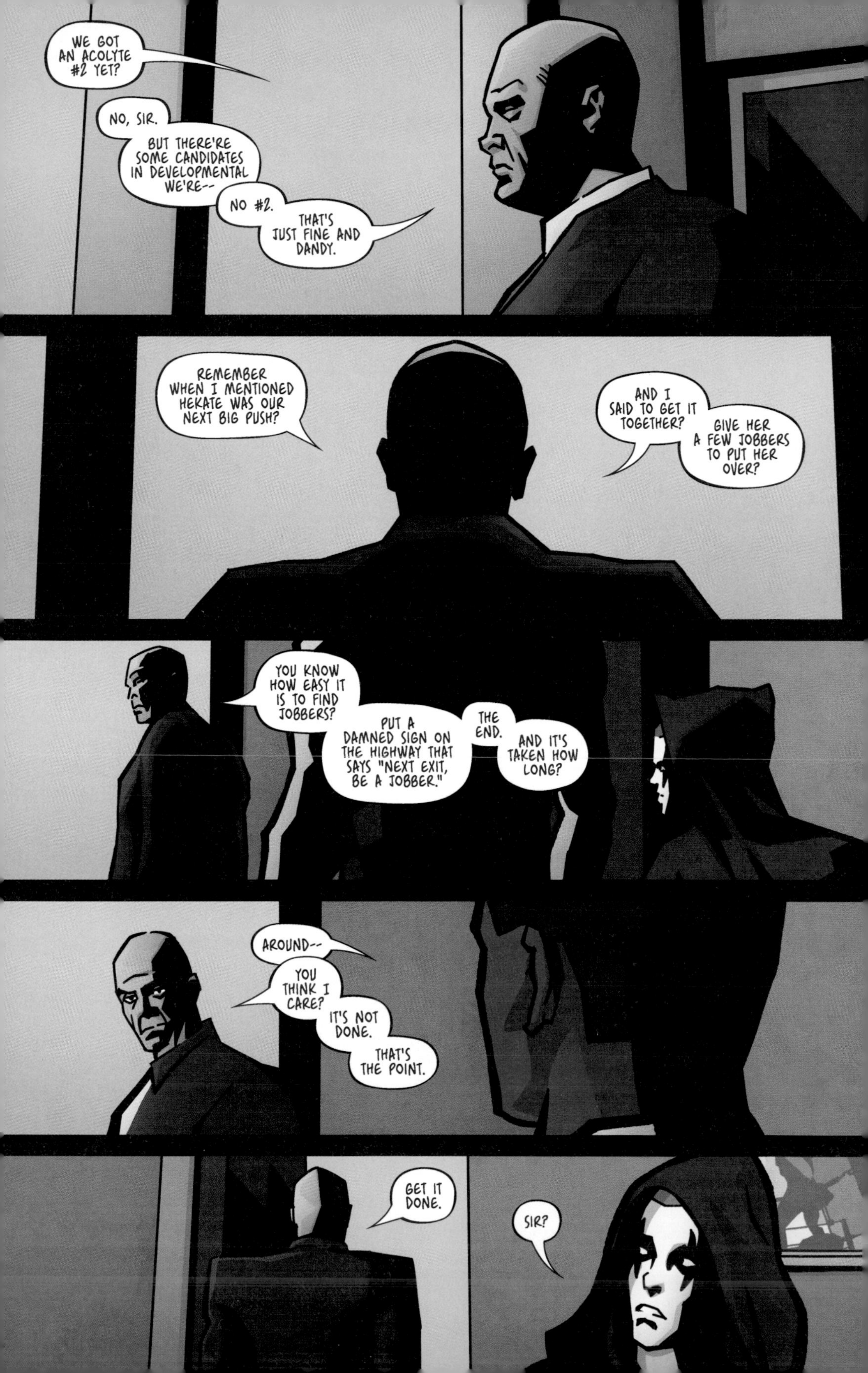
WE GOT AN ACOLYTE #2 YET?
NO, SIR.
BUT THERE'RE SOME CANDIDATES IN DEVELOPMENTAL WE'RE--
NO #2.
THAT'S JUST FINE AND DANDY.
REMEMBER WHEN I MENTIONED HEKATE WAS OUR NEXT BIG PUSH?
AND I SAID TO GET IT TOGETHER?
GIVE HER A FEW JOBBERS TO PUT HER OVER?
YOU KNOW HOW EASY IT IS TO FIND JOBBERS?
PUT A DAMNED SIGN ON THE HIGHWAY THAT SAYS "NEXT EXIT, BE A JOBBER."
THE END.
AND IT'S TAKEN HOW LONG?
AROUND--
YOU THINK I CARE?
IT'S NOT DONE.
THAT'S THE POINT.
GET IT DONE.
SIR?

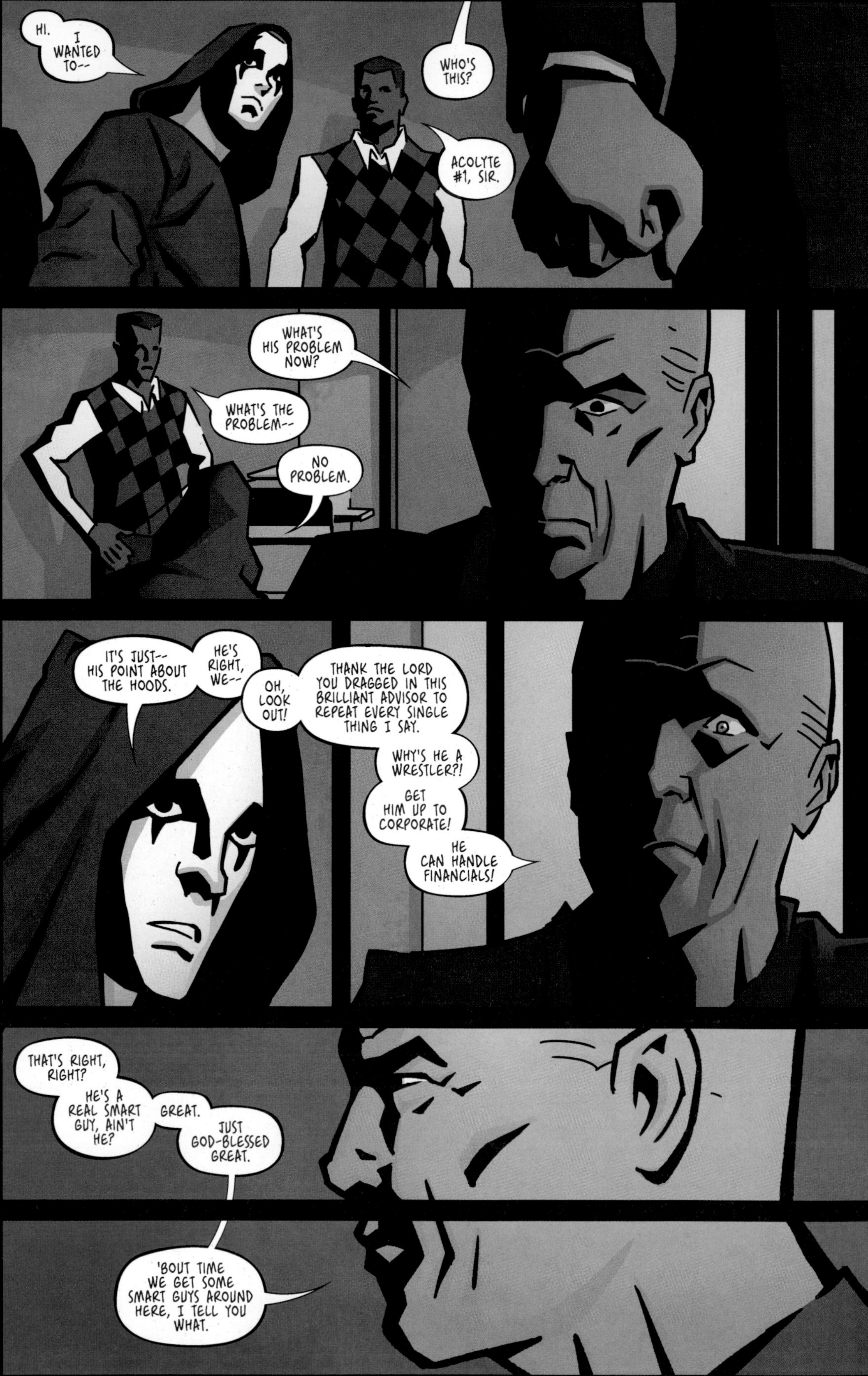
HI. I WANTED TO--
WHO'S THIS?
ACOLYTE #1, SIR.
WHAT'S HIS PROBLEM NOW?
WHAT'S THE PROBLEM--
NO PROBLEM.
IT'S JUST-- HIS POINT ABOUT THE HOODS.
HE'S RIGHT, WE--
OH, LOOK OUT!
THANK THE LORD YOU DRAGGED IN THIS BRILLIANT ADVISOR TO REPEAT EVERY SINGLE THING I SAY.
WHY'S HE A WRESTLER?!
GET HIM UP TO CORPORATE!
HE CAN HANDLE FINANCIALS!
THAT'S RIGHT, RIGHT?
HE'S A REAL SMART GUY, AIN'T HE?
GREAT.
JUST GOD-BLESSED GREAT.
'BOUT TIME WE GET SOME SMART GUYS AROUND HERE, I TELL YOU WHAT.

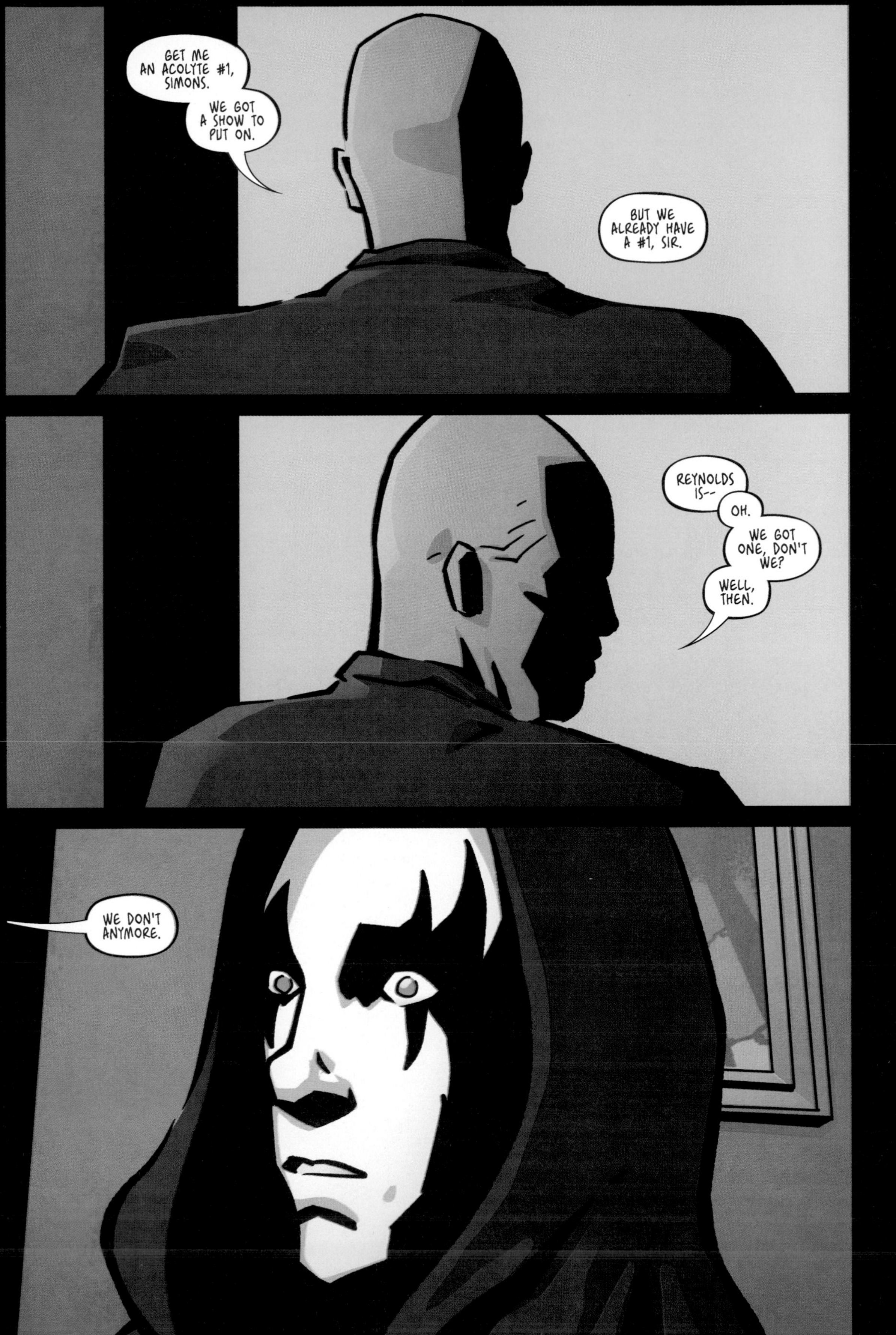
GET ME AN ACOLYTE #1, SIMONS.
WE GOT A SHOW TO PUT ON.
BUT WE ALREADY HAVE A #1, SIR.
REYNOLDS IS--
OH.
WE GOT ONE, DON'T WE?
WELL, THEN.
WE DON'T ANYMORE.

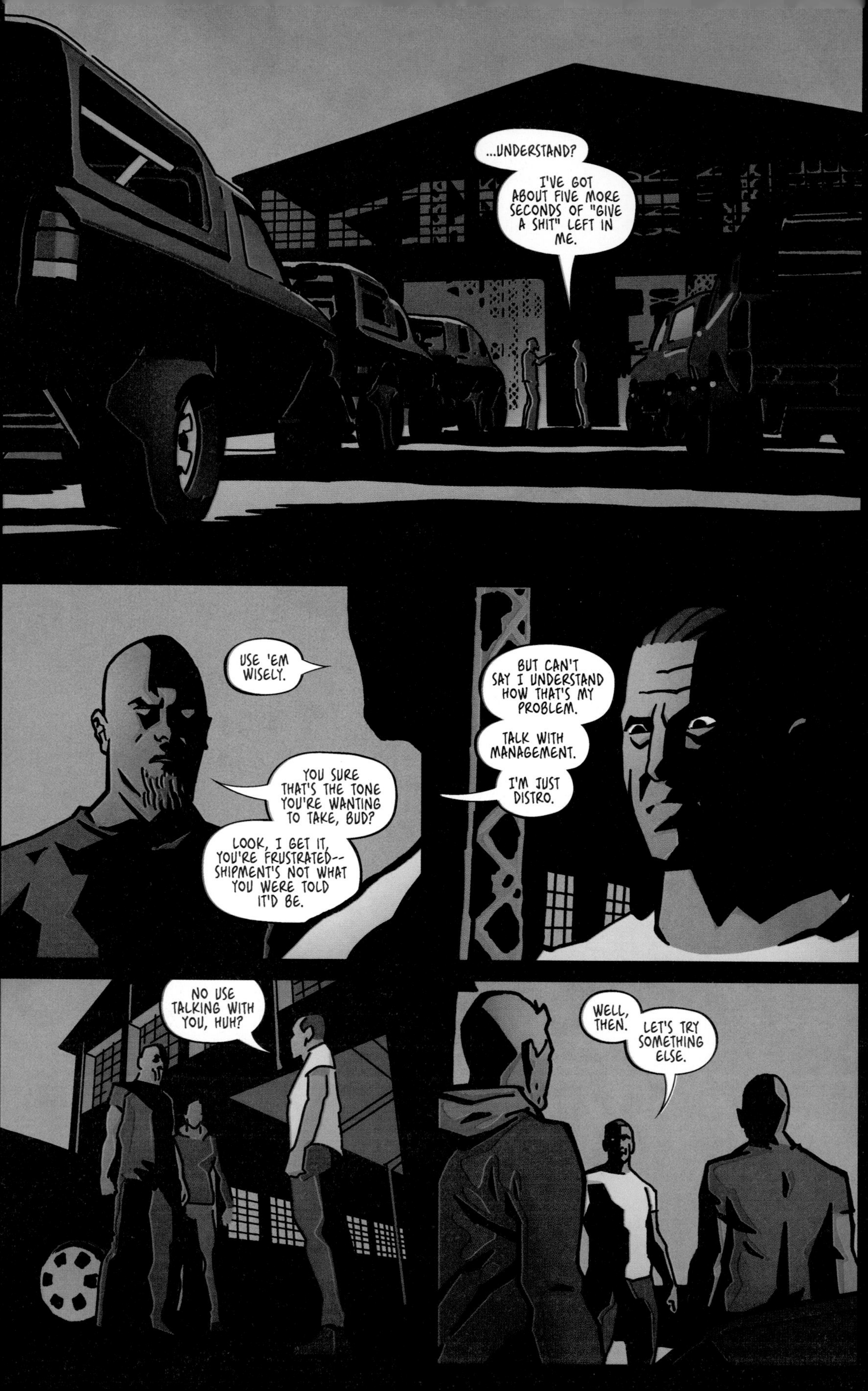
...UNDERSTAND?
I'VE GOT ABOUT FIVE MORE SECONDS OF "GIVE A SHIT" LEFT IN ME.
USE 'EM WISELY.
YOU SURE THAT'S THE TONE YOU'RE WANTING TO TAKE, BUD?
LOOK, I GET IT, YOU'RE FRUSTRATED-- SHIPMENT'S NOT WHAT YOU WERE TOLD IT'D BE.
BUT CAN'T SAY I UNDERSTAND HOW THAT'S MY PROBLEM.
TALK WITH MANAGEMENT.
I'M JUST DISTRO.
NO USE TALKING WITH YOU, HUH?
WELL, THEN.
LET'S TRY SOMETHING ELSE.

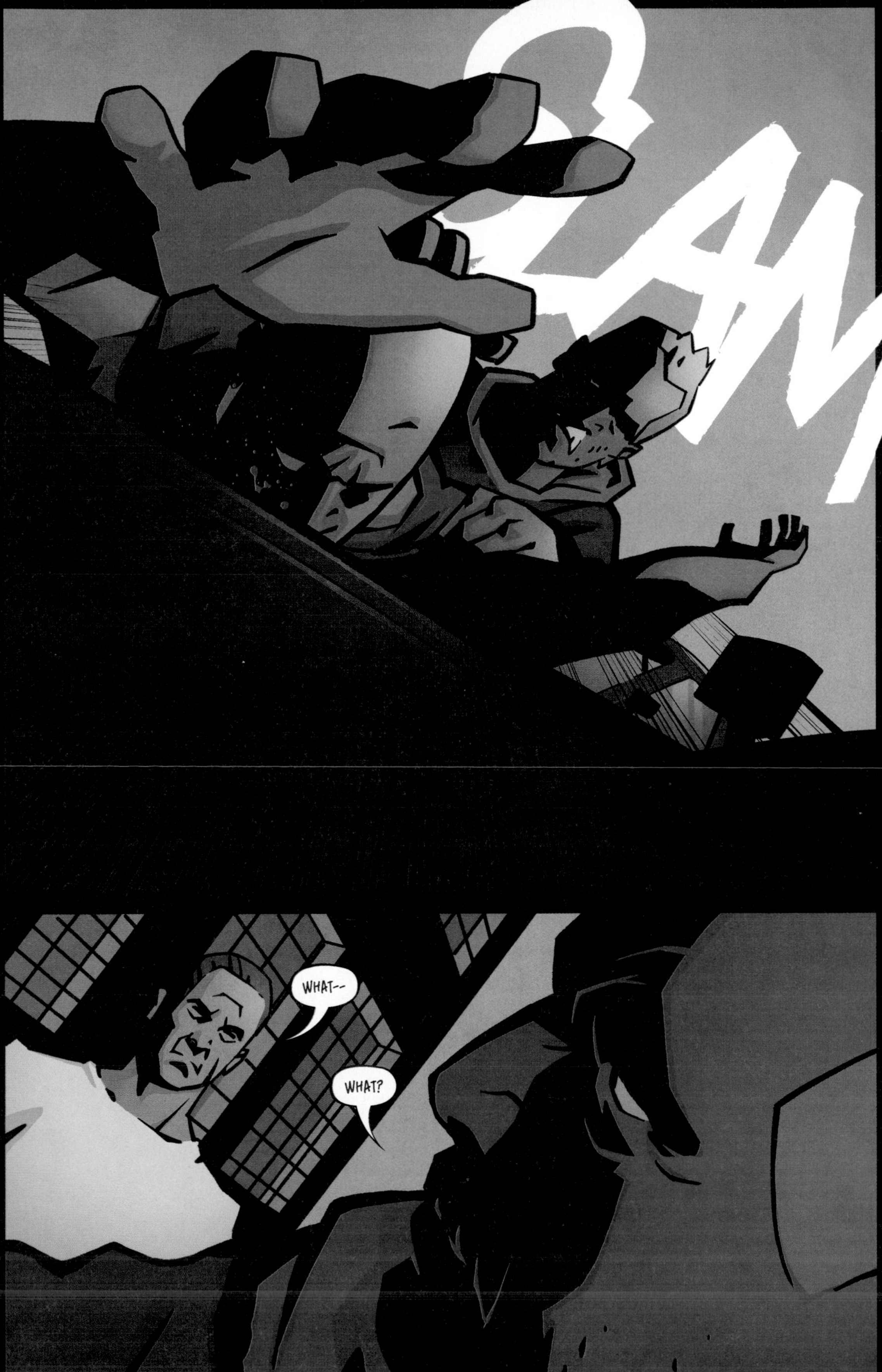
WHAT--
WHAT?

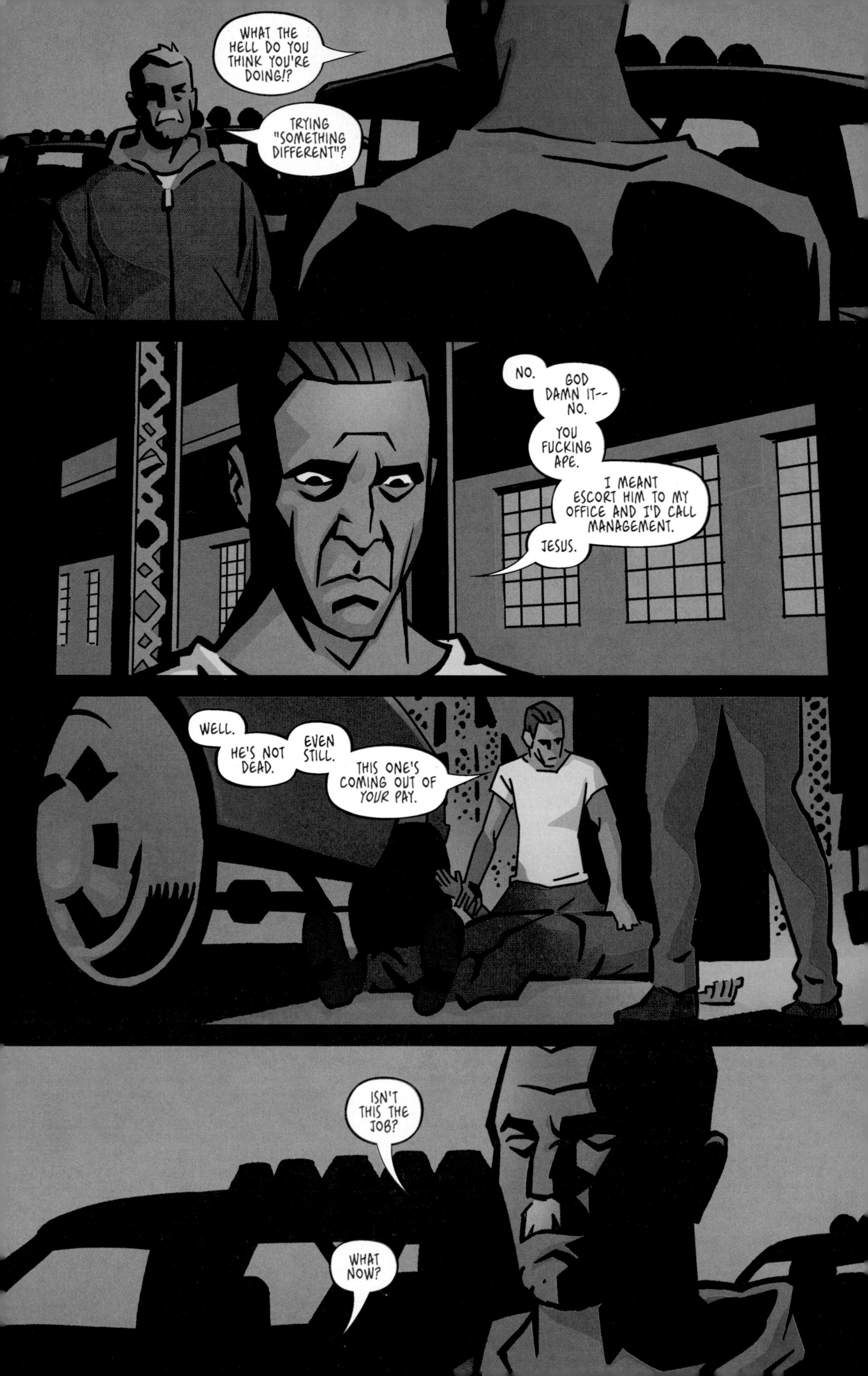
WHAT THE HELL DO YOU THINK YOU'RE DOING!?
TRYING "SOMETHING DIFFERENT"?
NO.
GOD DAMN IT-- NO.
YOU FUCKING APE.
I MEANT ESCORT HIM TO MY OFFICE AND I'D CALL MANAGEMENT.
JESUS.
WELL.
HE'S NOT DEAD.
EVEN STILL.
THIS ONE'S COMING OUT OF YOUR PAY.
ISN'T THIS THE JOB?
WHAT NOW?

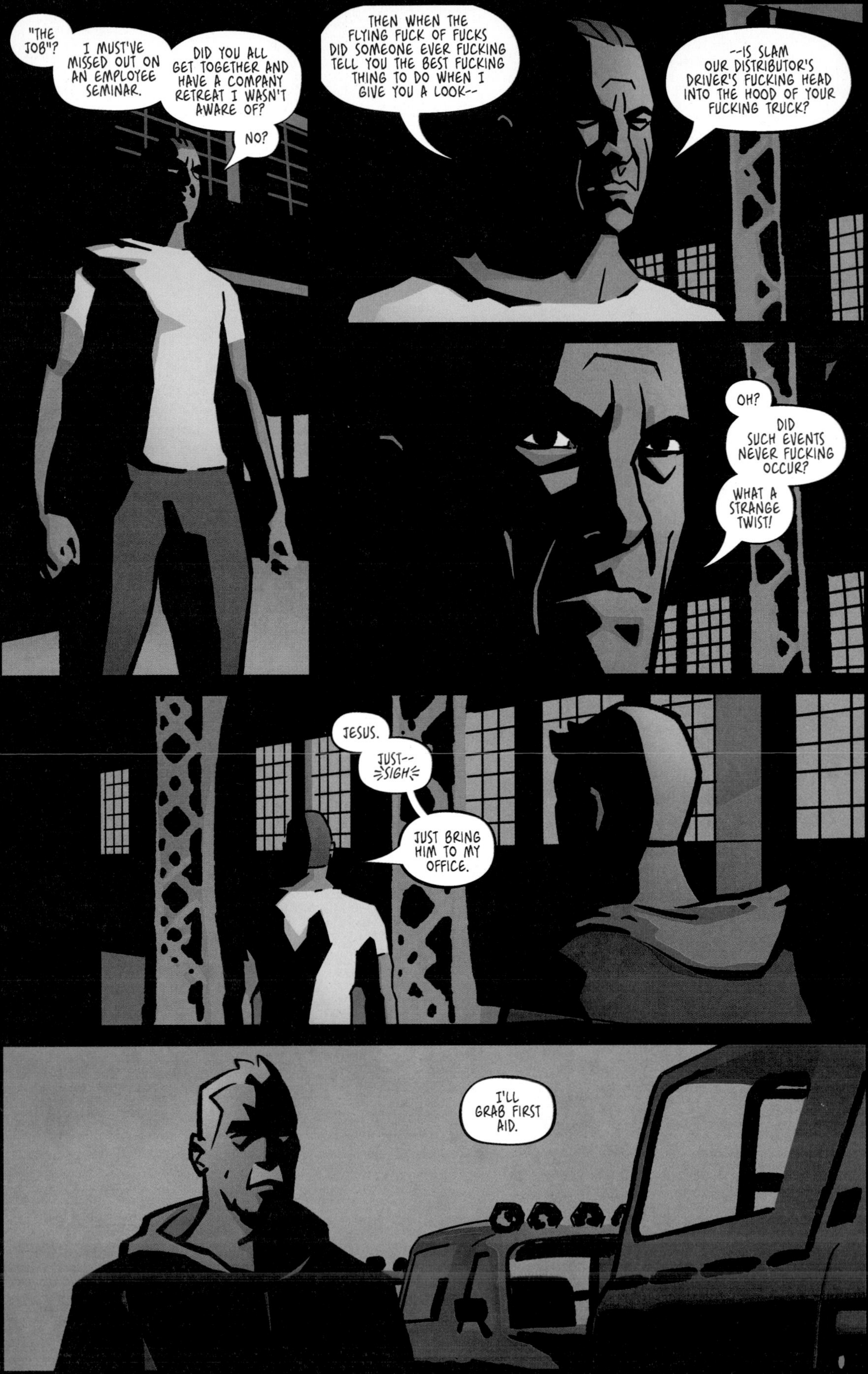
"THE JOB"?
I MUST'VE MISSED OUT ON AN EMPLOYEE SEMINAR.
DID YOU ALL GET TOGETHER AND HAVE A COMPANY RETREAT I WASN'T AWARE OF?
NO?
THEN WHEN THE FLYING FUCK OF FUCKS DID SOMEONE EVER FUCKING TELL YOU THE BEST FUCKING THING TO DO WHEN I GIVE YOU A LOOK--
--IS SLAM OUR DISTRIBUTOR'S DRIVER'S FUCKING HEAD INTO THE HOOD OF YOUR FUCKING TRUCK?
OH?
DID SUCH EVENTS NEVER FUCKING OCCUR?
WHAT A STRANGE TWIST!
JESUS.
JUST-- *SIGH*
JUST BRING HIM TO MY OFFICE.
I'LL GRAB FIRST AID.

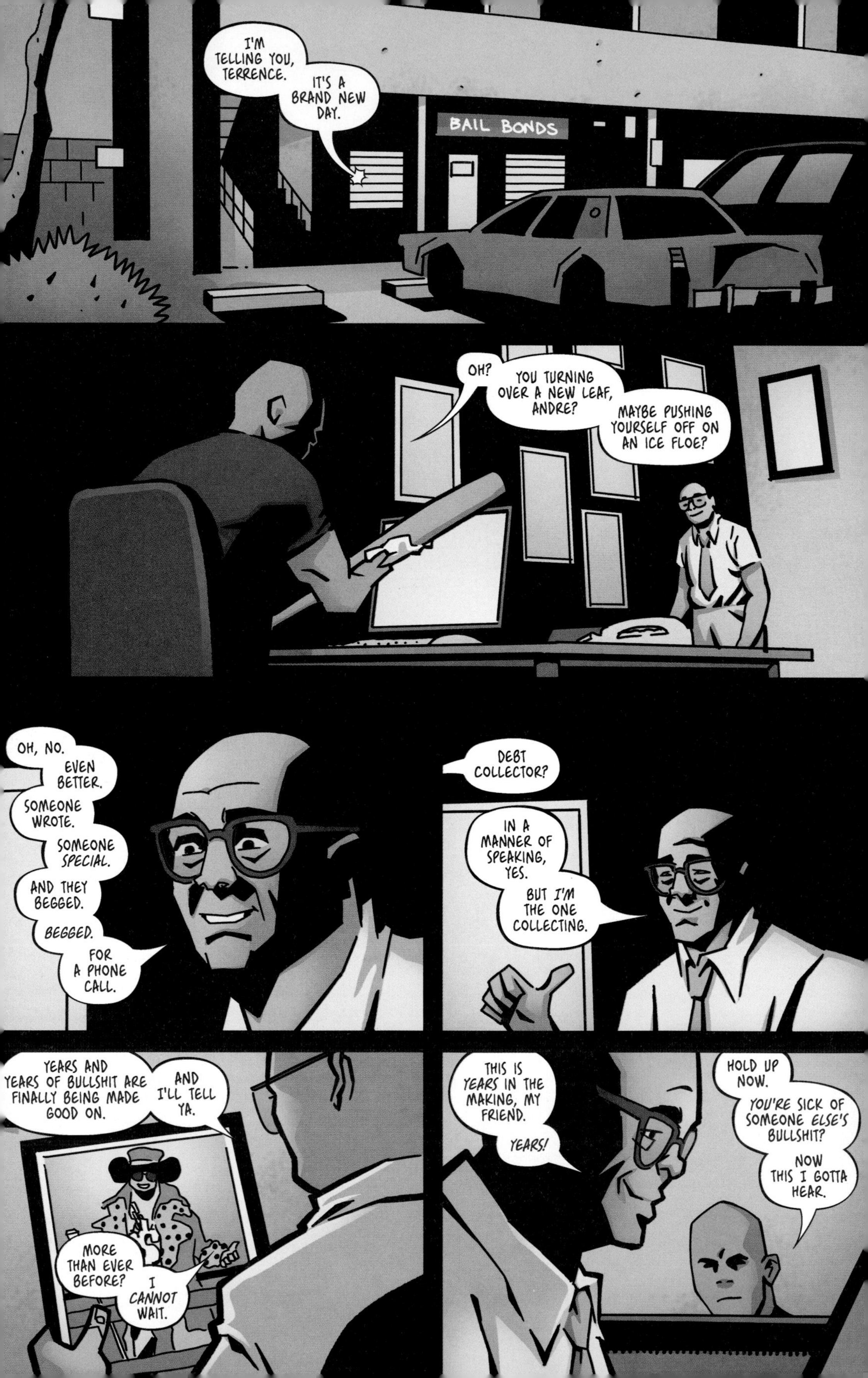
I'M TELLING YOU, TERRENCE.
IT'S A BRAND NEW DAY.
BAIL BONDS
OH?
YOU TURNING OVER A NEW LEAF, ANDRE?
MAYBE PUSHING YOURSELF OFF ON AN ICE FLOE?
OH, NO.
EVEN BETTER.
SOMEONE WROTE.
SOMEONE SPECIAL.
AND THEY BEGGED.
BEGGED.
FOR A PHONE CALL.
DEBT COLLECTOR?
IN A MANNER OF SPEAKING, YES.
BUT I'M THE ONE COLLECTING.
YEARS AND YEARS OF BULLSHIT ARE FINALLY BEING MADE GOOD ON.
AND I'LL TELL YA.
MORE THAN EVER BEFORE?
I CANNOT WAIT.
THIS IS YEARS IN THE MAKING, MY FRIEND.
YEARS!
HOLD UP NOW.
YOU'RE SICK OF SOMEONE ELSE'S BULLSHIT?
NOW THIS I GOTTA HEAR.

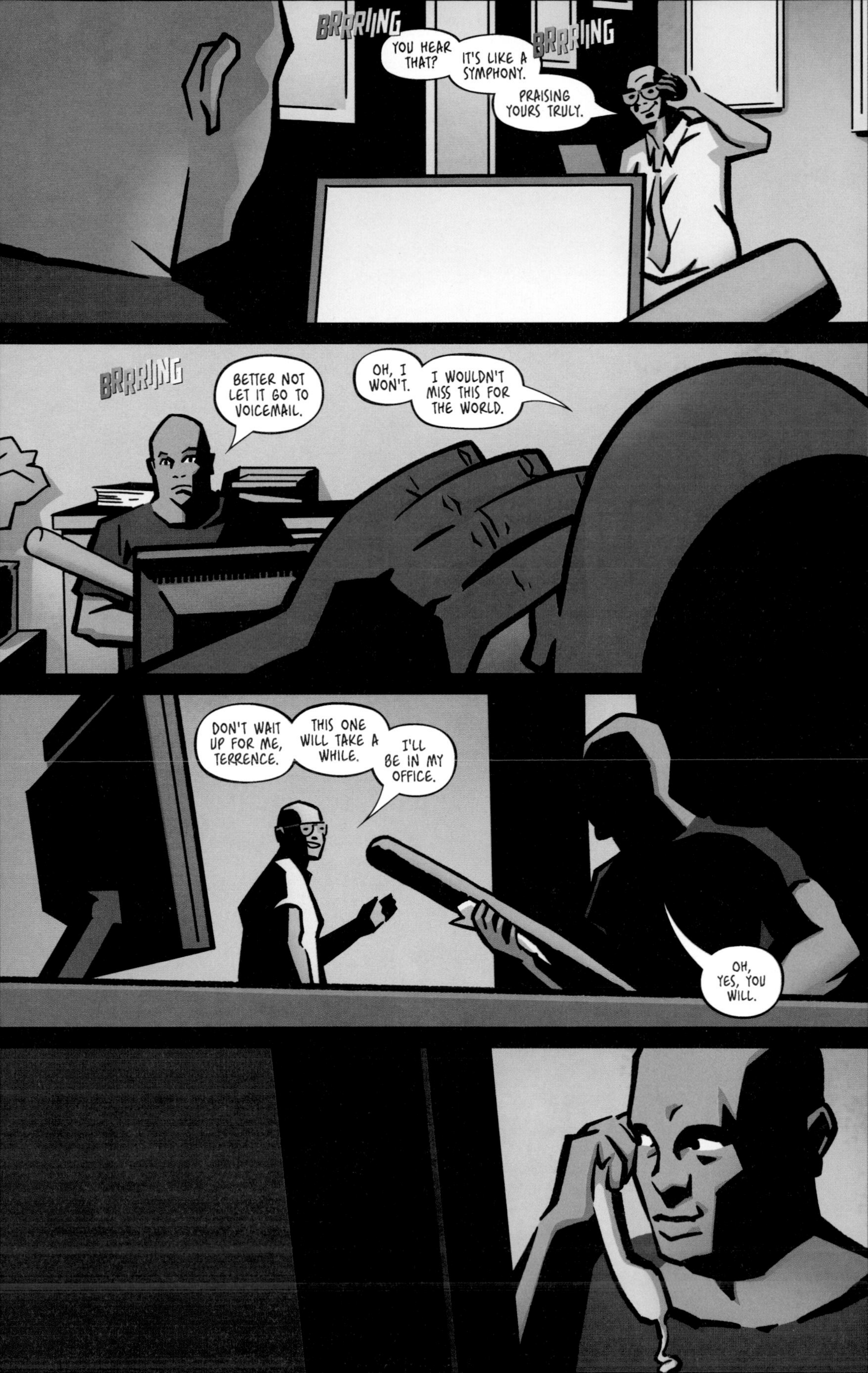
BRRRIING
YOU HEAR THAT?
IT'S LIKE A SYMPHONY.
BRRRIING
PRAISING YOURS TRULY.
BRRRIING
BETTER NOT LET IT GO TO VOICEMAIL.
OH, I WON'T.
I WOULDN'T MISS THIS FOR THE WORLD.
DON'T WAIT UP FOR ME, TERRENCE.
THIS ONE WILL TAKE A WHILE.
I'LL BE IN MY OFFICE.
OH, YES, YOU WILL.

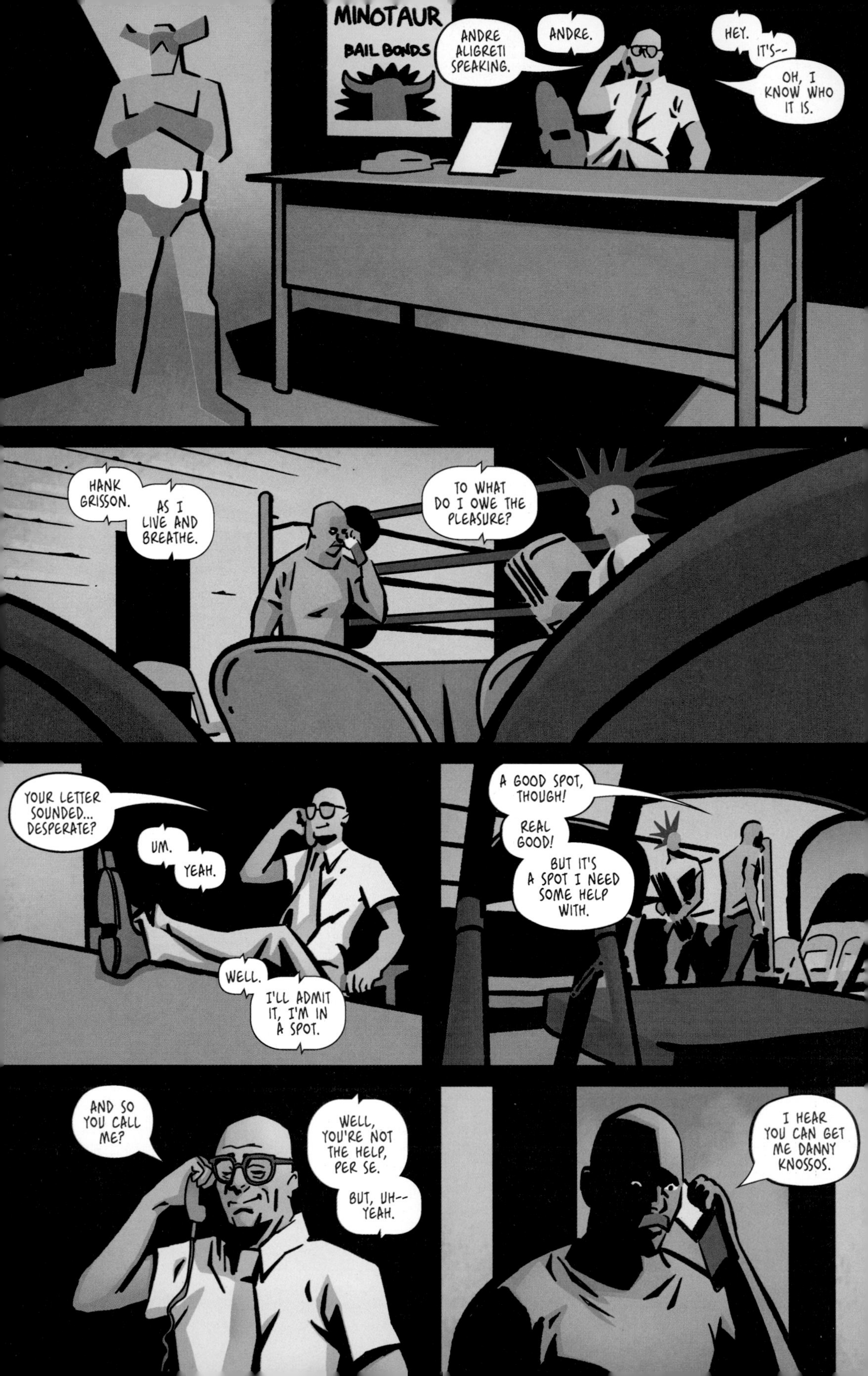
MINOTAUR
BAIL BONDS
ANDRE ALIGRETI SPEAKING.
ANDRE.
HEY.
IT'S--
OH, I KNOW WHO IT IS.
HANK GRISSON.
AS I LIVE AND BREATHE.
TO WHAT DO I OWE THE PLEASURE?
YOUR LETTER SOUNDED... DESPERATE?
UM.
YEAH.
WELL.
I'LL ADMIT IT, I'M IN A SPOT.
A GOOD SPOT, THOUGH!
REAL GOOD!
BUT IT'S A SPOT I NEED SOME HELP WITH.
AND SO YOU CALL ME?
WELL, YOU'RE NOT THE HELP, PER SE.
BUT, UH-- YEAH.
I HEAR YOU CAN GET ME DANNY KNOSSOS.

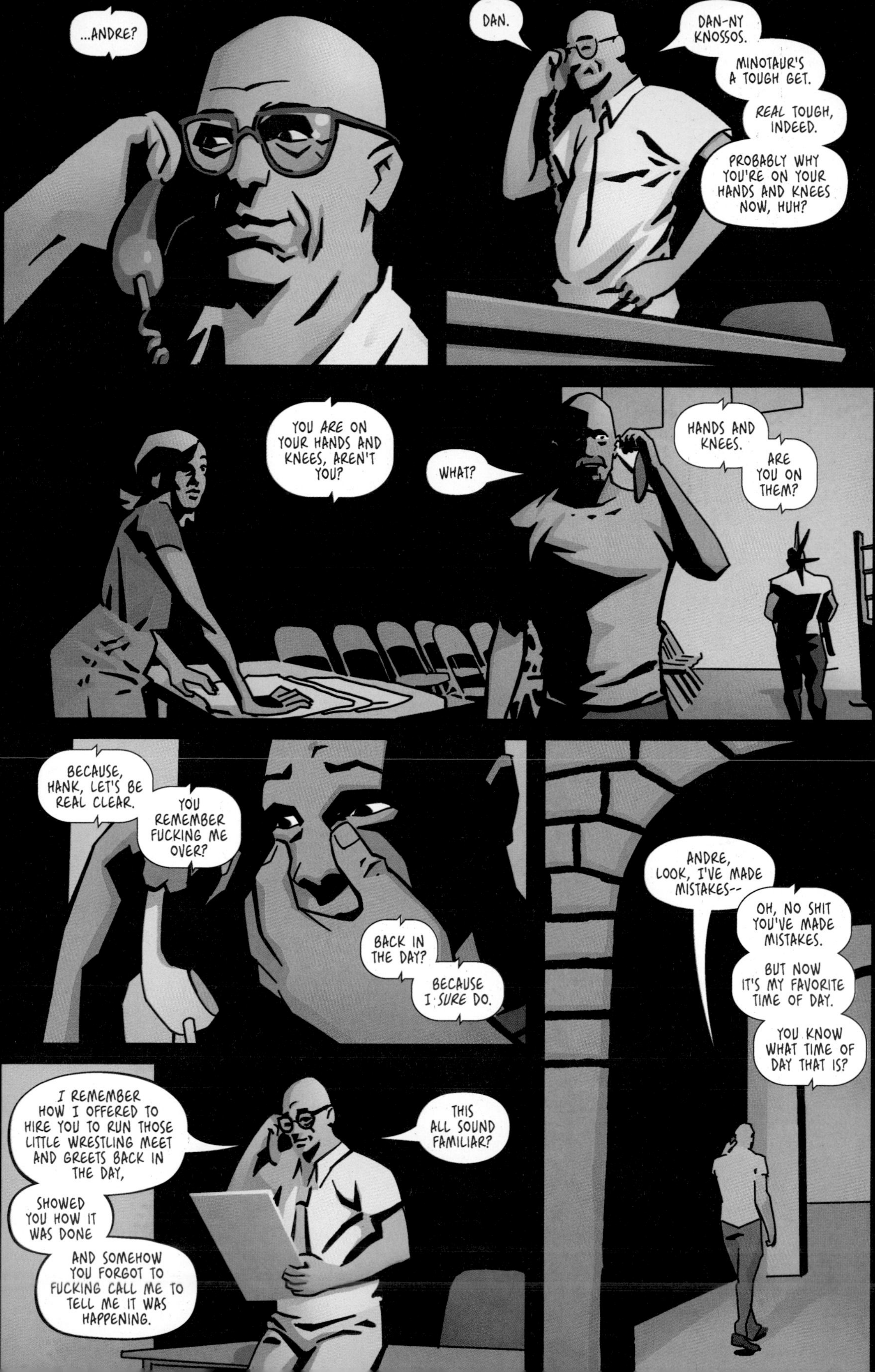
...ANDRE?
DAN.
DAN-NY KNOSSOS.
MINOTAUR'S A TOUGH GET.
REAL TOUGH, INDEED.
PROBABLY WHY YOU'RE ON YOUR HANDS AND KNEES NOW, HUH?
YOU ARE ON YOUR HANDS AND KNEES, AREN'T YOU?
WHAT?
HANDS AND KNEES.
ARE YOU ON THEM?
BECAUSE, HANK, LET'S BE REAL CLEAR.
YOU REMEMBER FUCKING ME OVER?
BACK IN THE DAY?
BECAUSE I SURE DO.
ANDRE, LOOK, I'VE MADE MISTAKES--
OH, NO SHIT YOU'VE MADE MISTAKES.
BUT NOW IT'S MY FAVORITE TIME OF DAY.
YOU KNOW WHAT TIME OF DAY THAT IS?
I REMEMBER HOW I OFFERED TO HIRE YOU TO RUN THOSE LITTLE WRESTLING MEET AND GREETS BACK IN THE DAY,
SHOWED YOU HOW IT WAS DONE
AND SOMEHOW YOU FORGOT TO FUCKING CALL ME TO TELL ME IT WAS HAPPENING.
THIS ALL SOUND FAMILIAR?

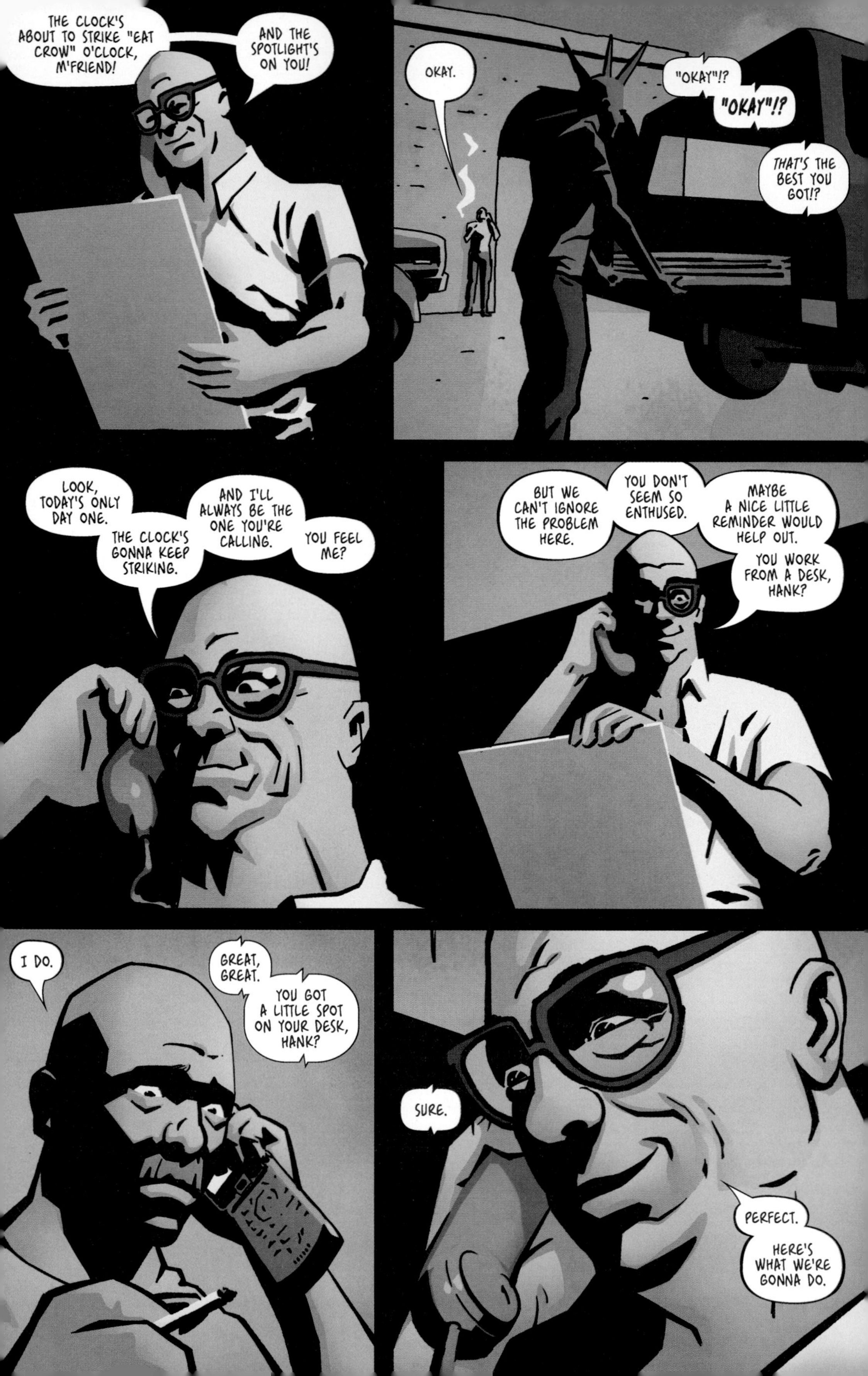
THE CLOCK'S ABOUT TO STRIKE "EAT CROW" O'CLOCK, M'FRIEND!
AND THE SPOTLIGHT'S ON YOU!
OKAY.
"OKAY"!?
"OKAY"!?
THAT'S THE BEST YOU GOT!?
LOOK, TODAY'S ONLY DAY ONE.
THE CLOCK'S GONNA KEEP STRIKING.
AND I'LL ALWAYS BE THE ONE YOU'RE CALLING.
YOU FEEL ME?
BUT WE CAN'T IGNORE THE PROBLEM HERE.
YOU DON'T SEEM SO ENTHUSED.
MAYBE A NICE LITTLE REMINDER WOULD HELP OUT.
YOU WORK FROM A DESK, HANK?
I DO.
GREAT, GREAT.
YOU GOT A LITTLE SPOT ON YOUR DESK, HANK?
SURE.
PERFECT.
HERE'S WHAT WE'RE GONNA DO.

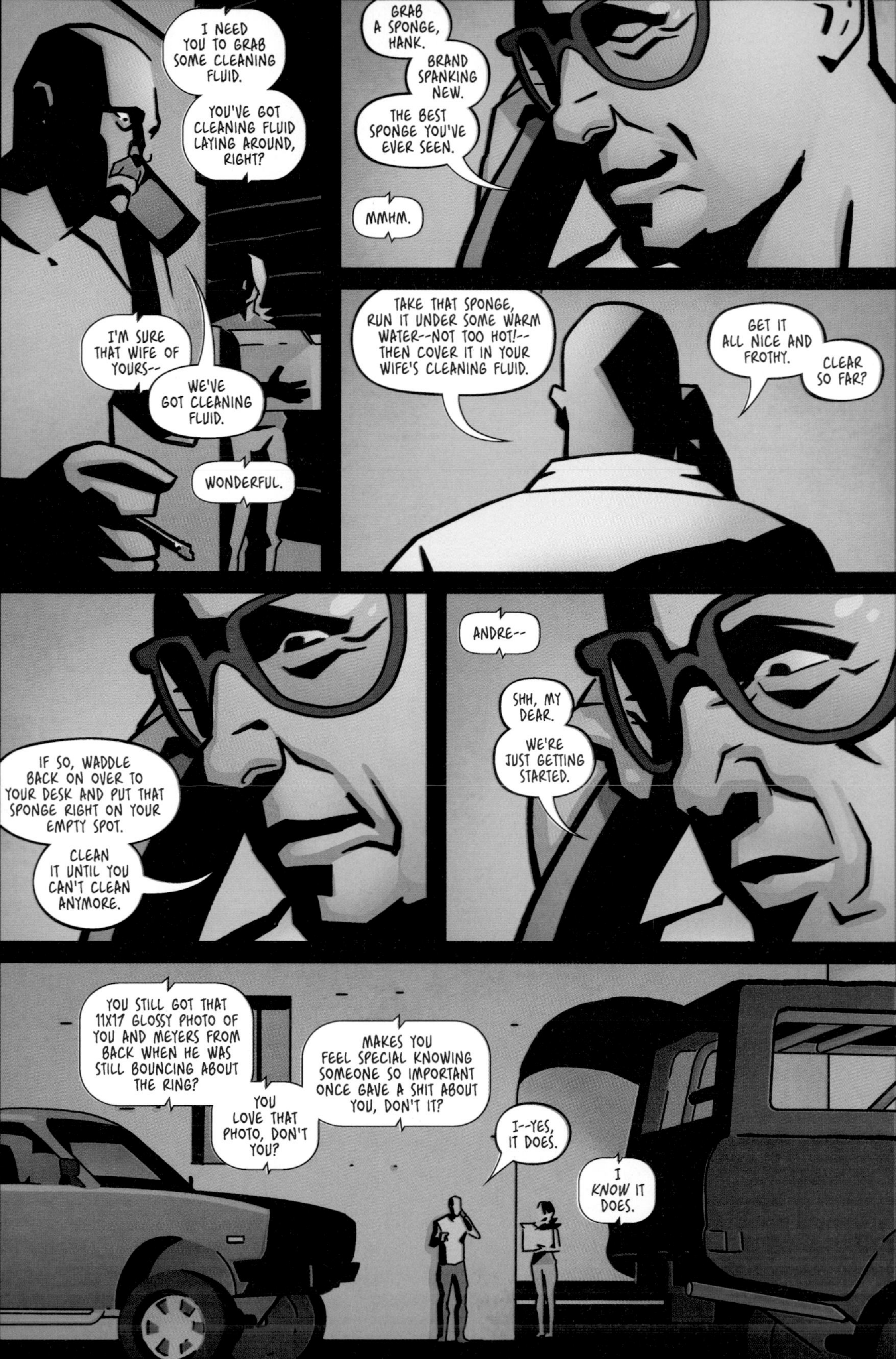
I NEED YOU TO GRAB SOME CLEANING FLUID.
YOU'VE GOT CLEANING FLUID LAYING AROUND, RIGHT?
I'M SURE THAT WIFE OF YOURS--
WE'VE GOT CLEANING FLUID.
WONDERFUL.
GRAB A SPONGE, HANK.
BRAND SPANKING NEW.
THE BEST SPONGE YOU'VE EVER SEEN.
MMHM.
TAKE THAT SPONGE, RUN IT UNDER SOME WARM WATER--NOT TOO HOT!--THEN COVER IT IN YOUR WIFE'S CLEANING FLUID.
GET IT ALL NICE AND FROTHY.
CLEAR SO FAR?
IF SO, WADDLE BACK ON OVER TO YOUR DESK AND PUT THAT SPONGE RIGHT ON YOUR EMPTY SPOT.
CLEAN IT UNTIL YOU CAN'T CLEAN ANYMORE.
ANDRE--
SHH, MY DEAR.
WE'RE JUST GETTING STARTED.
YOU STILL GOT THAT 11X17 GLOSSY PHOTO OF YOU AND MEYERS FROM BACK WHEN HE WAS STILL BOUNCING ABOUT THE RING?
YOU LOVE THAT PHOTO, DON'T YOU?
MAKES YOU FEEL SPECIAL KNOWING SOMEONE SO IMPORTANT ONCE GAVE A SHIT ABOUT YOU, DON'T IT?
I--YES, IT DOES.
I KNOW IT DOES.

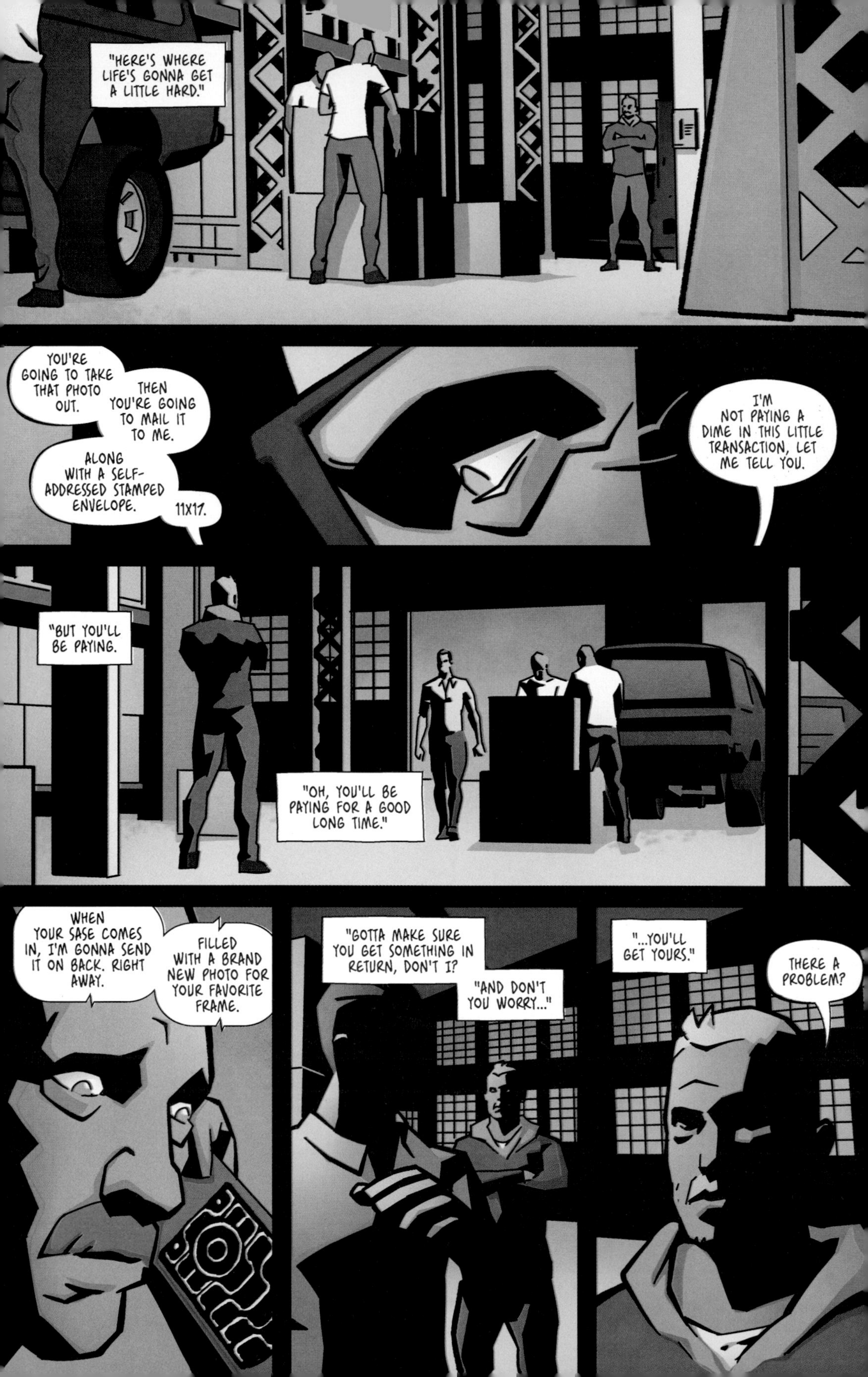
"HERE'S WHERE LIFE'S GONNA GET A LITTLE HARD."
YOU'RE GOING TO TAKE THAT PHOTO OUT.
THEN YOU'RE GOING TO MAIL IT TO ME.
ALONG WITH A SELF-ADDRESSED STAMPED ENVELOPE.
11X17.
I'M NOT PAYING A DIME IN THIS LITTLE TRANSACTION, LET ME TELL YOU.
"BUT YOU'LL BE PAYING.
"OH, YOU'LL BE PAYING FOR A GOOD LONG TIME."
WHEN YOUR SASE COMES IN, I'M GONNA SEND IT ON BACK. RIGHT AWAY.
FILLED WITH A BRAND NEW PHOTO FOR YOUR FAVORITE FRAME.
"GOTTA MAKE SURE YOU GET SOMETHING IN RETURN, DON'T I?
"AND DON'T YOU WORRY..."
"...YOU'LL GET YOURS."
THERE A PROBLEM?

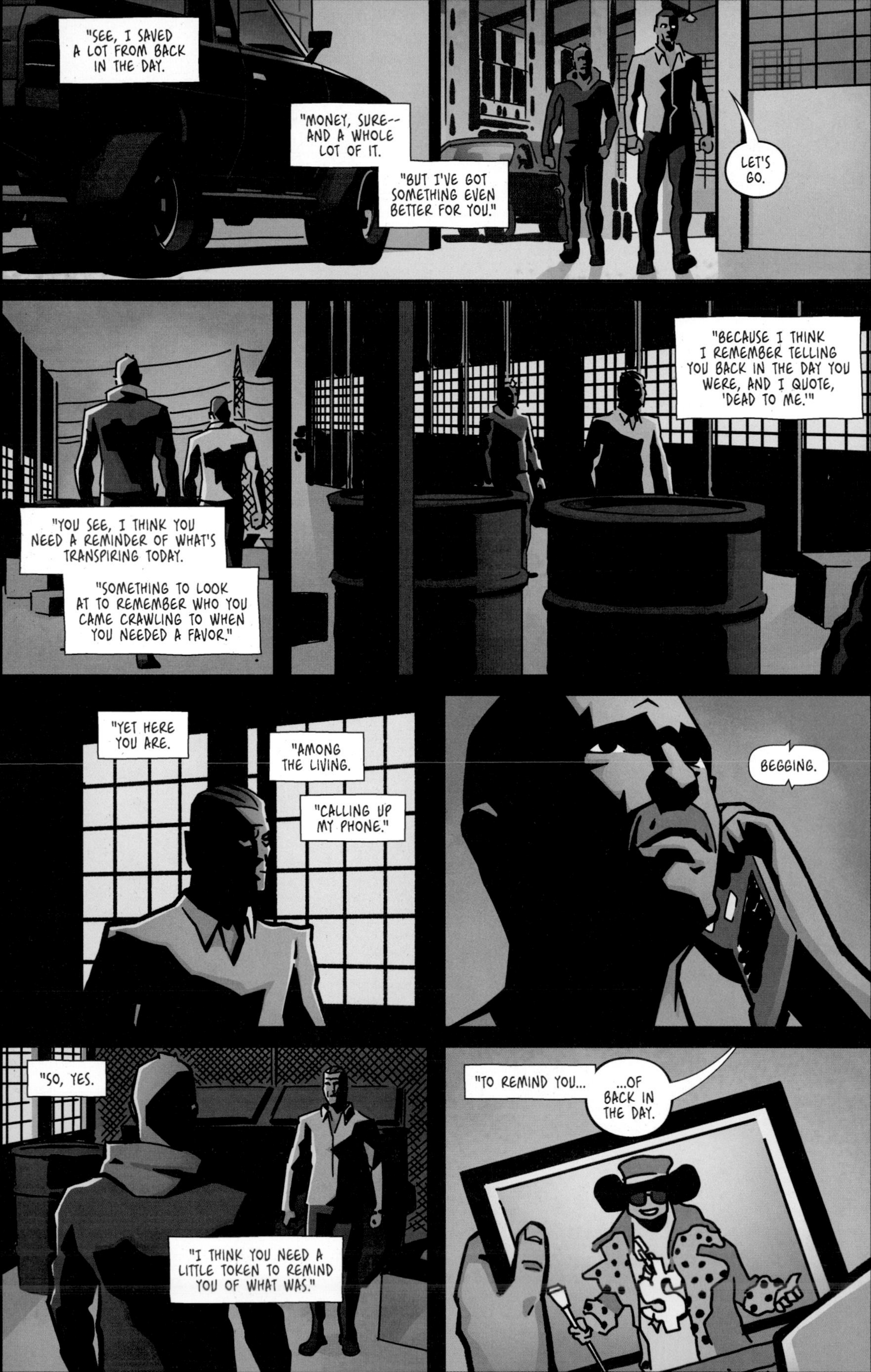
"SEE, I SAVED A LOT FROM BACK IN THE DAY.
"MONEY, SURE-- AND A WHOLE LOT OF IT.
"BUT I'VE GOT SOMETHING EVEN BETTER FOR YOU."
LET'S GO.
"YOU SEE, I THINK YOU NEED A REMINDER OF WHAT'S TRANSPIRING TODAY.
"SOMETHING TO LOOK AT TO REMEMBER WHO YOU CAME CRAWLING TO WHEN YOU NEEDED A FAVOR."
"BECAUSE I THINK I REMEMBER TELLING YOU BACK IN THE DAY YOU WERE, AND I QUOTE, 'DEAD TO ME.'"
"YET HERE YOU ARE.
"AMONG THE LIVING.
"CALLING UP MY PHONE."
BEGGING.
"SO, YES.
"I THINK YOU NEED A LITTLE TOKEN TO REMIND YOU OF WHAT WAS."
"TO REMIND YOU...
...OF BACK IN THE DAY.

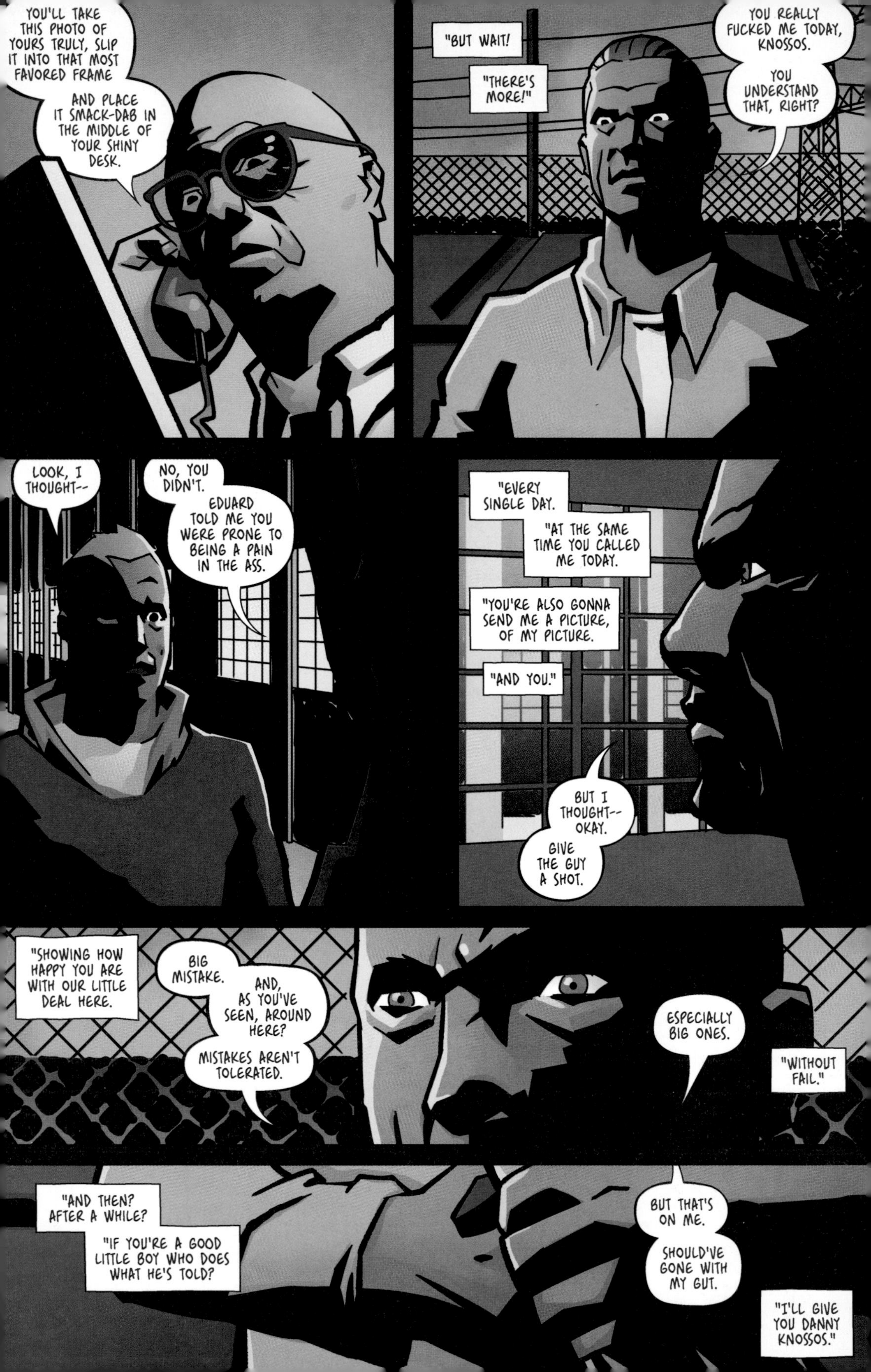
YOU'LL TAKE THIS PHOTO OF YOURS TRULY, SLIP IT INTO THAT MOST FAVORED FRAME
AND PLACE IT SMACK-DAB IN THE MIDDLE OF YOUR SHINY DESK.
"BUT WAIT!
"THERE'S MORE!"
YOU REALLY FUCKED ME TODAY, KNOSSOS.
YOU UNDERSTAND THAT, RIGHT?
LOOK, I THOUGHT--
NO, YOU DIDN'T.
EDUARD TOLD ME YOU WERE PRONE TO BEING A PAIN IN THE ASS.
"EVERY SINGLE DAY.
"AT THE SAME TIME YOU CALLED ME TODAY.
"YOU'RE ALSO GONNA SEND ME A PICTURE, OF MY PICTURE.
"AND YOU."
BUT I THOUGHT-- OKAY.
GIVE THE GUY A SHOT.
"SHOWING HOW HAPPY YOU ARE WITH OUR LITTLE DEAL HERE.
BIG MISTAKE.
AND, AS YOU'VE SEEN, AROUND HERE?
MISTAKES AREN'T TOLERATED.
ESPECIALLY BIG ONES.
"WITHOUT FAIL."
"AND THEN? AFTER A WHILE?
"IF YOU'RE A GOOD LITTLE BOY WHO DOES WHAT HE'S TOLD?
BUT THAT'S ON ME.
SHOULD'VE GONE WITH MY GUT.
"I'LL GIVE YOU DANNY KNOSSOS."

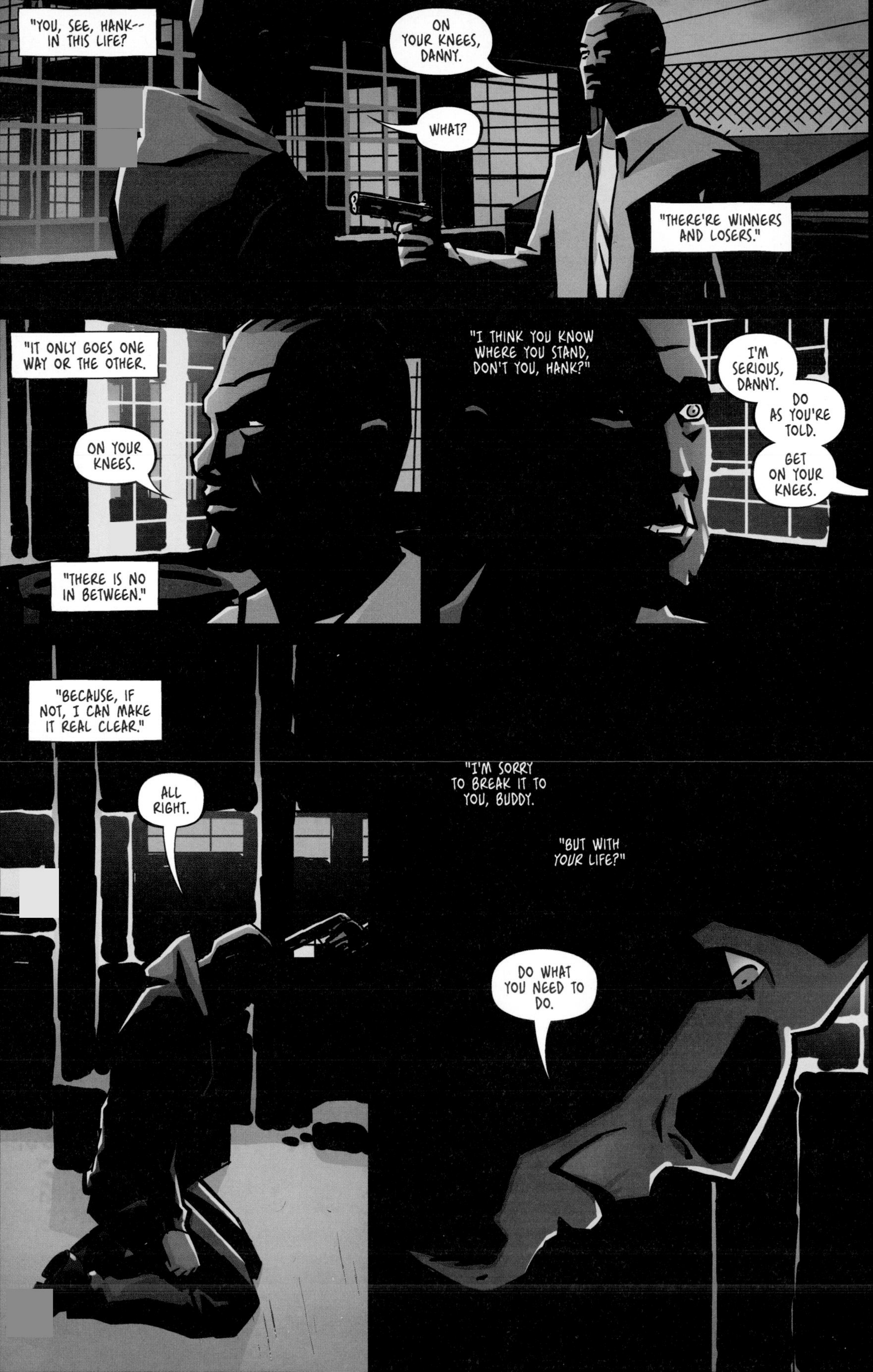
"YOU, SEE, HANK-- IN THIS LIFE?
ON YOUR KNEES, DANNY.
WHAT?
"THERE'RE WINNERS AND LOSERS."
"IT ONLY GOES ONE WAY OR THE OTHER.
ON YOUR KNEES.
"THERE IS NO IN BETWEEN."
"I THINK YOU KNOW WHERE YOU STAND, DON'T YOU, HANK?"
I'M SERIOUS, DANNY.
DO AS YOU'RE TOLD.
GET ON YOUR KNEES.
"BECAUSE, IF NOT, I CAN MAKE IT REAL CLEAR."
ALL RIGHT.
"I'M SORRY TO BREAK IT TO YOU, BUDDY.
"BUT WITH YOUR LIFE?"
DO WHAT YOU NEED TO DO.

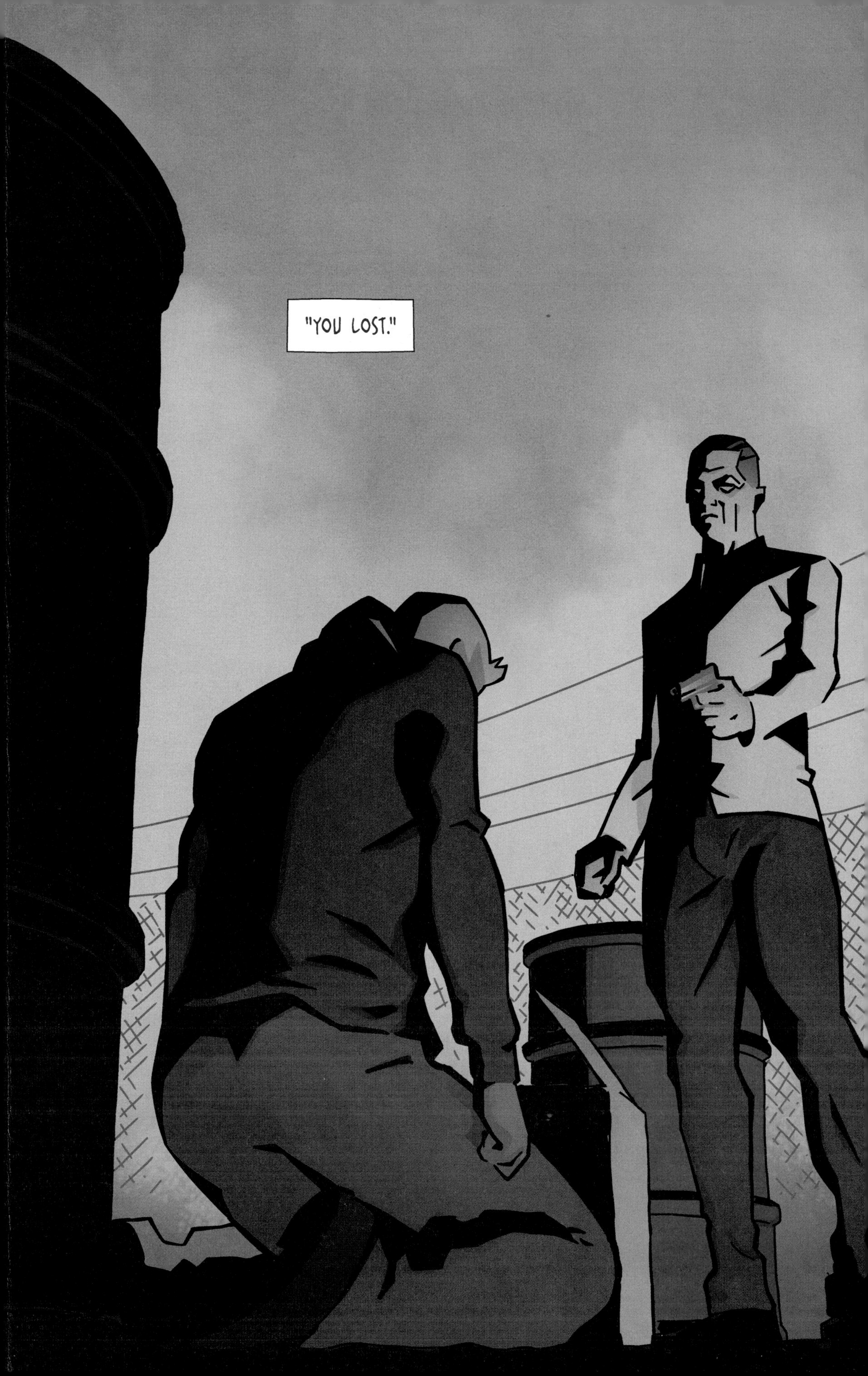
"YOU LOST."

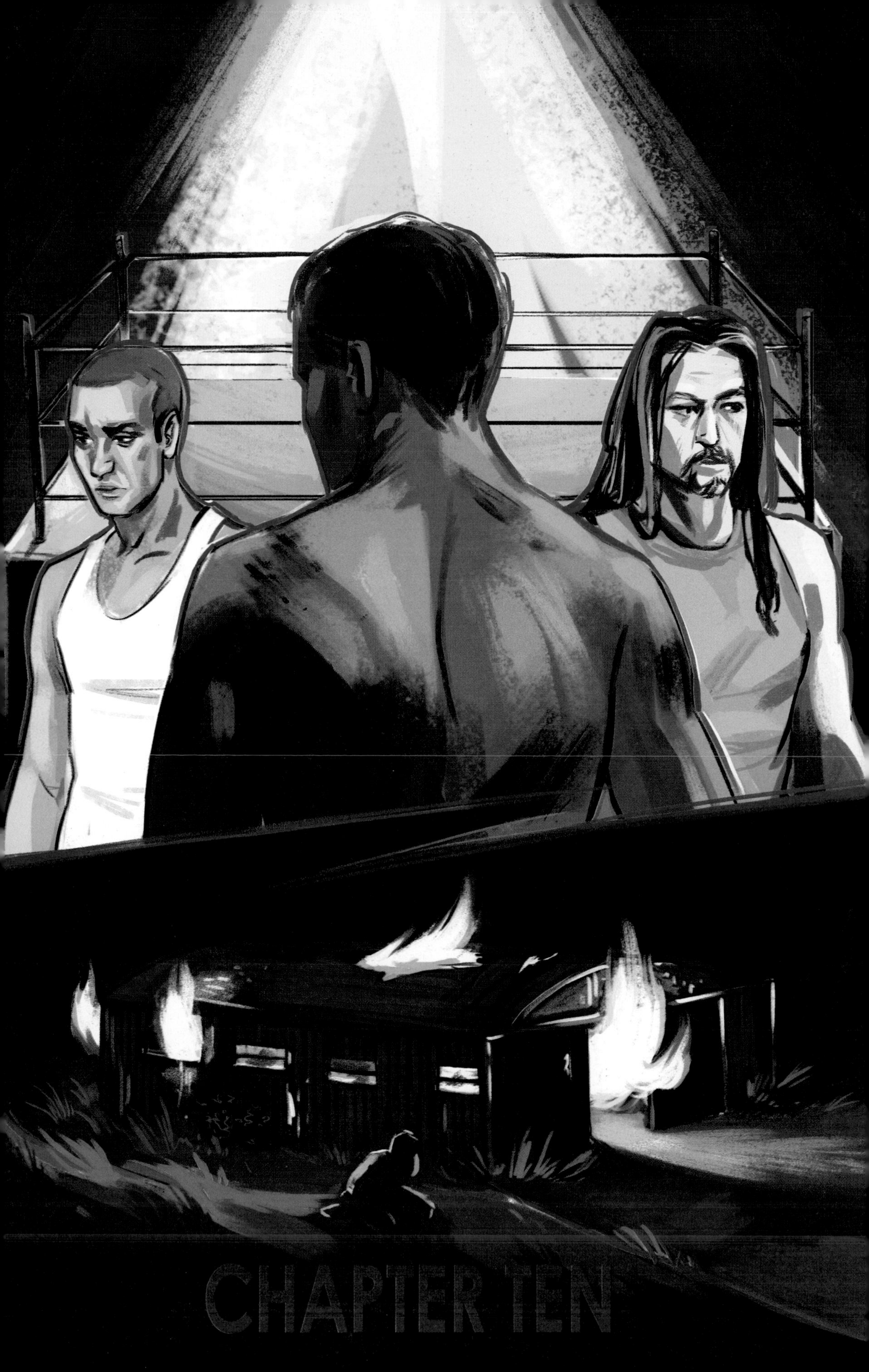

CHAPTER TEN

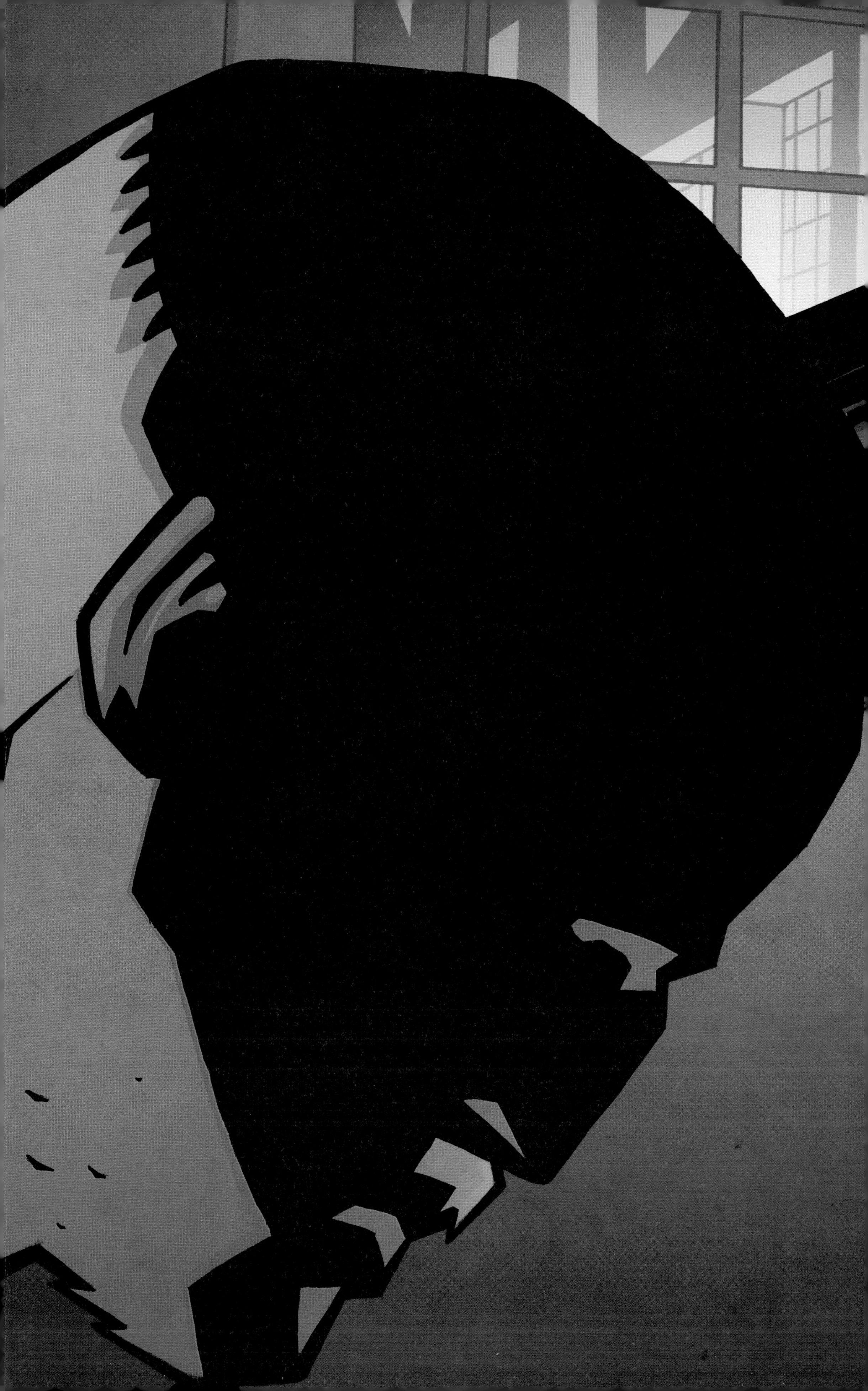

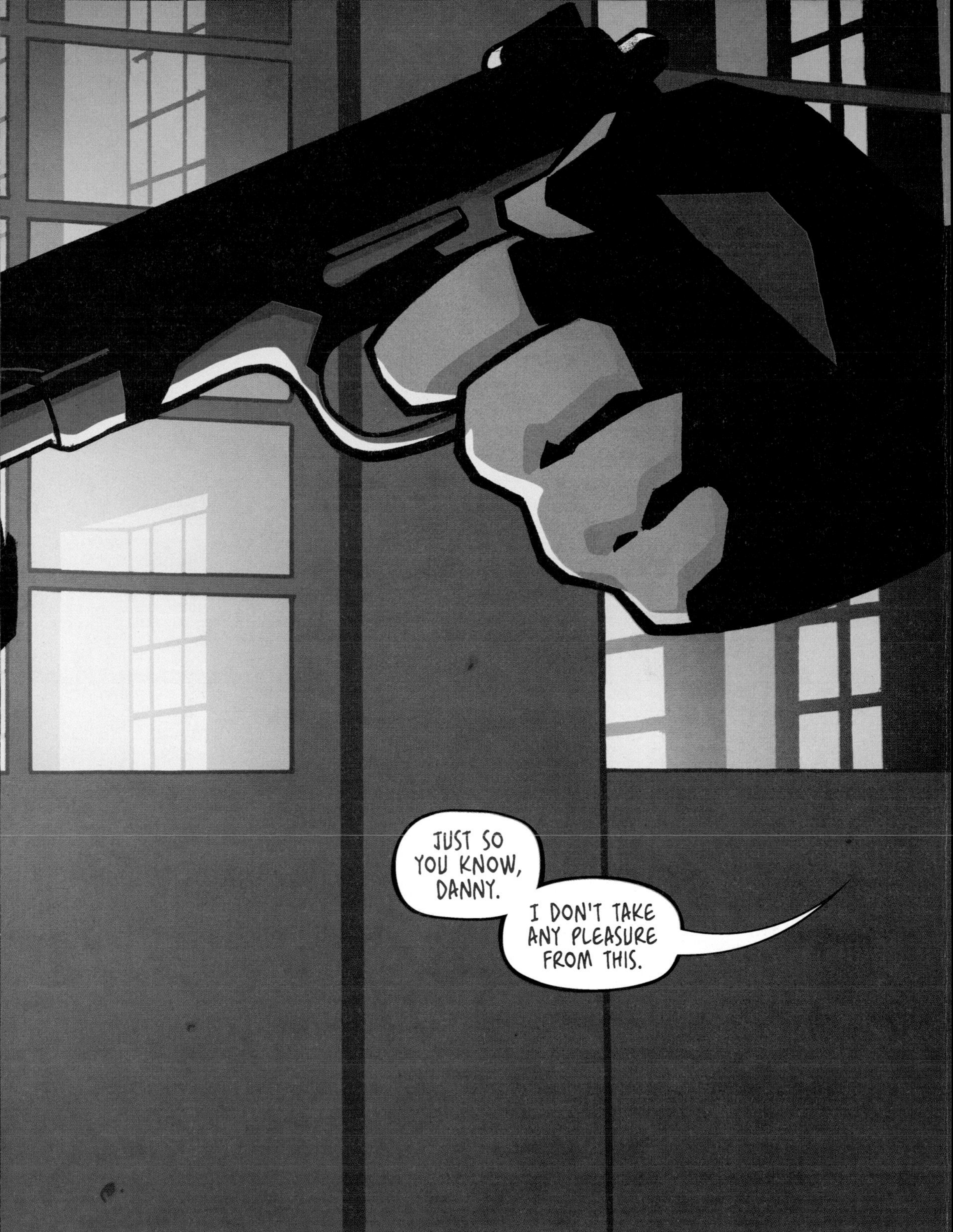
JUST SO YOU KNOW, DANNY.
I DON'T TAKE ANY PLEASURE FROM THIS.

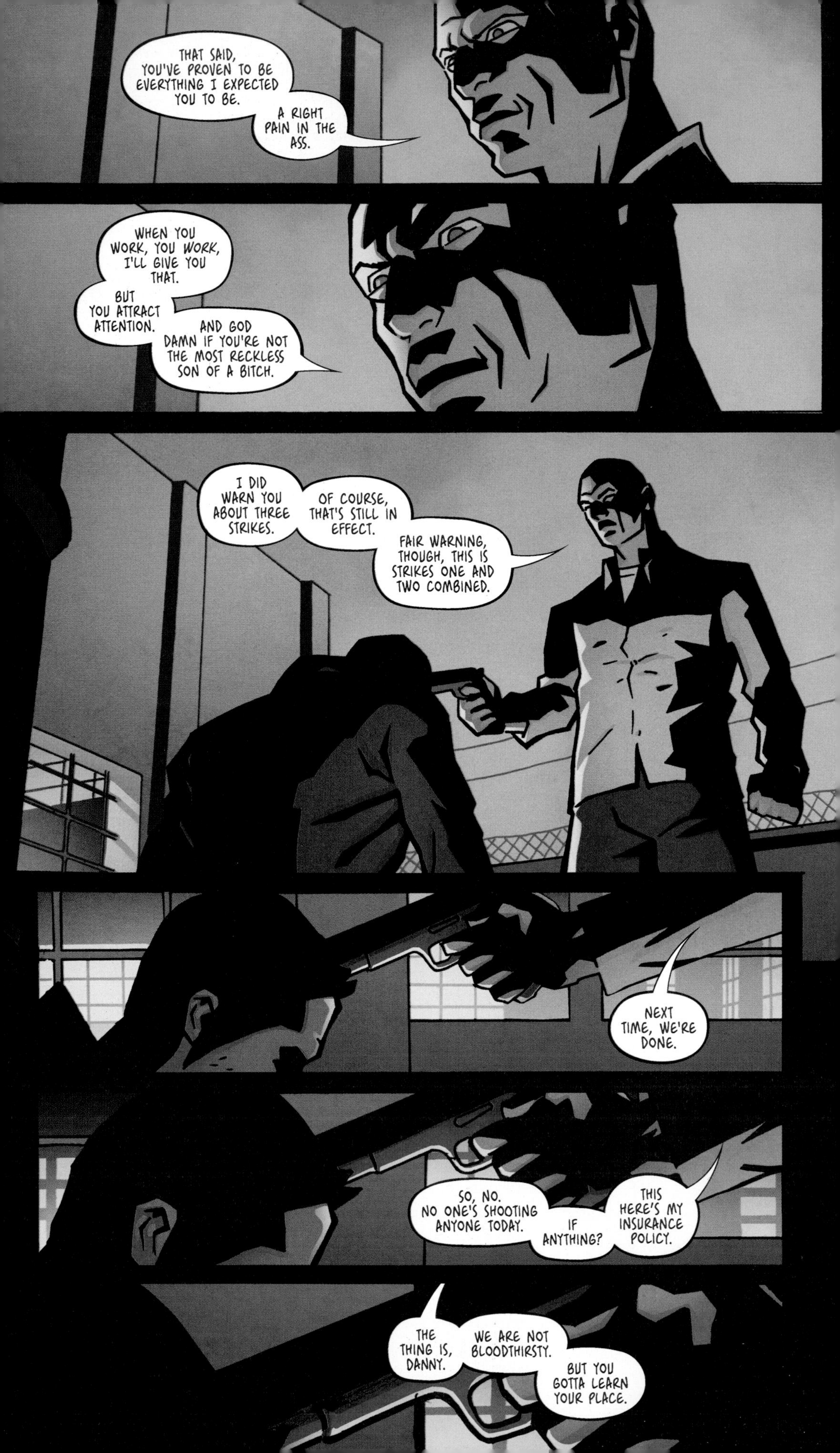
THAT SAID, YOU'VE PROVEN TO BE EVERYTHING I EXPECTED YOU TO BE.
A RIGHT PAIN IN THE ASS.
WHEN YOU WORK, YOU WORK, I'LL GIVE YOU THAT.
BUT YOU ATTRACT ATTENTION.
AND GOD DAMN IF YOU'RE NOT THE MOST RECKLESS SON OF A BITCH.
I DID WARN YOU ABOUT THREE STRIKES.
OF COURSE, THAT'S STILL IN EFFECT.
FAIR WARNING, THOUGH, THIS IS STRIKES ONE AND TWO COMBINED.
NEXT TIME, WE'RE DONE.
SO, NO. NO ONE'S SHOOTING ANYONE TODAY.
IF ANYTHING?
THIS HERE'S MY INSURANCE POLICY.
THE THING IS, DANNY.
WE ARE NOT BLOODTHIRSTY.
BUT YOU GOTTA LEARN YOUR PLACE.

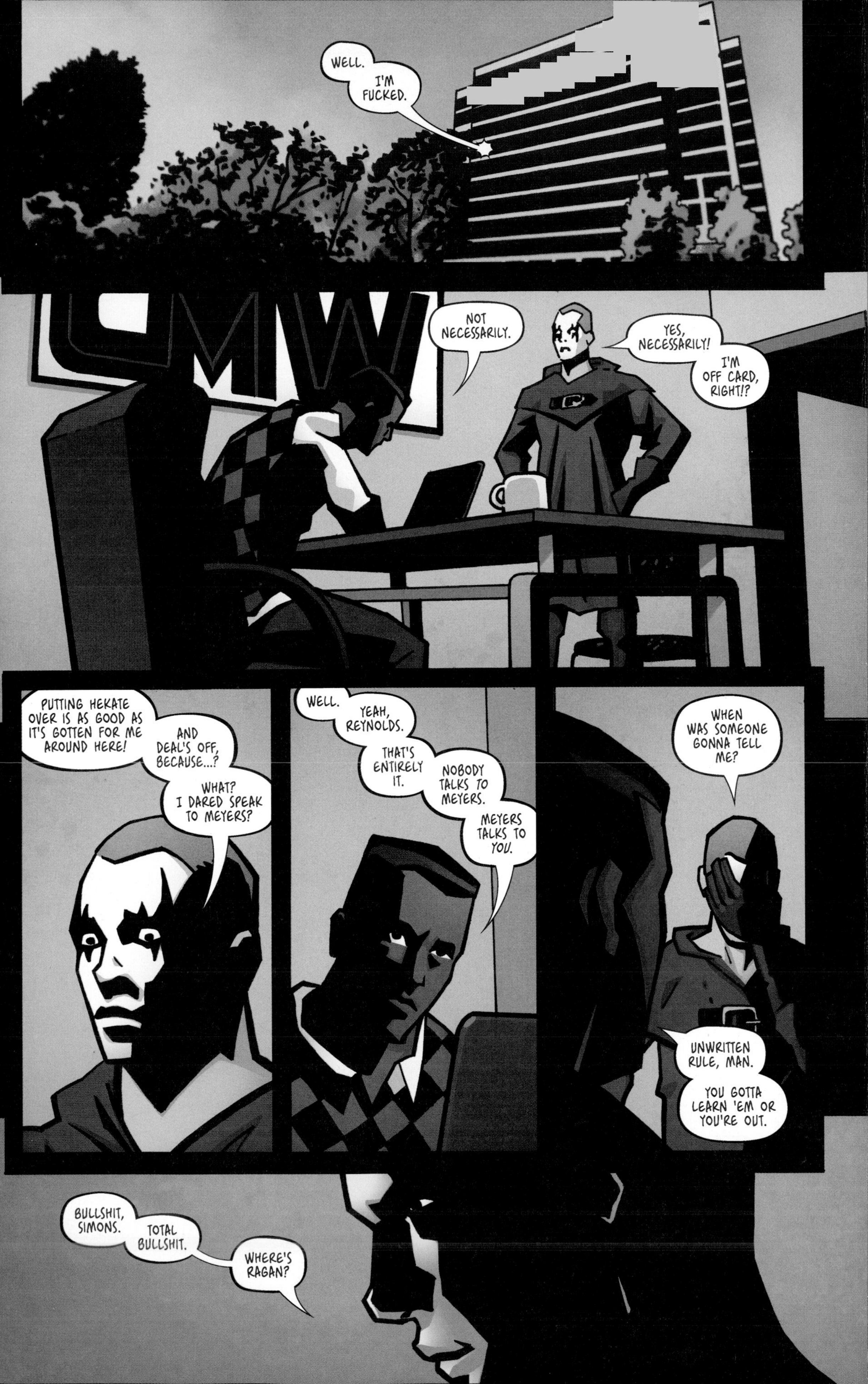
WELL.
I'M FUCKED.
NOT NECESSARILY.
YES, NECESSARILY!
I'M OFF CARD, RIGHT!?
PUTTING HEKATE OVER IS AS GOOD AS IT'S GOTTEN FOR ME AROUND HERE!
AND DEAL'S OFF, BECAUSE...?
WHAT? I DARED SPEAK TO MEYERS?
WELL.
YEAH, REYNOLDS.
THAT'S ENTIRELY IT.
NOBODY TALKS TO MEYERS.
MEYERS TALKS TO YOU.
WHEN WAS SOMEONE GONNA TELL ME?
UNWRITTEN RULE, MAN.
YOU GOTTA LEARN 'EM OR YOU'RE OUT.
BULLSHIT, SIMONS.
TOTAL BULLSHIT.
WHERE'S RAGAN?

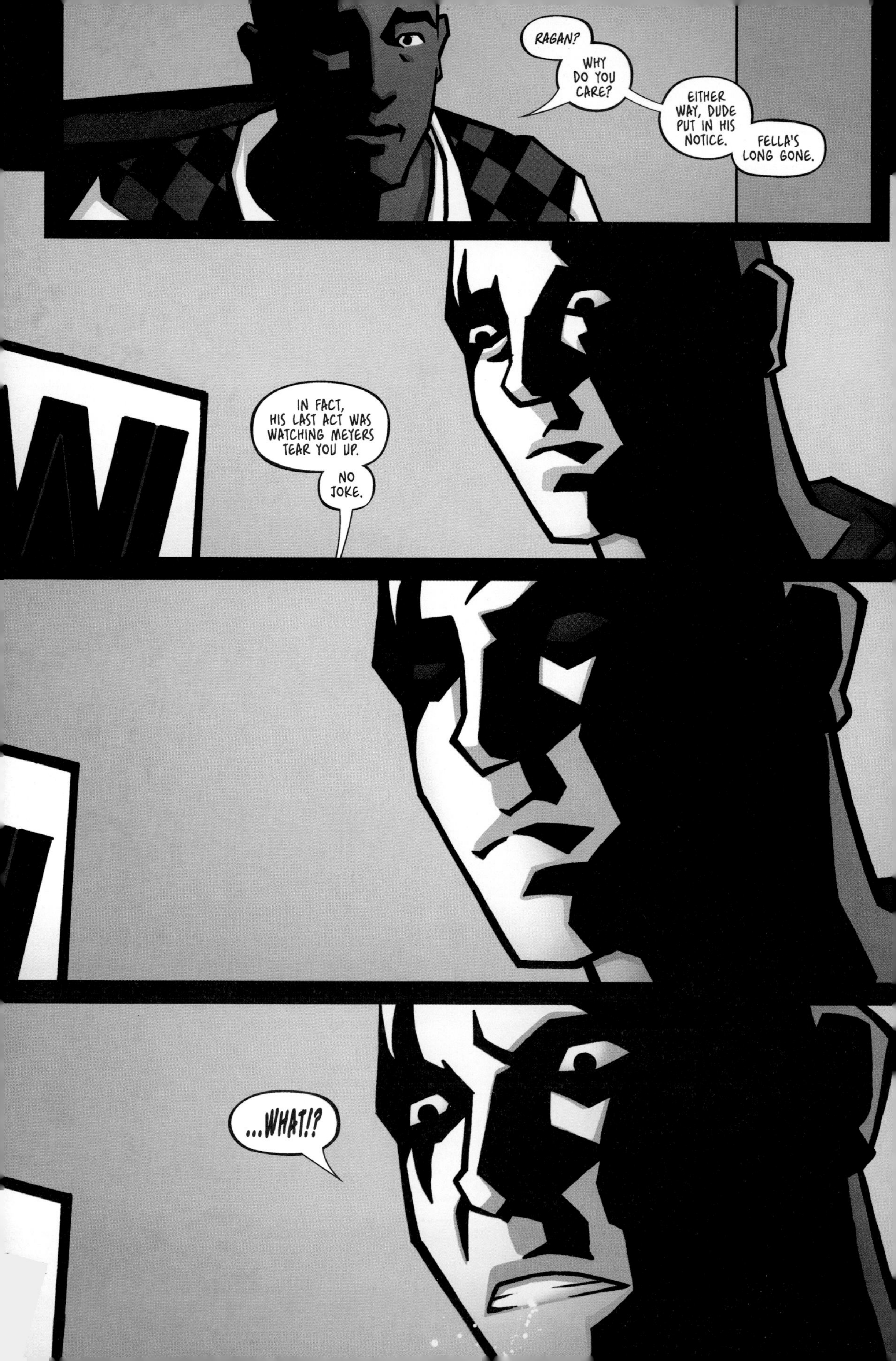
RAGAN?
WHY DO YOU CARE?
EITHER WAY, DUDE PUT IN HIS NOTICE.
FELLA'S LONG GONE.
IN FACT, HIS LAST ACT WAS WATCHING MEYERS TEAR YOU UP.
NO JOKE.
...WHAT!?

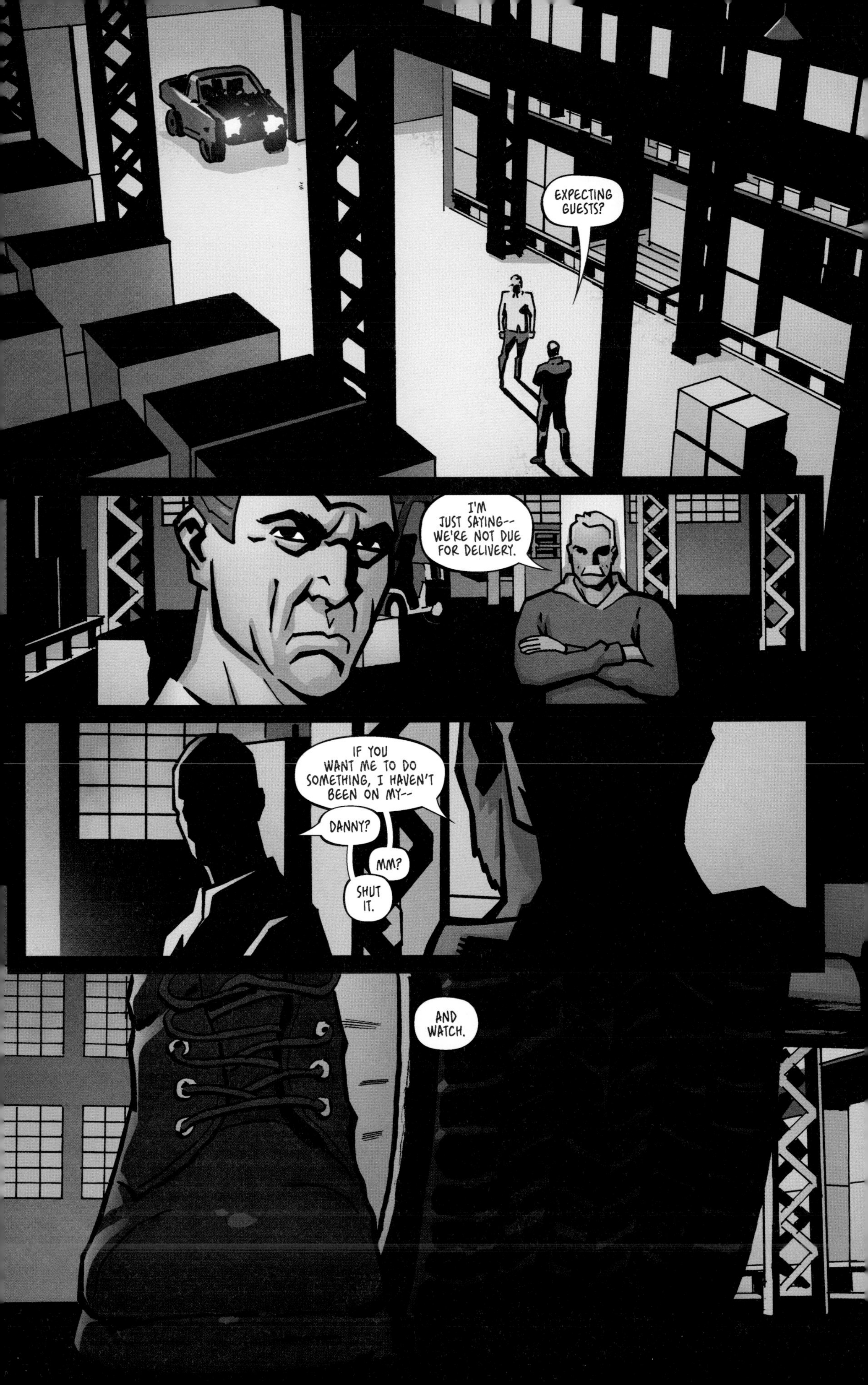
EXPECTING GUESTS?
I'M JUST SAYING-- WE'RE NOT DUE FOR DELIVERY.
IF YOU WANT ME TO DO SOMETHING, I HAVEN'T BEEN ON MY--
DANNY?
MM?
SHUT IT.
AND WATCH.

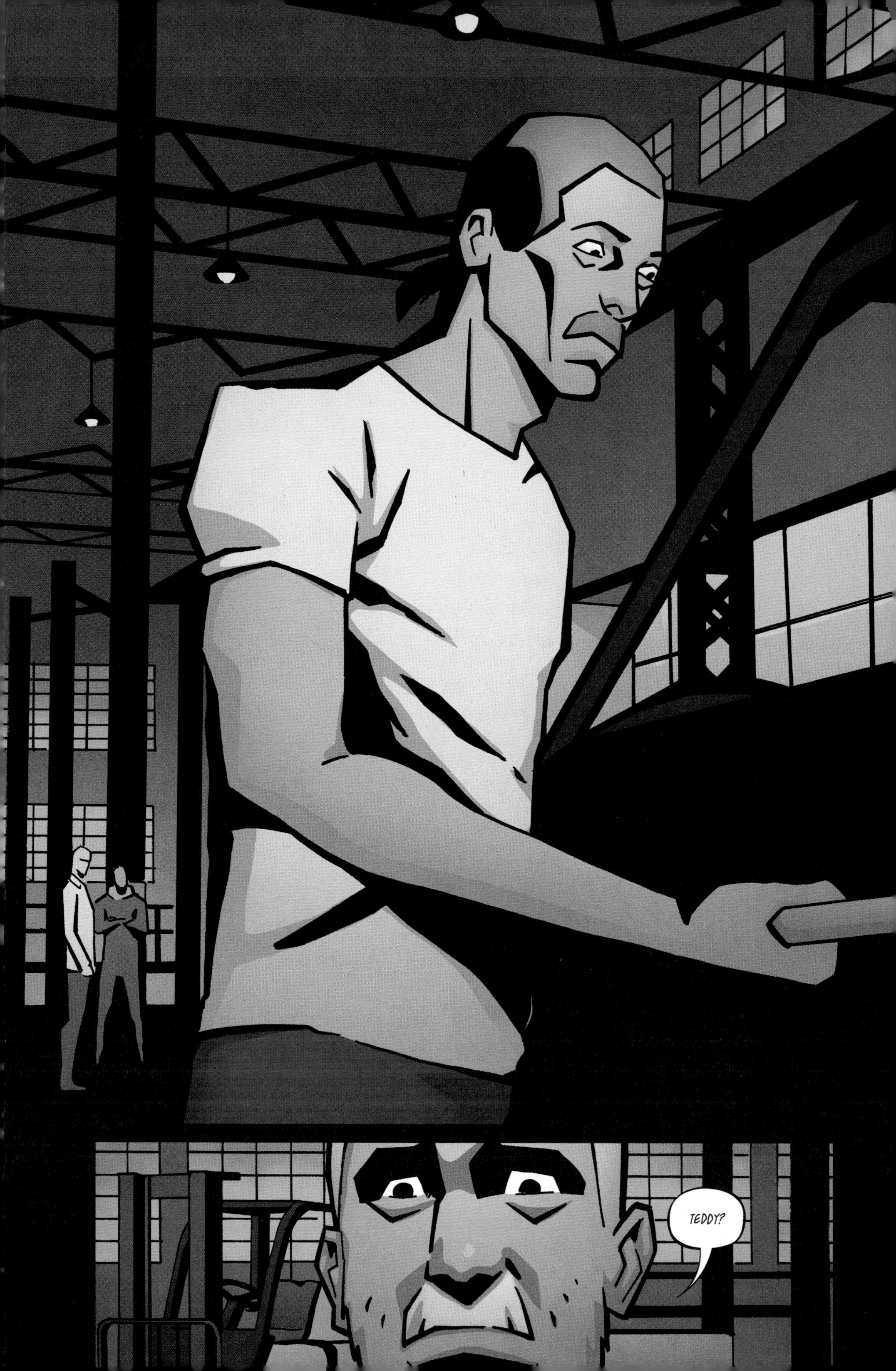
TEDDY?

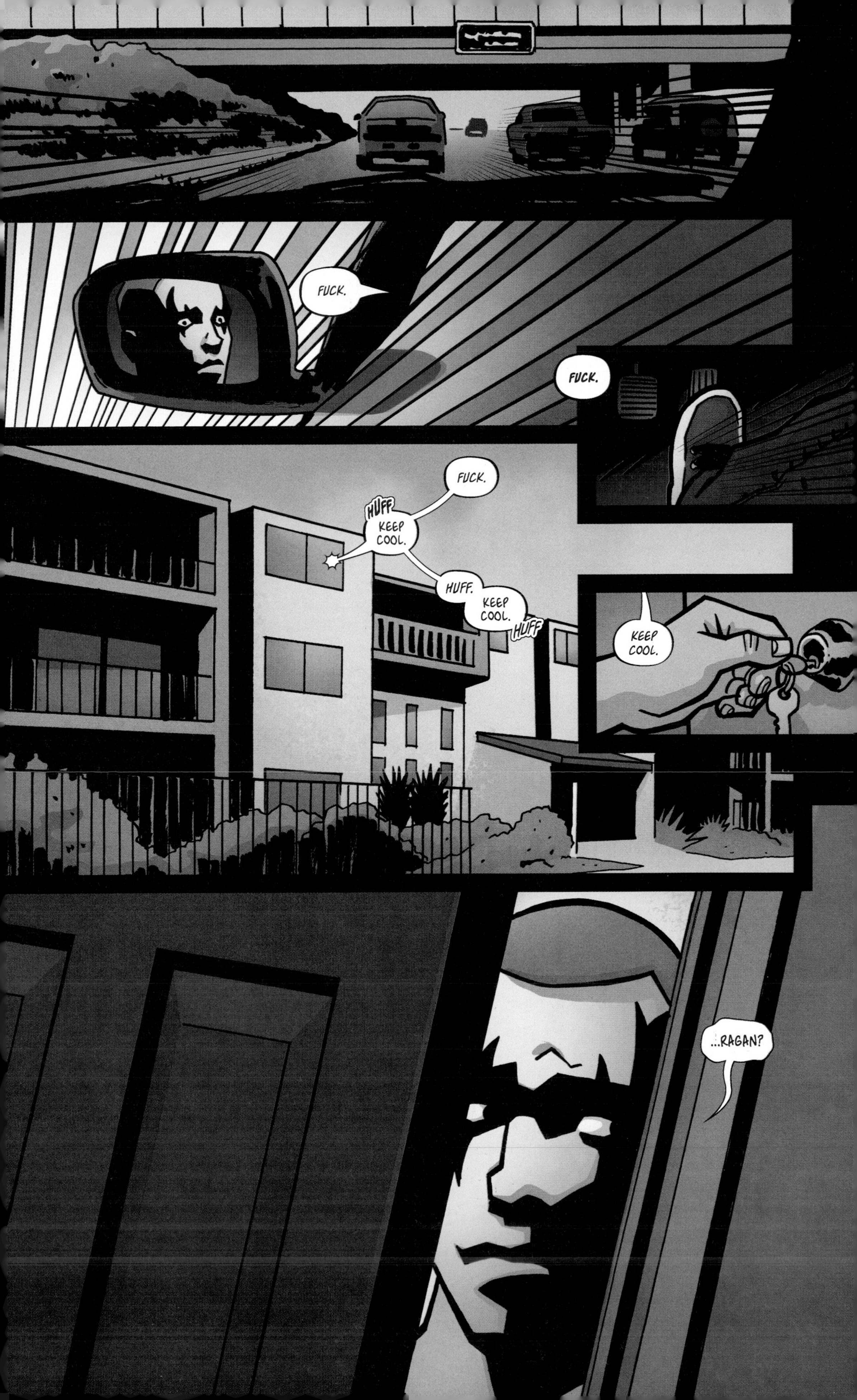
FUCK.
FUCK.
FUCK.
HUFF
KEEP COOL.
HUFF.
KEEP COOL.
HUFF
KEEP COOL.
...RAGAN?

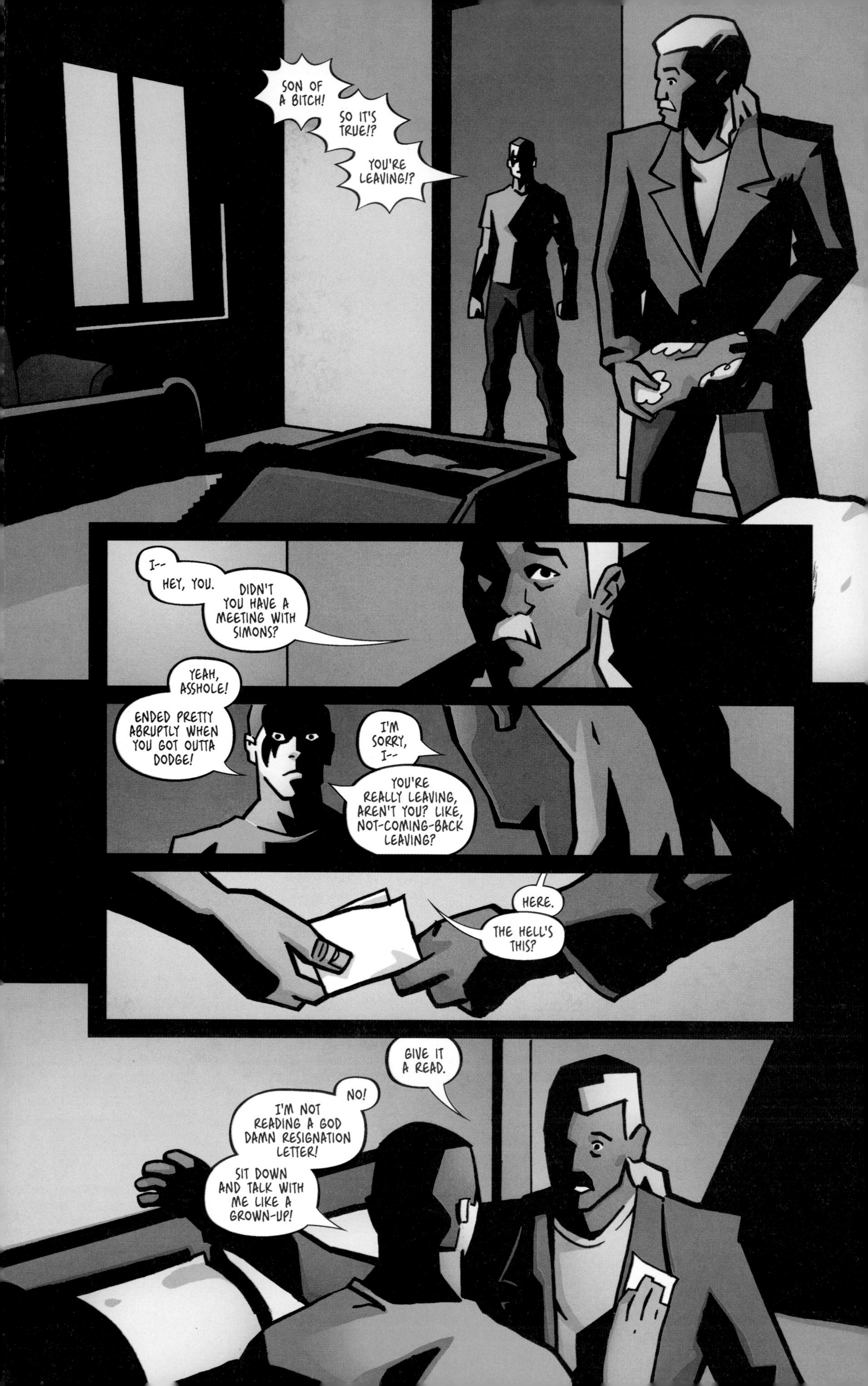

SON OF A BITCH!
SO IT'S TRUE!?
YOU'RE LEAVING!?
I--
HEY, YOU.
DIDN'T YOU HAVE A MEETING WITH SIMONS?
YEAH, ASSHOLE!
ENDED PRETTY ABRUPTLY WHEN YOU GOT OUTTA DODGE!
I'M SORRY, I--
YOU'RE REALLY LEAVING, AREN'T YOU? LIKE, NOT-COMING-BACK LEAVING?
HERE.
THE HELL'S THIS?
GIVE IT A READ.
NO!
I'M NOT READING A GOD DAMN RESIGNATION LETTER!
SIT DOWN AND TALK WITH ME LIKE A GROWN-UP!

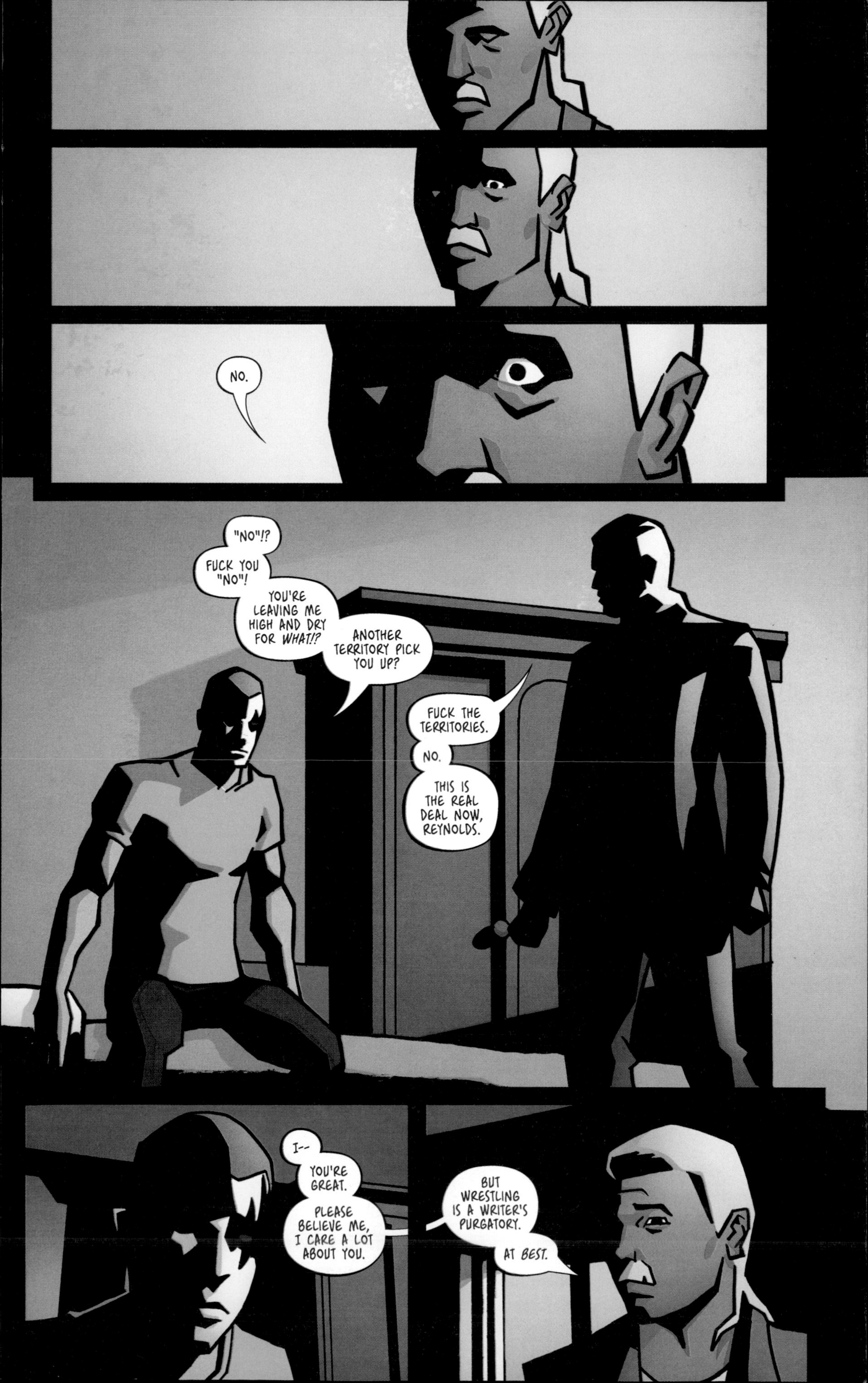
NO.
"NO"!?
FUCK YOU "NO"!
YOU'RE LEAVING ME HIGH AND DRY FOR *WHAT!?*
ANOTHER TERRITORY PICK YOU UP?
FUCK THE TERRITORIES.
NO.
THIS IS THE REAL DEAL NOW, REYNOLDS.
I--
YOU'RE GREAT.
PLEASE BELIEVE ME, I CARE A LOT ABOUT YOU.
BUT WRESTLING IS A WRITER'S PURGATORY.
AT *BEST.*

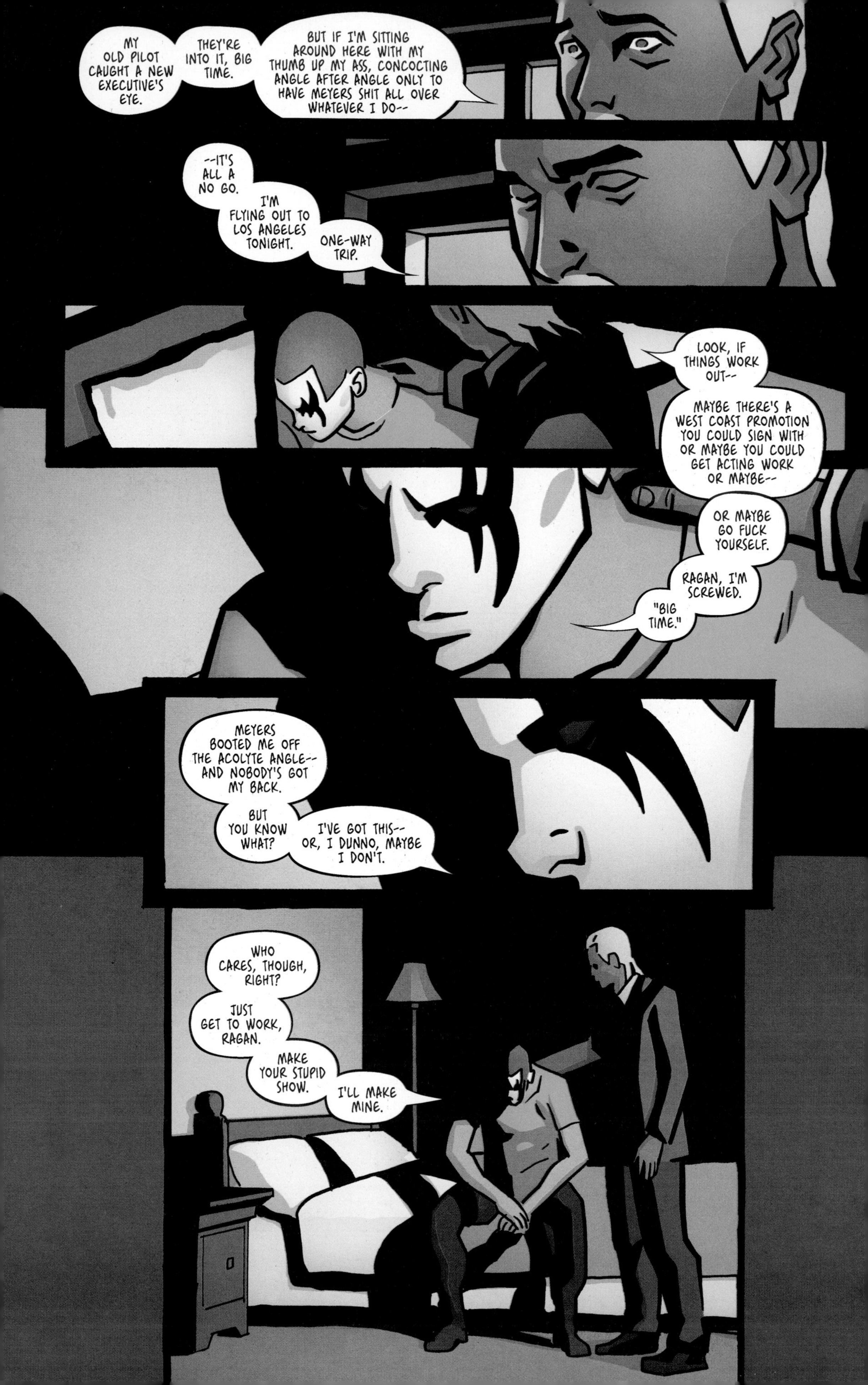
MY OLD PILOT CAUGHT A NEW EXECUTIVE'S EYE.
THEY'RE INTO IT, BIG TIME.
BUT IF I'M SITTING AROUND HERE WITH MY THUMB UP MY ASS, CONCOCTING ANGLE AFTER ANGLE ONLY TO HAVE MEYERS SHIT ALL OVER WHATEVER I DO--
--IT'S ALL A NO GO.
I'M FLYING OUT TO LOS ANGELES TONIGHT.
ONE-WAY TRIP.
LOOK, IF THINGS WORK OUT--
MAYBE THERE'S A WEST COAST PROMOTION YOU COULD SIGN WITH OR MAYBE YOU COULD GET ACTING WORK OR MAYBE--
OR MAYBE GO FUCK YOURSELF.
RAGAN, I'M SCREWED.
"BIG TIME."
MEYERS BOOTED ME OFF THE ACOLYTE ANGLE-- AND NOBODY'S GOT MY BACK.
BUT YOU KNOW WHAT?
I'VE GOT THIS-- OR, I DUNNO, MAYBE I DON'T.
WHO CARES, THOUGH, RIGHT?
JUST GET TO WORK, RAGAN.
MAKE YOUR STUPID SHOW.
I'LL MAKE MINE.

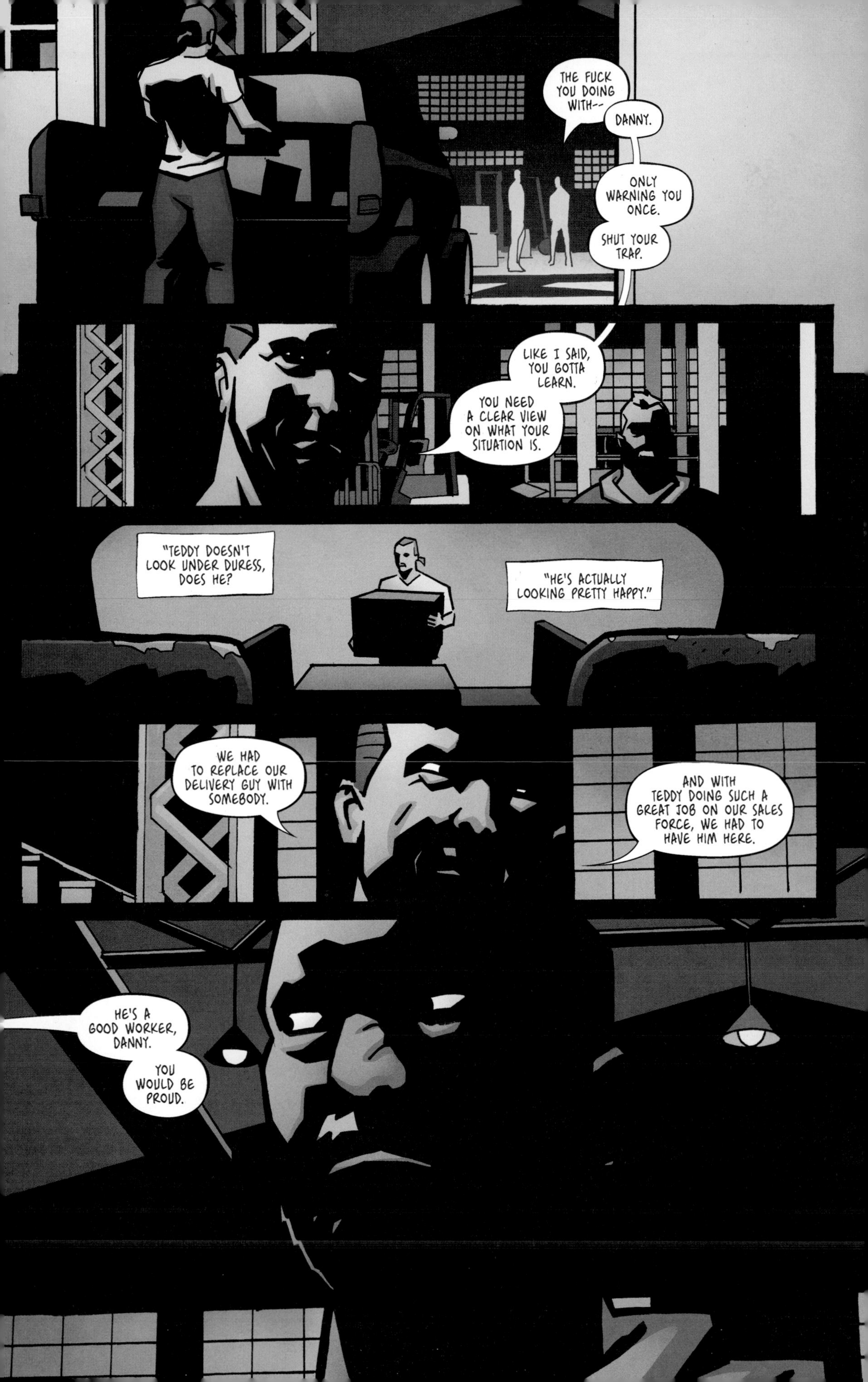
THE FUCK YOU DOING WITH--
DANNY.
ONLY WARNING YOU ONCE.
SHUT YOUR TRAP.
LIKE I SAID, YOU GOTTA LEARN.
YOU NEED A CLEAR VIEW ON WHAT YOUR SITUATION IS.
"TEDDY DOESN'T LOOK UNDER DURESS, DOES HE?
"HE'S ACTUALLY LOOKING PRETTY HAPPY."
WE HAD TO REPLACE OUR DELIVERY GUY WITH SOMEBODY.
AND WITH TEDDY DOING SUCH A GREAT JOB ON OUR SALES FORCE, WE HAD TO HAVE HIM HERE.
HE'S A GOOD WORKER, DANNY.
YOU WOULD BE PROUD.

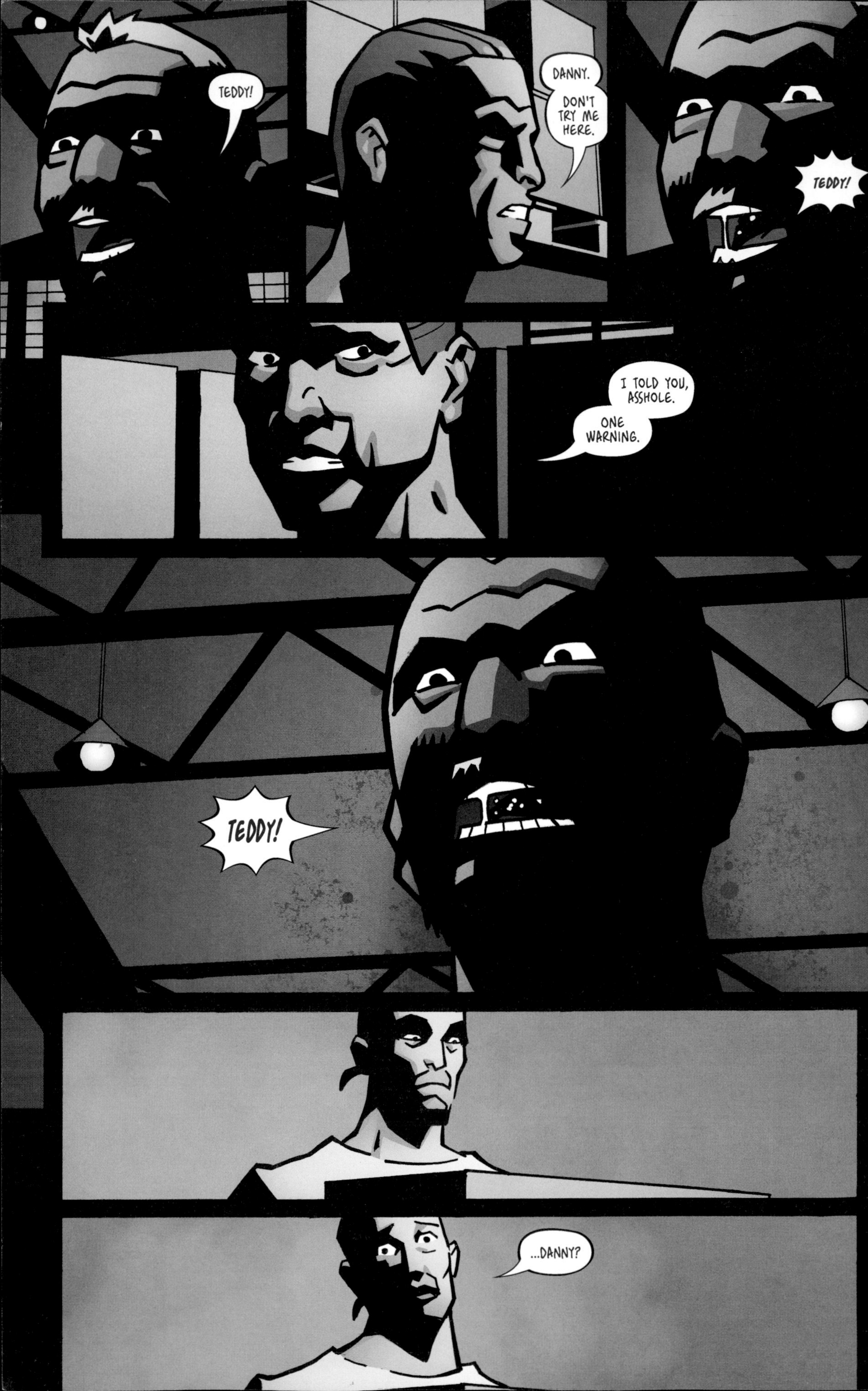
TEDDY!
DANNY.
DON'T TRY ME HERE.
TEDDY!
I TOLD YOU, ASSHOLE.
ONE WARNING.
TEDDY!
...DANNY?

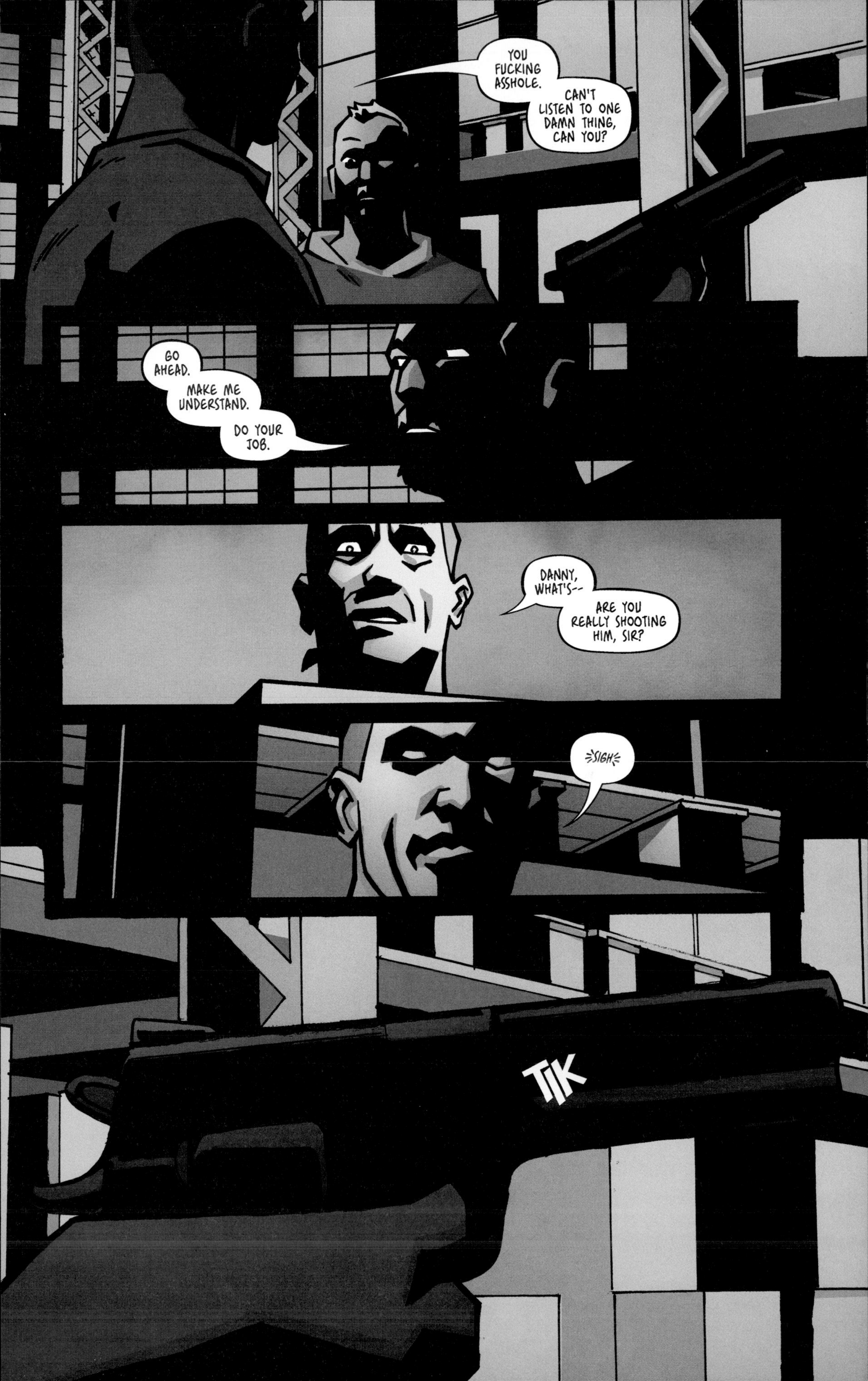
YOU FUCKING ASSHOLE.
CAN'T LISTEN TO ONE DAMN THING, CAN YOU?
GO AHEAD.
MAKE ME UNDERSTAND.
DO YOUR JOB.
DANNY, WHAT'S--
ARE YOU REALLY SHOOTING HIM, SIR?
SIGH
TIK

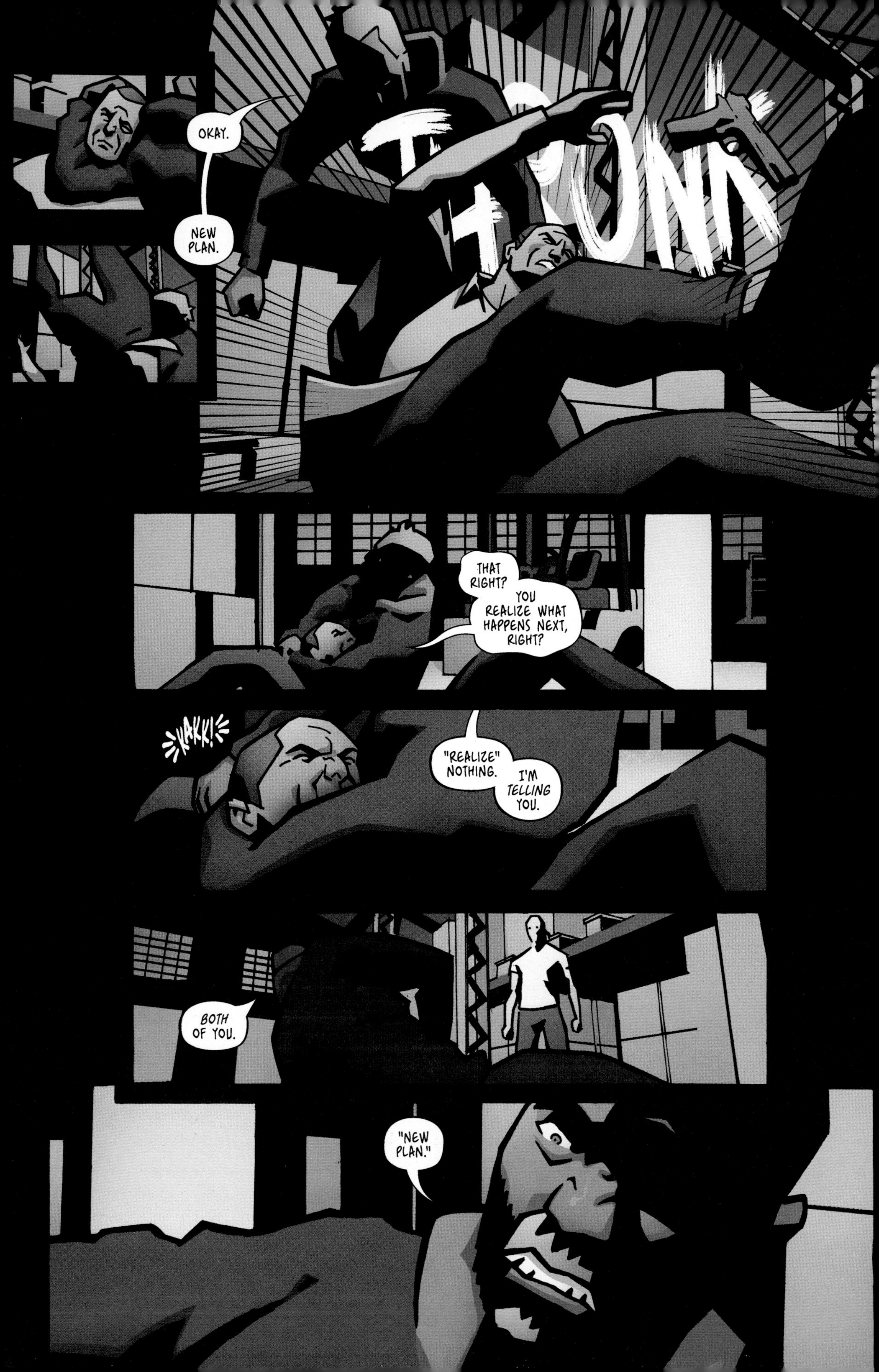
OKAY.
NEW PLAN.
THONK
THAT RIGHT?
YOU REALIZE WHAT HAPPENS NEXT, RIGHT?
KAKK!
"REALIZE" NOTHING.
I'M TELLING YOU.
BOTH OF YOU.
"NEW PLAN."

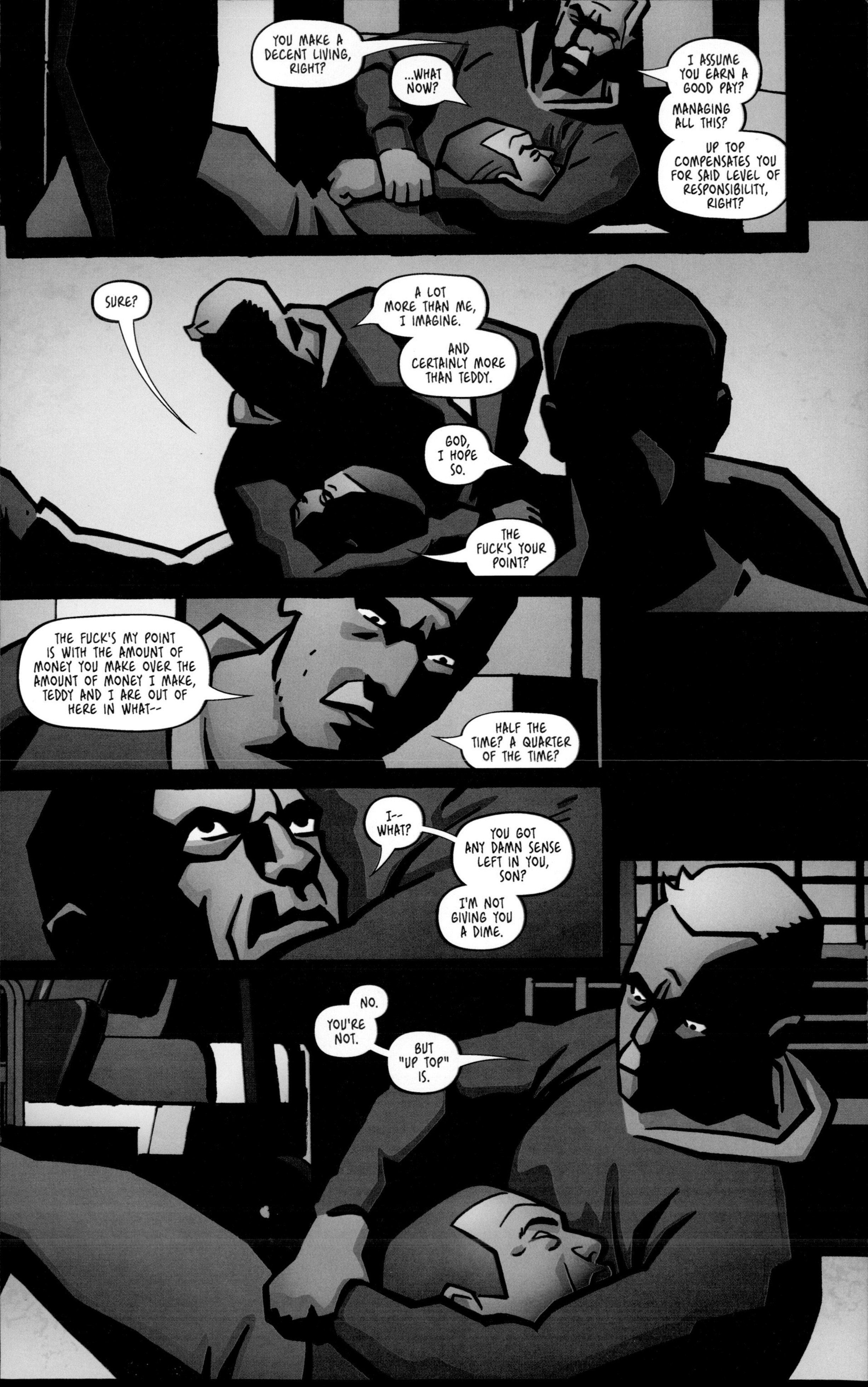
YOU MAKE A DECENT LIVING, RIGHT?
...WHAT NOW?
I ASSUME YOU EARN A GOOD PAY?
MANAGING ALL THIS?
UP TOP COMPENSATES YOU FOR SAID LEVEL OF RESPONSIBILITY, RIGHT?
SURE?
A LOT MORE THAN ME, I IMAGINE.
AND CERTAINLY MORE THAN TEDDY.
GOD, I HOPE SO.
THE FUCK'S YOUR POINT?
THE FUCK'S MY POINT IS WITH THE AMOUNT OF MONEY YOU MAKE OVER THE AMOUNT OF MONEY I MAKE, TEDDY AND I ARE OUT OF HERE IN WHAT--
HALF THE TIME? A QUARTER OF THE TIME?
I-- WHAT?
YOU GOT ANY DAMN SENSE LEFT IN YOU, SON?
I'M NOT GIVING YOU A DIME.
NO. YOU'RE NOT.
BUT "UP TOP" IS.

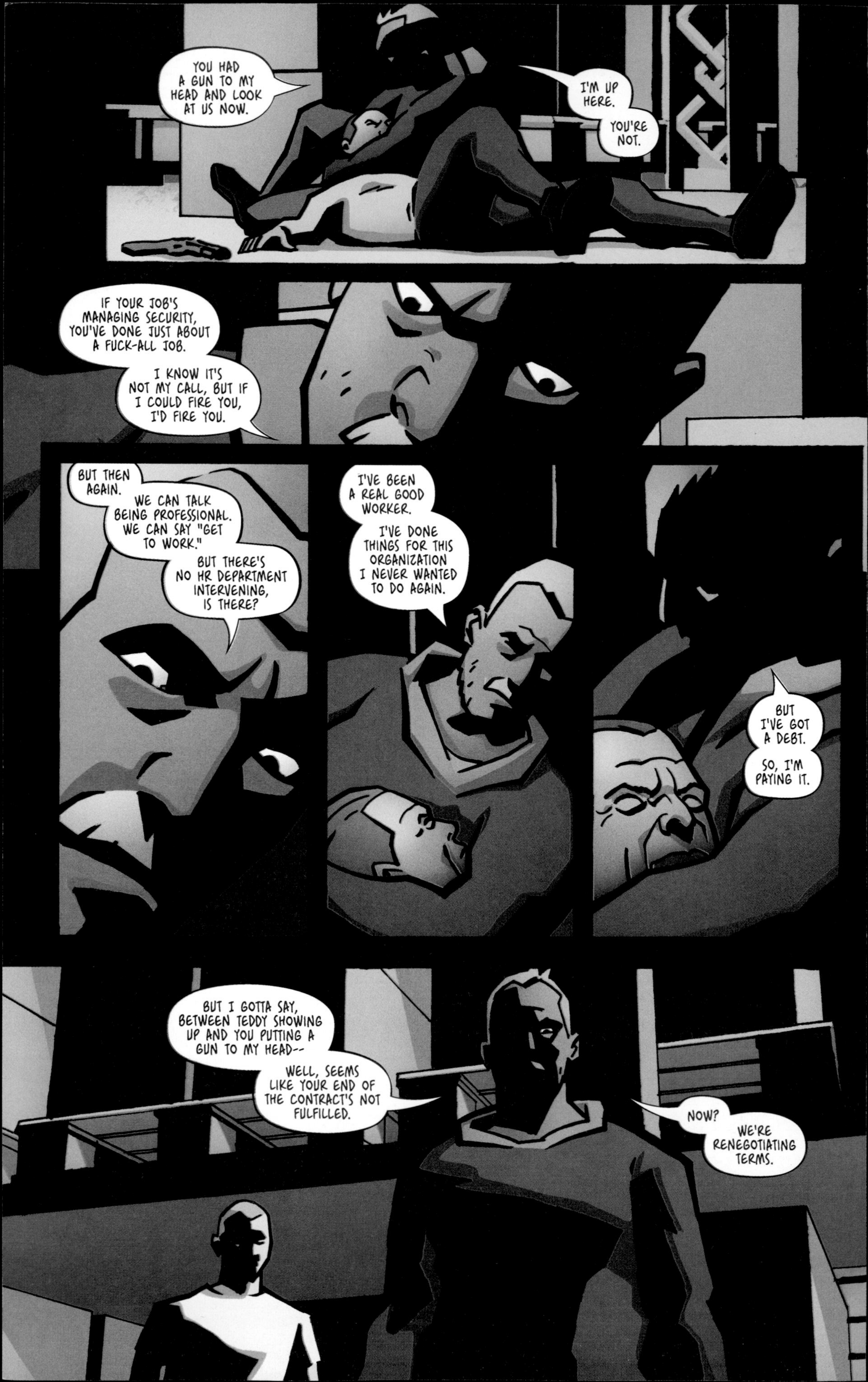
YOU HAD A GUN TO MY HEAD AND LOOK AT US NOW.
I'M UP HERE.
YOU'RE NOT.
IF YOUR JOB'S MANAGING SECURITY, YOU'VE DONE JUST ABOUT A FUCK-ALL JOB.
I KNOW IT'S NOT MY CALL, BUT IF I COULD FIRE YOU, I'D FIRE YOU.
BUT THEN AGAIN.
WE CAN TALK BEING PROFESSIONAL. WE CAN SAY "GET TO WORK."
BUT THERE'S NO HR DEPARTMENT INTERVENING, IS THERE?
I'VE BEEN A REAL GOOD WORKER.
I'VE DONE THINGS FOR THIS ORGANIZATION I NEVER WANTED TO DO AGAIN.
BUT I'VE GOT A DEBT.
SO, I'M PAYING IT.
BUT I GOTTA SAY, BETWEEN TEDDY SHOWING UP AND YOU PUTTING A GUN TO MY HEAD--
WELL, SEEMS LIKE YOUR END OF THE CONTRACT'S NOT FULFILLED.
NOW?
WE'RE RENEGOTIATING TERMS.

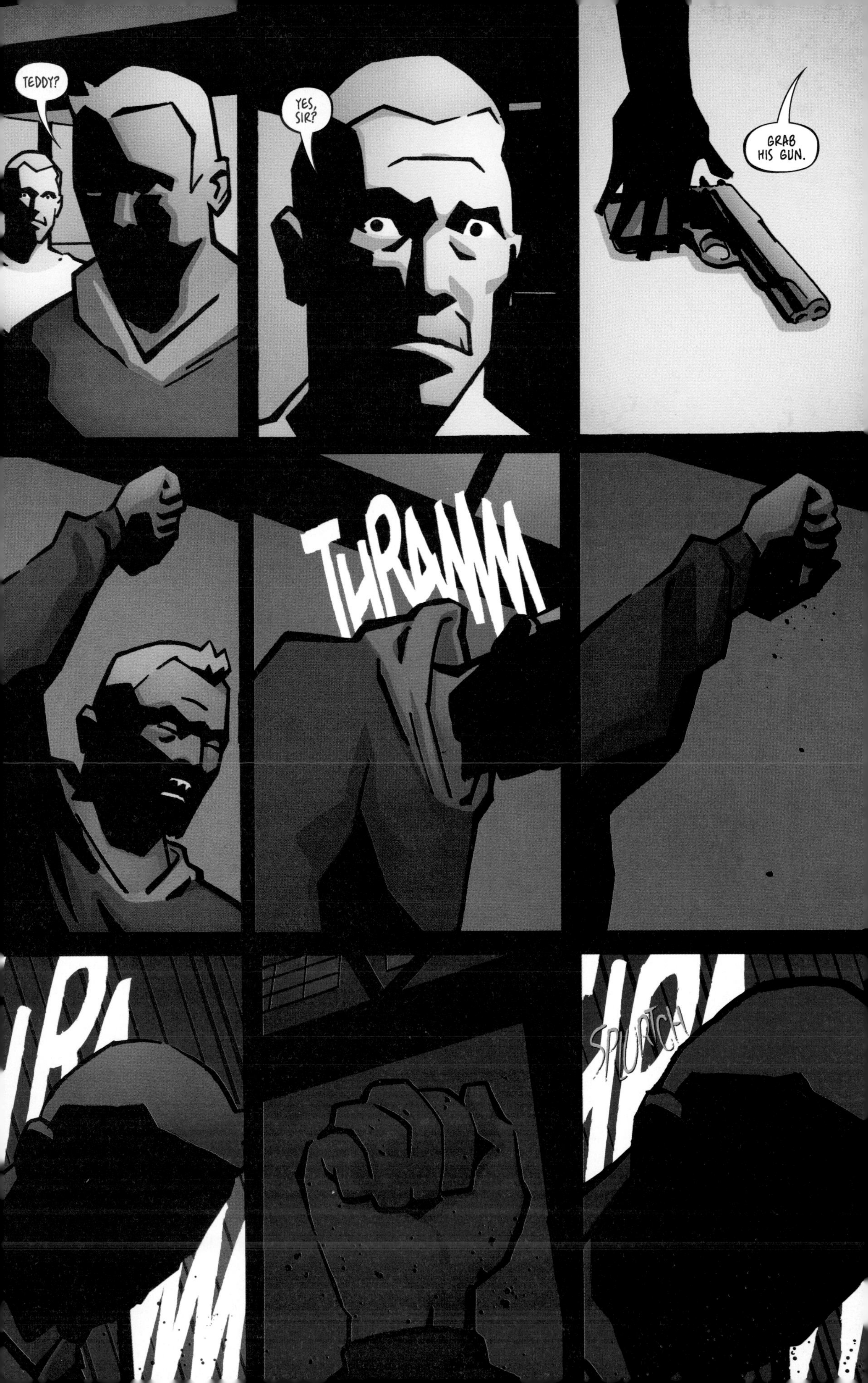
TEDDY?
YES, SIR?
GRAB HIS GUN.
TURANNM
SPLURTCH

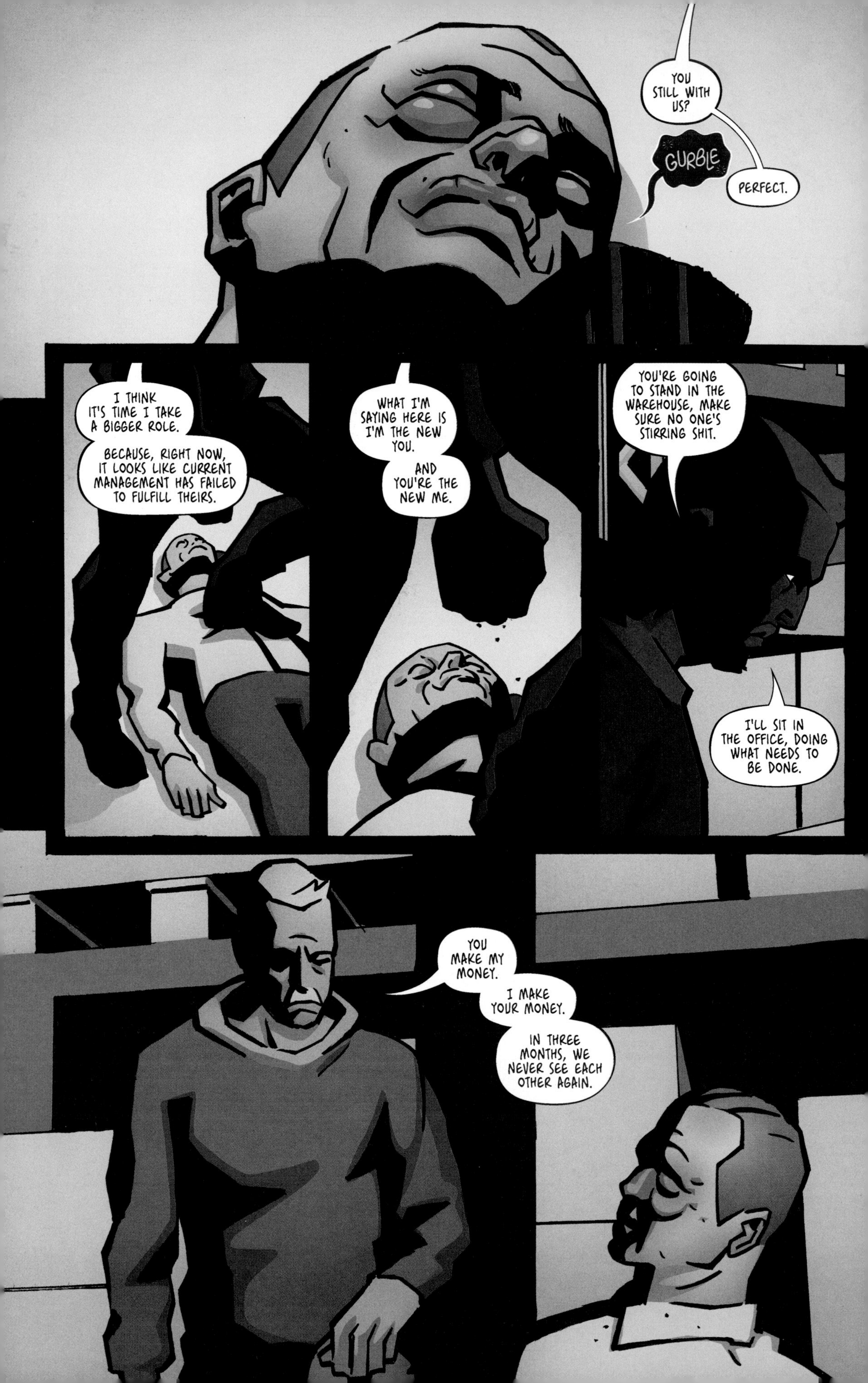
YOU STILL WITH US?
GURBLE
PERFECT.
I THINK IT'S TIME I TAKE A BIGGER ROLE.
BECAUSE, RIGHT NOW, IT LOOKS LIKE CURRENT MANAGEMENT HAS FAILED TO FULFILL THEIRS.
WHAT I'M SAYING HERE IS I'M THE NEW YOU.
AND YOU'RE THE NEW ME.
YOU'RE GOING TO STAND IN THE WAREHOUSE, MAKE SURE NO ONE'S STIRRING SHIT.
I'LL SIT IN THE OFFICE, DOING WHAT NEEDS TO BE DONE.
YOU MAKE MY MONEY.
I MAKE YOUR MONEY.
IN THREE MONTHS, WE NEVER SEE EACH OTHER AGAIN.

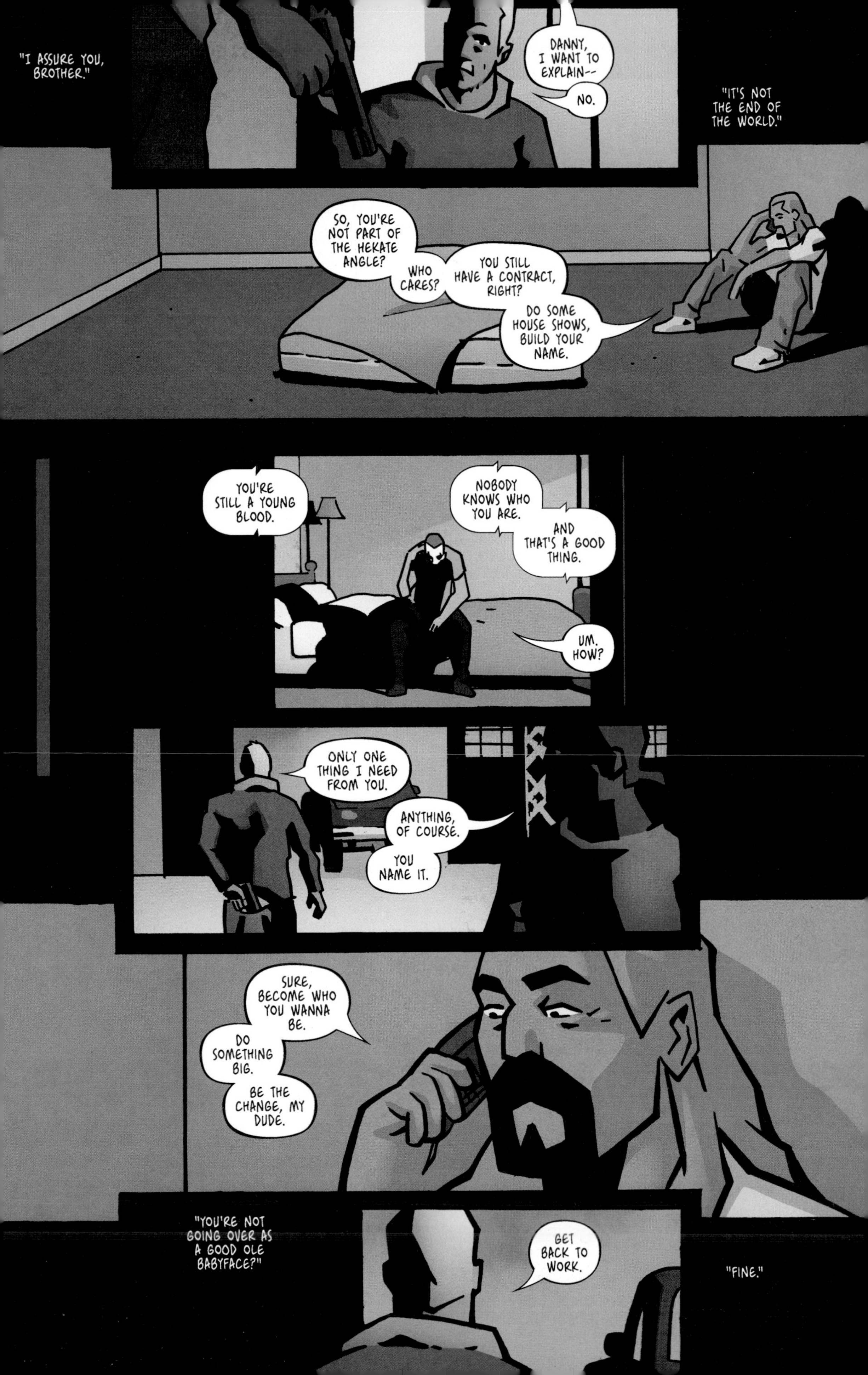

"I ASSURE YOU, BROTHER."
DANNY, I WANT TO EXPLAIN--
NO.
"IT'S NOT THE END OF THE WORLD."
SO, YOU'RE NOT PART OF THE HEKATE ANGLE?
WHO CARES?
YOU STILL HAVE A CONTRACT, RIGHT?
DO SOME HOUSE SHOWS, BUILD YOUR NAME.
YOU'RE STILL A YOUNG BLOOD.
NOBODY KNOWS WHO YOU ARE.
AND THAT'S A GOOD THING.
UM. HOW?
ONLY ONE THING I NEED FROM YOU.
ANYTHING, OF COURSE.
YOU NAME IT.
SURE, BECOME WHO YOU WANNA BE.
DO SOMETHING BIG.
BE THE CHANGE, MY DUDE.
"YOU'RE NOT GOING OVER AS A GOOD OLE BABYFACE?"
GET BACK TO WORK.
"FINE."

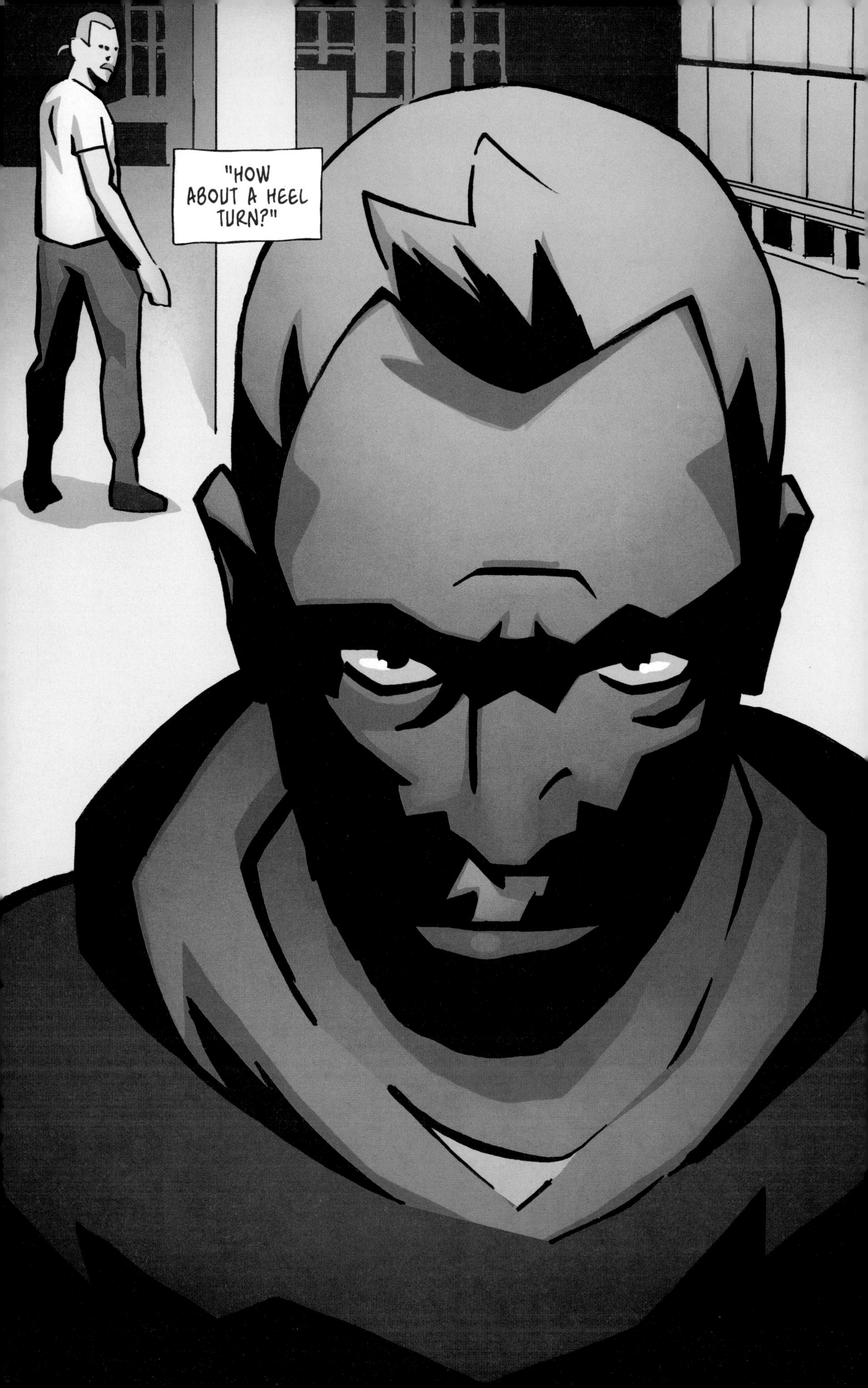
"HOW ABOUT A HEEL TURN?"

TO BE CONTINUED...

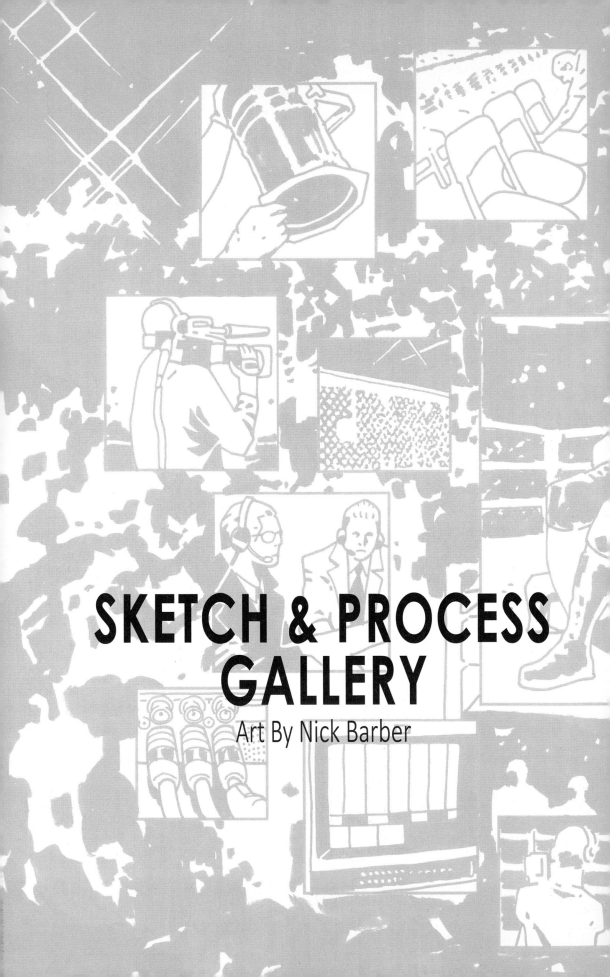

SKETCH & PROCESS GALLERY

Art By Nick Barber

ISSUE 6

Layout & Design

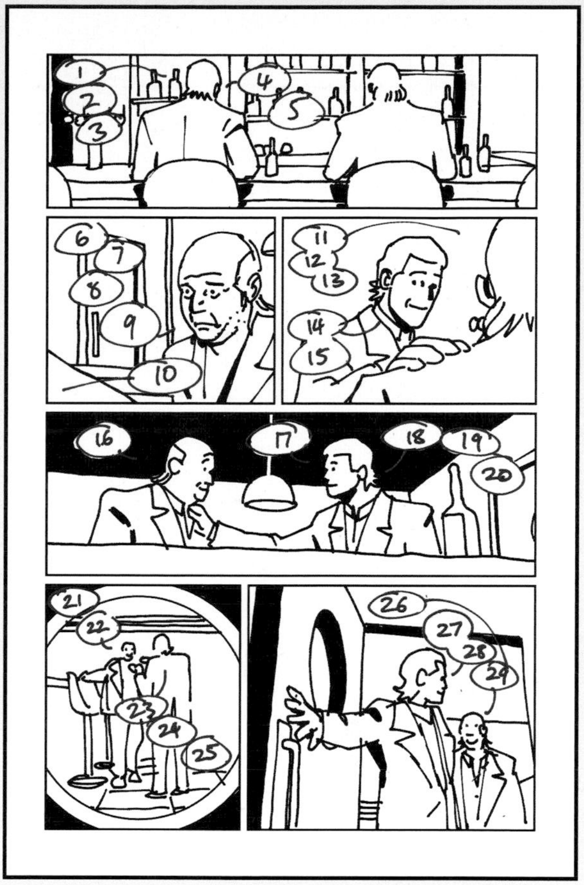

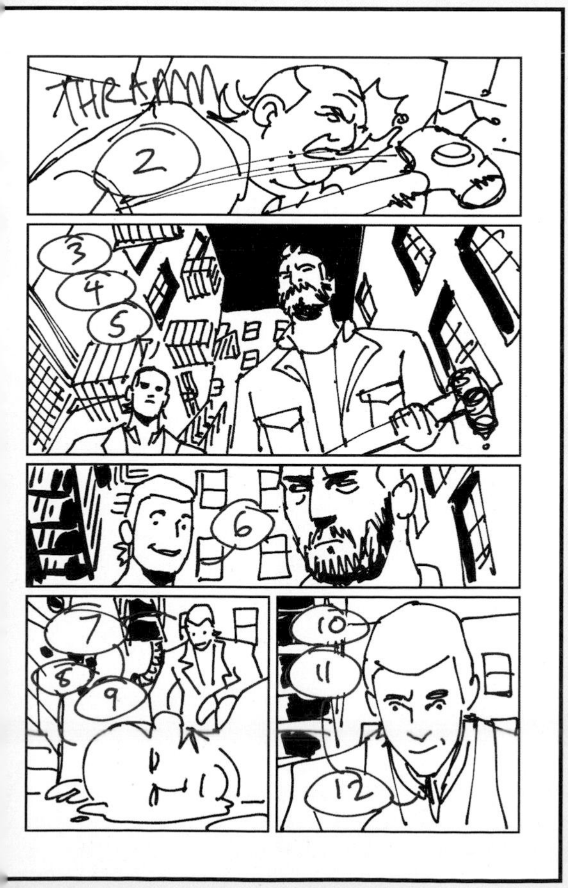
THRAMM

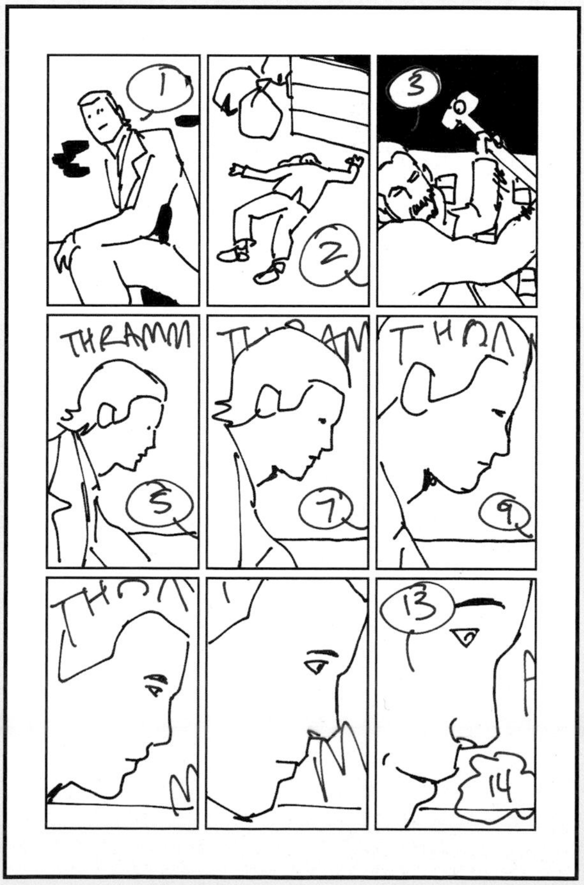
THRAMM

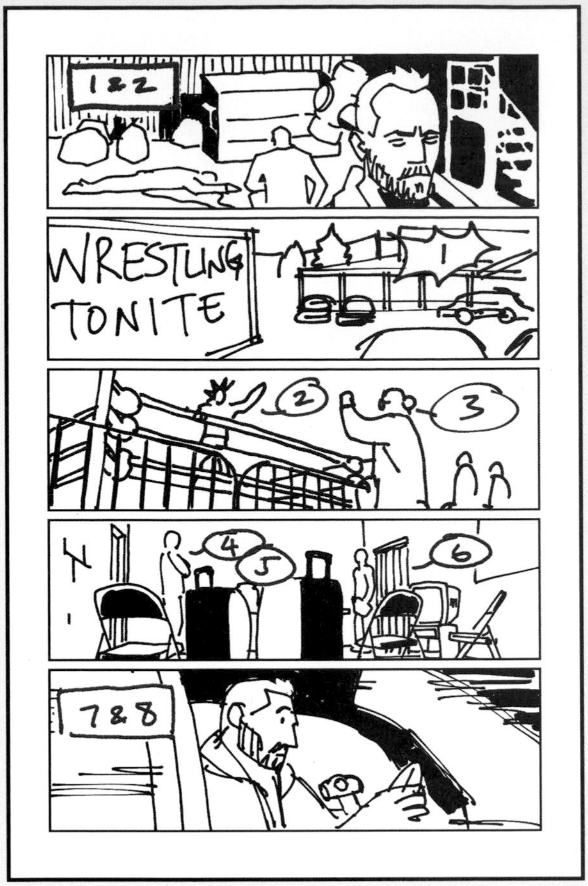
1&2
WRESTLING TONITE
1
2
3
4
5
6
7&8

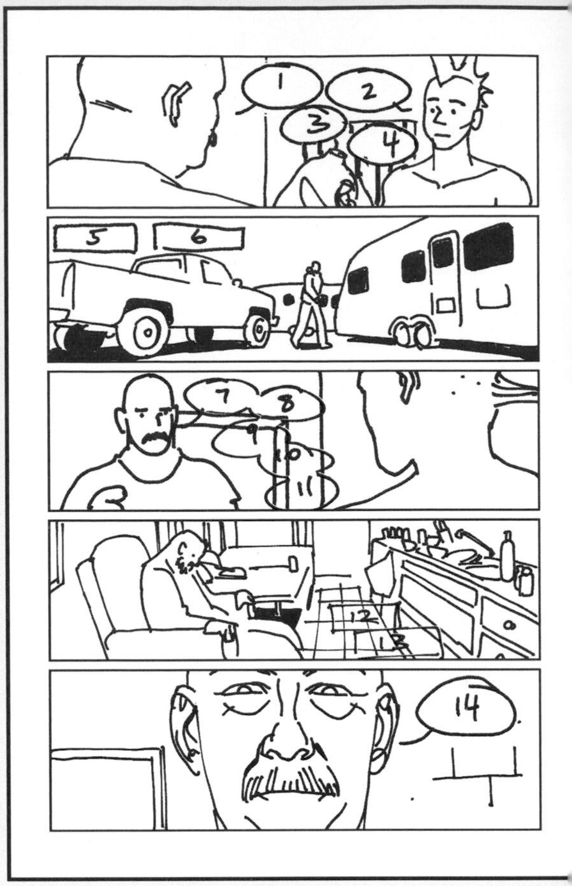
1
2
3
4
5
6
7
8
9
10
11
12
13
14

ISSUE 8

Pencils & Planning

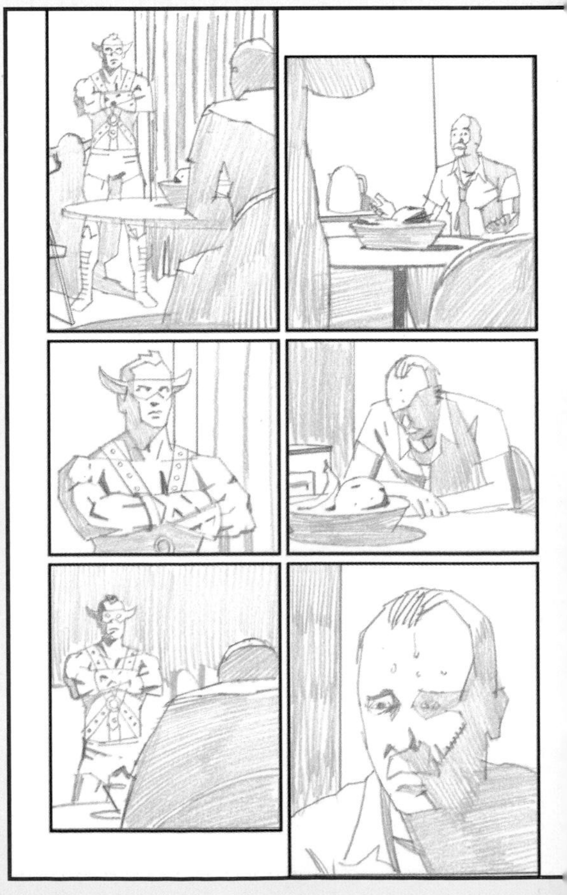

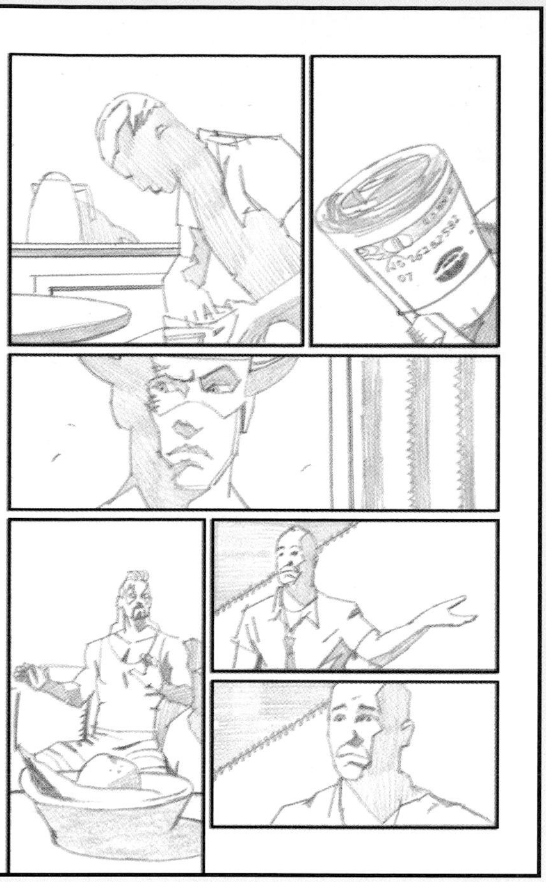
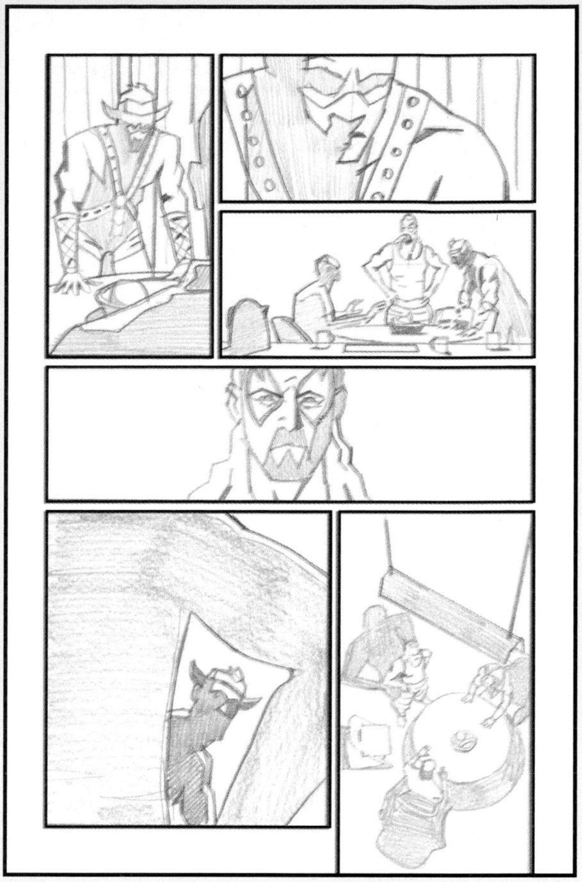
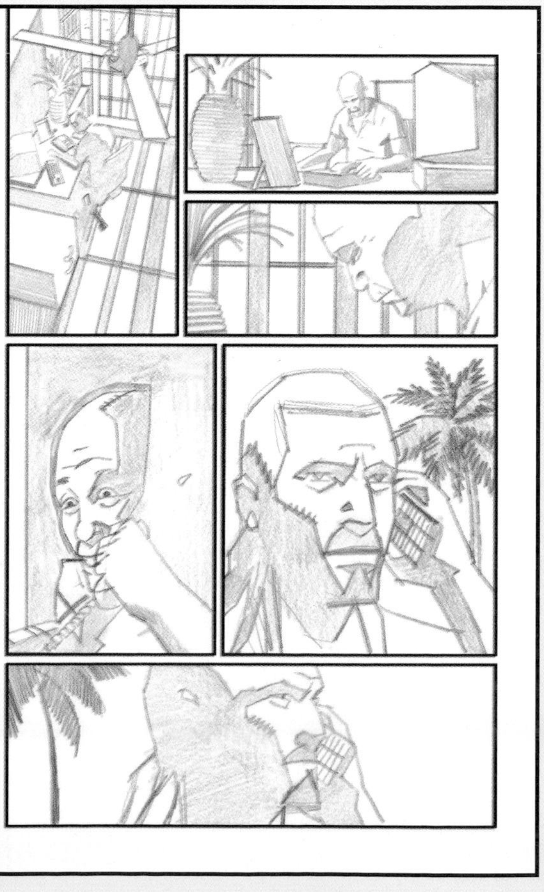
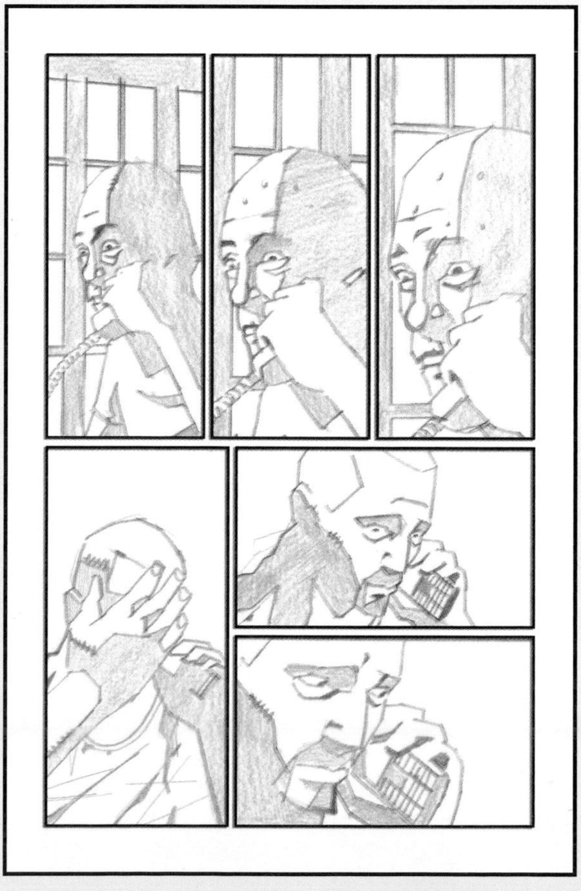

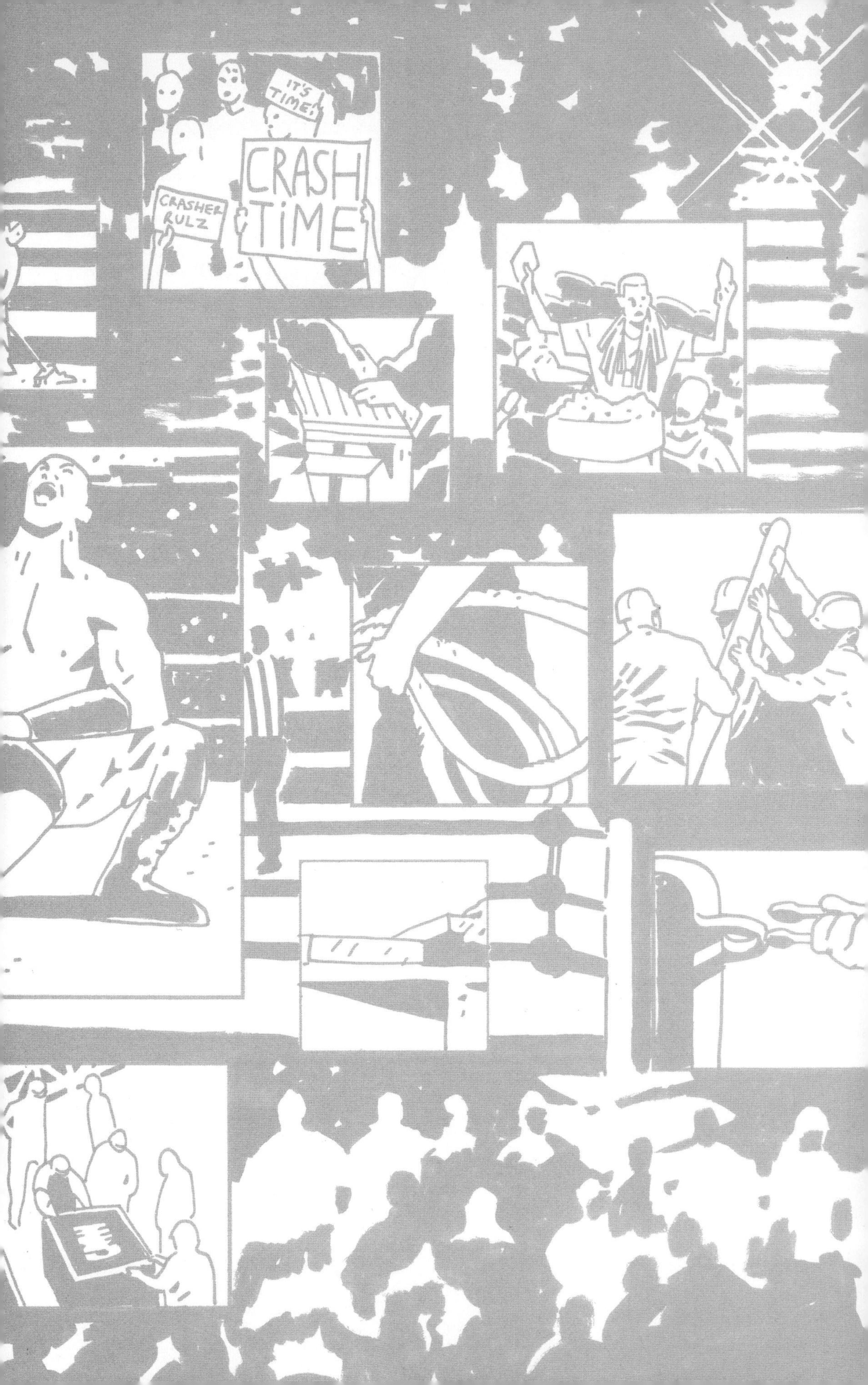

IT'S TIME!
CRASH TIME
CRASHER RULZ

JOE KEATINGE is the writer of Image, Skybound, Marvel and DC Comics titles including SHUTTER, RINGSIDE, GLORY, TECH JACKET, MARVEL KNIGHTS: HULK and ADVENTURES OF SUPERMAN. He is also the executive editor of the Eisner and Harvey award-winning Image Comics anthology POPGUN and the Courtney Taylor-Taylor penned ONE MODEL NATION.

NICK BARBER is from Auckland, New Zealand which means he has a funny accent and a penchant for second breakfast. Nick likes to tell stories and entertain people which he is now lucky enough to do for a living. RINGSIDE is Nick's first professional comic and hopefully the first of many.

SIMON GOUGH is a thirty-five-year-old man with a four-year-old's job, colouring in! Born in Birmingham, in the middle of the United Kingdom, Simon is now living down south in the sunny seaside hamlet of Brighton. Always eager to paint from a young age, and even more eager to read comics, it seemed only natural he would eventually, after many years of exploratory art education, intertwine those two loves into one (hopefully) booming career!

ARIANA MAHER is a Brazilian-American born in New Jersey who spent her formative years in Japan and Singapore. You wouldn't think any one person could talk about comic book lettering for hours... but then you meet her. By day she is an ordinary citizen but by night she transforms into a weird recluse obsessed with balloon tails and text placement. Her last reported sighting was the Seattle area. If spotted, approach with caution and/or more comics for her to letter.

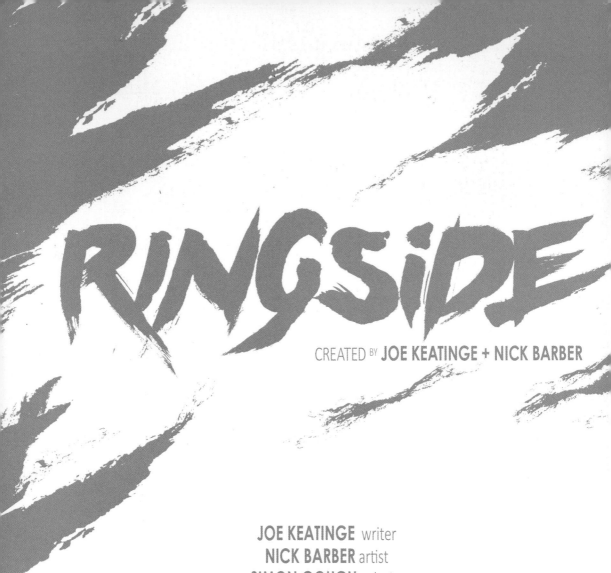

RINGSIDE

CREATED BY **JOE KEATINGE + NICK BARBER**

JOE KEATINGE writer
NICK BARBER artist
SIMON GOUGH colorist
ARIANA MAHER letterer
SHANNA MATSUZAK editor

design + layout by **ADDISON DUKE**
logo designed by **BRANDON GRAHAM**
special thanks to **DARREN SHAN**
cover art by **SANDRA LANZ**

IMAGE COMICS, INC.

Robert Kirkman - chief operating officer
Erik Larsen - chief financial officer
Todd McFarlane - president
Marc Silvestri - chief executive officer
Jim Valentino - vice-president
Eric Stephenson - publisher
Corey Murphy - director of sales

Jeff Boison - director of publishing planning
& book trade sales
Chris Ross - director of digital sales
Jeff Stang - director of specialty sales
Kat Salazar - director of pr & marketing
Branwyn Bigglestone - controller
Sue Korpela - accounts manager
Drew Gill - art director
Brett Warnock - production manager
Leigh Thomas - print manager

Tricia Ramos - traffic manager
Briah Skelly - publicist
Aly Hoffman - conventions & events coordinator
Sasha Head - sales & marketing production designer
David Brothers - branding manager
Melissa Gifford - content manager
Drew Fitzgerald - publicity assistant
Erika Schnatz - production artist
Ryan Brewer - production artist

Shanna Matuszak - production artist
Vincent Kukua - production artist
Carey Hall - production artist
Esther Kim - direct market sales representative
Emilio Bautista - digital sales associate
Leanna Caunter - accounting assistant
Chloe Ramos-Peterson - library market sales representative
Marla Eizik - administrative assistant

IMAGECOMICS.COM